These Shattered Truths

These Shattered Truths

SIRI SANDFORD

THESE SHATTERED TRUTHS

For information contact:
Siri Sandford
https://www.sirisandford.com

First hardcover edition April 2022

Library of Congress Control Number: 2022902573
ISBN 979-8-9857262-0-6 (hardcover)
ISBN 979-8-9857262-1-3 (paperback)
ISBN 979-8-9857262-2-0 (epub)

Cover design, book design, map, and illustrations by Siri Sandford

10 9 8 7 6 5 4 3 2 1

In dedication to my Mom, for patiently listening to me talk endlessly about this book and the many ideas in my mind. You have been my biggest supporter from the start, and I can never thank you enough.

Entrance to Metarock
Hidden Caverns
Dragon Isles
Wyntryn
Wyntryn Manor
Entrance to Rebynrock
Fynger Isles
Grymyr
City by the Sea
Capital of Grymyr
Goldryn
N
NW
W
NE
SW
E
SE
S

THE TWO CONTINENTS OF
Kanaleigh
Gladlyn
Crystal Lakes
Aysand
Eastern
Eventyr
Central City
Ygrette
Western
Eventyr
Southern Dunes

PART ONE

The Warped Library

The Sonder

"Mata ta chessya malla mey fin," Ava's mother would whisper to her. May the gods bless us until our end.

She would recite those words as the moon hovered high above them, on the nights when they laid on the manor's rooftop looking out at the stars. Those same nights it would be too dark to see anything but the snow falling and the stars resting high above them in the sky. Every time she spoke in that ancient tongue, Ava would ask, "why?" Because her family didn't believe in gods or goddesses. Her mother didn't worship anything beyond herself. In response to Ava's question, her mother would simply rub her thumb against her cheek and shake her head. The memories of those shared conversations with her mother are some of the few that have returned to her since the accident.

The memories only remind her of how her mother had always been distant and passive.

I should've known better, Ava thinks while staring out at the ocean below.

If she knew all of those months ago, the truth, the

lies, the deceit, maybe she would have done things differently. Made different decisions.

Now, a year later, sitting in a cold room, Ava knows she can never go back. Doesn't want to. Instead, she lets the rage dwell deep inside her heart and spread across her mind.

Ava is sequestered in a small room that sits on the eastern side of the Goldryn palace. Goldryn is a region on the western continent that is known for its agriculture and aquaculture. Since arriving in the humid region, Ava hasn't bothered to explore the city or try to learn about the culture. She misses Wyntryn too much, the snowy region to the north. She misses the stone walls of the manor and the horizon filled with mountains.

The door to her room slowly opens. A woman Ava faintly recognizes from her distant memories appears before her. After all that has happened, she isn't surprised by her recognition of the woman. If anything, Ava wants to know more about her.

The woman is lean, with a cool look of sympathy in her eyes. Her hair falls below her breasts. Long curled tendrils of pale purple and lavender. Her skin is a deep tan, descended from a race that originated in the western lands of Eventyr. The woman, a lady of the crystal lake, the daughter of a high lord that served beneath the Queen of Eventyr.

The woman tilts her head and examines Ava, eyes surveying her as if she hasn't seen Ava in a very long time. And she hasn't, not since before the death of her former mentor, Alys Wyntryn.

"Have I met you before?" Ava asks with a quiet, shaky voice.

"I'm Willow." She pauses, her eyes landing on

Ava's, recognition crosses her face. "You truly do look just like your mother." As Ava hears the words Willow speaks, her stomach falls. As if she has fallen off a cliff and doesn't know if she will land safely on her feet. Willow continues, "Well darling, I have heard so much about you."

"How do you know me?" Ava lowers her voice so that the Goldryn Queen won't be able to hear from beyond the sandstone walls. "How do you know my mother?"

Willow's eyes glint. "I'm here because of the boy you want to kill. He is a friend of mine, the same as you once were to me. I have information regarding your situation with him. Something you might find useful." Willow's voice is a merriment of smooth syllables that flow into whispers. Her voice is accented by the deep and ancient tones of the Eventyrians. Eventyr is a region on the eastern continent that is far from the palace where Ava now finds refuge. A place she at first thought of as a sanctuary but has turned out to be far from it.

Ava takes a steadying breath. "I don't want to hear what you have to say. He killed someone I loved. I will never forget about that … I can never forgive that." Ava has the urge to cry out. To throw the mirror across the room, set the world on fire, and scream until she loses her voice. And perhaps she has already done that, which is why she now feels empty. As if whatever anger she has is stifled. Her heart and mind so broken, so shattered, that she can't decipher what is the truth and what is a lie. Ava has been lost for the past year and has only spiraled more and more into a flurry of emotions as time goes on. And now it is an endless nightmare of nothing.

"Well Ava, then you'll find the information I have to share a relief. Information your lovely captor is trying to hide from you. Truths even your lost friend failed to let you see," she says. Willow lets a piece of parchment drop to the floor undetected. Ava looks off into the ocean beyond them as Willow continues. "I have a respect for your mother, and I owe it to her memory to keep you safe. Know that you can't trust anyone Ava, especially not within these walls."

As Willow moves to exit the room, Ava turns to watch her leave. That's when the raven-haired girl notices the ripped and folded parchment on the wooden floor. She bends down to pick it up, and as she opens it to read the words that are written on it with spindly handwriting, her heart stops. Her chest heaves, as she chokes out a cry. Not of relief, or sadness, but of regret. That her friend has died because of a single treacherous lie.

Chapter One

Every day life streams in, the dawn light shining through a window, hitting the floor, and bouncing through the room. Moving from one surface to another, and then another. Life is not easy.

There are days when grief avoids her. It let's her have a day of peace. Other times it torments her. Mocking her with daydreams and nightmares. Sometimes she wakes up and simply feels nothing but the urge to fall back asleep. To slip away into the darkness, hidden behind her own eyelids—safe from the world, from those horrible and unavoidable consequences.

It has only been three months since her mother's death. Three months since she fell flat on her knees and sobbed. Cried out for the one person who knew her, who protected her. The one person who could never come. Screamed into the night for her mother, but her mother was gone forever. And what followed her mother's death was inevitable. She lost her memories and was forced to hide from the world. She was even abandoned by her own father, who couldn't handle the grief of losing his beloved wife. And somehow in that grief had lost sight of what he had left to live for and ran away from his demons, leaving his daughter behind.

Ava wishes she could bring her mother back. Bring her back into the world, where she could be there with her, as lively as ever. Because maybe if her mother was there, her father might return, and her memories might come back too. But her mother will never return. It is only Ava, alone in that apartment. Abandoned by her father, abandoned by any feeling of sanity.

Left by seemingly everything—even the familiarity of who she once was. An empty vessel, left in this world to somehow struggle back into the thrumming of everyday life. The cycle of waking up, putting effort into her day, falling asleep, and doing it all over again. The steady torturous puppeteering of the life she is expected to live.

She sits on her bed, staring at the wall to the right. Watching the particles of paint blend together in her vision. Blurring into a mess of buzzing and liquid shapes. The wall as beige and bland as ever. The same as how Ava sees the rest of the world. Unexciting, uneventful, and full of empty sadness. She imagines herself sliding into the wall, into the paint, and disappearing.

Disappearing is an impossibility, so instead, she sits there staring at the wall and listening to the streets beyond her room on the third story of a bland apartment building come to life. She tries to push away her persistent worries and painful thoughts. She has been awake for hours, but she hasn't bothered to get up.

Today Ava has to live. Or at least try to live, because her mother can't. She has to get up and breathe the air that her mother can't breathe.

She presses her feet into the carpet and feels her

knees tense as she moves to stand. She pauses, steadily waiting for something to happen, to stop her from having to get up. But nothing happens. Air filters through her nose, tickling the top of her lip. Ava squeezes her eyes shut and grasps the quilt beneath her. Slowly, she lets go and stands.

The air conditioner buzzes to life, sending cool air through the vents. She moves to her window and pushes the light blue curtain open. Ava looks down at the city beyond her. The city is full of busybodies.

People cover the streets in red and blue, violet, and yellow. Hats of all kinds litter the heads of many, hiding their faces from the people passing by. Their hats slyly concealing their eyes, their identities. Grymyr is like that, disturbingly suspicious of every citizen. No one trusts anyone, not even their own neighbor here.

Ava slides away from the window and into a clean set of clothes, pulling herself together piece by piece.

She picks up her slim tracker and looks at the time. Four o-clock. Somehow, she has slept through most of the day. Ava flicks through the screens on the tracker and opens her voicemails. Her finger presses play on the most recent one, and her mother's voice chimes to life, crystallizing in the air around her. "Ava! You won't believe it, but that beautiful library on 32nd opened again! You remember going there as a little one, don't you? I can't wait to pick you up and then we can go straight there." Her voice switches to a more serious tone, the tone that always makes Ava's throat bob. "I need to talk to you about something. There's something aft—" it scratches out. Every time, the sound shakes into nothing. Every time Ava listens, it seems as if her mother doesn't want someone to hear those last few words. Or possibly it was a coded message, but something she can't even begin to decipher now. Her mother knew someone was coming after them, and someone did.

Ava wishes she knew what her mother had told her that day, maybe it would help her figure out what happened that night. She knows her mother picked her up because she was there during the car accident. But Ava can't remember what caused it, no one knew. Not even the city's officers who investigated the incident.

A knock sounds on the front door of the quaint apartment. Ava stares off through the doorway of her bedroom, not wanting to move, but knowing she should.

She reaches down for a hairband from the top of her dresser and twists her hair into a messy bun. There's another thud on the door. She takes a deep breath and walks through the apartment. The living room is the main space, with a few old pieces of furniture gathered into a sitting area before the front door. A small table with four chairs sits in front of the windows. There's a kitchenette that fits into the corner between her parent's room and the dining table. Ava walks past them to the door and pulls it open. Levi's half-smile shines down on her.

His hair rests shaggily across his forehead. He never bothers to brush through it, he does that enough with his fingers when he gets nervous. Levi pushes past Ava and collapses onto the couch. "Another day, another chance to put that beautiful smile back on your face!"

"I'm good, thanks." Ava lightly pushes the door shut. The hinges creak and she waits to hear the lock click into place. Ava sits down on the carpet across from Levi, letting her eyes fall to the dull rug.

"I know you'll never not feel grief from this, but it's been months. At some point you have to wake up and come back to the world," he says. His voice is hushed. His face is intent. He seems saddened to see her in this state day after day.

"I am here. I am back," Ava says.

His smile softens his disbelief. "No, I don't believe that. You barely remember me."

"I know, but I can't make the memories come back. They're ... lost." She brushes her fingers across the crevices of the carpet, trying to distract her mind, to find solace in the short pieces of wool twisted into a swirly intricate design.

He moves down to the floor beside her and lifts his fingers to Ava's jaw, pushing her chin up. She unwillingly meets his eyes. The green eyes that are filled with emotion. Emotions he seems to withhold from her. Levi knows she won't be able to understand—to remember despite how much she wants to. "They can't be lost, and if they are, then we will find them."

"What if I don't want to find them?" she asks. Her voice is barely a whisper.

The green of Levi's eyes dulls at the thought.

"I don't want to see it happen again. Whatever happened that night, ruined me. I can still barely breathe. If I were to remember, I don't think I'd survive. I want to know who we were, who you were. But it's gone and I'm starting to become okay with that," she says.

He turns from Ava. "I wish you weren't."

"I don't need the memories, Levi. I can still feel what I felt then. My emotions never left. My connections. You're still my friend. Even if I don't know how we met or what made me feel this way, it's that feeling, the air between us that's valuable." She reaches out towards him, but Levi shakes her off.

"No, not when you look at me like that." His face

contorts with his thoughts.

"You've been trying to help me remember for months, and we've gotten nowhere. Maybe it's better that we stop trying," Ava suggests. She hopes he will let it go.

"Just, let me try one more thing," he says.

"Fine, but if it doesn't work, do you promise to learn to be okay with me without the memories?"

He looks down at Ava's hand, still brushing her fingers along the swirls in the carpet. "Okay, I promise."

"What do you want to try?" Ava asks. She watches his eyes move back to meet hers.

"I want to take you to the library. The one your mother took you to when you were little. The one on the voicemail."

Her stomach drops. "I will do anything but go there."

"You have to leave. If there are answers to find, you know they are there. You know they are in that library, not in this apartment." His tone is serious, but it always is when they have this conversation. She knows she needs to go, but she would rather go back and stare at the wall. Getting lost in, nothingness.

"No. I can't—"

"You will. You need to go, Ava. I promise If there is nothing there that helps, I'll never push you again."

Ava believes him. But she doesn't want to leave the apartment and doesn't want to face real people. But she also knows that Levi is right. She can't stay hidden in this apartment forever. And the library from the voicemail might have the answers she needs. Maybe her mother left that message to give her a hint, a path to find her way back to the memories she is struggling to grasp onto.

Levi stands and shrugs. "There's no time like the

present."

"You want me to go now?" Ava pushes herself away from him, her back pressing against one of the armchairs in the sitting room.

"Wouldn't you rather get it over with than worry about doing it later?" Levi offers her a hand, but she glares back at him. "Come on, Ava, just one short trip. You promised."

She stands and walks back to her room. To compensate for the distance, she raises her voice. She says, "no, you promised to leave me alone if I do this." She rattles open the door to her closet and pulls a cloak from its hanger. She slips it over her shoulders and walks back to Levi. "Make this as quick as possible, please."

"Of course." He grins, throwing the front door wide open.

Ava aimlessly follows him through the halls, down the steps, and onto the sidewalk. She stares out into the misty day—cars flying past, horns honking. Lights flicker from all over the city and blend in with the late afternoon sunlight. The snake that once hibernated in her chest, comes to life with the growing anxieties she feels when faced with the world. It coils around her heart, growing tighter and tighter. A rush of anxiety. She feels the world close in around her. A blue haze darting into the outer fields of her vision.

"Come on, Ava!" Levi chimes. He hurries off to blaze a trail through the impertinent strangers.

She takes a deep breath and follows, hoping the snake will subside. There is the possibility that the library might give her the answers she's been looking for, but it doesn't make her want to go. Instead of having a hopeful outlook on the day, Ava wonders if this trip will only give her the answers she doesn't want to hear. Or rather, none at all.

They walk up to an old building hidden between various skyscrapers. The path to the library is cracked from the many years of weathering. Weeds spring up from the cracks in the concrete. They stretch across the rough gray surface of the rock, swallowing the path whole. Even the bricks of the library are entwined with ivy and overgrown landscaping. To the right is a gnarled and twisted tree. It casts an eerie shadow over the pathway.

The building they approach is made of old maroon brick. The library itself is five stories tall. In comparison to its neighbors, it looks like a speck in a city of giants.

A large circular window crests the top floor of the library. It's detailed and intricate, handcrafted long ago by a skilled craftsman. Even from the ground, Ava can see the scratches across the glass and wood. Beautiful markings with unknown meanings.

As Ava stares up at the large window, admiring its beauty. A figure moves up to the window. A shadow of a man, standing and staring directly at her. She meets the gaze of the mysterious figure, fear creeps up her spine. She shivers and reaches out to grab Levi's hand. He holds it firmly, giving her a comforting smile. But Levi doesn't seem to notice the strange figure, and Ava doesn't mention it to him as they walk beneath the shadow's gaze.

Ava examines the rest of the misshapen place as they continue. The door is tall and wooden, the red paint cracking at its seams. There are holes in the walls where bricks had broken and fallen to the grass below. Ava looks over to Levi as he says, "Well, this is it." There's a content grin on his face, but the destination doesn't deserve a grin. It is mangled and broken, a lonely artifact in a bustling city. There is nothing that earned this place a content grin. It needed someone to love it and bring it back to its former glory. Until then, it is only a place that speaks of an isolated sadness. A grave left behind in memorial of Grymyr's origin.

The only thing Ava likes about this place so far is the silence that spreads between the buildings. She appreciates the sound barrier created by the surrounding skyscrapers. The only sounds are their steps and the steady thrumming of her heart.

"So, this is it?" Ava asks.

"Isn't she beautiful!" Levi says. His voice is just a little too loud for the quiet atmosphere.

Levi says it as if this isn't his first time seeing the library. "You've been here before?" Ava asks. Furrowing her brows in confusion.

Levi slides his hand away from hers to open the door to the library. "Yes, I have. I came here after I heard that voicemail for the first time. I knew I had to come. If you couldn't find the answers for yourself, then I wanted to help you find them."

"That's a bit demeaning," Ava says.

"I didn't mean it that way. But you haven't left your apartment for more than food in months." He stands at the doors, one hand on the doorknob.

Ava grasps for a lie. "I know, I was joking. Let's go inside." She forces a smile for his sake.

He pulls the door open and holds it for her. She goes through and mumbles a, "thanks."

Once inside Ava looks at him. "You think this place

will help, don't you?"

His face is drawn. "Of course I think it will. I wouldn't push you to come if I didn't think it was important."

Ava nods, looking around the room. It is massive. A disheveled mess, but unlike the outside of the building, it is mesmerizing. Not eerie, but beautiful. All the complexities make it enchanting. The tallest bookshelves Ava has ever seen stand sturdy within the room. Books are strewn across the floor. Stacks of books overwhelm the space, toppling over pathways between shelves and piled high in the corners. From the ceiling hangs large creatures made of wood and metal. Around the walls, there are various sculptures of the gods and goddesses of other cultures from the two continents of Kanaleigh. It is interesting to see them there because Grymyr is known as the region that has broken away from the others. Cast aside its history to focus on technology and innovation. It is rare for places like this library to exist in the region.

Before her, there's an old lady sitting behind a reception desk. At the sight of Levi and Ava her eyes light up and she practically throws her book aside in haste. The old lady comes toward them in a speedy hobble. "Levites, Levites, look at you! What a striking young man." She croons, patting his hand with her own. "Now, I hear you have recovered nicely, yes? Next time I want you to tell me when these things happen. I mustn't hear it all from your mother."

Ava looks at Levi in shock. The friend she thought she knew so well has been hiding things from her.

"Yes, Ms. Ethelle I have. And you saw me last week, I was fine. Mother likes to exaggerate," Levi says to her. There's a kindness in his voice that makes it obvious that he has known this woman for quite some time. Which is odd to Ava, who thought he had only learned about the library through her. He is more familiar with this place and its people than Ava could have ever imagined.

The woman turns to her now. "Levites you have finally brought her, what a delight it is to finally meet you, sweet child." She winks at Ava.

Ava hesitantly smiles, an unsureness creeping over her. "Nice to meet you," she says.

Ms. Ethelle's face drops for a moment at the sound of Ava's voice, as if a ghost has just walked behind her. Ms. Ethelle forces a smile to cover her unexpected reaction. "Well dears, I have many questions for the both of you." She stares at Ava with interest, as if she is some rare animal, she has always wanted to see up close. Her eyes stray long enough to create an uncomfortable silence.

"I'm sorry Ms. Ethelle, but we are in a rush. We need to get home before dark."

"Ah, of course, you children are always in a rush. Do come by soon and talk to me, yes?" she asks, looking directly at Ava.

"I'd like that," Ava replies, before quickly walking away. She enters the closest path into the books. Levi follows close behind, instructing her where to go. Ava isn't sure what he is leading her to, but he seems to have a place in mind.

The library is a maze, art and literature cover the place from floor to ceiling. Always a new path hiding behind each corner. Ava can't imagine why this place, of all the buildings in the capital of Grymyr, had such importance to her mother. Her mother always had an appreciation for the forgotten and misfortunate, but this place seems like nothing but a relic. A hidden gem for historians, but a nightmare for any sane mind to explore.

Before Ava can process the collision of art, literature, and faulty memories, Levi moves ahead of her and pulls her down one last path leading to a stairwell. She pulls her hand from his grasp and looks around the small entrance to the stairs. "How much are you hiding from me?" she asks.

"I'm not hiding anything."

"There's definitely a lot that you have happened to not mention."

He runs his hand through his hair. "I know. It's … well part of it is personal, and you did know once. It's hard to talk about it when I have to explain everything again."

Ava looks away, the snake coiling tighter. "I am so sorry, Levi."

"Please, don't apologize. I've heard those words every day since the accident. I know you don't remember," he says.

"What do you want me to say?" Ava's own frustrations seep out with her words.

Levi looks up at the ceiling. "There's nothing you can say. There's nothing you can do. I only want to help you get your memories back so that we don't have to struggle through this. I know you didn't ask for this to happen to you. But it is so hard to be upfront about everything because you stare back blankly at me. Accuse me of lying. My best friend doesn't even know me anymore. Do you know how that feels?"

"No, I don't." She bites back her anger. She is angry because of how unfair the world is. But she knows it is unfair, and that there is nothing she can do to change the past. "How is this place supposed to help? I know it was in the voicemail, but it's a disaster. Whatever is hidden here will

be impossible to find."
Levi nods. "I don't think it's a book we are looking for. I think it's a person."

"A person?" Ava asks. She thinks back to the shadow gazing down at them from the window. The figure who sent chills through her.

"I can help you see her again, Ava."

Ava snaps to him, breathless. "What?" She fights the urge to laugh, but part of her believes him, actually believes in the impossible.

Levi steps towards her. "There is a way to see her. But you will have to trust me."

She shakes her head in disbelief. "That's impossible." She backs away, her gut telling her this is wrong. "She's dead. You can't speak to the dead. Have you lost your mind?" Somehow saying it out loud, saying her mother is dead and that it is impossible to see her breaks through something in Ava. It allows her to see through her muggy mind and to the simple facts. Her mother is dead, her memories are gone, and it is all in the past now.

"I haven't lost my mind. Trust me, okay?" he says.

Ava doesn't want to make this anymore difficult, so she nods. "Okay, let's get it over with."

"Come on." Levi turns and walks to the stairs. Right where Ava doesn't want to go. Towards the shadow in the window.

The staircase that reaches up through the cavernous library is small. It spirals upwards with small terraces that lead to dark hallways with various doors. The stairs themselves are steep and creak at every other step. The railing has missing bars and cracks along it. As Ava follows Levi up the steps, she hopes they will go anywhere but to the room with the circle window.

With each step, her mind jumps to random conclusions of what Levi means by saying he can help her see her mother again. She contemplates whether he might make her go through scrapbooks or videos to remember the past. Or whether he has set up a hologram of her mother to try to help. Whatever it ends up being, it doesn't seem promising.

The truth is, Ava is skeptical of Levi. Despite how good of a friend he is to her, he continues to give her reasons to question him. And with no real memories of him, Ava only knows what he tells her. She has to blindly trust whatever he says to be true. She doesn't even know where he goes when he isn't with her. He is a walking mystery.

The old stairs creak under them as they rise higher into the building; growing as they get closer and closer to the mysterious top floor. Ava continues to look down the hallways leading off into the various floors. Many of the passageways look boarded up and blocked off. This place must have been more than just a library at some point. And why did it supposedly opened again only a few months ago, after being deserted for years?

Levi reaches the top of the stairs first and waits for her. As she steps up beside him, he pushes open the door, and she walks in to see the large circular window. In-person it is twice the size she thought it would be.

The room is dusty and void of furniture. A ray of sunlight shines through the old glass making a shaky circular reflection on the uneven wooden floors. Ava can see various symbols that are scratched into the glass reflecting onto the floorboards. She moves closer to the window, wondering what the symbols mean. And they aren't only on the glass, they are on the wooden slats surrounding the window and on the empty bookshelves along the left wall.

When Ava turns to look at Levi, her eyes catch on a shadowy figure in the far-right corner. It begins to walk towards.

But the closer it gets, the more nerves run like wildfire through Ava's body. Because as the light touches the figure, its face comes into view. It looks just like her. How can it look like her? Her breathing becomes more rapid as she takes a step back. All she wants to do is run far away from it. Whatever it is. It's blue eyes, her blue eyes gaze back at her. Its face is exactly the same, but the expression is different. The aura. This reflection of herself is void of any life. It's terribly pale with sunken cheeks. She fights the urge not to gasp or scream.

She watches her face on an unfamiliar body glide toward her.

The face that reflects her own begins to morph into another. Right in front of her eyes, she sees its facial features physically change. She rubs her eyes and looks back at the figure. He now appears to be a young man. Close to her own age, but his face is thin and worn. With sharp cheekbones and hollow eyes. He has dark hair and green eyes. A dull, sage green. His body is lengthy and he's almost grotesquely skinny.

Ava can feel Levi's eyes watching her. Gauging her reaction to the strange man.

She simply stands wide-eyed, staring in shock at the man before her.

Levi is unphased by the fact that the man was wearing her face. But before she can ask him who this man is and how he can help, Levi introduces the strange shadow of a man. "Ava, this is Saira."

The figure stares blankly back at her. "Nice to meet you, Ava."

Chapter Two

"What are your intentions?" the guard yells in his face.

Rais smiles up at him. He doesn't feel like putting effort into answering his question, or any of the other questions they berate him with.

The palace before him hangs on the side of a cliff. Directly below it is a series of docks and bridges leading across the oceanside city. Rais stands at the base of the bridge leading to the main entrance of the palace. Two guards stand before him, their useless and baseless questions ringing out through the air.

"Answer me, kid. We don't take these threats lightly," the guard says.

"I made no threats, sir," Rais says. He looks past them to the gate at the end of the bridge. Normally he would take a more hidden route, sneaking his way past the guards and straight to the vicious Goldryn Queen. Although today he chose to present a more formal approach. To let Stygian be aware of his arrival. She has always been more honest when it came to unexpected affairs, but Rais is not seeking honesty. He seeks a reaction. Rais plans on gauging her responses in accordance with what he needs to know. He imagines Stygian is unaware of how easy she is to read.

His attention switches back to the guards, as one swings a sword toward his throat. Rais figures they were ordered by Queen Stygian to not let any Wyntryn's into the palace. He told them his name was Raiden, but he failed to mention he was the tenth protector of Wyntryn. If they figured that out on their own, it might explain why a gleaming blade is flying at him.

Rais slides his sword from its sheath on his back and meets the guard's blade with a loud clash of metal. It rings out through the air, an electric sound that sends waves of excitement through him. He pulls on his central energy, igniting his inner electricity. He sends it through his hands and into his blade. He swings the sword back, and instead of taking the man by the flesh, he meets the guard's sword once more. The man goes ramrod straight, electricity coursing through his veins. Rais steps back and kicks the man in the gut with one hard blow. The guard flies backward, his eyes going wide in shock. He lays on the bridge's cobblestone brick, flinching and shaking.

The other guard lets out an enraged call for battle and moves to attack. But the white-haired boy simply lifts his hand to stop him. "I already told you, sir, I am Stygian's old friend. She will understand if you go against your orders. Do me a favor, tell her the Sparrow is here. I will wait."

"To you, she is her Highness the Queen," he spits out. Despite his façade of bravery, Rais can see the fear soaking the man's mind. He is vulnerable to attacks of the mind, but Raiden has no interest in disheveling someone's mind for his own needs. That is a cruelty reserved for only those deserving of such pains. And he won't take that route now, because he has already put so much effort into going by this the proper way.

"Please let her Highness the Queen know I am here." He sheathes his sword and gestures for the guard to leave.

The Goldryn soldier steps backward, tripping over the other guard and falling onto the cobblestone. He has a look of horror as he stumbles back onto his feet. He hoists the guard up, supporting him as they stand together. Then they fumble across the bridge in slow, uncoordinated movements. When they finally reach the entrance, the soldiers by the door quickly move to get the gates open to let them through.

Rais leans on the railing beside him, patiently watching the doors.

As expected, they eventually open, and the guard Rais is waiting for comes hurrying down the bridge at a brisk pace.

"You can follow me, sir," he says. His breathing is unsteady.

It makes him wonder why such a powerful ruler would let such weaklings man her gates. He thought better of her.

He follows the guard down the bridge and through the palace gates. As they enter the mystical palace on the sea, Rais lets himself take a steadying breath. He has a long day ahead of him.

They walk through the halls of the palace, the bricks surrounding them shimmer teal and coral. The walls of the palace are made of thickly cut stones and have deep carvings of the ancient language strewn across them. Windows line the right side of the wall; large openings that are cut into the stone and lead to small outcroppings that look out over the ocean and the city below. Rais gazes out at the quickly darkening sky beyond the open windows. He watches as the Goldryn capital comes to life underneath the bright moon. Lanterns float up into the sky, streetlights set ablaze, and music begins to ricochet through the open air.

"Quickly now," the guard shouts at him. "The Queen hates lack of haste."

Rais pulls himself away from the entrancing setting and runs up the stairs after the guard. The man's uniform is a deep purple, with a symbol of a three-headed dragon cresting the back panel. He has a long sword holstered to his side, identical to the one the other guard had swung at Rais earlier.

The guard sees Rais staring at his weapon, and he slides his hand around it in warning. As if the scrawny guard can pose a real threat to him. Rais slips through the shields of the guard's mind. To his amusement, the guard truly believes he can avoid the same fate as his partner; the other Goldryn soldier Rais left withering on the stones of the bridge.

When they reach the top of the spiral staircase, there are two huge doors that encompass an entire wall. The guard walks over to a woman by the doors, and she gives him a nod. The dark, heavy wood swings inwards, revealing a large room encrusted with gems and overflowing with plants of all kinds. A woman stands before the throne, Stygian. Her gown looks like obsidian hanging from her thin frame. Her hair is pulled tightly into a braided bun at the back of her head and a shining maroon crown is nestled atop her dark brown hair.

"It's been so long, Raiden. I hope my mother hasn't corrupted you with her foolery," she says. Stygian easily disregards him, despite her knowing Rais since he was a toddler.

"Have you heard of her fate in Grymyr?" He asks, letting his manipulations begin. The Queen's mind is far too guarded for him to slip by. She has been building up her walls since she escaped from her mother's grasps. If he can't break through her mind with his own, then he will do it with words.

She sits back on the throne, her fingers wrapping tightly around the arms. A smile stretches across her face. "I have."

"Then you are aware that you are the accused?" Rais walks towards her, feeling a rush of energy charge through him.

Her smile doesn't subside, but her eyes show a disturbing lack of emotion. "You know I hated Alys, but I have no reason to murder her. Do you really think that low of me, old friend?"

He ignores her petulant question and asks, "do you not want vengeance?"

She lets out a short laugh. "No, no. Vengeance is for the weak, the blind. I have no interest in such useless endeavors. I have never known vengeance to bring the dead back to life."

"Do you know who did it?"

"I do, but I won't tell you. There's no need to send you off to kill someone else," Stygian says. Rais stares back at her, anger building in his gut. The anger he wants her to sense. She must feel it because she continues to speak. "If you're so desperate to know … it was a boy, in Grymyr. One of those annoying Society freaks Alys attempted to rescue years back."

"Levites," he says. That kid from the Society of the Collective. Rais had met him earlier that summer when going to Grymyr as the Wyntryn representative.

"Hmm. You have a lot of anger in you, Rais, I reckon you should work on that. It is not fitting for someone who wants to be king." She lifts herself from the throne and moves towards him. Her black dress slides across the stone, her threatening presence moving ever closer.

"I have no interest in being king," Rais corrects her.

"That's not what I see in your mind. I see a boy who was abandoned, in need of help. A purpose … let me give you a purpose. Wyntryn is without a ruler, and I have Wyntryn blood. I can help you take the throne. The other protectors of Wyntryn will have no choice but to listen to me because I am the daughter of the late Queen Alys." She reaches her finger out towards him, a purple fire twisting around it. Rais backs away, keeping a distance between them. He fights hard to hide his triumph because Stygian only sees in his mind what Rais is presenting to her. Her arrogance makes her oblivious to his tricks.

"What happened to you Syn?" His voice comes out hushed. "What happened in Eventyr that made you this way?"

"I met the only person who has ever seen me for who I am. An ally who helped give me this throne so that if my mother ever decided to come back for me, I would have a much stronger army than Wyntryn. And I would win." She lets her hand fall and looks around the room. A quiet breeze rustles in from the windows that crown the high ceiling. "What happened, was I became Queen. You and the other regions may think I'm evil, but my people respect me. That's more than Alys ever had."

Rais shakes his head in disbelief. "It was never a competition. She wanted her daughter. You chose to give up on her and follow this path."

"She lit the Eventyr forest on fire in search of a dragon's scale. She killed your parents! She even chose that damned girl over me. Claimed I could never match her prowess but look at me now," she yells. Her eyes gain a fire Rais had once seen in her mother.

"You killed my parents, Your Highness. You were a part of lighting that forest on fire. You want those talismans as much as any other person. You only allied yourself with Kalenti Alberona because she was in possession of the scale." He points to the crown upon her head, hoping what he told her is the truth. "You bargained your heart for that crown. You were not always like this."

"Why are you here then Raiden? What do you want from a heartless, selfish Queen?" she asks.

"I wanted to know if you went in search of your sister. I also wanted to see if you cared at all that your mother had such a horrible fate—clearly, you do not."

She raises her eyebrows. "My sister is a lost cause. I heard she was left an empty vessel after our mother's death. Even if I did care for either of them, they are nothing now."

"You are a cruel woman. I hope you realize that it was not me who was corrupted by Alys. It was you. Corrupted by your need to be superior." He turns to leave the room, but Stygian sends a flash of dark fire shooting towards him. Rais turns and meets her gaze as the fire dissipates into the air around him. "You forgot who trained me."

Walking away is a sweet victory for Rais. He has gotten all that he could ask for. He walks away knowing who killed Alys, and the shattered state that Stygian is in. Those two things are enough to quiet his own need for vengeance. Stygian is not one to have sudden bursts of anger—of any emotion. She has always been quiet, controlled. Her attacking Rais with his back turned only shows the grief she is really feeling. The grief she will never admit to anyone because she has committed her life to destroying her mother and everything her mother ever loved.

In addition to Rais' successes, he now knows the location of two talismans. The dragon scale is in the hands of the Queen of Eventyr. And the other, hidden in the mountains of Wyntryn. He is one step closer to completing Alys' wishes. One step closer to finding the talismans and returning them home to Wyntryn. And once he has those talismans, he can save his home from the terrifying beasts who have consumed the ancient lands.

The large doors shut behind him as he exits the throne room. He looks around for the guard who had escorted him there, but he is nowhere to be seen.

In the corner of his vision, he sees a glimpse of white fabric and turns to see Willow. She's as graceful as ever, her hair still stained the same lavender as when he last saw her. The lavender is in memory of her little brother, who died at a young age from an incurable sickness. She had told him once that it was her brother's favorite color. "Willow," he whispers.

"Rais," she says. Her face lights up at the sight of him.

"I thought I would never see you again." Rais pulls her into a hug.

She hugs him back and then pushes him an arm's length away to get a good look at her friend. "What are you doing here?"

"Never mind that, did she hurt you?" he asks. Willow shakes her head.

"You know it's not safe here in Goldryn. It isn't safe for any Wyntryns. Do you know she's been refusing refugees? Turning them away at the city gates," she says. Her eyes are wide, studying his face.

"I can protect myself." Rais narrows his eyes. "If anything, it is you who I am worried about."

"I am fine, don't you forget that I can protect myself too. The difference is that Stygian is after Wyntryns. I am protected here because of my loyalty and heritage. You are targeted because of yours," she says. "I want to catch up, but you should leave, get safely back to the manor."

"You deserve to come home too. Without Alys and the other mages there, it has become quite lonely. Everyone has retreated to the mountains or escaped to another region."

Willow pulls his hand with hers, holding it between them. Rais looks into her ethereal face. She has a mystical beauty but refuses any man who shows interest. Few knew, but she has been in love with a woman from across the ocean for years, but the woman turned her away long ago, leaving her to move to Wyntryn and train under Alys.

"Remember that you are not alone. I am forever indebted to you, to Wyntryn. I know Stygian took me, but I am no longer a prisoner here. She hasn't forgotten that we once were friends. I am safe, but you need to stay safe too." Her hands are ice cold. Rais so badly wants to slip into the Sonder to see if what she is saying is true, but he doesn't. He lets her thoughts stay hers.

"I will go then." He pulls his hand from Willow's and walks towards the staircase. He feels an urge to make sure they will see each other again, so he turns back to her to ask a question. The thought of her reminds him of their past. The days when they trained together in the ancient halls of the snowy manor in the woods. "Willow?" he asks.

"Yes?"

"Let us not become strangers?" He meets her pale purple eyes, and a sad smile falls on her lips.

"We could never be," she replies quietly, watching as her friend leaves.

Rais slips down the stairs. A feeling of utter loneliness crashes over him. He is destined to remain the sole protector of the Wyntryn Manor. Alone there, until the heiress is eventually called home.

Chapter Three

The evening sun shines down through the circle window. Reflecting the mysterious symbols across Ava's skin. She stares into the darkness. Her gaze locked with Saira's. The mysterious man who appeared with her face on his own. Despite the warmth that radiates from the window, a chill passes over her. Her heart stutters to find its rhythm in his presence.

Saira draws attention, but it is as if he isn't even there. Not present in the moment. Ava can't help but stare—watching him and the dullness in his eyes, the lack of warmth in his skin. A dead man walking. A person living on another plane of existence, grasping onto what he can in this reality. In this room. Somehow, she is seeing into him, through him. Like an open book. His mind draws her in. He reaches out his hand to Ava, but she takes a step back.

She is afraid to touch him. Afraid of what she might see. If he can reflect her face back to her, what else can he show her? What if by shaking his hand, he shows her all of the memories she is scared of. Memories that may hold even more terrors than the reality of losing her parents. Memories that are more painful than loneliness. Saira's gaze stays on her as she hesitates.

Levi gives her a sense of safety, but this unfamiliar figure screams the opposite. She can feel his desperation seeping through him and into the room.

Saira's hand hangs loosely in the air. Ava reaches out, letting his hand wrap around hers. His touch causes discomfort to spread through her. As soon as she can, she quickly pulls her hand away. She turns her gaze to Levi, who raises an eyebrow in question. She whispers to him, "what does he have to do with any of this?"

"Just wait," he says.

From seemingly nowhere a force penetrates her mind. A deafening scream leaves her mouth. It feels like a dagger is twisting into her mind. She moves her hands to her head, holding, grasping, begging for it to go away. Saira's voice rings through her skull. *You need to let go*, it calls out, clawing into her mind.

"Stop!" she screams. "Stop."

Blue shrouds her vision, and she falls into a world that is not entirely her own. It's the same room, same window, same books. But now it is only Ava, and Saira's empty face staring back at her. She stands up straight, her mind in a dream-like state, the pain is suddenly gone. She looks around herself, everything is blurred over in a haze of blue.

It is colder here, different.

The dream is gone in an instant. Another shattering pain rips through Ava's mind, and then she feels the wooden floor beneath her. Feels the smooth wood on the side of her face. A hand grasps her arm. "Ava?" Levi's voice calls out to her.

She gasps for air. She sits upright and pushes Levi away from her. "What was that?" she demands. She reaches her fingers up to the warm tears that stain her face.

Saira gazes down at her, and the same chill from before travels through her bones. He tilts his head. He is void of any perceivable emotion—an empty vessel of a man. "Ava, you have just experienced the Sonder."

"What is that supposed to mean?" Ava shouts at him. A panic flowers in her chest, spreading with steady grace, consuming her.

His voice is low, bone-rattling. "The Sonder is an ability accessed through the Plane of Verity. It is where your mind goes when you separate from your physical body. The Sonder is something attainable by those born into the bloodline of one of the original families in Kanaleigh. The bloodlines were made when the blood of mythical creatures was fused with human blood. Although now, generations later it can be attained by dying and being brought back to life."

"That's impossible," she whispers. "No one can be brought back to life."

"Those with access to the Sonder, can." Saira's features are of a boy her age, seventeen at best. But his eyes, his voice, come from someone who has seen life. Lived beyond a child's dreams. He continues to speak, interrupting Ava's thoughts. "I can tell this must shock you, but from my understanding, you have experienced the Sonder before. You are capable, but you can't seem to remember."

Ava turns again to Levi. "What have you told him about me?" Levi diverts his gaze from hers. "Why?" Ava demands. She gets up from the floor and straightens her spine.

Saira says, "I know you are confused. Let me explain."

"I don't want to hear your explanations!" she shouts. "I don't want to be here. I only want to find what my mother left behind for me."

"Why do you assume what she left behind isn't the information I have to share?" he persists, leaning towards her.

"I have no reason to trust or believe you. I do believe that my mother was smart enough not to entertain any conversation with you," she says.

Levi steps between them, putting his hand to Saira's chest and pushing him backward. "Ava, breathe. Give him a chance to explain. Then feel free to act as you please. And Saira, there's no need to be rude."

Ava nods at Levi in thanks. "I'll listen."

"The Sonder is a space minds can collectively go if they have access. What happened before, the pain you felt, it was because I was forcing your mind into that place. A place you didn't choose to go to yourself. You were fighting me, which is why it was so painful. When you give in, it doesn't hurt. With the Sonder, you can see into others' minds. You can access a collective of people, of information, with endless possibilities. You can retain your memories by using the Sonder as your asset. You can find remnants of your mother if you get close enough." He begins to pace. Ava watches, feeling unsteady on her feet. "I know, I know, you are thinking, why should I believe you? My convincing factor is simple you see. I died," he says with a timid smile.

Her mind snaps to attention. "I'm sorry, what?"

"I... died. So did Levi here. We both faced death and were brought back to life. It is a beautiful thing the Sonder. Giving mere mortals the ability to return from death. That is why I know your mother is out there. Not alive, most certainly dead, but her mind might have been trapped in the collective conscious. You only have to look in the right places." His words are placid.

The familiar snake coils tightly around Ava's heart. It stops her blood flow, spinning a spindle of dread inside of her. Saira's smile stretches further, as if in response to her emotions, her thoughts. But Ava knows it is insane to think he can sense what is happening within her mind. She gets the nerve to respond and tells him, "my mother is dead. Don't tell me I can find her when I can't. It's simply cruel. She is gone, and if she left anything behind for me, I doubt I'll find it with you."

"No, Ava. You are not listening to me!" His breathing is unsteady and wild. "My mind and soul are just as much existing in the Sonder now as they are here with you. Who is to say the part of your mother that was in the Sonder when she died, isn't there now? Ava, I can see you are scared—don't be. This is not scary. It is a relief. A blessing."

"I think I would prefer to believe that she is walking in the stars with our ancestors. Not trapped in this wretched world. The more you say the more I find it all entirely ridiculous." She spins on her heel, ready to storm out of the room, but Levi's hand catches on her shoulder. Levi pulls her towards him. "What do you want?"

"I'm only trying to help," Levi pleads with her.

"You think this is helping?" She throws her hand towards Saira. "He wore my face. He dug daggers into my brain!"

"What he's saying is true, or at least I believe most of it. I died too, Ava. I really did. If it weren't for Ms. Ethelle I wouldn't be here. I know this place because these people saved me. I thought they could help you too," he says quietly. Seeing Levi, feeling his sincerity is grounding for Ava. His voice helps calm her mind.

"You died?" she asks. Her emotions are substantially more tamable now than before.

"I was sick as a child and fell to a premature death. My parents thought I had a relapse last week, which is why Ms. Ethelle was so worried. But Ava, I can see into the Sonder. I don't really believe you can find your mother there, but it can reveal answers to you. It could return your memories to you." He grazes her cheek with his hand. "Please, give it a chance."

"I already did."

It is hard to not fall into Saira's scheme and listen to Levi. She can believe in the Sonder, believe they had both died, and that she might have died too. Somehow those things seem feasible to her. But Saira feels wrong. That place is simply wrong. Even if it did remind her of her mother's love for literature and mysterious creatures, she has no desire to be there a second longer.

Ava does believe that Levi is telling her the truth. She can see it in his eyes. She trusts him. He is the only person she has left, the only person who still cares. So maybe she has no choice but to trust him. And that blind faith in him gives her some acceptance of what they have told her, but her mind is still on fire from Saira's mental attack. She wants to go home, but she can't help but consider the suggestion. To use this Plane of Verity to try to access whatever is hidden deep within her.

"Levi?" she asks hesitantly.

"Yes?"

"Will you show me how to access the Sonder?"

"You feel others' emotions through the air, like

electricity reverberating from them, correct?" he asks. Still standing close to her, his hand lightly touching her cheek.

"I suppose so, yes."

He nods. "Then you've already accessed the Sonder. You just have to remember how to use it."

"Sounds a lot easier than it probably is." She steps away from Levi, staring directly at Saira. "Why can't I feel your emotions?" she asks on a whim.

He tenses. "I'm not surprised you can't access my mind."

"If the Sonder is a collective, revealing other's minds. How are they hidden?" She speaks slowly.

Saira tilts his head. "You have only learned of this now Ava, don't be surprised when it doesn't come naturally to you." His voice is clear and smooth.

"I don't mean to be rude, but you both said it yourselves, I knew how to access the Sonder before I lost my memories." She focuses on Saira. "And there is something off about you. You feel wrong."

He laughs but his face shows no amusement. "I feel wrong? You've only just met me. You know nothing about me," Saira says.

"If I understand what you've said about the Sonder, you can't be blocking your mind from me, because otherwise, I wouldn't be able to feel anything. Yet, I feel something. What are you hiding?"

"Ava," Levi warns.

"No. We came here for answers, I am searching for answers. You wanted me to listen to Saira, so I am investing in what he has to share." She pushes away the fear she feels towards Saira and lets herself recover the confidence she has repressed for the past few months.

"Ava, it's getting dark out. If you want to keep asking Saira questions, we can come back tomorrow."

The first and last time Ava left the apartment at night after her mother's death, something happened. She can't quite remember it, but Levi tried to explain it to her. He told her that all of a sudden, she froze in place. Levi guessed that a memory returned to her and that she didn't handle it well. It was bad enough that Ava doesn't want to go through it again or make Levi have to help her through it again.

She tears her gaze from Saira's and walks out of the room.

Ava is glad Levi offered up a chance for her to leave, but she still wants an answer to her question.

She feels empowered, better than she has felt in a long time. Whatever this Sonder is that she has accessed, that Saira forced her into, it unlocked something that has been hidden away in Ava's mind. Not her memories, but a repressed power.

She walks back down the stairwell and through the maze of bookshelves, Levi at her heels. She has a lot to say to Levi, but she holds her tongue. She decides to wait until they are outside of the library.

They move past the desk at the front where Ms. Ethelle sat before, her book is still open on the desk, but she is nowhere in sight. Ava slides her gaze away from the open book and continues past the desk, and out the front doors. As soon as the door shuts behind them, she turns to Levi. "How many other lies have you told me?" she asks.

"Ava ..." he says quietly.

"No. You answer me. How many?"

"Not here, not now. It's getting dark," he reminds her.

"I don't care. If I see them and break down, I will

survive. I've been living with this pain for months. The only thing that has carried me through it is you, but it turns out you've been lying to my face. Every day." Her eyes burn, her heart burns. A fire wells up inside of her. A hidden power fights to break through her mind. Escape from the Sonder into the world around her.

"I have lied, but it was all to protect you." He looks lost, distressed. His face sunken in.

"Protect me? I'm missing memories from most of my life. If you wanted to protect me you would give me truths. Things that I could know were real. Facts I could rely on. Something, anything to grasp onto." She begins to laugh, almost manic, tears starting to flow from the corners of her eyes and travel down her skin. "Gods! How am I supposed to trust or believe in anything or anyone, when you of all people lie to me?"

Levi's head drops. His hands press against his temples. "I am sorry Ava. I thought—"

"You didn't think."

She begins to walk down the rugged pathway to the street. She steadies her breathing, trying her best to calm down.

A car comes flying down the road, headlights shining.

She goes still. Her heart thunders in her chest. A deer in the headlights. She gasps, her lungs moving rapidly. Her body seems to tilt, falling faster and faster through the very ground beneath her feet. The snake buried in her chest bites down on her, sinking in its venom. Sealing her fate. Her own voice rings loudly in her head, filling her skull with unrelenting pressure. It screams for her mother. Somewhere beyond that deafening sound, is her mother's voice calling for her.

She stands frozen on the sidewalk in wake of the car. It has long passed, but the feeling is unrelenting inside of her. It refuses to subside.

"Ava!" her mother calls out. "It's okay," the voice reassures.

Levi's face comes into view, he holds her arms, then pulls her into a hug. "Close your eyes, it's gone. You're okay. It's months behind you now. You are safe. Nothing will hurt you now," he whispers into her neck.

That's why Ava trusts him. Despite his blatant lies, she trusts him because he helps her. He tries his best to protect her from the terrors she can't avoid. Unlike anyone else in her life, Levi will always be there for her. On the tormented days and on the peaceful days, he always shows up.

Chapter Four

Wind blows across the ocean in strong gusts, spraying water up onto the coastal streets. A calm air blankets the City on the Sea, the capital of Goldryn. Rais tours the city, twisting through the crowds while searching for a familiar face. He seeks a woman known as Nina. A tall, broad-shouldered woman with dark auburn eyes and a cold face. Her skin is darker than the sandstone but brighter than the rocky Wyntryn mountains. Nina has been a part of Rais' life since he first arrived at Alys' home.

Alys had sent Nina to Goldryn on a mission before her death. He hopes to find her there now. After their mentor's death, Nina chose to stay in Goldryn rather than return home. She never truly loved living at the manor. Never quite enjoyed having someone give her orders. It makes sense to Rais that she would end up staying in the city, making a life of her own.

People shove past him, setting their sights on the various places across the city that had only recently opened their doors at sunset. The city is alive at night, ebbing and flowing as the waves crash on the sandy shores. He walks through the streets, admiring the tan bricks glow under the moonlight. Torches are lit along every street, and huge bonfires are set up in each town square. The fire creates an aura of passion and beauty. Underneath the stars and glowing with the light of the fires, people sing and dance. Instruments of all kinds ring out into the night.

Young rouges run through the crowds, pickpocketing the privileged and scurrying off to the market tents. Despite the abundance of life on the streets, many of the homes look abandoned. They have dark windows, missing doors, and a sadness that seeps into the excitement of the night.

He finds his way to the market tents set up along the water's edge, watching as farmers set up displays of fruits and vegetables of all kinds. Poachers hang their recent catches and display meats wrapped in salt. Plants and flowers weaved into jewelry are sold in various tents. And he can see a lot of the same styles of jewelry being worn by many of the city folk as they roam the streets.

In the darkest corners of the city is where he suspects he'll find Nina. She is skilled with daggers and close combat. It wouldn't be a surprise to find her lurking around the pubs filled with others of similar talents. He's heard of the guilds of bounty hunters that work in secret for Stygian. Knowing her skills, it's possible she's been recruited to join one of the guilds.

The last time he had seen her, she wore her hair in numerous thick braids highlighted with auburn and gold. Her eyes were bright with a drive unmatched by any other woman who walked the Plane of Verity. She was high on a streak of successes and triumphs.

A year prior, Nina and Rais had completed their training. And that day he last saw her, she left the manor for Goldryn. It was her first solo mission. Before then she and Rais had gone on missions together. They would fight and capture the beasts that roamed the snowy woods of Wyntryn. They would go from village to village gathering what was left of the region's people. After that year was over, they had been successful in every task they were given. But what had driven Nina away, was the same thing that drove Rais to stay.

They found less than a thousand survivors on their missions. Many of the Wyntryns had fled the region entirely. They moved into Grymyr to join the workforce or the Society of the Collective. Many moved to the Isles to join the fisherman and pirates. Some escaped to refugee camps in Goldryn or crossed the seas to the eastern continent. Few remained in Wyntryn. Most of them hidden in the caverns below the northern mountains. The terror of the beasts on Wyntryn's lands drove them away, including Nina. She hated that she couldn't save them all and that they gave up and left, so she did too. But Rais stayed and found himself committed to bringing his people home.

What would Nina think of the Wyntryn he had left behind to come to Goldryn? What would she think of the chaos that had ensued after Alys' death? Without a Queen, the region descended further into madness. The soldiers and mages no longer had a leader, so they gave up the fight—left or went into hiding like everyone else. The manor he and Nina grew up in was once filled with young trainees but is now empty. Abandoned and slowly filling with dust. Only three cities remain in Wyntryn, and they are hidden below the mountains. Kept a secret from anyone beyond the Wyntryn people.

Goldryn on the other hand is as lively as ever. The streets awake with excitement and adventure. He may dislike the Queen, but she certainly did have the respect and love of her people. They will follow her to the ends of the world if she asks. It is no wonder Nina remains here. Hidden in the City on the Sea, living a life more fulfilling than anything Wyntryn can provide her.

He knows she is a great fighter with a keen mind, but she is horrible at covering her tracks. When they used to hide in the snowy forests of their home, Raiden would always find her by following the huge footprints she left behind. She never learned how to cover her tracks. He would find her the same way now, by following the clues she never meant to leave behind.

He can find them through the Sonder. Scattered clues around the city that steadily fade with time. Rais can see a trail of her that spins through the streets of the city. He follows the trail now, finding his way through the streets and to the busiest part of the coastal market. His mind buzzes with the thoughts of the many people pushing around him and browsing the tents. He can sense their pleasures, worries, and stressors. All their emotions tugging through their minds and seeping out into the air.

He pushes away the free-floating thoughts of the people and focuses on Nina's own trail of thoughts.

Rais pulls the hood of his cloak farther forward, covering his white hair. He carefully steps around the masses of people, until he stands before a particular tent set up along the market street. It is covered in a black velvet sheet. A sign hanging loosely above eye level, reads, Aysand Steel Blades.

The person behind the stand is shrouded in a black hood like his own, the only visible feature is their reddish-brown eyes. Like the redwoods from Wyntryn, dark and vibrant. "How much for this?" he asks. He holds up a curved blade with a carved wooden handle. A snake with sharp scales twists around the hilt.

"What brought you here?" they ask. They tug the blade from him.

"I want to buy that knife," he insists. "What is it made of?"

"Ancient oak. The rivets and blade are made of Aysand steel. I'll trade it for a blade of equal quality."

Rais pulls one of the knives from the inside of his dark blue coat and sets it on the table before the seller.

"I haven't seen this in forever," they whisper. Their northern accent leaks out into their words. "I thought you would have replaced it with a sharper blade by now."

"It was never mine to give away. Will it make a fair trade?" he asks.

The merchant nods, placing the Aysand steel knife before him. "What took you so long to come for me?"

"I was afraid you would turn me away."

"Let me wrap things up here, I'll meet you back at my place. It's right above the pub on 47th," she speaks quickly. "I won't be long."

Raiden slides his new knife into place in his jacket. He walks back into the crowd and finds his way to the closest empty street. He can feel the pressures of the people's minds slipping away as he moves quickly across the cobblestone. Small flames flicker from tall iron posts along the way. Plants crown the tops of buildings and ivy creeps up the bricks. Rais admires the way the city is built and decorated. He loves the way the people bring it to life. It would be nice if his own home was the same way. Rather, it would be fantastic if Wyntryn wasn't ablaze in eternal fire. That beasts of flame and horse didn't keep the land entrapped. It seems unfair that the people in Goldryn get to have this life. Especially when his own people are forced to fight for their lives every day. Few Wyntryn's have the ability to live without fear. There is a longing deeply rooted in him that Wyntryn will one day regain the same glory.

The salty air brushes past him in small gusts. In the forests beyond the city, autumn leaves begin to fall from the ancient oaks. Rais feels the changing of seasons like the movement of a sword. It's smooth, easy, and predictable. He lets his mind slip into the Sonder, comforted by the cooling air. The Plane of Verity is quiet. As the blue haze envelops him, a silence blankets the street. The only sounds are distant, reverberating from the crowded market that is far behind him now.

In that silence, he feels a darkness, much sharper than the cool breezes of the coming autumn. An unnerving mind leaks from an alleyway up ahead. He can only imagine that mind being possessed by some sneering and vile creature.

Electricity flies through him in anticipation. As he nears the alley he can feel whispers of emotions, muggy and tangled. They slip out of its mind and into the Sonder in a sticky web. He pushes toward it and tries to feel its thoughts. Though nothing legible trickles out into the web, only mindless and dismantled thoughts. He steps into the alleyway now. The only light is the moon shining over the rooftops.

The stones of the alleyway are covered in a thick green moss that floats in standing water. Rais walks through the muck, feeling for the muddled mind hidden in the dark. Its thoughts still flutter in and out of the growing web in the Sonder. The mind feels so real, yet he sees no physical presence in the alley.

A figure falls from above, upon him in seconds.

He retracts his mind from the Sonder, centering himself in the alley. He sends lightning through his fingertips, igniting the air around him. The man's foot kicks out into his chest, but he doesn't falter. He reaches forward sending strikes of lightning through the tortured man. Rais twists into his mind, intruding into his thoughts. The web of mindless muck so close to his own is disturbing. Whatever happened to this man is beyond inhumane. He pulls away from the man and retracts his mind. But his energy continues to buzz through his skin. "What did she do to you?" he asks.

The man's mind seems to clear for a moment, a clarity crossing his features, before falling back to the same hardened gaze as before. The man bends his knees and lunges at him. Rais invades the man's mind again, commanding him to freeze. To not move a muscle. In the man's stagnant state, Rais searches the spiderwebs of his thoughts. He tears through the tendrils with ease, in search of the man's true consciousness. Not the one forced upon him that spreads like sticky glue. Rais pushes a thought forward, *why?* Rais detracts from his mind to look the man in the eye.

His icy blue gaze slowly fills with life. Rais can tell he's fighting down the cobwebs that still plague his conscious. *Why?* he pushes forward again.

"To find what you know," he croaks out.

"You have been following me since I left the palace. What do you think I know?" Rais asks.

The man's face is pale, lifeless. "They took my mind. I became lost in the plane, and …"

"What do you think I know?"

The life in the man's eyes retreats into him. He fights out what words he can. "All I know of is the woman with dark eyes. You gave her a blade connected to a power source. I felt it ... what is it from?" he gasps out.

Rais pushes back into the man's mind and tells him to forget his mission to follow him. He turns away from the man, pulling his hood back over his hair. He conceals his mind from the Sonder and walks away from whom he assumes to be Stygian's spy. The man will only stop following him if he remains ignorant to Rais' presence, as to not remind him that he was given a mission to follow Rais.

Hopefully, he will also remain ignorant of the dagger Rais gave Nina. Because the knife is connected to a power source. All the mages trained under Alys were given daggers of that kind. Ones that are connected to a powerful fountain beyond the manor's walls. The knives were each enchanted in a way that allows them to draw energy from that sacred place. The one Rais gave Nina, was her own. She had left it at the manor, and Rais brought it with him in the intention of giving it to her himself.

Raiden stands outside the pub on 47th street. The lights flicker, neon greens flashing against the pale assortment of flowers that trickle down the front of the building. Knowing his friend, she has most likely already settled herself inside. He breathes in the salty air and shakes his tiredness away. It had been a long trip that morning to get to the palace. It is impossible to alate from one place to another within the city, so he had to travel by horse. The days of riding have left his legs and shoulders aching. He can't remember the last time he had ridden for more than a day. Riding horses has never been a habit for him. He has always preferred to practice his swordsmanship or meddle in the Sonder. And with all the exertions of energy recently, he has reached his limits.

He stands before the pub, drowning with the weight of reaching those limits. His body sags against him. His muscles aching and his mind overstimulated. It forces him to try twice as hard to focus on the next task at hand. He is going to try to convince Nina to come home to Wyntryn.

Rais enters the pub, and a familiar voice rings out, "Golden Sparrow!" He turns to the Wyntryn diplomat. The man is towering, a body carved from stone. Eieran has a deep laugh that rattles the glasses on the surrounding tables.

"To think I would run into you here," Rais says.

"To think I would run into the Golden Sparrow. And to think you would dare turn down my offers of diplomacy twice. You are a legend, son," he bellows. His white hair shakes against his chest.

"Cousin," Rais says. His thoughts are haunted by the state of that poor man's mind in the alleyway. "I ran into a peculiar man in the streets today. He was covered in webs. His mind ... truly mangled."

Eieran nods, letting out a sigh. "Yes, there have been more and more as the seasons change. I suspect it is the Society sending them here."

Rais furrows his brows. "Not Stygian?"

He watches as Eieran fights his amusement at the question. "No, no, not her. She has evil in her, but she would never shatter an innocent mind."

Rais senses a presence approaching him. He turns to her. "Nina."

"Ah your cousin is here," she spits. "Let's go, Rais. My place is upstairs." Eieran moves to get up, but Nina tilts her head in warning. He smiles awkwardly and leans back into his seat.

"I will find you before I leave, cousin. I want to know more about what the Society has been doing."

He follows Nina through the people, who are drunk with the entrancing aromas being handed out by the waitresses. Nina even reaches out and takes one for herself. She pops the cork off with her thumb and breathes in the flowy purple air. It causes her body to relax into fluidity. She tosses the glass to the side, ignoring it as it shatters on the wooden floor. Rais looks to the glass on the floor, fighting his urge to clean it up. She is so disrespectful of simple kindnesses. But Rais likes that about her, the freeness of her spirit and the opposing hardness of her personality.

They reach an open doorway that leads up into a set of rickety stairs. Between the walls of the stairs, the slurred voices of the people in the pub soften. "Is selling knives a lucrative business?" Rais asks.

She shakes her head. "No, it's not. But I prefer it over being an assassin. And living in Goldryn is expensive for foreigners."

"You can always come home," he suggests. She turns to him with tense eyes.

"That's real funny, Sparrow, but no."

He pushes his hand along his neck. "Have you heard about the attacks? About Alys?"

"All of it, yes. Wyntryn is not my problem anymore. Alys doesn't rule my life. If anything, I am finally free." She pushes through the door at the top of the stairs.

"Free?" Rais snaps back. "You signed a blood oath. And what about the freedom of the citizens that have been killed by the monsters that we were assigned to eradicate?" He quickly follows her into the dark room.

Nina turns to him, her eyes ablaze. "Who will come after me to hold me accountable? You?"

"Please, it is not about accountability. It is about helping the helpless. We were trained for this."

"We were trained yes, but did we choose?" she asks. Her body is timid and her mind stronger than it had been when he last saw her. Rais has no access to her inner thoughts—she shuns him through the Sonder.

"We were not forced to sign the oath. You could have run away then, but you stayed," Rais says.

She smirks. "Sure, but the pressure was a force. Go home Rais, you don't belong in this part of the world. You want me to do what you want to do. You are perfectly capable of doing it yourself."

Rais doesn't disagree with what she says, but he did choose. He's proud to be a protector of Wyntryn. But it's a lonely position. "If I am entirely honest, I want my friend back. There are thousands of reasons for you to return, but that is my real reason for being here," he says.

Nina bites her lip. "You have and always will be my Golden Sparrow. But friends don't have to walk the same paths in life."

"What if I told you I know how to get the first talisman?"

"I wouldn't believe you."

He lets the friendly haze of the Sonder gather around him and pushes his mind's eye to her. She doesn't let him breakthrough at first but eventually gives in to him, letting his memories spread through her own. "See what I see."

Her eyes go wide. "The arrow," she whispers.

"I also have reason to believe that Kalenti Alberona has possession of the dragon scale. But the arrow is in our own arena. We could take back the region with it."

"We could really save them."

"If you want to join me, you can choose to do so Nina. You know where to find me," he says. Rais turns from his friend and leaves. He wants her to come home, but he knows he shouldn't continue to push her any further.

He walks back down the stairwell and into the pub to say his farewell to his cousin. Hopefully, he too, will join him in Wyntryn one day and help save their people. Eieran is one of the highest-ranking diplomats in the region, but he spends more time working outside of Wyntryn than in the region itself.

"Cousin?" Rais asks. Eieran sits slouched in the chair that is far too small for him.

Eieran shifts to look at him. "There is much to tell you, but there is not a need yet to gather the other protectors. You should know though, that the Society has not stopped attacking. I am here to gather information on those webbed minds, as you called them. The Petrichors are investigating the hidden cities for similar influences. You should keep an eye out too, cousin. But since you have exposed yourself to Stygian, it is best you leave now."

Rais pats Eieran's shoulder and shares his goodbye. Between Stygian, Willow, and Nina, he has seen everything he needed to see in the City on the Sea. With his goal completed, he only intends to take his sacred information back to Wyntryn. To the manor where he was raised. He has always known the Society is a threat. They created the Atane, the beasts that have been destroying Wyntryn with fire. Stygian even claims that it is the officer Levites who was the cause of his Queen's death. The same Levites who is supposedly friends with Alys' daughter Ava.

After leaving the pub and heading to the stables on the northern end of the city, he goes straight to his horse. She was originally Alys', a prized black beauty of a creature. The horse whinnies when he appears by the stall. He pushes the door open and lets Oberyn come to him. She leans her head down to his chest. Rais runs his fingers through the horse's thick mane. "Time to go home."

Chapter Five

Ava stands in the doorway of the warped building entrapped in a city of skyscrapers. She lets go of the door and it hushes shut behind her. The room is silent. The wooden desk before her is empty. There is no sign of a shadowy figure haunting the shelved halls. The floorboards creak below her with each footstep. She flinches at each one as the noise reverberates through the room.

She left earlier this morning for the library. She isn't sure what she is looking for, but Ava supposes she will know when she finds it. She wants to make her trip quick so that she can get back to her parent's apartment before Levi does.

Conscious of the instability of her own mind, leaving the apartment alone may have been a bad decision, but for her, it is a necessary one. She needs to face her demons. To find whatever her mother left behind on her own. Ava is the only one who can solve the mysteries of her own past. Which is why she is there now, brushing her fingers through the dust that coats the dismantled library.

The main room is remarkable, an ancient artifact

left behind in a growing technological city. Ava used to devour books. Her room is covered in various stories she once read. Although, books are a rarity in Grymyr. The news she's seen claims that most books on the continent were burned to ash in the third resurgence of the Great War. The war in which the Wyntryns and Goldryns were eradicated, nearly twenty years ago. Their countries were torn apart by mythological beasts that were born and bred in Grymyr's government labs. Ava has only heard whispers of the travesties, but if any of it is true, then she is grateful for the library. For the safety it gives the thousands of books that remain there.

The books are piled high, leaning towers of forgotten literature. Many of the stacks and shelves have collapsed with age and cover many of the pathways between bookshelves.

Ava finds her way to a row of shelves that aren't blocked. Both sides of the shelves in the pathway are lined with symbols. Letters or words from an ancient language foreign to her. They are identical to the symbols that cover the circular window in the attic.

She steps up to the closest bookshelf, following the symbol's simplistic lines with her eyes. She runs her finger across the engraving in the wood. The symbols draw her in, asking her to follow them. They feel alive. The very shelves tell her a story in a language she can't comprehend. She closes her eyes and follows the feeling that the symbols give her. They light a fire within her. It runs through her veins, her mind, vibrating at her fingertips and spreading through her. She pictures the feeling as a bright bursting blue. It reaches down into her gut and pulls her along the maze of shelves. The symbols take her on a journey through the books. Time passes by swiftly.

She steps into empty air and loses balance. Her eyes fly open as she looks down at the staircase before her. She catches herself on the railing with a steadying hand and takes quick mouthfuls of air.

She finds herself on a wide staircase that leads down to a lower level of the building.

The same symbols that were on the shelves and that window, are also on these stairs. They are carved thickly in two straight lines. One on the sixth step down and the other directly above on a wooden beam.

Ava steps down the first few stairs, stopping when she hears voices coming from the lower level. She bends down to sit on the wooden steps. Far enough down the staircase to see through the railing, but high enough to blend in with the shadows. Through the wooden poles, she can make out two women arguing. One woman Ms. Ethelle. The other is a younger woman, with dark hair and pale white skin. From her perch, Ava can barely hear what they say and she is too nervous to get any closer. The woman juts her finger at Ms. Ethelle in a harsh way. Her face contorts with words Ava can't distinguish.

They are surrounded by ornate lamps and four red velvet chairs. The rug below their feet encompasses much of the room. A deep red layered with floral patterns of gold and black. The room is cleaner than the main room of the library. All the books are organized neatly on the shelves. Even crystal chandeliers hang from the ceiling. There are various doors hidden between the shelves lining the walls. Each one is unique in color with a large symbol in the center of frosted glass.

As Ava leans down to examine the doors, her hand slips from the railing and her elbow hits the wooden step. The dark-haired woman's head snaps towards her. Ava pushes herself up and scrambles back up the stairs. Her nails catch on the uneven boards and sharp pains shoot through her fingers. She tries to reach out to the symbols on the bookshelves. She needs them to guide her back out of the books, but she can't grasp onto them. They don't call to her anymore.

"Who's there?" the woman calls out.

Ava runs through the shelves, jumping over books and crumpled papers. She hears the woman running up the steps after her. Ava sees an opening on the bottom of a shelf, so she drops to the ground and slides underneath. She stands up on the other side and backtracks through the stacks, hiding between jumbles of books.

The woman continues running down the other line of shelves. Ava's back is pressed against an angled bookshelf. Her heavy breathing and racing heart are on the verge of giving her away. *What was she afraid that I overheard?* Ava thinks.

As soon as the footsteps pass Ava again, and the woman goes back down the staircase, Ava releases a stifled breath and comes out of hiding. She slips back through the bottom of the shelf and looks for the symbols again. When she finds them on a bookshelf farther down the path, she follows them through the trail of books—eventually finding her way back to the front of the library. She glances around warily for the woman or Ms. Ethelle. Rather than staying to search for answers, she decides to leave. She pushes through the front doors and moves down the stone pathway. She passes under the crooked and mangled tree that grows from the side of the path.

Luckily for Ava, it's still early morning, so it is likely that Levi hasn't arrived at her apartment yet. Since she doesn't want to take any chances, she takes off down the sidewalk. The city is busy in the morning. Cars and people take up every open space. She weaves through people and crosses roads as quickly as her legs will allow.

She lets out a sigh of relief as she finally reaches the entrance to her building. A gust of wind throws her hair in her face as she unlocks the gate with her pin number. She opens the gate and walks through the small garden to the glass front doors. She enters and waves at the man behind the counter. In the early days after her mother's death, he would tell her stories about her mother and father. She passes by him to the elevators and takes one up to the third floor. The metal doors open, and she steps out into the hallway. Down the hall, slouched against the wall is Levi. He looks up at her as she walks toward him.

"Hey, I've been waiting for you."

She smiles to hide her frustration. "Yeah, sorry. I thought I would try to get out on my own for once. After yesterday I realized that I was too fragile and needed to break through that barrier."

"Don't apologize. That's amazing, I'm proud of you." He smiles back at her, but it drops quickly.

She pretends not to notice and simply replies, "thanks." Ava unlocks the door and holds it open for Levi. She pushes it closed behind her, letting the lock click into place. Levi tosses a satchel onto the floor by the sofa. "What's in the bag?" she asks.

"Turns out my parents are maniacs when it comes to forgotten literature. I was thinking that maybe some of these titles might conceal some needed information on the Sonder." He sits on the floor and dumps the contents of the bag out onto the rug.

Ava sits down across from him. Her heart and anxiety burnt out from the morning's events. Despite her belief that there are answers out there somewhere, each time she looks, she finds nothing. And her belief falters evermore.

She wants to be okay with who she is without her memories. But not knowing has been hurting Levi, and she doesn't want to put him through that. But she is also scared. Terrified of what she might find. This morning when she went in search of answers, she didn't even know what she was searching for. She was desperate for anything, but somehow okay with nothing. Her heart and faith are so diminished because of her contradictory emotions. Because everything inside of her is mangled and destroyed.

She sits across from her friend, the boy who knows more about her life than even she does. When he smiles at her, she smiles back. Glad to have someone, and deathly afraid of losing him. She tugs at the papers and pages, skimming, but not retaining. She would like to draw her mind away from her thoughts and focus on the books. But she can't. Her mind refuses to stop churning.

Ava eventually sets the books down and goes to her parent's room. It is the first time she has opened that door since her father left. She walks along the bookcase on the wall, keeping her gaze from straying to the reminders of her past littered throughout the room. She comes across a journal with her mother's name scrawled across the spine. Ava pulls it out and brings it to the living room. She sits down in the same place and opens it up. She flips through the pages until she comes across a letter addressed to her.

When the ocean comes, let it take you. When the river swarms, let it carry you. When you lose yourself, find the water and follow the current. Even if you do not know where you must go, you will always find your way. The current knows, and you are the current. Ever flowing, ever raging, ever soothing. My darling girl, you are the light of my world. Your mind as endless as the depths of the sea, and your heart is as large as the ocean. My love for you never fails.

The journal is filled with short poems and letters written to her mother's loved ones, people she had met in her lifetime. And the letter she reads—the one of oceans, was written for Ava.

She laces her fingers through the journal's pages, savoring the feel of the paper and the words written on the page. Her mother wrote that she had a mind as endless as the depths of the sea, and a heart as large as the ocean. Salty tears sting her eyes. She wipes them away before they can slip down her face. Her mother had her faults, but Ava could always see past them. Because it's her mother, and how can she not love her mother?

She finds another poem a few pages after the one of the oceans, but it is listed to have been written by an Aran Petrichor, not by her mother. The poem is lovely but sad. She lets her eyes go over the words again and again.

A songbird flies only to be taken away by time. In a manor, she flew until the wind pushed her away too soon. Too soon, they cawed, too soon they wept. Our structures now weep with the loss of our niece.

Who is Aran Petrichor, and what happened to his niece? She closes the journal and slides it onto the rug—pushing away the feelings that surface at the thought of her mother.

Hours pass by, and they still sit there on the rug. Levi is seemingly unphased by her lack of reproach to his idea of going through all the old books. Ava simply hopes that Levi will find something so that she can stop reading the books herself.

"You seem better," he says. Levi looks up at her with a crooked smile. The skin beneath his eyes is dark, and he seems to sag into the carpet.

"What?" Ava replies distantly. Her mind is still lost in her mother's letter.

He chuckles and hands her a small piece of paper. On it is a singular symbol painted onto the parchment in dark blue ink. A thin dragon twisted into a circle, with an arrow piercing through the dragon's lower left side, and three dots blotted along the upper right side. "That symbol, it's in a lot of these journals."

"What does it mean?"

"I'm not entirely sure," Levi says.

Ava stands and stretches her arms above her head. "This is exhausting," she says. Ava watches as he flips through one of the books. She hates keeping the events from that morning from him, but she wants to be able to have something for herself. Something that he doesn't know. But still, she doesn't like lying. It doesn't sit right with her. Even if the lie isn't that big of a deal, she is still uncomfortable keeping things from him.

"I need to tell you something," she says, surprising herself.

He sets the leather-bound book down. "What is it?"

"This morning, I didn't go out to just leave the apartment. I went to that library, and I was hoping to feel or find something that would help. I did find something, but it wasn't what I was looking for. There were these symbols on the shelves, and they led me to a stairway leading down to a lower level. When I was going down the staircase, I saw Ms. Ethelle and another woman down there arguing over something. I don't know what, but that woman came after me. And I know it's not much of anything interesting, but I don't want to lie to you." She feels relieved getting it off her chest. Those short few hours of hiding it from him were a burden.

"I thought you'd gone out to get some fresh air." He rubs his upper arm. "How did you find the shelves with the symbols?"

Her brows furrow. "I'm not sure. I suppose I felt them. They were speaking to me, and I followed their voice. It sounds crazy, but I closed my eyes and followed the feeling I got from the symbols," she explains.

"That's not crazy."

"That symbol you handed me. It looks like the ones on the shelves, on the circle window. What if they're connected?" She picks up the piece of paper she'd left on the floor. The symbol of the dragon being pierced by an arrow. "Whatever these symbols mean, they must have something to do with my mother, with the Sonder."

She walks around the sitting chairs to the windows that line the far wall of the room. She stands at the largest window in the center and pulls the curtains open. Ava reaches to the edge of the windowsill and flicks the locks over. She pushes the windows open and listens to the sounds of the city. She leans against the windowsill. The cracking paint pokes her skin. The curtains billow inward and her hair flutters away from her face. Ava breathes in the fresh air and lets out a long breath. Her shoulders heaving with the mental strains that pull against her.

Levi walks up behind her, pushing her dull brown hair behind her shoulder. She straightens her back, a quiet discomfort spreading over her. He leans in towards the crook of her neck. His breath tickles her skin and sends sharp tingles through her. His fingers brush the back of her neck, and she can feel his rarest impulses reverberating from his mind. She turns her head towards him, Levi is so close to her. The edges of his freckles in her peripheral. She doesn't move to get any closer, not wanting to entice him further. But she doesn't push him away either. She doesn't pull away when his fingers lift her chin towards him. Or as his mouth tilts down towards hers. Their breath mingles between them. A minuscule distance between their lips, a tightening thread of anxiety moving through them. Her heart thunders in her chest. She can feel his too, practically jumping against his ribs.

She swallows a shaky breath. A sound shockingly clear when being that close to another person. She can't remember a time when she was this close to another person or if she has ever been. In midst of her thoughts, Levi moves ever so closer. His lips grace hers. She edges upwards, letting their lips connect. For a second, she wants to remain there. To stay in that moment. But to invite him to continue will only hurt Levi.

She pulls away, turning her back to him, to gaze out the window at the silver and black buildings stretching into the sky. Crested by puffy gray clouds.

Levi breathes out an awkward laugh. She doesn't turn to look at him. Rather she lets her head fall as she stares down at the hardwood floors.

"Sorry," he says blankly. She feels him move away, the air around her growing colder with every inch that grows between them.

The door opens, and footsteps sound in the hallway.

She shakes off her fear and runs after him. "Levi!" Ava calls from outside of the apartment doorway. She lets go of the door with her fingers and continues farther down the hall, "Levi! Levi, wait." He stands still, not turning to look at her. "It's not that I don't feel that way about you, it's that there's a lot happening in my mind. I can't understand it sometimes." She stares at the back of his head, desperate for him to turn around. "Please, don't abandon me."

He turns to her, not moving any closer. He stands in the hallway, unmoving. A sadness blankets him, sweeping off his mind in waves. "Every day I offer my heart and soul to you. I always show up. Always at your door, every single morning. It's exhausting. I know you're hurting, but it's been months. And it's hurting me now. You don't feel the same, you don't remember, and the worst part is ... the worst part is that you can't even control most of it. I am angry at you. I am angry that you're hurting me and that it isn't even your fault."

"Maybe it is." She meets his eyes, an entrancing forest green. She can't look away. She holds onto his gaze because she desperately wants him to stay. It would be great if she could speak through to his mind, apologize without needing words. Instead, she tries to share it all through that single stare. "Levi," she whispers. A tear falls down his cheek as she says his name, leaving a shining path on his skin. A brightening red rims his eyes. His face shows the struggle to fight back the tears, but they are unfortunately inevitable.

Ava takes a breath, her ribs shaking. "You know I love you right? Just not in the way you want me to. I have feelings for you, I do, but they're buried under so many other feelings. You're my best friend—"

"Stop," his voice cracks out.

"Will you be here tomorrow?" she asks. Her body slowly shakes with each rise and fall of her lungs. Their eyes still connected in a sorrowful gaze that neither of them can break.

He squeezes his eyes shut and then walks away.

Leaving her standing there, selfishly asking for him to keep giving her his all. And not returning the favor.

Chapter Six

Raiden travels through the mystical forests and meadows of the Goldryn landscape and then on to the broken-down towns and pine forests of Wyntryn. Past torn up villages and trampled homes. The beauty of the coast fades into the cold barren mountains leading to the Wyntryn Manor. As the days pass, he feels the strain on his body growing. His inner thighs and ankles are sore from the steady switch between a walk and a canter on Oberyn. More than anything the boy needs rest. Yet his arrogance keeps him from stopping, and he knows it too. But he doesn't want to miss the chance of Alys' long-lost daughter returning. Any blood of the Wyntryn family is connected to that manor. Ancestral ties that are burned into the very soil beneath the trees. He knows that one day she'll be called back home. But her memory had been desolated by Alys. Alys claimed that it would protect her, but Rais had warned her that it could do the exact opposite. He didn't want her to lose her memories. Didn't want her to forget him or the world they grew up in.

He rushes back home now in the hopes of seeing

her. But there is the possibility that he has already missed her. Despite his need to get back to the old stone manor, his body is giving way to sleep.

Oberyn stumbles on a divot in the snow and Rais jolts forward. His loss of balance throws his horse off even more. He steadies himself back into the saddle and rubs the base of his palm against Oberyn's neck.

As he feels Oberyn lose her balance again, he decides to give up on his pursuit and rounds the trees to the nearest village. It is a small grouping of buildings sequestered in a clearing not far from one of Wyntryn's tallest mountains. The village is one of the few still standing. It only survives due to the abundance of skilled mages who live within it. They are protectors of the mountain, and many have signed a blood oath to the lands of Wyntryn. An oath that promises to protect Wyntryn, its creatures, and the royal bloodline with their lives. If the oath is ever broken it is rumored that the ghosts of the ancestors they have sworn to protect, will hunt the traitors down and shatter their minds.

Rais doesn't believe in those consequences, but he does believe that a blood oath should never be broken. That in breaking it, it will ruin one's moral character and dignity, and thus shunning themselves from the Sonder.

He rides Oberyn into the village of powerful minds. The shacks they live in are covered in thick layers of snow. He slows Oberyn down and dismounts the beautiful mare. Her pelt is slick with frozen sweat. He leads her to the stables on the far end of the village and slides a rope around a loop in her bridle. Rais unlatches the girth holding the saddle in place. He loops the stirrups up on the saddle to keep them from hitting Oberyn as he pulls the saddle off her back. The horse shakes in relief. Her pelt pressed and hot where the saddle had laid.

Rais quickly brushes her down. He then pulls furs from the side satchels out and throws them over her shivering muscles. He rubs the star between her eyes and walks off through the stable and into the snow. The village is quiet, but not empty. The thoughts of the open-minded men and women flutter through the air. And he can feel the barricades of the stronger minds resisting his.

Finding his way to the inn, he pushes the door open. A small lady sits at the front desk. A sword twice her size is strapped to her back and her eyes are dark. A woman who has faced many horrors.

"I'm looking for a room, and I'd like to pay for the stall I used in the barn," he says to the young brunette.

She doesn't meet his eyes, but she shuffles around the desk for a key. "You are one of the Queen's mages, aren't you?"

"Yes," he says.

"There are stories about the boy with golden hair and golden eyes. Here on the mountain, they praise you as a hero of our land, but there are many who hate you for not saving our Queen." She hands Rais a key. "Your room is second down on the top floor. The stairs are in the hallway past the fireplace.

"Thank you. And the heiress is still alive, we are not without a Queen," he tells the woman.

She nods. "I believe it, but we are Queen-less. For she is not here to save us now."

Rais tosses a satchel of gold coins on the wooden counter and heads to his room. He is used to the small comments made by the remaining Wyntryn citizens. Some fall to their knees and beg him to save them. Others put a hand to their sword and swear at him. Some thank him for his service. Though he always looks past the comments because he understands their erratic feelings. He feels it too. He blames himself for the Queen's death and for his friend losing her memories.

He twists his key into the lock and opens the creaky wooden door. The room is quaint. Only a small bed in the back corner. All he wants is to lay down and not have to move until sunrise.

He pulls his belt and straps off and lets his sword fall to the floor. His body falls just as carelessly onto the mattress. The blanket only covers half of him. Leaving his feet hanging off the end of the bed. His eyelids are heavy, and he easily falls into a deep sleep.

Rais wakes to the clashing of swords and the roars of Atane. The genetically modified beasts were released by Grymyr in the war. He shakes the sleep from his mind and reaches down for his sword. He slings the strap around him, tightening it as quickly as he can. He slams the door of his room open and runs down the stairs. In the foyer of the inn, there are children cowering in the corner. The woman from earlier stands before them, holding her sword out. Ready to take down any attacker.

Rais breaks his gaze from the woman and sprints out the front door. An Atane rushes towards him, he doesn't have time to reach his sword, so he ignites his energy. Sparks of electricity fly out around the animal. It screeches and fights Rais' hold. Rais pulls his sword out and slices the animal's neck. It collapses to the ground before him. The beast's muscles flinch from the excess electricity running through it.

A man from across the village yells, "we need mages in the south of town!"

Rais raises his hand to the man and runs towards the south end. The horses in the stables are slamming themselves against the stalls in terror. Loud screams of people echo into the winter air. Rais runs faster, pushing his legs to their limit, fighting the pain from the days of travel away, and focusing on the need to save these people. Up ahead a group of beasts circles the town's irregulars.

He pulls on his stores of energy and pushes the electricity through his hands. Gathering the energy into a large sphere in front of him, he sparks it to life and pushes it towards the beasts. His palms face upwards, his fingers straining with the effort. He pulls the ball apart and slides it around each of the Atane. One by one they fall and wither to the ground. He holds the lightning in place, feeling his own body straighten and tighten. The men inside the circle pierce the animals with their weapons until there is nothing but silence. Rais releases his hold on the beasts, feeling an empty pit grow in his stomach.

He walks towards the men and women, all gasping desperately for breath. A man with dark features and thick curly hair steps towards Rais and takes a knee. "Thank you, Sparrow."

Rais gestures for the man to stand up. "There is no need to thank me. You all got them here in one place. There would be no way to take them all down if they were separated."

"They were different this time. These were all fire breathers. Normally they have differing abilities if none at all, making it easy to take them down. Luckily, Em was able to keep the fire at bay." He gestures to a burly woman with light eyes.

"All fire breathers?" Rais thinks aloud.

The woman from the inn walks up behind him. "Which is why we need the heiress. Wyntryn blood is all that is left of our own fire mages." She looks to Rais. "The only combatant for fire is fire. Everything else only holds it at bay but can't destroy it entirely."

"She is alive, I know it. She will come home to us. I will make sure of it," Rais says to the group. His sincerity leaks into the air around them.

The man before him looks to the mountain. "We are sworn to protect our land and people for as long as we live, but our fates draw nearer every day."

Rais wants to stay in the village to help protect them, but his duties are to the Queen. Alys left it to Rais to help piece the heiress' memories back together. Being here will only delay the help they all desperately need. He needs to get the talismans and he needs to bring their heiress home. "You all made an oath, don't ever let that commitment falter. Queen Alys would not want us to give up. If you ever need help, reach out to our ancestors. They will send signals to those with the ability to save you," he commands.

The man nods before him. "We will send a signal if we are at risk of being overrun. We appreciate your help, Golden Sparrow."

"My name is Raiden." He opens his palm to the man.

He places his fist in Rais' palm, "Erka."

"Thank you for protecting these people, Erka. In the morning I must be on my way, unfortunately, I am needed elsewhere."

Erka sheathes his sword and goes to help the other irregulars gather the Atane bodies scattered throughout town. As Rais heads back to the inn, the people pile the bodies so that they can burn them from this world and bless the land with their ashes.

Rais sleeps until morning and awakes to the sun shining through the dirty windowpanes. As soon as he is awake and bathed, he goes straight to his mare.

In her small hay-filled stall, Rais sees that Oberyn had gathered quite the attention of the townsfolk. Her pelt is brushed clean—her mane and tail neatly braided back. He smiles at the sight of his sleeping horse. She had attached herself to Rais long before he took over ownership. Always following him through the fields beyond the manor and asking him for treats.

Rais wakes Oberyn up and pulls off her blankets. He puts her pad, saddle, and bridle back on. Because of the thick snow deeper in the region, he decides to put protective wraps on her lower legs. He leaves the stable with Oberyn following him out. Once outside he places his foot in the stirrup and swings his leg over the saddle. She shifts beneath his weight and Rais pats the side of her neck.

The morning air is sharp with frost. Rais pulls his cloak tightly around him and begins his ride back to the manor. The fire in the southern part of the village burns bright behind him as he rides away.

The ethereal manor stands alone in the clearing. The sun casts a glow across the grounds. All the windows are dark. The sign by the front entrance hanging loosely by only one of the chains, swaying in the wind. Loneliness passes over him. A realization of how desolate his life and the lives of the Wyntryn people have become. He will spend the next days, weeks, or even months walking the halls of the manor—alone.

Rais dismounts from his horse and brings her to the

stables to rest. He takes care of her and then heads to the manor. Its rough stone walls reach high above him, three stories of rooms and balconies. Rais slides his hand across the metal handle. A shiver runs through him. He pulls the door open and steps into his dusty home.

The back foyer smells of jasmine and wine. A memory of the secret parties that were once thrown there. Where Rais and his friends would try forbidden aromas and laugh until their ribs strained.

He walks through the ghosts of his memories, a longing for the happiness he once had. He shakes off the nostalgia and moves up the grand staircase to the second floor. Walking through the hallway of portraits that stare through him, he goes to his favorite room in the manor. The study. It is one of many, but this one, in particular, holds a place in his heart. It is where he first met his person, the girl who made everything right. The one who taught him it was okay to move on from his past.

Rais strays through the room, taking in every bit of it. The shelves of books, the green velvet furniture, the wrought-iron windows. He goes to the fire and sends a bolt of electricity out into the dried wood. It sparks into a steady blaze. Slowly warming the air.

He senses another mind in the manor. Letting the hazy blue encompass him, he feels for the person who it belongs to. He lands on a presence right outside of the study. He glances at the glass doors. There's a figure moving close to look in through the glass. Rais pushes himself against a bookshelf not visible to the figure and watches their eyes fly across the room. He can feel they are scared, confused, and … he knows this mind. It's different and tangled up in a web, but he can feel the remnants of who she once was. Ava.

Rais rushes to the door and stands in front of it, breathing quickly. His mind flies in every direction. His heart practically jumps from his chest. She came back, she's here.

He opens the door and stares at her. She faces away from him now, her dark hair a mess behind her. She grasps onto the railing as he moves onto the balcony. His heart drops at the sight of her, feeling how she has changed.

"Hello," he says. He wants her so badly to turn to him. He prays that it won't take long for her to remember.

Chapter Seven

The library rises above Ava. The sounds of the city echo between the buildings. Her eyes burn against the smoke rising from the construction not even a block away. Ava is at the library to see Saira. She wants to learn more about the Sonder. About how to control her mind. She owes it to Levi to try since he spends so much time trying to help her. Especially since he has yet to knock on her door since their fight. Since she turned him away.

Ava got so used to him being there for her every day and making fun of her lack of smiling. Oddly enough, him mocking her usually made her smile. Even if it's only been a few days, it's been long enough for her to miss him. Ava decided to go to the library because she thinks the Sonder will help her find a way to connect to him. To understand him better.

She walks into the library and is greeted by the now-familiar smell of mildew and dust. She smiles at the arcane structures above that reach down into the library.

They are elegant. Floating above the chaos. Perfect above the bookshelves, crowned in layers of dust. As she finds her way to the stairwell, she can't help but glance up at the metal dragon. Its eyes glow with life. And the most intriguing aspect of it is the arrow that slices into the dragon's skull. It is wedged into the left eye socket. The dragon tells its story from high in the library. Its wings bent as if it had been shocked by the hit and lost its hold in the air. The metal creature is created to look like it's falling, but it stays stagnant in the air. Held up by thin wires.

She pulls her gaze from the sculpted beast and finds herself before the stairwell. Her nerves are on high alert. Her chest flutters with the adrenaline. She is not fond of Saira, but he is the only person she knows who can help her find a hold in the Sonder. She lifts her shoulders and pushes them back. Then she starts up the stairs, freezing every time one of the steps lets out a screech underneath her weight. Part of her doesn't want Saira to know she's coming, but she also fears surprising him.

"Ava?" Levi's voice echoes from one of the darkened hallways. She turns to it, her squared shoulders falling as she sees him. "What are you doing here?"

"I came to see Saira. I want to learn more about the Sonder."

"Oh," he says quietly. Levi leaves the shadows to face her. "You can ask me."

"Are you sure?"

He shrugs. "I'd rather you ask me than Saira."

"Okay … how long have you had access to the Sonder?" she asks.

"Since I was six or seven. But I never had a footing in it until two years ago. Saira has helped me learn to enter the Plane of Verity and how to keep my mind balanced in both at once. What I'm not good at is crossing over, it's not exactly a pleasant experience."

"What do you mean, crossing over?"

Levi runs his hand through his hair. He says, "when you physically go to the Sonder your mind is capable of reaching others. You walk amongst the faint souls of those around you. It's hard to tell if they are other irregulars or normal people. Only those with the ability to cross over onto the Plane of Verity without damaging their mind can see the difference. They are also the only ones able to alate."

"Alate?" Ava asks. She recognizes the word. It is a part of the ancient tongue of Kanaleigh, but she can't for the life of her remember the meaning.

"You alate when you step through the Plane of Verity and into another place. Those who are capable can enter the Sonder here, and when they walk through, they can walk out the front doors of the library. Saira can alate, but he never leaves the attic."

She has many more questions, and even though Levi said he prefers she ask him—she is drawn to the attic. Saira's mind pulls her there. And she can't resist it. A fish seizing the toggling bait. "Well, thanks, Levi. And I'm sorry about the other day."

His eyebrows raise and he shakes his head. "Okay, Ava."

She looks down and continues up the stairs. Taking each step without a second thought, until he is right before her. When she forces her gaze upwards, Ava is face to face with Saira's pale features. His voice coats her mind. *You are here to learn how to enter the Sonder, aren't you?*

"Yes."

A blank smile stretches across his porcelain skin. "You can speak to me through the Sonder, Ava, mind to mind. You were once capable, and you are now. Release your mind from its tethers and send it forward to me. My mind is open now, so it will be no trouble."

Ava closes her eyes and feels for that slippery blue haze that once coated the world around her. When it doesn't come, she reaches out to the symbols on the window and feels her mind slip into a foggy haze. She does as Saira instructed and tries to break through the tethers of her mind. But nothing happens, she feels the same.

Saira's icy voice cuts into her mind again. *Let go. Draw on your energy and relax into it. You have barely even entered the Sonder.*

Ava tries to relax into the world around her. She pushes away the anxiety that tenses her muscles. There's a release inside of her. And her mind flows out into the Sonder in waves. *Can you hear me?* she says to Saira.

Yes, very good. Now control your mind. Pull it back in, block me from entering so easily.

She tries to pull the folds of her thoughts back in, but she can't. Her eyes flutter open and she sees Saira staring intently at her. It feels as if phantom hands grasp onto her shoulders, and she is pulled backward. Her body flies through the doors of her own world and into the Plane of Verity. A plane of blue wisps. She can still see Saira, faint in front of her, emotionless. He raises an eyebrow as she falls backward, and when she lands on a foreign surface, she can't see him anymore. She closes and opens her eyes again, and she is no longer in the library. She is someplace entirely new.

She feels an ache in her spine as she pushes herself into a sitting position. Her hands scrape against cold stone. Shivers spindle through her body as she's hit with an icy wind. She looks around the stark landscape. The trees are mostly barren except for the few towering evergreens.

This world is covered in a glistening white. As perfect and beautiful as the dragon in the library. The landscape is gorgeous, but falling through itself, deserted.

Ava forces herself to stand, her body crying with small pangs. She stands on a stone balcony. A dull shade of gray. She turns to look behind her and sees that she is on one of many ledges covering the face of a massive manor. Its structure is aged and lonesome in the sea of trees. The windows of the manor are decorated with iron intricacies. The door before Ava is covered with the same iron. She looks through the glass panes, into a small room with a blazing fire. A pain shoots through her skull, and she catches herself on the balcony railing. She closes her eyes against the headache, begging it to recede.

"Hello." She stands rigid, tightening her hand against the cold stone railing. She wishes to return to the room with the circle window. The old rickety floors with the empty shelves.

"You refuse to grant me the courtesy of a hello?" the deep-toned voice says from behind her. An amusement twists through his words. She turns to the sound. A tall man stands in the doorway. He looks down with a smile on his face.

Did he drag me here? she can't help but wonder.

The man has light hair and stunning gold eyes. He has a scar that stretches from the soft skin above his jaw to the base of his neck. His skin is tawny and smooth, with high-set cheekbones.

"Do you know who you are?" he asks. His fingers run through his snowy hair. She doesn't resist the urge to say her name. His presence is like Levi's, she can feel deep down that he is no danger to her. But she should know better than to trust a stranger.

She begins to tell him her name, but her body begins slipping back into the Sonder and away from that secluded balcony. The world goes fuzzy again as she is pulled through the Sonder and back into the dark library. The room spins around her. Ava steadies herself on her hands and knees. She has the desire to retch on the wooden floorboards. She gulps down nausea and lets her eyes adjust to the dark room. What the hell had just happened to her?

"Ava." Levi lifts her chin and meets her eyes. "Are you okay?"

"No," she stammers out. Her breathing is shaky.

Saira's voice floats out from behind Levi. "We know now that you can alate. How, exciting."

"Exciting?" she asks. "Someone pulled me away from here! I didn't choose to do it!" The nerve of Saira. Ava only keeps listening to him because she needs answers. But if she had what she wanted, she wouldn't waste any time getting far away from Saira.

"Well, you know how to handle yourself. You let me drag you right on back," Saira says. "You are quite impressive really. To be able to alate before you can even shield your own mind. You are a curious case." He bends down beside her, and Levi drops his fingers from her chin. "Now tell me, where did you go?" he asks. His sharp voice cuts through the air between them.

"You don't know?" Ava asks.

"No, I simply followed your mind. I don't know the place you went to. What did it look like?"

Ava feels the need to keep it to herself. To not let them know about the golden-eyed boy. So, she lies. "I don't know. Everything looked, hazy."

Saira narrows his eyes. "Odd indeed." He bends

ever nearer to her face. "There was no man?"

"No," she says. Lying through her teeth. Why would Saira ask if there was a man? Maybe he's only asking her questions as a façade, to hide what he knows.

"You were completely alone?"

"Yes," she insists.

"Leave her alone Saira. I'm going to take her home." Levi pushes Saira away from her and helps Ava up.

She shoots a glance at Levi. Worry is plastered across his face. She wonders how long she was gone, how Saira was able to bring her back. Ava turns to Levi as they walk out of the room. "Levi, how did he—"

"I told you he is capable of a lot more than me. And in case you're wondering, you were only gone for a minute or two. We're lucky he was able to pull you through the Sonder."

"How did you know?"

"I couldn't feel you anymore," he whispers.

"The Sonder confuses me ..." She isn't sure how to say it. How to describe everything she has seen since first stepping foot in this library. She had just been pulled through her very reality and to a place she can only assume is very far from Grymyr. She's never seen snow in this city before and assumes much of the region is like that too. "It's so vibrant and complex, and yet it's birthed from the simplicity and vastness of death."

The vastness of death. *Did I die too?* It's a thought she's had before. One that's terrifying. A thought she can't help but believe.

"That's why Grymyr despises irregulars. They have too much power. People who are meant to be gone—are real and given the ability to tamper with the mind. It's dangerous. That's why the Great Wars began. To destroy those who were never meant to be alive in the first place."

Ava's gaze moves to Levi. There's something bone-chilling about his words. There are people in the city that are killing irregulars. Her mother was killed by someone in this very city. Ava has always known that her mother's death wasn't really an accident. But she has no inclination of who did it. Possibly these dangerous people Levi speaks of are the ones at fault.

"That's horrible," Ava says. Grymyr is a despicable place. The streets are filled with life, but they so easily take it from others. They pretend to be a place that protects their people, but aren't the irregulars living in the city also their people? "Irregulars are still alive. We are still as alive and real as anyone else."

"Yes, but the irregulars wanted to destroy Grymyr. So, Grymyr protected themselves." He speaks with an intensity she has never heard from him before.

"Levi, we are irregulars. Do you agree with the government?" she asks.

"No, but we aren't meant to be alive," he says.

"I don't agree with that. What about the ones who were born this way? There's no way to excuse the killing of others. In the war hundreds of cities burned to the ground, hundreds of thousands of people were murdered. All because they were born or forced into a livelihood that they didn't choose."

Levi seems to pause at this. "It was horrible. Every war is unfair. We should just hope it never happens again. And please Ava, do not use the Sonder in public. You could get yourself killed."

"Who would kill me?"

"There are people, that work for the government. They are people trained to eradicate irregulars. You need to be careful, especially if you don't have control yet."

He mentioned those people again. People with the intention of killing irregulars like her. Like what she believed her mother to be. Ava gets to the bottom of the staircase and lets her eyes fall to her friend again. "Do you know if my mother fought in the war?"

"I imagine she did."

Ava finally has the heart to ask Levi what has been circling her mind. "My mother was an irregular. Did these people, who work for the government, kill her? Try to kill me?" Ava's mind spins around the thoughts. Her brain struggles to bring up memories buried deep within her.

Levi's mouth falters, his jaw clenched as he thinks of how to respond to her. "I don't know. But it's possible."

He is holding back from her. She can tell his words aren't his natural responses. He has an emptiness similar to Saira in that moment. A grim and desolate tone. And beyond her conversation with Levi, all she can think of are those bright golden eyes.

Like any other day, she is in the same disheveled and warped library with Levi. He is finally letting her see what's hidden down some of the hallways off the windy staircase reaching up to the attic. They have a slight awkwardness between them still, but Ava tries to push past it. To make it feel like nothing had happened between them at all. They are just best friends, who love each other in different ways.

"Levi, what in the world is the purpose of this room?" she asks. She looks around. It's the size of a broom closet. The window is boarded up and it is covered in spiderwebs, with a lone chair sitting in the center.

"Don't ask me." He lifts his hands in defense. "I'm as oblivious as you are."

"Sure, you are."

Ava had pushed away the memories of what happened days before. She's tried to forget the mysterious boy with golden eyes. But she can barely stop thinking about him. Her only distraction is Levi's bright smile and his over-exaggerated hand gestures. There was something about that manor, that person. However she got there, she knows it was for a reason. And she wants to know why.

"Hey, now that we're finally here not to see Saira. Why is he so blank, so empty?" Ava asks out of the blue.

Levi loosens his grip on some books he found in another hallway and lets his hand fall to his side. "I don't know, but there's definitely something wrong with him. He's … off." His face is drawn as he says it.

Ava raises her eyebrows. "Like how he never leaves that attic?"

"Exactly. I personally don't trust him, and you probably shouldn't either," he says.

"I don't, but he might be able to help me open my mind enough to access my memories." As she finishes her thought a shout echoes down the stairwell. "What was that?"

Levi stares back at her with as much surprise as she feels. They rush through the door and down the hallway, winding through the maze of fallen beams and spiderwebs. They stare up the stairs as voices drift down from the attic.

They stand silently, listening to the arguing voices of Ms. Ethelle and Saira.

Levi wraps his arm around her and pulls her down

the flight of stairs, pushing them underneath a shadowed alcove to hear without being seen.

"Saira, I keep you here for a reason. You know that. Do not make me regret that decision. You will not go hurting that girl. You know who she is. She is not some irregular scum you can dig your claws into," she snaps at him. Her voice twists through the air.

"If I did have any clue, why would I care?" His voice is cold, entitled. Not at all the Saira she had met and known this past week. He lets out a short laugh. "Ethelle. If I was that much of a problem, you wouldn't let me spend time with Levites." Ava feels Levi stiffen beside her. She reaches out and grabs his hand, hoping it will provide some comfort.

"I let you be near Levites because although you deserve every ounce of torture, it would be cruel to isolate you entirely. If you ever, ever hurt him, you will regret the day I—"

"No Ethelle. You will regret that day. Not I."

Their voices stop fogging the air around them and light footsteps scuttle against the old wooden stairs. They get closer to them with every step. When Ms. Ethelle reaches the floor they are hidden on, she continues right on past. Either she doesn't notice them or pretends not to. They stand there in silence in the shadow of the stairway for a long while. Neither of them speaks.

Ava supposes they are both trying to wrap their minds around what they overheard and what it can possibly mean. Levi doesn't give her any hint or any idea of how he feels. But he continues to hold tight to her hand as they walk back down the creaky stairs. As they tread downward, Ava looks up the winding staircase. To the reflection of the light drifting down from the circle window.

From that delicate window, and the shadowy figure who remains trapped inside.

Chapter Eight

The days pass with ease. Ava has pushed back her concerns of the new world she has entered and that odd argument between Ms. Ethelle and Saira. Each day she sees Levi and they share an awkward conversation on their way to the library. At the library, she learns from Saira the ways of the Sonder. After overhearing the conversation between Saira and Ms. Ethelle, she didn't want to ever talk to him again. But if Saira knows something about her, she wants to know what it is. She wants to know what it is Saira wants to glean from her. As far as she's aware she's never met him before, but maybe her mother knew him. And if that's true, then she can excuse putting herself at risk.

Another benefit of meeting with Saira is that he is teaching her how to use the Sonder. The simple tactics open her mind to the mystical world of irregulars. He teaches her to tether herself to the world, and how to not slip away into the Sonder. So that she can't be consciously dragged away again. They spend hours meditating, communicating. Saira's emotionless presence steadily becomes more familiar. Every day he seems more human to her; less of an empty vessel. Levi sometimes sits in on her meetings with Saira, his nerves leaking into the room around them.

When Ava was leaving the library yesterday, Levi stopped her. He asked her to stop meeting with Saira. Told her he doesn't like the idea of him being able to pick and prod at her mind. Ava listened to him, but she's not going to stop. She first went to the library to find answers. Levi himself told her those answers were with Saira. Ava has been ignorant to the world around her for far too long. So, she is going to do whatever it takes to get the answers she needs.

There isn't much she can do to protect herself from Saira, but she appreciates that Levi worries about her. Even when she can't see him, she can feel him nearby. Levi can't seem to resist her, despite how poorly she has treated him. Ava isn't sure how to feel about it. She wants to spend time with Levi like she used to, but she's afraid it won't be the same as it was before.

She sits now on the floor across from Saira, deep in mediation. She focuses on the thrumming of her body. Her energy reverberates in the air. She reaches into the Sonder and feels for the mind across from her. She settles over Saira, feeling for his thrum. It is quieter and more rigid. Like a box falling unevenly down a hill. There is no pattern or consistency. It is faint, and she can barely grasp onto it. As soon as she thinks she has a hold on him, he slips away. Ava lets out an exaggerated sigh and breaks from her meditative state.

Saira's eyes flick open, and he stares blankly at her. "You are barely stronger than you were yesterday," he says.

She has the urge to roll her eyes but resists. "I haven't learned anything new in the past few days. How am I supposed to get stronger?"

"You need to focus."

"I am."

Saira stands and gestures towards the stairwell. "You are welcome to leave and come back when you are willing to admit the truth."

He has done this before. Commanded her to leave when she became an annoyance to him. Ava never tries to stay long anyway, because she is only there to find out more about the Sonder and how Saira might connect to her past. Despite that, Saira still gives her an unnerving feeling that settles in her bones.

"I don't have to prove anything to you," she says flatly. Saira's eyes follow her as she stands and leaves the room.

Ava reaches the bottom of the stairs and has the urge to find her way back to the basement. To the entrancing symbols that paved the way through the bookshelves. Since she was followed by the pale woman, she hasn't gone back. She never saw or sensed that woman again, but she can sense Ms. Ethelle below her now.

She pulls herself into that deeper state of mind, into the Plane of Verity. As she walks through the library, she becomes aware of a steady beat from the symbols. She follows their voice, lighting a pathway through the books.

Ava finds herself standing before the stairs going down into the basement. She takes one step down at a time, the temperature growing colder as she descends. Walls close in on her mind and shut her out of the Sonder. It's an invading feeling, blocking her from sensing anything other than herself. She is reverted to her basic senses, cut off from the Sonder.

She breathes out her worry and steps out onto the hardwood floors. The room is lit up by ornate chandeliers that are evenly placed throughout the room. Someone sits in the chair facing away from her. In the same place where she had seen Ms. Ethelle and the dark-haired woman arguing.

Ava wants to try out her new abilities and see into the person's mind, but something stops her here. As if the room is a barrier to the Sonder. She moves towards the red velvet chairs and the woman turns her face to the side. Ava recognizes the rough lines of Ms. Ethelle's face. "You trespass here, dear."

Ava tentatively moves to the chair across from Ms. Ethelle. She sits down and folds her hands together. She lets her gaze stray across the woman's smile lines and her dull purple blazer.

"I have noticed you come here without Levi now and study with his brother."

"His brother?" Ava asks. Her whole body seems to freeze. She can't believe she saw through that fact. But if they are brothers, why does Levi not trust him? What happened between them? She turns her gaze to the dark rug at her feet. Levi lied to her again. Not even that, he has been lying to her. Both of them have been lying to her face, for weeks. She's never trusted Saira, but Levi? This lie beats out all the rest. What else have they been keeping from her?

"Yes, dear. Saira is his brother. I am surprised you did not know." She flicks her hand and continues. "Anyhow, I am curious why you are here. This room is meant to be hidden from outsiders."

Why is Saira here, in this library of all places? Since they are brothers, it only means that there is so much more being withheld from her. Ava looks around the room. There are curious symbols painted on the doors. Why are there so many doors? She can only imagine what they all lead to.

Her mother mentioned this place in the voicemail. She specifically mentioned this library, but was it a warning or a clue?

"What is this room?" Ava asks.

Ms. Ethelle smiles now. Her lips thin as she says, "you don't know why you're here do you?" Ava breaks eye contact with her. "This room is one of many underneath the library. Only those meant to be here, find their ways here. They are drawn to it, drawn to certain doors within the room."

Ava looks around at the doors between bookshelves, each with a unique symbol plastered on frosted glass. "I am not drawn to a door. I was following the symbols."

"I know dear. I sensed you on your way here many weeks ago. I have been meaning to ask what you overheard that day," Ms. Ethelle says.

"Nothing. As soon as I was here, I was leaving." Ms. Ethelle nods, her eyes surveying her again, the same as when Ava first met her.

"Why can't I enter the Sonder here?"

"There are many anomalies in the world dear, you should learn to not question what you can't understand." She pushes on the arms of the chair and stands upright. She gestures for Ava to follow her. "Come now, you have other places to be."

Ava walks beside her to the bottom of the stairs, where Ms. Ethelle turns to her and says in a hushed voice, "never stop searching those who search you." Ava stares back at the woman. "Now go on girl, go on. You have places to be that are not here."

Her phrasing is odd to Ava. The way she says it, doesn't make any sense. What reason does Ms. Ethelle have for warning her; could she be referring to Saira or someone else entirely?

"Wait," Ava pushes the word out. The old woman pauses, tilting her head at Ava's sudden reproach. "Who was that woman, the one with dark hair and pale skin?"

"That was their mother. She works here in the library, like many others, but you should not take the chance of being seen down here. Go on now. As I said, there are places you are being called to that are not here," Ms. Ethelle says. She swishes her hand towards Ava.

Ava stumbles up the stairs and out of the building. She is confused by the whole ordeal. She could tell Ms. Ethelle was purposefully skipping over her question about not being able to enter the Sonder down there. She also warned her of people who might be searching her. Beyond that, Saira is Levi's brother. She has to repeat it to herself over and over again in her mind. Almost not believing it to be true.

All of the symbols that lead to the staircase make it seem like it is an entrance to something. And it's so well hidden within the books. Could the library be something other? A cover-up—like how her mother's voicemail is a façade for what she was really trying to tell Ava.

After leaving the warped library, Ava returns home. To her parent's apartment in the center of the bustling city. In the apartment, she draws all the blinds closed. Her room now shrouded in darkness and cut off from the world. She goes to her bed and lies down. Her body sinks into the fibers on her comforter. As much as she wants to fall asleep, her mind is far too awake to allow for that.

Sunken into the mattress, she stares up at the ceiling. The popcorn pattern shifts as the sun forces its way through the thin curtains of her bedroom. She reaches up towards the ceiling with her right arm. Her fingers trace unnoticeable patterns between the uneven textures of the white above her. She lets her hand fall back to her side as she closes her eyes.

Ava pictures the balcony she had been dragged to. She draws it out in her mind's eye. The concrete railing with the flowery engraved textures. The horizon in her image is clouded by snow-covered evergreens. The mountains curl their jagged edges across the corners of her vision. She turns to face the shadow of the man that stood behind her. He is tall. She can't picture his face entirely, but she remembers his voice and his yellow-tinted eyes. The echoing bliss of his presence casts shadows across her face. The safety she felt, the same feeling she has with Levi. Except with this mysterious boy, he felt uncertain of her. But she can't imagine why.

How can she feel a bond with someone she has never known?

She is swept into a tide of thoughts. Bombarded by thoughts of her mother. And as soon as they enter her memory, her mother appears behind the mysterious man and takes her hand. She leads her through the gorgeous hallways of the manor and out into the snowy landscape. Onto a pathway leading through the snow-covered hills.

Her mother looks down on her, her doe eyes encompassing Ava. In the vision, she feels small. Like a ghost of the girl that she is now. Ava lets the dreams of her mother take her through the snowy trees and foothills beyond the mansion. She walks through the snow as her younger self, at her mother's side. Her mother takes her to a clearing where dozens of bursting lights float through the air. The orbs shine in the space around a huge fountain. They cast light blue beams across the running water. Her mother turns to her and leans down to kiss her forehead. Ava hears her voice speaking through her mind, "my beautiful love, my life, you burn brighter than you may ever know."

Ava jolts upright, opening her eyes and letting her surroundings fade into her vision once again. She's sitting on her bed, the sun casting a dull glow through the curtains as it descends below the city's buildings. Her mother's words sounded so real. They send chills up and down her spine. They remind her of who she was, who she is now. And everything that she is missing in her memories. It is hard for her to grasp. The familiarity of that library, the words of Ms. Ethelle, the emptiness of Saira, the lies Levi keeps spinning her in, and the unknown world that seems to be consuming her. Had her mother really taken her to that snow-ridden place or had it simply been a figment of her imagination? A way for her to cope with the loss of her mother.

Whatever it had been, she knows she has to return there. To that massive stone building in the middle of nothingness. Like the library, something or someone is telling her to go there. She has to return to that balcony, to that frozen land.

She quickly quiets her worries. Ava feels right in this choice, to go back. The terror of being dragged there still rakes through her. But this time it will be by choice, and in that choice, she is not fearful. She trusts herself to be careful and trusts that this is the right decision. She wants it to be. Just as she wants Levi to be safe and trustworthy. She wants to know that by going to this strange place she may learn more about her past and future. It may help her remember. She has the ability to investigate now, and she's determined to utilize that ability. To use the Sonder to at least try to recover from the past year. If she can't find answers or what she is meant to find, maybe it will help her move on.

She rubs her forefingers against her temples and furrows her brows. Her gut isn't only telling her to go back there, she wants to. To find that pathway, that fountain her mother led her to.

The snake in her chest squeezes her heart. She will do anything to see her father and mother again. Even with the absence of her memories of them, the emotions remain. She remembers how happy they all were. How much her parents loved each other—loved her.

When she closes her eyes, she tries to remember what it feels like to alate. How to walk through the Plane of Verity and out to a particular place. She keeps her eyes closed and reaches out into the vastness of the Sonder. The blurry blueness slowly consumes her. Ava focuses on the balcony, on the chill of the winter air, and the feeling of her hands on the rough concrete. She remembers the feeling of her shoulders being pulled through the dark room atop the library. She searches for that pull, that open door in the Sonder. She pushes herself towards the balcony and falls through the folds of the plane. It feels as if an infinite wind is pulling her through a tunnel.

She feels cold stone beneath her hands. Her eyes flick open, and she touches her face, her stomach, making sure this is real. She looks around at the shimmering snow-covered landscape and at the balcony she kneels on. With a jolt, she realizes she actually did it, and her whole-body lifts with excitement. Her mind is tired, and her body is weakened, but she feels amazing. She stands up on wobbly legs.

Alating this time feels better than before, smoother even. It is far more exhausting, but she is mentally clear. Whereas before she felt jumbled and unaware of herself. The snake that had tightened around her heart begins to loosen now. It is a relief. Her body shivers in the stagnant air. She stands there for a moment in the cold and lets herself relax. Thankful to have a break from the pressures of her own mind.

The sound of a door slamming rings out through the air. Ava turns towards the glass doors expecting to see the mysterious man, but there's no one there. Only a closed door. She grabs the handle and turns it. The door creaks and she steps inside the room. Light cascades through to the dusty interior. There's a fireplace and velvet chairs. A dusty green sofa sits between the chairs in front of an old fraying ottoman. Along the walls are built-in bookcases, every space is crowded with a book or some little figurine. A green tapestry hangs before one of the shelves. A twisting dragon is stitched on it, with two opposing figures holding flames in their hands. The room reminds her of the old rickety library in Grymyr. Except this seems older, fancier even. It's warm, not a strange space, but a home. It is touched by the golden age of some long-forgotten era, a place filled with memories she cannot begin to fathom.

She lets her finger glide across the bookshelves. They are coated in what appears to be years of dust. She wonders why this place is where she was brought. Was it that mysterious man that took her here or something other? Ava looks around the room as she rubs the dust from her fingers. The home seems abandoned. If this room is in this shape, she can imagine what the rest of it must look like.

Glorious in its lonely aging—gathering time and showing the effects of years of wear and tear.

She hears faint footsteps from beyond the room. She breathes slowly, her chest rising and falling as the footsteps grow closer. Until they are upon her. A rattle sounds from the doorknob, but it stops. The floorboards creak under the weight of whoever is out there as they move away from the room. She hesitantly reaches for the door and opens it, placing her hand against the door frame.

Ava clutches the smooth wood with one hand and leans ever so slightly out into the hallway. She sees a painting of a woman staring from across the hall. She looks down in the direction of the sounds of the person retreating down the hallway. Her eyes slide over the portraits that line the walls. They resemble the style of painting that is famous in Ygrette. Poised, smooth, and leaking sadness.

She turns from the entrancing portraits and moves into the hallway where she can see the man from before descending back down the stairs. Against her better judgment, she follows him. She knows he must be aware of her presence, but she doesn't let it bother her or scare her back to the apartment. She continues on—pushing down her nerves.

When she gets to the top of the stairs, he's standing halfway down them. Paused, staring ahead. She can feel his own hesitation. But she doesn't know why he would be nervous. She steps down towards him, her body fighting her with every step. He finally turns towards her, and his eyes meet hers. She stifles a gasp—they are golden. She knows this from seeing him before, but they are more detailed this close. Brighter in the light. He looks young, her age maybe, with tawny skin, proper posture, and deep-set eyes.

He doesn't move and neither does she.

"You," he whispers. Gentle happiness crosses his face. The air stays so steady and quiet that she can hear her own pulse beating through her body. She doesn't know how to respond to him. She looks over the railing at the huge foyer and marbled floors. Tall windows cover the face of the room around two large doors. Beyond the windows, she can see the forests surrounding the manor. It reminds her of the dream she had of her mother.

She begins to explain, her eyes still on the trees outside. "I dreamt of this place. Parts of it, that I have no way of knowing about. I came back because ... because something is asking me to be here. It was begging me to come back."

"What do you know?" he asks her. She looks back in confusion. "Follow me."

"Where are you planning on taking me?" she asks. Her tone is sharper than she had intended. Ava's unsure of whether she wants to go with him or not. He's a stranger, but she is also a stranger in his house.

He stares blankly at her for a moment. "You look cold, I was going to get you tea."

Ava stills, wishing she hadn't been so rude. She nods at him, and he turns around. She follows him down the stairs and to a kitchen. He takes her to the back where a small rickety table lies. He gestures to a chair for her to sit down. She watches as he grabs a kettle and fills it with water. He doesn't put on a burner to heat it up, instead, he places his hand on the edge of the metal and it lets out a faint ring. Steam rushes from the kettle and he pours the water into two cups. Ava stares in amazement at the electrified water set before her.

"Thanks," she says. Ava lets the teabag sit there,

and then lifts the cup to take a sip. But she pauses and looks back up at the golden-eyed boy before her. He hasn't drunk from his tea yet. "Is it poisoned?" she asks.

"If it was, you think I would tell you?" He stares back at her.

"Well, you haven't had any of yours. So, I figured …" He reaches over and takes her cup, sips the tea, and then slides it back to her. "Right."

Ava doesn't even know why she asked, but she supposes it was instinct. She also barely understands why this boy has reacted to her in such a way. She is a stranger who has shown up twice in his house, and he is so calm.

"How did you find your way here?" he asks her. In her vision, her mother led her through this very manor. How was she able to envision it so clearly, so exactly? "I pictured what I had seen when I first got pulled onto that balcony," she tells him.

He looks intrigued. "Fascinating. You were pulled here?"

"You weren't the one who brought me here?" she asks.

"No. That was not me," he says. He looks out at the falling snow.

"Well then, how did I get here?"

"You were called," he suggests.

"And who are you?"

He looks down at his hands that are clasped together on the table. "I could ask you the same thing."

Ava's brows furrow. She reminds herself that she's here because of her mother. She gulps and taps her finger against the side of the chair. "Is there anyone else I can ask about why I was brought here?"

"No." His tone turns cold. He pointedly glares out

the window. It doesn't seem like he is going to lighten up enough to help her. So, she stands up and walks towards the door leading out of the kitchen. "Where are you going?" he calls from behind her.

"Out."

"Out there?" He gestures to the winter storm brewing beyond the glass.

"Yes," she says. It seems dumb to go out into the cold, but she wasn't miserable on the balcony. If this person doesn't know how she got here and can't give her any clues, then she is going to listen to her mother. Find and follow the path she took her down.

"Are you a fool?"

"Maybe I am," she says as she continues out of the kitchen. She briskly walks through the hallway he took her down and into the large foyer. On the banister hangs a large trench coat, so she plucks it off and slings it over her. She pulls it tight around her and opens the door. Outside, there is a wind growing steadily stronger.

Flecks of white patter her hair and face. She doesn't remember it being this cold on the balcony, but she pushes past the uncomfortable feeling and goes down the front stairs. She hugs her arms around her and starts off towards the opening in the trees. Identical to the path she walked in her dream.

She shivers uncontrollably underneath the jacket. She pushes on, fighting the icy air that consumes her lungs. She always thought winter was her favorite season, but she's beginning to question her own reasoning.

The pathway she follows shows faint footsteps along it, and it narrows as the trees grow denser. Beyond the trunks, she can see the sharp peaks of snow-covered mountains. The trees pull to the side, turning sharp angles with each gust of wind. Her hair blows all around her, growing wet with the falling snow. The gusts slashing cold across her frail body. The path ahead is hazy. The wind blows snow heavily across the pathway. She stumbles farther through it, her feet dragging more and more.

She breaks through a line of trees into a clearing. There is no snow there, and in the center of the clearing is a stone fountain. Despite the freezing temperatures, the water still runs freely through it. There are small splashes as water falls to the lower sections. It is the same fountain from her dream, but here, there are no drifting orbs. No peculiar blue lights. Only a fountain and the onset of dizziness.

The place is … wrong. She shouldn't be there. She turns to leave, but the snow has somehow grown even higher. Layering and layering. The world seems to spin around her. Her stomach flips and bile rises in her throat. She stumbles towards the fountain to sit down.

What is wrong with me?

Her body is lethargic, and her movements grow slower. She clutches her hands to her head as a pressure grows. Tensing and tightening in her skull. There's a shadow moving through the snow ahead, but she can't focus her eyes on it. Before she can sit down, she collapses to her knees. Her body gives way beneath her. Her mother's presence is not there at first, only a restricting nauseating feeling that grips onto her. Her body is frigid. A blue mist spreads around her and a loud thrumming shakes her head.

Through the haze she sees her mother reaching out to her. She's warm and Ava's cold. Ava reaches for her mother, but before she can, firm hands grab her from behind. They pull her away from the fountain, away from her mother. "Mom!" she screeches in desperation. The headache in her mind grows stronger. Arms wrap around her and pick her up. They fade into the hazy blue. She can barely see his golden irises through her cloudy mind. Before she can say anything to him, her mind fuzzes out. And all she sees is darkness.

Ava wakes up in the dusty room with the green tapestry. She has a blanket on her and there's a bright fire burning before her. Without looking for him, she can sense his presence. He keeps a careful watch on her.

She pulls the blanket tighter around her. She isn't sure if that was really her mother or not. But it looked just like her. Ava can see the shadow of her mother in her mind. What would have happened if she was able to grab onto her hand? Was it even possible to touch a ghost? Maybe it was a figment of her imagination, brought on by those horrible headaches.

"She wasn't really there."

"How would you know?" Ava asks. A pain still flickers behind her eyes. It pulses in her skull. She can feel him watching her, but she keeps her eyes on the fire.

"Why would you go there?" he asks. His words cut through the dry air.

Great, ignore my question.

Ava bites the inside of her lip. "I told you before, I had a dream of this place," she says quietly. She is tired and heavyweights seem to pull against her, asking her to lay back and rest.

He seems to talk to himself as he asks, "why would you dream of that?" He moves from the chair he was sitting in and walks to the balcony doors.

"What is that place?" she asks. There was no snow around the fountain, and yet all around the clearing, the snow was falling quickly and heavily.

"It is a sacred place, only a fool would go there if their mind is not capable of handling the pressure."

"I get that I am a fool. But why would I dream of it? If I couldn't handle it, why would I be called there? Called here?" she asks. Frustration seeps through her skin.

"I wonder the same thing, Ava. Know that it isn't safe there, at least not for you now. It may take your mind time to recover from what you were put through."

"How do you know my name?"

She can feel him freeze—she looks to him now. Watches him clench his jaw and consider what to say. How did he know her name? Did she say it before and not remember?

"I know you," he says.

"You know me?" To say she is stunned is an understatement. She has no recollection of him, no memory. But she supposes that she doesn't have that with anyone anymore.

"Yes," he replies. "You were ... are the greatest person I ever knew." His voice is strong, but she can see his eyes growing glassy.

"How can you know me?" she asks.

"We have known each other our whole childhood ... this room is actually where we spent the most time. Playing games with each other's minds rather than doing our assignments or showing up for training. We were determined to discover everything ourselves." His eyes alight with nostalgia, reminiscing on his fond memories of her. Memories she wishes she could touch.

"Did you know my mother?" she asks. She tries to push past the fact that she can barely understand the girl he is talking about.

"She was my mentor."

"Oh …" Ava says shortly. Her gaze strays away from him to the carpet. "Then do you know?"

"Yes. I know."

"I don't remember." She laughs, her eyes straining with tears. "I don't have anything but some semblance of what it felt like to be with her."

Ava wants to remember her mother. She even wants to remember the accident itself. It would be painful, but it would be real. Not some recollection that Levi shared with her. And all Levi has ever done is lie to her, so why should she trust anything he has ever told her?

"Never mind that now," he says. He probably wants to avoid making her and himself more upset. "What was in your dream?"

"It was my mother, walking me into the woods. To that fountain. Except it was filled with these orbs, but I think they were souls. It's what made me come back, that memory or dream."

The real fountain looked exactly like the one from her dream. She must have been there before. It's weird to think that she once spent time in this manor. A place that is vastly different from her parent's apartment in Grymyr.

"You saw souls there and thought it was a good idea to go?" he asks.

"I believed it would lead me to my mother, to answers, to something," she whispers.

"Please, don't go there again."

"I won't." She looks to him. His emotions sweep off in waves. His mind is open to her. She can feel a love from him, one she can't comprehend. It's eerie. He sits down in the same chair from before, and they stay there, staring at the fire for what feels like hours.

Ava pulls her knees to her chest, settling underneath the blanket. She asks, "what's your name?" She realized that she never really asked.

He shifts in his seat. He says, "Raiden."

"Raiden?" she asks mindlessly. "That's your name?" It feels kind on her tongue, familiar, but distant.

"Yes," he says. Before getting up and walking to the door. He turns back towards her. "You can come and go as you wish. I know it's a lot for you to understand right now, but you need to come back here eventually. The people need you. I need you." He speaks from a place of desperation, but she doesn't know what he means when he says the people need her.

She can't begin to fathom how deeply her relationships spread, how much she lost in the accident. She didn't only lose her mother, she lost so much more. What she is mourning day in and day out is not only her mother. It's her memories. It's the people, the feelings, the life she lived.

At least now she knows more than what Levi can tell her. She knows more than Saira will ever teach her. She is tethered to this place. She found a part of her life that is missing.

She stands up from the couch and lets the blanket fall to the ground. She gazes at the room. The books, the tapestry, the fireplace, the velvet furniture, the ornate windows. She takes it all in, before entering the Sonder and going back home.

In the apartment, she lays back down on her bed. Closes her eyes and lets the weight of the day drift off her. She falls into a fitful sleep, with one word circling her dreams,

Raiden.

Chapter Nine

Rais stands on the balcony outside the study, staring out into the night sky. He sees Ava in his thoughts and memories. She's in the halls and out in the fields. Visions of them running through the trees. After seeing her in that state, he can't shake the feeling that something is vastly different about her. Her eyes are darker, her hair duller, and she holds herself differently. Most vibrant of all is the insatiable anger dwelling within her.

He was the same way when his parents died in a fire when he was a child. Alys told him he was a kind and happy child, but he never remembers feeling that way. The pure childlike bliss. He only remembers the anger and the way grief tore him down and ripped him apart.

Ava lived in bliss for a long time. But she moves slower now as if pulled down by the weight of her own thoughts. She has become older, faded. A blur of who she was before. When he stood before her that day, he could feel her anger spewing from her mind in chunks. A deep set and unconscious anger. It seems to coat her mind and drown her. The trauma she had experienced, it would have broken any normal person, but she came out of it stronger. She was never able to alate before, but she alated to the manor by choice. And as soon as he left the room, despite her lethargic state, she was able to alate again. Her mind is unblocked and uncontrolled, but her abilities are heightened.

Rais wonders if the prophecy is true. If in death, Ava arose with an energy in her unmatched by any other irregular. He only hopes that Stygian won't succeed in her end of the prophecy and that Ava will be the one to come out alive. And be the one to rescue their beloved region.

He retreats back inside. Grateful for the embers of the fire that burn on in the study. They stretch heat across him as he goes out into the hallway. The walls are covered with portraits of the Wyntryn original bloodline. Couples of long ago facing each other from either side. His old mentor had thought it romantic, but Rais doesn't see it that way. It's cruel how the couples face each other, and yet it is impossible for them to reach their second half. A wall of air, space, and time dividing them. Years of dust and decrepit memories keep them from each other.

He strolls through the haunted hallways. Down the stairs, and to one of the most peculiar rooms. One lined with thick metal and a large square carved out of the floor that's filled in with cushions. The room sits in the lower east wing of the manor and has windows at the very top of the walls that let in small sprays of moonlight.

He steps to the edge of the cushions and falls onto his back. Rais pulls Ava's dagger from its sheath at his side and twists it mindlessly in the air. Ava accused him of poisoning her. He chuckles into the desolate room and leans his head back. His skull beginning to ache, his laugh slowing. His lungs rise and as they fall, he lets out a short breath. He has to fight against the tears that line the edges of his eyes. He is alone in this ancient mausoleum. A place that barely feels like a home to him anymore. Rais has no one but himself, and the hope of Ava and Nina returning.

Unlike his raven-haired friend, he does not have the opportunity to simply alate away. He is doomed for a much darker and unforgiving destiny. To prepare her for a war she might not survive. To risk his life in search of talismans capable of destroying his mind by simply holding them in his possession. But he is willing to do anything to save Wyntryn, to save future generations. He wants to save Ava too, but she is the only one who can do that. She will have to stand on her own, but until then he will do his best to protect her.

In hopes that one day he won't have to be alone anymore.

Rais has been roaming the manor for hours. Hours that turn into days, and still Ava hasn't returned. His thoughts are clouded by the endless hazy blue that spreads into his vision over and over. After she left, he began to lose track of time.

It was the same after Alys' death. He had roamed the manor for hours. Hours that turned into days, and days that turned into months. Until he found a letter from the Princess of the Dragon Isles, which told him the location of a talisman that she had hidden deep within the Wyntryn mountains. That is when he left and went to Goldryn to recruit Nina and see Stygian, but before then, he was lost.

The first month after Alys' death was easy. The work staff were still there, still marking the days on the calendar as they had always done. Then the staff director told him that they hadn't been paid since early summer. They didn't know why, and he certainly didn't know either. He thought it was odd how long it had been since Ava and Alys had last visited, but he didn't question it at first. Then, more weeks passed by, and the staff grew lazy because they hadn't gotten their paychecks in weeks. Eventually, the calendars were abandoned. Any sense of time lost. Ava still hadn't returned, and still hadn't bothered to send him letters. He wasn't sent on any missions, so he stayed at the manor—mindlessly walking the hallways and reading forgotten literature. Eventually, the manor staff left and went on to other work. Eventually, everyone left. He was left there alone, with no one.

When he heard of Alys' death he was in the barn, and a bolt of lightning went right through the roof and into the stall he was standing in. Luckily there was nothing in the stall, but him when the roof caved in from the blast. At the time he didn't know that Ava had lost her memories. He learned about that when he opened the letter Alys had left for him. Somehow, she had predicted it.

Rais knew Alys' death was coming, but for some reason he never expected it to happen. Never expected Ava to lose her memories, at least not so soon. When news of Alys' death spread through Wyntryn, everyone gave up. They didn't know Alys had been aware of her coming death. That she was planning to give herself up to the Society, planning for her own daughter to lose her memories, and planning how to save her people. He only knew of her plans because after her death was confirmed, he opened the letter she wrote him.

Alys brought Rais to the manor after his parent's death and had caretakers at the manor raise him. But now, what was once a bustling home is desecrated. Building dust and diminished to nothing but an old Gothic manor in the middle of a winter wasteland.

Now months after Alys' death, in that empty manor, he can't help but find peace in the loneliness. He hasn't been stressed in months. He isn't expected to push his mind past its breaking point in training. He isn't expected to perform like a perfect soldier. He has been connected to the Plane of Verity since a toddler, the perfect specimen for Alys to mold and shape to her liking. But he is free from that now. He doesn't have to follow orders—he is free to make his own.

He may never escape the burdens that Alys put upon him, but if he can live out whatever time he has left in the presence of Ava, he'd be more than thankful for the life he lived. For now, he will continue to roam the manor and watch as more dust builds with every passing hour and day. And hopefully someday Ava will find her way back again.

He stands in the left-wing of the stone palace. There isn't as much dust there because it is a spot he frequents. The room is the back foyer of the manor, it leads out to the stables. After the staff left, he continued to care for the horses. He enjoys being around them because he can't reach their minds through the Sonder. He can't hear the stray thoughts they fail to hide or have to worry about how they perceive him. They are understanding creatures and they don't expect anything from him. But after all of Alys' students left, the only horse that remained was Oberyn.

He walks towards the large glass doors. Metal carvings of plants creep across the scratched surface. He looks out the doors to the barn. The roof has a large chunk missing that lets snow fall through to one of the empty stalls in the stable. The hinges on the doors are rusted and cracks stretch across the wooden slats. Somehow in the months since the staff left, the estate had gone from supreme elegance … to this. Slowly falling apart every day.

He grazes the frosted glass with his fingertips. His nerves prickling at the touch. *Time is a fickle thing.* It takes, and takes, and then runs right by you, leaves you in the dust. And when you look behind at where you thought it was, it's gone. And all you are left with is rotted memories slowly fading from view.

"Rais." He turns to face the memory of Ava.

She smiles at him. A goofy grin that shows her teeth. He watches himself walk to her and pass her a dagger. "Is this what I think it is?" she asks.

"Yep, Alys left it with me before leaving for Metarock."

She slides it from its sheath and brushes her finger across the flat side. The dagger is short but sharp. With twin dragons that twist around the crossguard and slide along the sides of the hilt. "She told me once I would never earn it. She even told Eieran that I didn't deserve to get my mage's coat."

Rais sets his hand on hers. "Why do you listen to her? She holds everything your sister did against you. You are doing everything right. You have to learn that your mother will never let herself see that."

"I just— " her voice catches. "I want her to be proud of me. I want to be enough. I mean, I can't even alate. This manor is filled with the best mages not only in this region but across the continents. Compared to them, I'm so incapable."

"I wish you could see what I see."

She slides the dagger back into its cover. "And

what's that?"

"I see an amazing girl, who will be an amazing Queen. You are brave and caring. You would risk your own life to save the people you care about. You deserve this dagger and the mage's coat. This dagger means the ancestors can work through you. You may not have enough power to alate, but when you need the energy, the ancestors will give it to you."

The memory fades away and Rais looks through the glass to the snow-capped mountains.

He whispers into the quiet unearthly structure, "that is what you are now Alys, lost to time, and fading from view. Even this home you built is forgetting you, covering your traces with each tick of the clock. That is why you molded me into what I am, right? Because you were afraid you would never be able to stop time. Now here we are, and I have nowhere to go but here. You have even given me orders in death, to fix the mess you left behind. Before I know it, I too will be nothing but dust within these walls."

He closes his eyes and steps away from the glass doors. He wants to leave the manor, but he is tethered there. His mind isn't yet ready to run away from it, at least not until Ava returns.

Chapter Ten

She feels as if she has woken up from a dream. The coat that she's still wearing, is the only proof of it being real. Her hands are stuffed in its pockets. She admires the beautiful stitching along the shoulders and folds of the coat. The embroidery swirls into itself with symbols similar to those at the library stitched largely at the tops of the shoulders. She pulls one of her hands from the pocket and touches the fabric, running her hand down the length of the coat. It cuts off before her knees and is much too large in the arms. And for some reason, she leaves it on.

She wants to wear it and share the same warmth reflected in those golden eyes. Because for so long, she has felt anything but warm. Ava remembers the silent, cold rage held deep within Raiden. The sadness in his eyes when she looked at him like a stranger. She wants to understand that sadness. Wants to know why she meant so much to this stranger. If she had her memories back, everything would be so much easier.

Raiden, the mysterious boy from her past. The boy who she was once friends with. If his emotions feel that powerful, she can't imagine what he has gone through in comparison to her own sorrows. She wishes she could understand the Sonder better so that she could reach out to those emotions within him. And better understand her own.

She slips her hand back into the pocket of the coat as she walks down the city streets to the library on 32nd. She is going to see Ms. Ethelle again. Levi has been lying to her about Saira, and she can only assume there are even more things being kept from her. Possibly secrets from her own past.

She wonders what Levi would think of her excursion to that secluded manor. She isn't regretful of lying to him about it, especially when he hides so much from her. She realizes that it's impossible to know if she even met Levi before she lost her memories.

She has emotions associated with Levi, but they are not like the ones she felt leaking from Raiden. She never saw the memory of emotions inside of Levi. Now that she thinks of it, she might feel like she can trust Raiden, but she is still cautious of him. Even with the reassuring feelings, she doubts him. When she is around Levi, especially all those months ago, she blindly held faith in him. What if he was placing those thoughts in her mind? Is that even possible?

She shivers at the thought, but she knows Levi. He's always been there for her. Sure, today he didn't show up to meet her, but that seemed to be happening more and more frequently. And there's no way Levi would hurt her, even if she didn't know him before she lost her memories, he's her friend. She has a love for him, for his kindness, and how he cared for her for all those months.

Ava rounds the corner to the creaking library, devoured by the city climbing up around it, and follows the rugged path leading underneath the tree. She glances up to the circle window, but no shadow sits behind the glass and stares down at her.

Going through the library, she finds her way to the basement stairs again, but before she can go down the steps, she hears a peculiar sound. Ms. Ethelle careens around the banister of the stairs and begins running up the steps.

"Run! Get out of here while you still can," she calls up to her. Her aged voice shakes with heavy breaths.

"What? Why?" Ava asks. Her pulse quickens, sending adrenaline through her.

"He's been freed," she gasps out. A loud clash sounds from across the library. "Can't go that way now," she mumbles. Ms. Ethelle grabs her by the wrist and yanks her down the stairs.

"Who, who's been freed?"

The old lady is breathing hard, her gray hair going in all directions. "This way," she says, pulling her with a surprisingly strong grip. "Saira. He has a powerful and uncontrollable mind. That boy is a walking amplifier, and shatters minds with ease."

"Saira?" Ava asks. She spins to look towards the stairs, the noises getting closer and closer.

Ms. Ethelle opens a door with a large painted circle and two lines going through it. "Go through here, and don't stop running until you get out," she says. Ms. Ethelle pushes Ava through, and Ava stumbles back, falling onto the wooden floorboards. "I sent Levites through here not long ago, he will meet you on the other side." She holds up a finger as if she's forgotten something and runs to a bookcase across the room. Ava's mind is swirling.

"What are you doing?" Ava calls to Ms. Ethelle. Her panic rises as the woman fumbles for something on the shelf. Ms. Ethelle needs to give up on whatever she's looking for and get out of that room. If Saira is as dangerous as Ms. Ethelle makes him seem, she needs to run. Ava needs to run.

The clashing gets closer, then his feet hit the stairs. Heavily clunking against the steps.

Ms. Ethelle finally grasps onto a leather-bound book and runs towards the door. Saira appears at the bottom of the stairs and lets out a horrific and inhuman scream. Ms. Ethelle throws the book through the door. "Run!" her voice scratches out. "Go, now, you are all they have left!"

Ava scrambles onto her feet and searches for the book in the dark room. The door slams shut. The room is suddenly pitch black. Her breathing is loud and unsteady. She grasps onto the book and holds it tight to her chest. Her feet start moving and she's running as fast as she can down the hallway. Her out-of-shape body straining against her. Her lungs fighting for air.

"I see you," Saira's voice calls out from behind her. "Don't think you can fight me, Ava. I have barely taught you how to think," he yells. Disturbed laughter escapes his throat.

Ava keeps running, the hallway turning into a tunnel. She can see a faint light shining down at the end from an opening overhead. But before she can get any closer, a sharp pain rings through her skull.

She lets out a scream and falls to her knees. The book clatters away onto the muddy floor. "Dear oh dear, did that hurt?" Saira sings. Another pain stabs her in the head, this one twisting into her. It sets her whole body aflame with a burning ache.

He's still far behind her, so she pushes through the pain to her feet. Ava grabs the book once more and stumbles farther ahead. Another pain crashes over her. She yells into the dark against the pain, tears beginning a steady stream down her face. "Let me go!"

He's right behind her, and he grasps the back of her neck. She's lifted into the air. "I'd rather not, you don't belong in this world. You are nothing but a nasty irregular," he sneers, edging his lips close to her ear. "Did you know, I created those beasts who storm your homeland day after day, after day." His mouth stretches into a smile against her skin.

"What did you do to Ms. Ethelle?" she chokes out.

"Nothing really. She broke the rules of the Collective, so I broke her. She should have known better than to let her mind weaken enough to set me free."

Ava twists from his grip. A genuine surprise crosses Saira's face, but rather than catching her again he sends another painful wave through her mind. It paralyzes her. She falls against the wall, her body singing with pain.

A thump sounds from the end of the tunnel. "Leave her alone Saira."

She watches Saira's face drop, and a dagger thrown by Levi sinks into his shoulder. "You're such an annoyance, brother."

Levi glances down at Ava, uncertainty crossing his face when Saira calls him brother. He then looks back at Saira and grabs hold of Ava. He pulls her through the hazy blue and into the hallway outside her apartment. He pulls the key from her pocket and opens the door. Levi helps her inside, but she falls to her knees on the carpet. He bends over her, brushing the hair from her face.

Ava's fingers are still tightly wrapped around the book, but Levi doesn't touch it. He sits there and looks down at her, worry written all over his face. When Ava can finally see straight, she forces herself to think. She winces at the pain shooting through her skull. "I'm okay," she says.

"No, no you're not."

"Do you want to tell me what that was?" she asks, looking up at him. Her brain hurting too much to force an emotion.

"He's my brother, and that building is not only a library. It's the home of a Society. The Society of the Collective. The government here in Grymyr highly dislikes irregulars so they created a Society of irregulars built to destroy those who don't conform. Saira and I are a part of it. It's the only way we can live in this region without being executed. That's why I told you to be careful. And to not let anyone see who you are," he explains. His brown hair falls before his face. She tentatively reaches up and pushes it away. So that she can see him, see the curves of his face.

"That explains the lies," she says. Not quite comprehending what he tells her. Her stomach turns. She feels sick. Her gaze is steady on his even skin, but an emptiness spreads through her. She is done with the lies. Even if he can explain them. She is tired of the anguish, the sadness, the anger. She has spent every second since her mother's death being drowned by her own thoughts and emotions. *Is it too much to ask for some temporary relief?* She wants to scream at whatever is beyond their world. At the puppeteer pulling the strings.

He nods. "My brother hasn't been entirely sane his whole life, but he hit a breaking point when the Grymyr government started using him as an assassin. He was forced to kill his best friend. After that, he lost it. He tried to kill our mother because she's like us, an irregular. He continued to warp into insanity, losing his tether to this world and falling deep into the Sonder. That's when they decided to trap him in the attic. The symbols all over that window are tied to Ms. Ethelle, our great aunt. But as she grew older, and Saira grew stronger, he was able to break free."

Levi acts as if she wasn't just attacked by his brother. His tone is cool. *Why is he so okay with this? His brother tried to kill me.* Her hands shake and her breathing is uneasy. Ava looks down at her hands and tries to still them. But they don't stop shaking, and her body only feels more unsteady with every passing second.

She tightly closes her eyes then opens them. Levi has been forced to lie to her. She moves to her knees and reaches out to his face. She rests her hands on his cheeks. He doesn't seem to notice that they're shaking or that she can barely breathe.

"That's horrible ... you've been living with all this pain, and I've been so selfish," she says. She lets her forehead meet his, to steady herself more than to comfort him. They sit there, silence stretches between them.

For so long she never saw him, but in that moment, she sees him for who he is. Seeing into his mind in a way she never has before. Even so, how is he so calm?

He wraps his arms around her and pulls her into a hug. Levi moves to kiss her forehead. "I'm sorry to drag you into this mess," he whispers. She's nestled against him, finding comfort in any touch that isn't Saira's. The back of her neck still stings with the memory of his hand. Her mind still burns with the memory of his attack.

"It seems I was already in it," Ava says. Her mind is

still distant. Her eyes not quite focusing on her surroundings.

Levi pulls away from her and stands up. "I have to go back, to see what's left of my aunt and Saira. I'll have to report back to the Collective ... so stay here please. I'll come to check on you when I'm done."

Ava nods and watches him leave. He is so casual about the Society of the Collective. It must have been horrible having to hide something so prevalent in his life from her. And no wonder he hated her going to Saira for help. He is a monster, and she clung to him like a mentor. Even if she never saw Saira as a mentor, that's what Levi saw. Levi only watched from the outside, not knowing what she was really thinking.

She turns now to the leather-bound book she let fall beside her when she reached out to Levi. Scrawled on the top of the leather is the symbol of a dragon on fire, with an arrow piercing through it, and three circles stamped on the other side. She picks it up and unwraps the leather tied tight around it. The strip of leather falls into her lap. Her fingers trace the rough-edged pages, and she lightly flips the cover open to the first page.

Written in a beautiful cursive is, Alys Rosaline Wyntryn.

She brushes her thumb against the dried ink. It's her mother's journal. Ms. Ethelle threw her this journal, her mother's journal. Ms. Ethelle knew she could be killed at any moment, and she risked her life to get this to her.

Ava holds the journal like it's made of the most delicate glass. She flips through the pages one by one. Silently reading the sentences her mother built. The cathedrals of wavy handwriting scrawled across the paper. Every page is an update, a snippet of her day. Whether it's boasting about her daughter or complaining about a nuisance. It brings her mother to life in her mind. The beautiful brown-haired woman with striking eyes. Her tall lean figure stands in her mind, dressed in the black suit described in one of the journal entries. The entries don't talk of the manor, only of the days she spent in Grymyr, in this apartment. It's as if whatever she referenced happening in the region of Wyntryn is meant to be a secret. At least to those who might get their hands on this book.

Ava pauses when she reaches a break in the journal. A page folded over. She pulls it open and begins to read the entry. It's different than many of the others. It's not about the little activities of the day or how her husband and daughter were doing, it mentions the Society.

Ava hears the words like an echo in her skull, a warning from memories past. As if her mother is reaching out to her through the journal. Her words carve a path for her lost daughter. To help her solve the riddles swimming in her head.

Written on the page, "… Ava has been seeing a boy from the Society, Levites. I didn't encourage her to move on from Rais, but it seems her father did. I told her last summer that she's not allowed to see Levites, but she refuses to listen to me. It's not that I dislike the boy, my issue arose when I sent Rais to infiltrate the Society. He overheard Levites' brother Saira plotting my own murder. In the room with him, was Levites. There is evil in that boy. He may have not been born with it, but his family pushed it into his mind. Muddied the water with lies. And he is taking my own daughter down with him. The Society is going to kill me, and Levites is a part of …"

Ava collapses into herself. She falls backward, her feet moving quickly behind her. She throws the door open and rushes down the hall. Her lungs swelling, her throat taught. Her body neglected by the need for air. She has a need to feel snow on her face. To throw off her jacket and stand in the deathly weather.

She pushes the door to the stairwell open. Her mind betrays her, allowing her to step through the Plane of Verity. But she doesn't notice. She loses balance, falling to her knees. Her hands slam onto the rough ground. People rush around Ava, too busy to see her there. She doesn't even notice. Her eyes are still closed. Her mind clouded. But there is no snow in Grymyr. No cold to soothe her aching mind.

She pushes her hands and knees against that sidewalk and screams.

A scream so loud her voice doesn't even crack. So powerful her whole body loses mobility. She simply screams until her voice is hoarse. Until her body moves from heaving and shaking to a quiet murmur. She sits back on her heels, staring at the cars flying by. And now, when the headlights shine before her, and the water from the sky pours down upon her, dark clouds heavy above—she doesn't freeze, she breathes. Her mind calm. Her eyes flick around the city surrounding her. This time, in her moment of pain, no one is there but herself. That is all she needs to feel the power within her once more. Because as she looks around, all she sees is fire. A beautiful blue fire, alive and real underneath the pouring rain.

PART TWO

The Wyntryn Manor

The Plane of Verity

Ava's eyes are intent on the piece of parchment in her hand. Willow turns back to Ava. The woman's eyes are large and doe-like, the iris' a pale lavender. The roots of her hair are as dark as midnight, but she has the rest dyed a subtle purple. She is smooth, stealthy, a silent hunter. But she isn't here to hunt Ava, she hunts for something other. A goal, but Ava can't figure out what it is. Despite how hard she tries to enter the mysterious woman's mind.

"Why are you telling me this?" Ava asks. Only a strip of light shines upon them through the window.

"Because he needs you. You need him too, you know it. You know the Queen only wants you because you're powerful. Your occurrence is one in a thousand years, darling. And you know he doesn't care about that—he sees you for what's inside." Her words twirl into the air between them as if blessed by some ancient goddess.

"I am not anything special."

"Have you heard the prophecy? The one of the two all-powerful sisters, destined to destroy the world or each other? A test of fate, of control. It is one of the ultimate questions of our race, do we use our power to take control of the physical or the mind? Many believe we aren't meant to exist at all, this prophecy is the end all be all. How do we live or how do we die?"

"And what if I choose nothing? What if I choose that I'm better off not controlling anything? That prophecy you talk about is meant for children. A story mothers tell their kids to scare them. To make them think there are punishments for our actions."

Willow gawks at her, her darkly painted lips widening in a disbelieving smile. "After all this time being surprised by the peculiar, and you still believe it is all a story for children? Open your eyes, Ava. You are not living a fairy tale. You have a destiny. You have people relying on you to leave this place alive. Would you truly give up on thousands of people because of your own personal torments? I'm truly sorry he died, it's treacherous, but there are those who are still alive," she says to Ava.

Chapter Eleven

"Willow," someone calls from the hallway.

"Leave it at the door, please," Willow says. She sits with her legs crossed, looking out at the ocean below. The night is chilly, and the sky is lit up by raging fires scattered throughout the city. It's been a long time since she's seen a night without light pollution degrading her view of the stars.

She brushes her hands against the rough stone of her wide windowsill. The scars on her hands tug against each crevice. She lifts her hands from the stone and holds them tightly together. *I despise that woman.*

When Willow first went to Goldryn, it was not by choice. She was caught in the rip current of Stygian's wrath nearly two years ago. And Stygian had bled her until she had given up every last secret she held. Willow has considered if it would have been better to die with the secrets, but she can't change the past. Nothing can change the past. She looks down at the scars. Her once smooth skin, dark and torn.

She isn't a slave of Stygian's, but she is a weapon.

A tool that the Queen uses whenever she needs it. Willow has a gift, unlike any other irregular. She can break through any mind, no matter what walls someone has built up. By simply touching someone, she can see into their mind and soul.

Another benefit Stygian gleaned by taking Willow was Alys' wrath. Alys was quite fond of Willow and housing the daughter of an Eventyrian high lord gave Alys good political standing. But from Willow's perspective, Alys didn't care much about who her allies were. The thing about Alys is that she was a very complex woman. She could either rip you apart until you were nothing, or she could make you feel like you were the most important person in the world. There was often no in-between. The only real thing that she cared about was keeping her region safe, but besides that, everything else was up in the air. No one knew what she was thinking or planning, except for Rais and Eieran. The Hynrule's were close to Alys.

Rais went to Willow often to confide in her. And those secrets he told her, are the ones Stygian ripped from her mind. Willow may never be able to forgive herself for that. For breaking the trust of her closest friend.

Willow knows Stygian hates her allegiance to the Sparrow, so she doesn't reach out to him anymore. She doesn't want to be Stygian's weapon. She hates being forced to rip into people's minds. Nevertheless, Willow is loyal to Stygian. And Willow stays in Goldryn, even though she shouldn't. There is something about the Queen that makes her want to stay. She sees the pain in Stygian and wants to help her. Against her better judgment, she risks her safety to help the woman.

She untwists her legs and moves away from the cool breeze flowing in from the window. She goes to her door and opens it. Her dinner sits on a wooden platter. She picks it up and brings it to her desk.

Willow looks up at the mirror hanging on the wall. She runs her fingers through her loose curls. The lavender is fading out of her bleached hair. She will have to go to the market to get new dye. She kept it lavender in honor of her little brother. He died of a sickness before she left for Wyntryn when she was sixteen. Her brother loved the color because it was the same color as their eyes, pale purple.

It has been years since his death, but she will never be able to escape the grief. It will always tug at her heart. An endless pull. When she thinks it has left, she has an unexpected memory, and then she finds herself falling apart all over again. The tightening in her chest returns and she feels like the world closes in on her. It cuts her off and leaves her drowning in an obsidian ocean.

She brushes her hair back with her hands and ties a thick black ribbon around it. Then she slides onto a stool and stares down at her dinner.

She pokes it and then stands back up. Even though the fruits are bright, and the fish is warm, she has a lack of appetite.

Willow slips out of her room and into the warm hallway. She steps through the halls, listening to the soft whispers that spread from around the palace. She passes by the room full of flowers and plants; the greenhouse that is built into the side of the castle. She continues to the throne room. The wide double doors are already open. Dark purple drapes are being hung along the walls with Stygian's crest, a three-headed dragon.

Willow nods to the workers as she passes and moves towards Stygian. Her heels clicking lightly on the marble floor. Stygian turns to her and dramatically sighs.

"Thank the gods you're here." Stygian slinks towards her. "My dear Willow, I require your specialties." She narrows her eyes, looking her up and down. "I know you still refuse to meddle with people's minds, but Grymyr has reached out to me."

Willow steadies her breathing. She says, "I do not wish to harm anyone."

Stygian twists a hair around her finger. "I understand that darling, but this is for something you will want to help with."

"You think this person is lying to you?" Willow asks.

"Why should I believe that anyone would not attempt to lie to me? Especially over this, something that would please us both ever so greatly."

"What did they tell you?"

"Grymyr wants to offer me a talisman in turn for my support in taking over a hidden city in Wyntryn."

Willow almost lets her façade slip. Grymyr knows about the hidden cities? Alys was so serious about keeping them secret, that she removed the memories of the hidden cities from Stygian's mind. She gulps. "What city?"

"It's called Rebynrock. And you know, I do like the idea of being able to take what's mine. If I get a little extra in return, even better," Stygian says. The Queen tugs at her necklace. The crystal is pale pink. Stygian scowls at Willow after seconds of her refusing to speak.

"Fine. I'll help. Take me to this messenger?" Willow asks.

Stygian lifts her chin and grasps onto Willow's wrist. Willow flinches at her touch, but Stygian doesn't seem to notice.

People still touch Willow without a second thought.

It's as if they forget she can see right into their mind when they do. Maybe it's not that people forget, but that they trust Willow. Or rather, they like the idea of someone else knowing their thoughts, without them having to share them.

Stygian drags her to the lower levels of the palace. They find themselves in the main room of the armory. A guard with obsidian hair stands before them. "Aliras, take Willow to the Society commander," Stygian orders.

"Yes, Your Highness," he says. He dips his head to Stygian, then turns to retreat down the stairs. Aliras is one of Stygian's most trusted guards. If she asks him to fetch, he fetches. Not that he wants to, but because he is afraid of what would happen if he didn't.

Willow glances to Stygian before following Aliras down the stairs. "Aliras, is there anything I should know?" she asks.

Aliras shrugs. "He's only told us what he was commanded to say."

"And what's that?"

Aliras stops before a door and gives her a sympathetic smile. "You'll know soon enough." She reaches for the knob, but he catches her hand. "Be careful. You may be powerful, but he's a Society commander. We have no clue what he's capable of."

"I'll let you know if I need help," she says.

Willow enters the room. In the center of the damp cell is a chair. On the chair sits a dark-haired man with reddish skin. He wears the Society's signature uniform; black plated armor with hidden crevices befit for all their unique technologies. She steps towards him and reaches for his shoulder. His eyes follow her. Her fingertips barely have to touch him before the walls of his mind fall. "Commander Damon."

"Hmm?" He looks up at her. "Are you here to negotiate? I have set my terms quite fairly."

"Yes, you will give our Queen a talisman in turn for troops. But that won't do," she says. She continues to carefully search through his thoughts.

Damon's head tilts and he narrows his eyes. "Grymyr wants Wyntryn, so we will not change our terms."

"I am aware that is what you believe. But Stygian has Wyntryn blood. The protectors of Wyntryn will side with her before they even give you a chance. Your people will be massacred before you even step foot in Rebynrock."

His mind is filled to the brim with twisted thoughts. It is the same with every Society member she has come across. Their minds are slowly corrupted to the point of insanity. Their thoughts become a webbed mess, and they slowly lose themselves to the Sonder. It is a disturbing and sad sight, but there's nothing she can do to save him. He chose this path.

"Do you not know how powerful the Society is?" he asks.

"Oh, I am aware. You are so powerful, that you need help from Goldryn to even stand a chance. Your technological inventions will not save you from the finest mages in all of Kanaleigh. You have heard of Alys Wyntryn, haven't you?" She says this because irregulars have flocked to the manor in hopes of being trained by her for years. Willow is one of those people. Every mage who has been trained by her has proven to be extremely capable of handling the Sonder.

"We killed that slimy—"

"If I were you, I would stop talking. That woman you speak of is the mother of the Goldryn Queen. If you want her support, you will tell me your true intentions. And do not think that you can hide anything from me. You can try, but I will simply take the thoughts myself. And trust me, the pain will be, unbearable."

He presses his back into the chair and lifts his chin. He slides his tongue across his teeth. "Alright. Grymyr wants the heiress."

"Ava Wyntryn?" Willow asks. Ava is an old friend of hers, but she hasn't seen Ava in over a year.

"Yes."

"Why?"

He holds his tongue. Willow presses her fingers to his forehead and begins to plow through the spiderwebs. His jaw clenches and his eyes widen. "Like you said the protectors will only listen to Wyntryn blood ..." he says. She pulls her hand back. "One of our commanders has been retraining Ava in the Sonder. She's been going to him willingly, and we want to convince her to ally with Grymyr."

"Last I heard, Ava lost her memories," Willow says.

He nods. "Yes, but that doesn't matter. We don't need her to remember."

"Why involve Stygian, if you want Ava?" she asks.

"We don't know how to get to Rebynrock."

Willow smiles. She walks away from him and pulls open the door. Aliras leans against the wall across from her. "Come on, I got what I needed," she tells him.

He moves into step at her side. "And?"

"It's in Stygian's best interest to take Rebynrock herself."

The Society has Ava and they are planning on taking Wyntryn. Willow will have to find a way to reach Rais and warn him. If he knows Ava is in the Society's grasp, then it's in the Society's best interest to go into hiding. When Rais unleashes his true power, he is a force to be reckoned with. And he will do anything for that girl.

It may be time for Willow to return to the manor.

Chapter Twelve

Rais sits on the carpet of the hallway. The mid-day sun casts his shadow across the floor before him. He sighs and rests his head in his hands. His thoughts spin in circles—a marathon slowly coming to an end. Only minutes before he had tried lighting a candle on the wall with his power, but his energy had built up so much over the past few weeks that he lost complete control. Rather than a small spark to the electrical line, he sent a large strike of lightning down in the hallway. It caused a boom that sent all the paintings along the walls crashing to the floor. He can barely believe he was so reckless. He usually portions off energy each day, so that he can retain control over his powers. He supposes he lost track of himself.

His mindless outburst only adds to the stressors already plummeting his mind. That's why he's sitting there, head in his hands, upset at nothing but himself.

If his old mentor were there, she would chastise him for destroying her coveted art. He wouldn't blame her either, they are all masterpieces, irreplaceable originals. And yet here he is, gazing through his fingers at them. At the irreplaceable paintings scattered across the ornate runner that was imported from the Southern Dunes.

Over the years Rais has learned much about the world, the Plane of Verity, the mind and yet, even now he still feels lost. There are still thousands of questions that torment him. Answers he doesn't have and concepts he can't even begin to understand. And what he can't help but wonder, is if Ava can help answer the questions. He knows she's forgotten so much, but Alys said she would come back more powerful than before. With a stronger connection to both worlds.

He trusts Alys' predictions, and Ava's mind did feel different. But what makes him doubt the growth in her abilities, is how destructive the fountain was to her physically. That place can be walked by minds who can protect themselves. Minds with enough power to earn the respect of the ancestors who walk there. But they attacked Ava's mind as if she shouldn't have been there. When weak or unprotected minds enter that clearing, the power of the ancestors can eradicate one's mind entirely. Being in the presence of the fountain can cause anxiety, hallucinations, as well as other severe ailments. And Ava's mind is free, running unprotected from the world around her. So easily malleable by forces of greater natures.

Nearing the end of Alys' life, she began to avoid the fountain. Even began to ignore their ancestors. Possibly that might explain why they acted in such a cruel manner towards Ava. They may see Ava and take out the anger they have towards her mother on her. Rais hopes that isn't true, but he can't help but think through all the possibilities.

The wrath of their ancestors has no end when it comes to Alys. That's why he thinks it might have a connection to Ava. Because Alys had been known for her cruel tactics. There was a time when one of her students discovered materials with information that was restricted from them, and when Alys found out, she wiped the girl's memory clean. Rais spent the day with the girl, piecing her back together. He had to enter her deepest subconscious and connect hundreds of pathways individually. But there was only so much he was capable of repairing at such a young age. It took months for Alys to realize the severity of her actions. When she did, she did her best to fix the remaining damage and returned the girl to her parents. But that doesn't excuse Alys from her cruelty.

Truthfully, the late queen had always been morally gray. Her reactions are extreme to all things. It was confusing for anyone who knew her personally because she was a kind person. At her core, she cared more about Wyntryn than herself, but she made such torturous choices. Despite Rais' respect for his past queen, she was the one responsible for burning down his family's village. She set it ablaze with the help of Stygian. That was long before they separated from each other and Stygian changed her allegiances to the Queen of Eventyr. In the time since Alys brought him back to life, he found the heart to forgive her. But there are many who can't bring themselves to look past her deeds.

Rais pushes himself onto his feet and picks up one of the paintings, raising it back up onto the wall. As he's centering the frame, he feels her enter the manor. Her footsteps sound from down the hall, and he drops his hands from the picture, turning to her.

"What happened here?" she asks. He meets her blue eyes. She shifts her braid over her shoulder and looks around with false confidence. He can sense her heart beating rapidly and her lungs moving unsteadily.

"I may have let my energy build up too much," he says. He eyes her curiously, he notices flecks of ash scattered across her hair and … his coat. Her gaze lands on him then flicks to the portrait he had hung moments ago. She moves towards it and gazes up at her ancestor's haunted eyes.

"It's beautiful."

He stares at her. "What happened to you?"

She freezes. That's when he recognizes the tear stains on her cheeks, trails darkened along her faint freckles. The sight of her certainly doesn't help him calm his worries.

"Why are you covered in ash?" he asks.

She looks on at the painting, a strength he hadn't seen in her before solidified in the core of her mind. "Raiden," she says.

"Ava," he replies. He can't tell if she was saying his name in question or simply stating it. But he doesn't mind hearing it roll off her tongue. He used to hear her say his name all the time, but now when she says it, there's a lack of familiarity. To her, he is nothing but a stranger in an empty manor.

"How did you create this mess with energy? It seems unrealistic that you were so fired up, that you began ripping paintings off the walls." She looks to him now. Her eyes inspect the abnormality of his own.

"Many irregulars can be mages, capable of harnessing their energy into elemental power. For someone like me, who's taught myself to store physical energy, when I go too long without releasing it, I lose control," he says.

"You're a mage then, of what?" she asks. Rais can tell she's speaking over what really torments her mind at the moment. She's not willing to say what made her return to the manor.

"Air, but my power appears most often in the form of lightning."

"How do you know if you're capable of harnessing energy?" she asks.

He smiles. "If you need help, I can help you."

Rais remembers when they were first learning to control their energy. He always tried to hide his true abilities from Ava. She was never able to draw on enough energy to conjure anything more than a small flame. Whereas Rais could draw on energy for hours on end before reaching a limit. It's why he moved up the ranks so quickly. Alys took a liking to him and was eager to train him into her perfect little soldier.

"What do you define as a need?" She pushes the subject ever further from what he knows she's really asking. She's hiding something from him, and he's determined to get to the bottom of it. He wants to know why her mind is shaking from stress and why she's covered in dirt and ash. Why there are tear stains on her face and clouds in her eyes.

Despite his curiosities, he doesn't want to manipulate her into telling him. He would rather her tell him because she wants to. So, he lets his urge fall back, and answers her honestly. "Anything you're not able to handle on your own."

"Well, I came here because I need something," she says. She turns her head to look over her shoulder as she walks back down the hallway.

He moves to her side, following where she leads. "And what would that be?"

"Answers."

His smile grows as his interest is peaked. "You have questions?"

"That's how you get answers," she says. Ava rolls her eyes at him. For someone who portrays herself as kind-natured, she is surprisingly harsh with her boldness. But beyond that boldness, there's something off. Something she trying desperately to keep at bay.

Rais is used to her hiding her emotions. Before she lost her memories, she often tried to hide when she had arguments with her mother. Rais was always able to tell. Whether it be the slight flinching of the skin below her eyes or the tightening of her jaw. When she's upset and forces a smile, her eyes never smile with her. The glassiness a dead giveaway.

Rais could try to reach out to her thoughts through the Sonder, but he never does that with Ava. He doesn't want to ever breach her privacy. He'd prefer she confides in him on her own because she wants to, and not because she has to.

"What about a trade?" he asks.

"Explain."

"I answer your question, and you let me show you something."

She takes a second to contemplate. "Fair enough, but my questions come first."

"Keep them to a minimum and you have a deal." He reaches his hand out to her.

She grasps it and says, "deal."

Rais steps around her and leads her down the main staircase to one of the manor's old training rooms. It is one of the rooms with metal walls and a cushioned alcove in the center. Alys had used them to train students to harness their energy. They'd train until they could barely see straight. The windows are high up because they are meant to prevent distractions, but nonetheless, they always found a way to distract each other.

Rais steps into the cushioned area and settles against the heavy fabric. He waits for Ava to sit down across from him. She is seeming to slowly relax within the walls of the manor, but Rais still wants to know why she is stressed.

He looks up to the ceiling and says, "ask away."

She shifts around on the cushions. "I want to know how to trap someone's mind in a room."

Rais' gaze switches back to her, his mind suddenly present in that moment more than it had been before. "Trapping a mind is extremely difficult. To do so is to risk your own. It takes an immense amount of power and can be as dangerous as bringing someone back to life. To trap someone's mind you first have to trap your own."

She is deep in thought, staring intently at her hands. "Why would you need to do either?" she asks.

"You save someone from death when they still have a life to live and deserve the chance to keep on living. You trap someone's mind because you lack the heart to kill them, but their actions deem unfit for them to live amongst others." He knows she's not really seeking an answer to that question, but he still responds.

"What about taking memories?" She twists her hands around and around. "Why would someone do that?"

A shiver passes through him. "To save thousands."

She looks to him, her brows furrowed. "Why do people keep saying that to me?"

"What exactly are they saying?" He wants to ask who, but he doesn't want her to get accusatory and leave the manor again.

"I've been told numerous times now, that I need to stay alive because people need me. That my people need me, but I don't have people."

It's difficult to be around her. With each sentence, his heart sinks a little more. The girl he knew is gone. But he still cares for her, whether she remembers him or not. The fact that she came to the manor today, is enough for him. It hurts, but he would rather be with her than apart. Even without memories, there are so many things about her that are the same. She may not know it, but he can still read her like an open book.

"You do," he says. Not necessarily to her, but to himself, thinking of the destroyed villages. Of the danger Wyntryn people face in refugee camps and in their own region.

"I do?" she asks.

He realizes he said it out loud and supposes he should at last try to explain it to her. "Your mother, Alys, was Queen of Wyntryn."

"Wyntryn was destroyed in the war. There's few surviving anywhere but in Grymyr."

Rais can't help but feel sympathy for her. For the lies that have been spun in her delicate mind, the mind that is struggling to understand the world it woke up in. "No. We are in Wyntryn now. This is the home where your ancestors, the Wyntryn bloodline have been born and raised for generations. You're right, the war killed many, but this region is full of survivors. Of your people."

"My mother was really the Queen?" Her words come out wobbly. "How could he not have told me?"

"Who?"

She blinks at him. "Levi." At the sound of his name,

her face drops and so does his.

"You've been speaking to Levites?" He practically shouts.

She flinches at his sudden outburst. "Yes, he helped me after my mother's death. But he … I'm here now, because …" He can feel she's at a loss for words. Her open mind is groggy.

"Is he why you came here today?" Rais remembers the brother, Saira, the one he met when he had a mission in Grymyr, had his mind trapped in an attic. "Levites' brother has been trapped in a room for years, is that why you asked me those questions?"

She looks lost—confused. "I trusted him," she says. "He pretended to be my friend, to love me … but Ms. Ethelle gave me my mother's journal. And I read in it that Saira and Levi are responsible for killing my mother. It mentioned you, and I think you're the only person I know who hasn't lied to me. That's why I'm here, really. Yes, I wanted to figure out if I could trap him myself, but I know that's useless …"

"Trap who?" Rais asks. He leans towards her, grabbing her hand. "Ava."

"Saira."

"He escaped?" Saira is far more dangerous than she may know. He is a Society commander and an incredibly powerful one at that. The Society's niche is shattering people's minds. It is a task that takes a massive amount of energy, and very few can wield it without assistance. Saira is someone who doesn't need any assistance. His power alone is enough to completely eradicate one's consciousness. Besides that, he is known to be unstable. His choices and actions are erratic.

"Yes. He attacked me, not even an hour ago," she

tells him.

His anger builds to a crescendo and it takes all his control to hold himself there before her. To not crush her hand with his fury. That disgusting and vile creature attacked her.

She must feel it in his mind because she forces him to meet her eye line. "There's no need to be rash." She seems to fall into her old self, calming him as she had always done before. "Hey, look at me, I'm okay. If anything, I'm better than okay. I asked about energy because I may have set part of the Grymyr capital on fire."

He snaps back to himself. "You did what?"

"I read that journal entry and lost control of myself. When I looked around me all I saw was fire. Levi warned me about the Society, people who would hunt me down and kill me if they knew I was an irregular."

"You came here for safety then?"

"Yes. For a lot of reasons, really."

She has no clue how much it means to Rais to hear that she set the world on fire around her. That she did it with ease, with an unawareness. It meant that she didn't lose her memories for nothing. It meant Alys didn't die for nothing. Wyntryn really had a chance of fighting through and surviving if the prophecy rings true. Ava might have a fighting chance. For years she was barely capable of harnessing her energy. She could light a candle, but never part of a city. And since her hair is slick with water—an entire part of the city in the rain.

"Hey," he says. A blissful smile alighting his face.

She looks to him, the memory of emotion from before fading away now. "Yes?"

"You can stay here as long as you like. Ask me as many questions as you need to. I'll make sure next time you set Grymyr on fire, it's because you choose to. And I'll be there to watch."

She may not understand what he feels for her. She may not remember who he is or the times they spent together, but he wants to know who she has become. He wants to make sure time doesn't steal away what memories they have yet to make. And he can't wait to set the world on fire beside her. In that moment he can see the fire burning deep within her soul, and he knows that it will only continue to burn brighter.

Chapter Thirteen

Her feet swing off the edge of the four-poster bed. Ava isn't used to such luxuries. Let alone an entire mansion filled with rooms and mysteries. Only hours have passed since she learned she could harness energy into bright blue flames. Since she learned Levi had a part to play in the murder of her mother. Yesterday she was attacked by Saira. And only hours have passed since she was told her mother was Queen of Wyntryn, and thousands of people will begin to look to her for guidance. She is only seventeen, barely old enough to feel okay on her own. And yet she is faced with so many burdens.

Her eyes are heavy and there's an ache that stretches up the backside of her neck. The moon is high in the sky. The is night already old, but her mind refuses to shut off. Ava has tried for hours to fall asleep. But instead of dreaming, she's been staring up at the ceiling for who knows how long, and now she lets her feet swing back and forth off the side of the bed. She still hasn't grasped onto reality.

In Grymyr she felt like she was finally understanding things, finding herself, but of course, she was thrown into another loop that has spiraled her back into madness. She wishes it was easy to be alive. That life would stop throwing her around like a rag doll. She wishes she could at least be given more than five minutes to breathe, with no challenges or worries. Only five minutes that are void of mourning and sadness.

Ava can't stand to think anymore. So, she pushes off the bed and lands softly on the wooden floorboards. Her feet ache at the touch. She pulls Raiden's coat from the doorknob where she left it and walks out into the hallway. The manor is impossibly quiet at night. Only the sound of her bare feet shuffling across the rug. She makes her way to the third floor and finds a door to a walkway between the two wings of the building. She steps out into the night air, her bare skin reeling against her. But she ignores her body's cries and continues across the stone.

She gazes out at the stars, wondering if her mother can see her. If her mother watches her from up there. She can't even remember who she was before, but she knows she adored her mother. And that they had a deep love for each other. What would her mother would think of her now?

There is one memory she retains from when she was small, it's a blur really, but it's more than nothing. A hint of what her childhood was like.

In the memory, she sits on her father's lap while her mother reads her a story. She doesn't remember what the story was, but she knows the cover had a knight in shining armor, riding atop a white dragon. Ava said, one day she would be as brave as that knight, and her mother told her she was already brave enough to do anything she set her mind to.

The hazy memory soothes her. She settles in that

moment, one of the few islands of her life left in an ocean of deserted waters.

She hears the door from the other side of the walkway creak open, but she doesn't look to see who it is. She knows Raiden is the only other person in the manor with her. She keeps her eyes on the stars as he comes to stand beside her.

She begins to tell him the memory but stops before she gets to what her mother said. Because it starts to fade, and she can't quite grasp what her mother's exact words were. Her breath catches in her throat, and Raiden rests his hand over hers on the railing. He sends thoughts of reassurance to her, an understanding that makes her feel less alone.

His voice stretches out into the open air. He says, "you know I have this memory of you, that I have never been able to shake. We were not a day over twelve, and you stood atop this very bridge insisting that if you thought hard enough, you could fly. I was terrified. I genuinely believed you were going to climb up on the railing and jump. For the life of me, I begged and begged you. I even started crying, and before I knew it you were bursting out laughing. In this strong and beautiful laugh. Utterly mocking me, but I could never be angry at you. And right after you started laughing, I did too. We shook on this bridge until we could barely breathe. Our chests aching, both of us gasping for air. Afterward, you looked at me, smiled, and jumped off the bridge. I was petrified, but somehow you had noticed that if you jump at the perfect place, you could land on the roof below and slide down to a balcony on the opposite side of the bridge. You told me that I screamed like I had seen a ghost."

Ava stares at him with wide eyes, entranced by his

story. In the tale of them from years ago. "I was horrible," she says.

"No, no, it was genius," he comments quietly. "You should know it will be perfectly fine if you never get your memories back. Because you are still you. I can feel it in your mind, the openness. The way you respond to the world around you. You are still Ava, with or without your memories." He is so intent on her as he says it. Her whole-body flutters with his words. Right there next to her, he isn't a stranger at all. Compiled emotions from his memories pour out around them. He's letting her see and feel them. Ava sees him for who he is, sees him as he sees her. Someone she has cared for her entire life.

"Even if you say I'm still me. I feel like that girl you tell me about, is so distant. A ghost that's always near me, but I can never catch hold of her."

"Have you tried to get your memories back?" he asks.

"Levi tried to help. He said I could reach them with the Sonder. Something about them being hidden in a cage in my mind that I can open if I find it. And Rais, I'm sorry you lost me—lost what I was to you." she tells him.

"I never lost you, Ava. We always said life is ever-changing. We have simply had to adapt to what life gave us. You have lost far more than I have in this past year, so you do not have to apologize to me for that."

She may not know him the way he knows her, but she would like to. There is an inherent familiarity about him. She really does feel as if she has known him her whole life. But she couldn't answer a single question about him. Because she truly has no idea who he is.

Ava shifts her hand next to his on the railing. The warmth of his skin on hers. "You answered my questions earlier, so what do you have to show me?"

His face brightens with a golden sheen. He says, "do not feel pressured to go, but I want to take you to see what's left of Wyntryn. They are your people, and even if you never take the throne, it might be a connection to your past, to your mother."

Ava gulps, and nods. Unsure of how to feel about the suggestion. "I need time, but I want to go."

"What if instead, I teach you how to control your fire?"

She smiles at that. What she felt in the moment she set the air itself ablaze is incomparable with anything she has ever felt before. "I'd like that."

They stand in silence for a few minutes, watching the night sky. But Ava's toes are going numb and she decides sleep is the best remedy for the pains of the past day. She ushers her quick goodbye to Raiden and heads inside.

The next day, she wakes up in the late afternoon. Ava follows the path to the kitchen that she remembers from weeks prior. She finds the kettle dirty in the sink and washes it. Dries the outside and refills it with water. She places it on the stovetop and fiddles with the little gauges until she gets one of the burners going.

"You know, you can always heat it up yourself." Ava glances in the direction of his voice as Raiden appears in the room. He sits at the small rickety table with an apple in his hand.

"I don't know how to."

He stands and walks to her, setting the apple down on the counter by the oven. "I can show you."

"Fine," she says. Curious to what he means. She assumes he wants her to make the flame herself, but she's never done it consciously before.

He turns the burner off and holds his hand out to her, palm facing upwards. "Focus your energy right above your palm."

She holds her hand out in the same way he does and stares at her palm willing it to ignite.

"No. You will never achieve anything that way." He reaches out and holds her hand with his. His thumb presses against the center of her palm. "You feel that? Do not push your will or thought to it, push your energy. When you run, what source do you draw from to keep moving when it gets difficult? Take that source, your physical energy, and push it here to this point." He lifts his thumb above the skin. "Now push it upwards to my thumb. There, perfect."

She meets his eyes, drawing her focus from her energy. "What about making it into fire?"

"You have to ignite it through the Sonder. Once you have the energy where you want the power to come alive into our world, you must let your mind enter the Sonder and set it aflame. Make sure you tether yourself to our reality first, whether it's the temperature of the air or the feeling of clothes against your skin. Make sure it is impossible to lose control," he explains.

She nods and he removes his hands from hers. She keeps her hand steady before her and focuses her energy right above the palm of her hand. She pulls on the veil of the Sonder and falls into it. The gentle blue consumes the world around her. She sends a signal down to the energy, and it bursts to life. Even as the Sonder fades out of view, the fire burns a bright iridescent blue. She stares in amazement at her creation. It tugs and spindles in her palm, moving with a life of its own.

"Perfect," he says. His cheeks push up with a small smile.

She keeps her eyes on the flame and presses her hand to the side of the kettle. The steam quickly squeals from the kettle, and she yanks her hand away. The fire disappears into the air. A black circular stain is left on the side of the kettle where she pressed the fire.

"Is there a way to control its heat?" she asks.

"There is, but that might be a lesson for another day. I am honestly surprised that you held the flame on for so long after leaving the Sonder."

"Is that unusual?"

"Not unusual, but it is difficult. I suppose your subconscious might remember a lot of the lessons you had when you were younger. We all learned the basics, but few were ever able to achieve any of it. Most abilities fail to develop until irregulars are past their twenties," he says.

"How is it for you?" Ava asks. She remembers the ease with which he heated the water before and the mess he created in the hall upstairs.

"I have been able to access my abilities since I was quite young. Although I was not considered an expert until two years ago," he recalls.

"Two years ago?" she asks, "you were only …" She searches for his age. Ava is so sure she knows it but can't seem to put her finger on it.

"Sixteen." He pours the water into a cup for her and drops a teabag in, then hands it back to her. "That is why I am still here, and no one else is. After completing my training and signing my oath, Alys began calling me her Golden Sparrow. A Sparrow, in Kanaleigh, is a term used for the person considered all-knowing and powerful under the crown. Someone to be used by the King or Queen to carry out their dirty work."

Ava can't imagine the pressure he must face. Someone so young expected to perform twice their age. Burdened with responsibilities no one should have to endure alone. "Is being the Sparrow good or bad?"

His eyes narrow at the thought. "Both." He takes a breath and explains, "those close to me use it as a nickname and say it mostly out of respect to me earning the role. Many see it as a threat, others see it as something to worship. Someone once called me Queen Alys' dog. It's not a pleasant role to have."

"I don't understand why she would give the title to you. If it came with so much hate and expectations. You were so young, and you still are so young." Ava is baffled by the thought of her mother doing that to him. Whether it was meant as a kindness or not, she is sure that there must be hundreds of others as capable as Raiden.

Raiden doesn't seem to take offense to her comment when he responds to her. "I am not fond of the title, but it is who I am. And it is who I will always be until I die. She chose me because she saw something in me that she did not see in anyone else. If anything, I am thankful for it, because it means I got to be the person who was here waiting for you to be called home."

The thought occurs to her again that Raiden may have been the one to pull her here to the manor. "Were you the one who brought me here?" she asks.

"No. I assume the ancestors brought you here. Alys left me with a series of requests upon her death. One of those was to help you take her place. In the letter she told me you would be called here when you were ready," he says. His hands slightly shake at his sides.

She still struggles to understand why her mother would put so much on him, but she doesn't ask about it again. She can tell he struggles with the same question. Despite her own lack of understanding, there is another more pressing question plaguing her mind. Why would Levi kill her mother and then pretend to love her?

"I need to return to Grymyr," she blurts out.

Raiden's brows furrow. "There is no way I am letting you go back there. If they are not aware that you know by now, then they will find out soon enough and follow through with whatever they are planning for your fate. You are the heiress to a region controlled by irregulars. In the end, they will not let you live."

"I have to talk to Levi, to give him a chance to explain himself."

"To explain what?" Raiden asks. His voice steady regardless of his anger. "He killed your mother, and I am sure he is responsible for a myriad of deaths."

"I can't believe that," she says.

"Do you want to know what is happening to your people at this very moment?"

She stares back at him, anger welling up in her chest.

He lowers his voice. "They are being killed and eaten by beasts created in Grymyr. Beasts fabricated by the Society. Hundreds of thousands are already dead because of the Atane. When you first saw me, I had just arrived here from helping save a village from an attack. This is not something that can be solved by you getting yourself killed over emotions. You are the last of your bloodline able to fight for the Wyntryn people. Without you, without your fire, they will all die. I will die. There will be nothing left of this region but ashes and stone."

Her brain can't handle the information he throws at her, so she shakes her head and averts her gaze. She says, "then I won't die."

Raiden stares at her in disbelief.

She turns away from the intensity in his eyes, begging for her to stay. She keeps walking and steps through the Sonder and into her parent's apartment. The world overlaps, fading from cold to warm. The noises of the city flow into her senses. The faded furniture and wallpaper of her home coming into view.

Ava lets out a shaky breath and kneels on the ground, holding her head with steady hands. Somehow, she is meant to be a Queen, a savior to her people, and she can barely save herself. *I will have to take it one step at a time.* Day by day. The people of Wyntryn will have to fight on until she can be ready to fight for them. And for her to be ready to start on that new journey, she has to close the one she is on now. She is intent on learning Levi's true intentions. It isn't fair to leave him with no reason and no chance to explain himself.

As her body and mind finally settle in the new atmosphere, she feels another presence in the apartment. She stands and walks towards it. Through an open door, she sees Levi in her parent's bedroom staring down at a photograph.

"Levi?"

He adjusts the frame on the dresser and runs his fingers through his hair. "Did Ethelle give you the journal?" he asks.

"She did."

"So, you know now?"

"Yes."

He's silent. She can feel a sadness leak from him into the room. "I wanted to be the one to tell you, but I never found the right time."

"Why?" she whispers. "Why?" Her voice catches in her throat, cracking as her thoughts explode again. Her voice rising as she says, "why would you do that? Why act like my friend? Why would you let me think I loved you?"

He finally meets her eyes, and she can see him breaking apart inside. He shatters like a fragile glass underneath the truth. "You—"

"Levi," she begs.

He blinks away his tears. A solemn gaze darkens his green eyes. "I had no choice."

"No choice?" she yells.

"They kill any irregular who won't conform to their rules. You either join the Society or die," he says.

"You think I haven't figured that out?" she asks. A subtle laugh escapes and she looks to the ceiling. "That is no excuse to kill someone, anyone. You would value your own life over others?"

"No, that's not what I'm saying."

"But it is," she insists. "You chose to live and did nothing to stop the fate of others. Tell me, were you there when she died?"

He is frozen in place in front of her. The pale afternoon light shines down between them. She stares back at him, begging for an answer, but he doesn't want to.

"Were you?" she asks, praying he wasn't.

"Yes."

"And did you do anything to stop it?"

"I'm sorry."

"Gods!" Her voice cracks out, and she begins to shake uncontrollably. "You watched us die?"

"Ava, I …"

"Show me." The snake hardens in place in her chest, a permanent resident of her pained soul. "Show me your memory of that day."

"No, I won't put you through that."

Out of all the times he chooses to care, he chooses now. Did he care when he lied to her over and over again? Did he ever worry about how it would hurt her? "I will never forgive you unless I know exactly what happened that day."

He nods, a tear falling down his cheek. He steps towards her, and she flinches. Levi's eyes fill with a deeper pain than before, and he forces his feet forward until he stands before her. He reaches out and presses his forefingers to her temples.

She closes her eyes, and her vision alights with a darkened scene.

Levi watches from the trees, his body covered in a thick black suit. He wears a tracker on his ear that lets out a piercing voice every few seconds, sending him updates and reports. His vision is on the road, right on the outer suburbs of the city. He tells the person through the tracker, "car heading this way, confirming the identification of two inhabitants." A short pause. "One Alys Rosaline Wyntryn. One Ava Beckett Wyntryn. Should we draw Beckett out before completion?"

A radio buzzes into his tracker, "they are both targets."

Levi presses a button on his suit, signaling another person to set the plan in motion. As her mother's car comes whipping down the highway, another car flies from the trees, its headlights shining. It collides with her mother's car, sending it into the air. The car spins and lands upside down on the highway.

Levi watches as her mother throws her door open and rushes to the other side of the car. Her mother drags her from the car and lays her out on the road, her cry echoes into the night. A loud and wretched scream. The cry only a mother makes when she loses a child.

Ava watches through Levi's eyes as her mother bends over her limp body. Levi runs from the trees shouting her name. The tracker in his ear screams at him to stop and return to his station. A bullet whizzes by Levi and hits her mother dead on. She drops to the ground beside Ava. Ava sees herself through Levi's eyes slowly coming back to life. Levi falls to his knees by her side. He stares into her blank and confused eyes. Her face is bloody and quickly bruising. A man tightens his grip on Levi's shoulders and pulls him away from her, screaming at him for bringing her back to life. But he wasn't the one who brought her back to life, her mother did.

She opens her eyes to the faded apartment shrouded in the afternoon sun. Levi's hands drop to his side, and she meets his gaze. "What happened to you?"

"They put me in charge of your case, to make sure you never find out about your past," he says. "They wanted to shatter your mind, but Ms. Ethelle convinced them otherwise."

Levi might be the only reason she is still standing today.

"And who shot my mother?" She forces the question out. Gagging on the words.

"Saira. He was made the head of that mission, but he recklessly killed one of our own after and was locked away in the attic again."

She can barely look at Levi, barely see the boy she

thought she loved in him. He looks dangerous to her now, not charismatic and innocent. Even if he didn't kill her mother, he's responsible for her death. He could have done something to stop it. He could have stopped the deaths of many people, but instead, he stood by and watched. Even had a hand in participating. What would have happened if he told the person through his tracker different names? If he didn't give confirmation of their identities?

"Goodbye Levi," she whispers into the room.

He has a look of understanding on him but tears still fall from his eyes. "Where will you go?" he asks. Desperation falls from him in waves.

"Home," she says. Ava finally feels like she has closure over her mother's death. She might be able to survive without the terrors that have wrecked through her mind for months. For once, she doesn't feel like she needs Levi's support or comfort. She can handle the world on her own or at least try her best to. A smile crosses her lips. "I'm going home."

Chapter Fourteen

Willow leans across the railing beside Stygian. She keeps her hands folded together as she explains her discussion with Commander Damon. Stygian listens intently, but Willow isn't sure what Stygian is thinking. She doesn't dare try to figure it out either.

"What should I do?"

Willow almost laughs. "You are asking me?"

"I always ask you when it comes to these things," Stygian says.

"I know, but this has nothing to do with me. It is not a decision I should weigh in on." Willow always has to remind herself of the horrible things Stygian has done. Because sometimes Stygian surprises Willow with how annoyingly human she is.

"I trust you Willow. I have done unforgivable things to you, and yet you remain loyal to me. Your sensibility is far more trustworthy than mine."

Willow bites the inside of her lip. Her trusting Stygian is a far cry from being sensible. "I think Wyntryn is unprotected and without a Queen. If you want to do the right thing, you should help protect those people. You may have given up your birthright, but the protectors might learn to accept you again." She says this because Ava can't be there for Wyntryn and those people need a leader.

"They all hate me," she says.

"With good reason," Willow adds. For a second Willow fears she's poked an angered bear, but Stygian doesn't seem to notice the bite behind her words.

Stygian lifts her chin. "What should I tell Grymyr?"

"Tell them you'll help, but let them know they have no right to take the Wyntryn throne. The talisman is safer in your hands than in your enemy's."

"I am allied with Grymyr." Stygian turns so that her back is pressed against the railing.

Willow watches her. She doesn't know whether it's a good idea to push Stygian to go to Wyntryn or not. But she knows Rais is far too young to be expected to save the region himself. Possibly having Stygian help, will allow him to relax and give him a chance to save Ava.

Stygian pushes off the railing. "I'll take their offer. You say they don't know the location of Rebynrock. Do you?"

"Yes," she says. She has to trust herself. And something is telling her that showing Stygian the location of Rebynrock is the right decision. She presses her fingers against Stygian's temple and shows her a direct path to the entrance into the mountain.

Stygian gives her a small nod of thanks, before slipping back into the palace and disappearing.

There is an odd divide within Willow's heart. A piece is at home in Eventyr, the other lies within her now, in Goldryn.

Willow is the daughter of the high lord of the Crystal Lakes. She is the heiress to his position. If she was ever to return to Eventyr, her father would marry her off to the first high born he runs into. She prefers to avoid that. Especially since her heart lies elsewhere, in the hands of Kalenti Alberona.

Willow met Kalenti before she became Queen. She had left her family's estate and was on her way to meet Alys Wyntryn when she ran into Kalenti. Willow thought someone was trying to attack her, and she ended up pinning Kalenti to a tree with a knife in her hand. After their inconvenient introduction, they became good friends. Willow traveled with Kalenti to the capital. But they were interrupted by a wildfire. A fire caused by Alys and Stygian.

It's interesting to look back now. She thought she loved Kalenti, and maybe she still does. But Kalenti loved another. And after all this time, rather than living in her home region with Kalenti, she now lives in Goldryn. With the Queen who burned down Eventyr's largest forest.

"Willow."

She looks behind her to Aliras. "What?"

"What did you tell her?" he asks. His tone cold.

"What's happening?"

"Stygian ordered me to gather our largest troop at the border with Wyntryn. What did you tell her?"

Willow didn't expect her to plan for a real war. All she meant was for Stygian to protect the Wyntryn people, but clearly, she had other plans in mind. "I told her the talisman is safer in her hands than the enemy. I said she should help protect Wyntryn."

"Why do you put such faith in her?"

She steps towards him but falters. When Stygian had grasped her wrist that afternoon, she had seen briefly into the Queen's mind. She hadn't thought much of it at the time, but now a horrible feeling is creeping up her spine. She saw a memory of Stygian arguing with her mother. The argument that had ensued when Alys stripped away Stygian's last name. Stygian is hungry for vengeance, and sought reason with Willow. And Willow practically placed the Wyntryn crown upon her head. "What have I done?"

Willow runs past Aliras. She leaps down the steps. The guards watch her unsteadily, but they've probably learned not to worry about her. Willow's heels cause her to slip on the sandstone, so she kicks off her shoes and continues out into the courtyard. Across the courtyard the guards begin to lower the gate to the city. Willow sprints and ducks underneath the closing gate. She barely clears it. She stands on the bridge, her knee aching from sliding across the stone. Willow glances back at the palace, and the gate begins to raise. Someone is coming after her.

She doesn't have time to get out of the city, but she has enough time to get to Nina. Willow forces herself to run.

"Stop!" Stygian shouts from behind her.

Her feet slow. She turns to the Queen.

"What are you doing Willow?" she asks.

She doesn't know what to say. She's made an awful mistake. Leave it to her to put trust in people who make horrible choices.

"Darling, I am only listening to what you told me. I am not going to attack Wyntryn."

"Then why are you sending so many troops?" Willow asks.

Stygian moves towards her. "Because I will never trust the Society. They did kill my mother."

"You could care less about Alys."

Stygian raises her brows. "Why does it worry you?

You have told me yourself that you have no interest in returning to Wyntryn."

"I don't."

"Is this outburst about Rais? I will not hurt him if it bothers you," she says.

"So you are planning on attacking?" She watches Stygian carefully. Her features are cool and her energy is calm.

Stygian smiles. "Trust me."

Willow brushes her fingers across her scars. She should not trust Stygian. "I'm sorry for making you feel I didn't trust you," she lies.

"If you have an issue, talk to me first," Stygian commands.

Willow smiles. "Of course. If you don't mind, I need to buy new dye from the market before the sun rises."

"Very well."

Willow forces a light expression as she turns from the Queen. She keeps her pace steady and walks in the direction of the market. As soon as she feels Stygian's mind recede, Willow slips down one of the alleys. She follows it towards 47th street. The neon light of the pub sparks on and off in the distance.

Willow enters the establishment and pushes her way through the people. They sway to a melody that hurts Willow's ears. She makes it to the staircase and runs up the steps. When she opens the door, Nina isn't there.

Willow retreats down the stairs and into the dining area. She goes to the bar and hits her fist against it. "Max!"

Max moves over to her. "Make it quick girl, what's up?"

"Nina?"

Max shrugs. "Check her market tent. If she's not

there, I know there's some guilds trying to recruit her."

"Thank you."

Before Max can reply, Willow is already halfway to the door.

She finds her way to the market set up along the coastal streets. She pulls her mind into the Sonder and searches for Nina. She senses her nearby but can't quite grasp onto her location. Willow gets closer to the lines of tents and moves in between them searching for her. She doesn't have time for this. It won't take long for Stygian to become suspicious of her. That is if she isn't already.

One of the tents nearby is selling dye. If she wants to sell her story, she has to at least bring dye back with her. She goes up to the tent and points out a subtle purple to the seller. He wraps it up for her and places it before her on the table. Willow hands him some gold coins and grabs the wrapped jar.

She continues down the line of tents until she notices one selling Aysand steel knives and swords. Nina has connections with a trader in the Isles who imports Aysand steel. If any of these tents are hers, it's this one.

Willow goes up to the tent. The owner is making a sale with someone. "Excuse me, Nina?" she asks.

Amber eyes meet hers. Thank the goddesses.

As soon as the man buys his knife and leaves, Nina pulls her into the tent. "What are you doing here?" Nina's hand strays against her wrist. Willow is the only person Nina's ever allowed to see inside her mind. There was a time when Willow visited Nina at the pub every chance she could get, but it hasn't been that way for some time. There is no solidified reason as to why they fell away from each other. It was simply the tide of time; it swept them in different directions.

"Stygian is making a deal with Grymyr."

"For what?"

"For Wyntryn," Willow says.

Nina's mouth gapes open. Willow tilts her head in worry. What hurts Wyntryn, hurts Nina. And Willow has led Stygian down the path of destruction. One that will inevitably hurt Nina's home.

Nina takes a step back and runs her fingers along the base of her neck. "When?"

"She has already ordered soldiers to gather at the border."

"You're kidding me." She practically spits out. Willow can see the disgust in Nina's face. "Did you try to stop it?"

"I—" A pain flickers behind Willow's eyes. The way Nina is looking at her is unbearable.

Tyral vaye malla Stygian's feya fin. Willow begs the goddess Tyral to end Stygian's wrath.

Nna studies her face. "Gods. Why would you help her?" She knows her far too well.

Willow averts her gaze. "I wasn't thinking."

"Clearly."

"Look, the Society has Ava. She lost her memories and they're trying to manipulate her into some sort of weapon," Willow explains.

"I'm guessing you saw into the mind of a Society member?" Willow nods. "Then you know how to save Ava?"

"No."

"Do you know anything that doesn't hurt Wyntryn?" Nina asks.

"I didn—" Willow wants to explain, but the truth is she did know. She saw into Stygian's mind. She should've known better.

Nina scrunches her nose and lets out a shaky breath. "You think you are all high and mighty Willow. You think your heart is bigger than everyone else's. You are so blind to the pain you cause."

Someone loiters by the front of the stand. "Hello?" they ask.

"Get out!" Nina shouts at them. She pulls a cloth that falls over the front of her stand. She turns to Willow. "Tell me about this deal."

"The Society is offering Stygian a talisman in turn for Goldryn's help in taking Rebynrock. I didn't tell Stygian, but I saw in the Commander's mind that the Society has already crossed into Wyntryn."

Nina leans against the table. "I should have never left," she whispers.

"Please don't tell Rais what I've done."

Nina's eyes flash at her. Her anger swelters into the air around them. "If Rebynrock falls because of you, then I will not keep it from him."

At least that means she won't tell him at first. "Thank you."

"You are lucky I like you Willow. Because there are a lot of weapons at my disposal right now," Nina says.

"I'm sorry. But as soon as I realized my mistake, I came right to you. If you can get to Rais and any of the other protectors, you might be able to stop this."

"Run back to your owner Willow. I'll take care of it from here."

Willow backs out of the tent. The words hurt, but Nina's anger is entirely warranted. Stygian asked her what she should do. Willow could have said anything, but she chose to push Stygian down this path. Even if it wasn't what she was expecting, she should have been able to suspect Stygian's intentions.

She finds her way back to the palace and up to her chambers. She lays down on her bed and prays to the goddesses that she didn't just sign Wyntryn's death certificate. "*Chessya ayatha reyani fin. Rynal vaye malla,*" she whispers. She continues to repeat the blessing until she falls asleep.

Chapter Fifteen

Ava steps into an olive and brown room overlooking the city of Grymyr. Her brown hair is the last part of her to fade into the Sonder. And then she's gone, as quickly as she came. He fights the desire to follow her because he knows deep down that she might lose faith in him if he oversteps. He must have faith in her, too. To return, to not abandon him or Wyntryn. He simply has to hope that she follows the path where she is needed most. And trust that she will put her faith in him as he has with her.

Rais slowly makes his way up towards Ava's old room. It's the same room she uses now, but part of him is still trying to cope with the loss of the girl he once knew. She is so similar and yet so different. All the things he loved remain, but she's darker now. Invaded by misfortune and trauma.

He enters her room and picks up his coat from where she left it on the floor. He pulls it over his arms and fastens the buttons in the front. He opens the armoire in the corner of the room and pulls out one of Ava's own coats. It has the same two symbols on the shoulders as his, but there's less embroidery and it's shorter. Smaller in the waist too, with buttons running down on the opposite side. He sets the dark blue fabric on her bed, and leaves the room, shutting the door behind him.

His walk continues, slow and lethargic, to his own room on the opposite side of the manor and one story up. When he finally makes it there, he pulls his favorite sword off the wall. He lays it across his lap and begins running a sharpening block over the blade.

His eyes catch on an out-of-place paper on his desk. He figures Ava possibly found her way in here and rummaged around, but when he picks it up it's a paper he doesn't recognize. A letter addressed to him. He opens the parchment to see a short letter from the Society of the Collective requesting his presence at their main headquarters on the day of the rising moon.

The festival of the rising moon is celebrated across both continents, in honor of the changing of seasons. Although in Wyntryn, the seasons are much different. It turns from fall to winter now across much of the continent, but in Wyntryn signs of winter have already been present for more than a month. He folds the letter back up and sets it down cautiously. He gets up from the chair, slides the sword into its holster, and pulls the strap around his chest. The sword hangs heavily at his back.

He wonders how long the letter has been there, and who delivered it to his desk. Raiden pushes his mind into the Sonder and feels for a nearby mind, but he can only locate one—Nina's. He pulls himself from the Sonder and listens for the hushed footsteps sounding up the stairs. He walks out into the hallway and moves towards her. Nina's auburn eyes are intent on his. "Rais, thank the gods," she says. Sweat dribbles from her forehead. To alate to

Wyntryn, she had to have traveled through the entire City on the Sea. Because you can't alate from within the city's walls. "I ran from the city as soon as I heard."

"Heard what?" he asks.

"About the mountains ..." She puts a hand on her hip and leans against the railing.

"Tell me."

She slides her deep blue hood off and pushes her hair back with a sigh. Her words come out breathy. "Stygian is using irregulars from the Society to raid the hidden caverns. Rebynrock is being attacked by mages from both regions."

Raiden falls back a step. He has to close his eyes to keep from wavering. The worry of who put the letter on his desk fades into the background. Rebynrock is one of the smaller caverns, but if Goldryn and Grymyr were to find the others, Wyntryn would truly be gone forever.

He gets the grit to respond to Nina. "How long ago did it happen?" he asks.

"As far as I know it's only just happened, but as soon as I got word I came straight here. I tried to contact some of the other students who trained with us, but most of them have scattered across the continents."

"Well, we have an advantage with it being on our land. If we can keep them from learning the locations of the other cities, we can keep ahead of the other regions." He waits a second to let Nina to catch her breath. "We also have a Queen now."

"Do we?" She asks, dismissing his comment.

"She is still getting her bearings. Although, you should know Alys was right in her predictions. Whatever happened to Ava when she died and lost her memories, made her more powerful. She lit an entire part of Grymyr on fire, in the rain." He still can barely believe it. It would have been so amazing to see. Although, he doubts Ava feels the same. Since the fire was created through her wrath. Anger that was entirely warranted.

She shrugs. "I never thought Alys was lying to us. I've just never really liked Ava. She's a little too self-focused for my taste."

"Have you met yourself?" he retorts.

She rolls her eyes. "I know, I know, but come on Rais, who wouldn't like me?"

"Me."

"You begged me to leave paradise to come to help you live out your epic journey fantasies," she says, emphasizing *epic*. As if Wyntryn being in mortal danger is anything of the sort.

"You were not living in paradise," he corrects.

Nina begins to retreat down the stairs. "Living above a pub, selling Aysand steel, bounty hunting here and there, it is a dream. You need to see the bigger picture. It's the simple things that are enjoyable, at least I wasn't lonely or having emotional breakdowns every day."

"Real funny Nina."

She shoots him a broad smile. "I try my best, Sparrow." She shifts towards the front door. "Unfortunately, I have to go. I came here because I figured you deserved to learn about Rebynrock in person and I thought you'd have a mission to send me on."

"Give me a minute, and I'll think of something." He raises an eyebrow and Nina scowls back at him.

"I'll gladly throw a punch at one of those Society clowns, but I am not going after that talisman."

"Alys asked us both to find them," Rais reminds her.

"I know, I know. But Alys is gone. I am no longer tied to her. Plus, Ava is far from being a Queen. Just because she can conjure some energy for once, doesn't make her a diplomat." Nina taps her finger against the banister.

"Where will you go then?" he asks.

"Wherever feels right, but I can't honorably live in the region that is destroying my home. And maybe along the way, I might run into the painite talisman," she says. Nina runs her hand down one of her braids then tosses it over her shoulder. The haze of the Sonder begins to spread around her.

The painite talisman was mined from the tunnels beneath the Metarock Mountain in western Wyntryn. The last known location of the talisman was in a small village along the Grymyr border. But that was more than twenty years ago. If Nina has an inclination of where it might be, then that can change the course of Wyntryn's fate.

"I'll see you on the other side?"

She huffs in amusement. "See you on the other side, loser."

Chapter Sixteen

She untwists her hair from the braid, letting it fall down her back in one fluid motion. The manor halls are silent and she can't feel Raiden's mind nearby. Ava enters her room, stepping over the fallen portraits to get there. On her bed lies a midnight blue coat, replacing the one she had left there earlier that day. She picks it up and runs her fingers along the soft embroidery on the shoulders and lapels. The same symbols that are on Raiden's are on this one. Circles with lines crossing through. And instead of the swirls of embroidery, on hers, there are two dragons in white thread that twist from the collar of the jacket down the lapels. The smells of jasmine and sweet cinnamon lift off the jacket and into the air.

Her heart warms at the scents. The aromas swirling in the air make her think of a forest on fire. Fire that flickers and bends in a soft wind—ricocheting the harsh smoke of burning wood and spicy herbs. A memory comes to her, coating her mind.

She grabs the coat with one hand and follows the memory through the manor. It pulses and vibrates in her head, fighting to surface in her consciousness. The thoughts lead her to a room on the bottom floor. It's a large room, but the dark, warm tones make it feel cozy. As she turns to the two glass doors leading out into the snow, the memory breaks through. It crashes through her like a winter storm.

In the memory she spins through the room, drunkenly laughing and giggling at the phrases spewed by her friends. A girl with lavender hair tosses her a ball of water, and Ava can't seem to grab it in the air. It splashes through her fingers and onto her hair and face. A young Raiden runs towards her and falls to the ground in laughter. He takes a large gasp. He says, "you look like a sea monster from the Isles!" Ava rolls her eyes and moves to him, issuing a sarcastic punch. He catches her fist with his hand and pulls her to the ground with him. She rolls to her back, looking up at the ceiling. Her inhibitions are gone, sunken away by the scents they inhaled from small glasses. Glasses she recalled were bought from one of the cooks after he returned from a trip to the market two villages over. In her memory she lets her head fall to the side, meeting Raiden's golden eyes. They lay there on their backs sharing thoughts through their minds.

"Get a room," a girl shouts from across the room.

"Get a life," Ava yells back. She directs the words to a girl she now recognizes as Nina. A girl with tight curls and a smug smile. The memory ends when her mother slams the door open ... and, well, Ava can't remember what happened next.

As she fades from the memory, she's still standing in the cozy room, looking out at the snow.

Beyond the glass doors, there's a building. Ava moves closer to the frosted glass to get a better look at the misshapen structure. A scraggly fence reaches out from the sides, closing in a large part of the land. She's never noticed it before.

Ava pulls up her hand to look at the jacket she found on her bed. She shrugs it on and feels the shape conform to her body. It must have belonged to her whenever she resided in the manor.

She pushes the iron and glass door open. Her boots instantly sink into the thick snow. She forces her way through one step at a time, following a path already marked by deep footprints. One's she assumes to be Raiden's because as she nears the building, his mind becomes present in the Sonder.

Ava fumbles her way through the snow until she finally makes it to the large doors. She slides one open and squeezes through the small opening. She gazes over what she can assume is a barn. There's a row of eight stalls on either side, but they look empty. One is even full of snow from an opening in the roof above.

A nicker sounds from the end of the stable, so she walks towards it. Inside the stall on the farthest end is a large black mare and ... Raiden. He stands in the stall, completely entrapped in his own head while he brushes the horse in slow, steadying motions.

"I didn't realize there was a horse out here," she says.

He breaks his focus and looks to her. The memory returns, and she feels that hopeless joy she felt back then.

"Are you okay?" he asks. Raiden must have come here to distract himself.

Her head still aches with pain, but she feels good. At peace with the world around her. Prepared to take those first steps into moving on. "Yeah, I'm okay. But the truth still hurts."

"Do you want to tell me about it?"

"Not really, but I should." She wishes the scene she saw through Levi's eyes would go away. That it could be replaced with that wonderful moment in the manor from years ago. But that vision, Levi's memory, refuses to subside. It sparks inside of her mind, shocking her when she least expects it.

Raiden bends his head in acknowledgment and reaches out his hand, offering her the brush. "Brushing a horse never hurts."

His smile brightens her mood, and she takes the brush. She slides the stall door open and steps into the wood shavings. The horse bends its head to her, and she lets it sniff her hand. Ava runs her fingers up the horse's broad face.

"I see you found your coat," Raiden says. His voice quiet.

"Yes, and you found yours." She glances quickly to him but moves to the other side of the horse to begin brushing its soft coat. "What's their name?"

Raiden stands still on the other side. "Oberyn. She used to belong to your mother, but she eventually became mine."

"Oberyn," Ava whispers to the horse. The horse's ears flicker back and forth in response to hearing her name. Ava sinks into the feeling of the horse's aura. She lets herself be grounded by the tall animal.

"I went back to my parent's apartment in the city. When I got there, Levi was already there. I asked him to tell me the truth." Ava doesn't want to tell Raiden that she thought she loved Levi. Even if it was in a forced and toxic way. And it is not as if she has an obligation to tell him. Raiden doesn't need to know. So, for now, she will keep it to herself. Because more than anything, she wants to leave it in the past. If she doesn't think of it or say it, then it will stay forever buried within her. Maybe, for now, that's okay. But she does tell him the rest. "He was there when my mother and I died. I asked him to show me his memory of it, and … I saw myself die. Heard my mother's scream, and then I saw her get shot."

Ava's breath catches in her throat. "Levi didn't do it, but he could have stopped it. He could have made a decision that would have saved my mother's life and mine. Because when I died there, that old part of me died too. I still feel her, inside of me, but I'm not the same as I was then."

"No one is the same as they were, we all change Ava. I see you for who you are now. No one expects you to be the same after everything that has happened. Memories or no memories, you are who you choose to be. You are the only one who needs to accept that."

She stops stroking the horse and walks back to him to look him in the eye. "I had a memory resurface. Of you and me, what was I to you?" she asks.

He watches her, his eyes glazing over. "You were everything."

Ava doesn't break eye contact, doesn't ask him to elaborate. He does that on his own.

"You were my person, and I was yours. In a manor full of people who did not understand us, we understood each other. When you left for Grymyr to be with your father every summer, I had other friends I spent time with, but none like you. What we had, was different. It was real," he explains.

"What about now?" she asks.

"I am whatever you want me to be. Right now,

your people need you. And I can help you save them, so if that is all you want me to be, that is who I will be for you."

She bites her tongue, unsure of how to feel or respond. That memory brought back a semblance of the feelings she had for him, but they are in the past. And who she is now isn't sure how she should feel or if what she feels is more than friendship. She thought she loved Levi, but seeing those memories, hearing Raiden now, she can't comprehend the emotions. She blinks her gaze away from him. "I feel like I've just met you. But I've also known you forever, and it's hard to decipher my own mind right now. If it's okay, I would appreciate a friend and someone to help me figure out how I'm supposed to be a person that people look to for guidance. I'm not built to be a Queen, and I don't know where to start."

"We can figure that out together then. Although, there is something you should know," he says.

"What is it?"

"In Wyntryn, there are a series of caverns once used to gather energy for the villages and towns. Old mining tunnels that were abandoned long ago. They are a secret to the rest of Kanaleigh, and when the war began, many of the people living in the region retreated to the caves. Built them into thriving cities. And I recently got word that one of the three has been taken by the Society," he says.

Ava shakes her head. "Are there no defenses?"

"There are, but not in comparison to Grymyr or Goldryn. We are allied with the Isles, but their armies are dismal. The hidden cities are meant to be, well, hidden. No one was prepared for an attack of this magnitude."

"What do we do?" Ava asks. She feels useless in this world, especially in comparison to people like Raiden. With a developed mind and control over his abilities.

Someone with influence and power.

"We make sure you're prepared to represent the people, and then we go and fight. First, we can negotiate. I'm sure our diplomats have already begun that process, but no other region will listen to someone with little power. This continent was built on five sustaining bloodlines, for centuries each region has been run by its own blood. They will listen to you."

"But I have no clue what I'm doing." She pulls the brush against Oberyn's neck. The repetitive motions soothe her thoughts. She asks, "how will I even know what to say?"

"Can you speak through the Sonder?"

"Surprisingly, yes," Ava tells him.

He nods. "Then if you need help, I will help you. As the Sparrow, and you the heiress, my oath is sworn to you. I will stay by your side."

"You better not," she says. "If you think I'm a mess here, wait until I'm thrown in front of people far more intelligent than I am."

"Have faith in yourself. You may not remember, but you are quite the leader."

She gawks at him. "I'll believe it when I see it," she says, pausing before continuing, "can we make sure I have better control of my powers before we go?"

"Sure, but you should get some rest first."

"Good idea." Ava looks around nervously and hands him the brush back.

Raiden's mouth lifts into a smile, probably feeling the emotions leaking from Ava's mind. She turns away and leaves the stall. As she walks quickly through the barn, she realizes how vulnerable her mind is. How willingly she let Saira invade it. Levi may have targeted her because of how unprotected her mind is. If she has to negotiate the release of one of the Wyntryn cities, she can't risk anyone invading her mind. Especially if she will be dealing with people from the Society who are experts in that field.

She has to start building walls and protecting herself so that she can better protect her people.

Chapter Seventeen

Ava's fire rises higher than before, but it quickly falls as she loses focus. Rais has been trying to help her, but she doesn't seem to understand how their abilities work. Rais holds a hand up to her before she attempts to spread the fire again. "You are going to hurt yourself if you keep at it. The way you are drawing on your energy is like punching with your thumb tucked below your fingers. To become an irregular, life must first be taken away. Then we are reborn through energy. That energy comes from the very ground we walk on. From the life that flows through Kanaleigh. We can only draw on our abilities because we are made of energy. It is why we can enter minds and speak through the Sonder. We are all living because of the energy that moves through Kanaleigh. The Sonder isn't a place we go to. The Sonder is Kanaleigh, the life that flows around us, invisible to everyone but irregulars." Rais kneels in the snow. He pulls tendrils of electricity from the ground. Lightning pulses against his skin.

"What about the people who are born as irregulars?" she asks.

"Those born with abilities, are different. They are innately connected to the Sonder because of the blood that runs through their veins. In some instances, the energy that flows through them is strong, allowing them to be more capable than someone who was brought back to life." He stands and the spindles of lightning move with him. "Now, when you feel you are tired, rather than drawing energy from within yourself, draw it from your surroundings."

"I can do that?"

He chuckles. "Yes. As I said, we are alive because of the energy that comes from Kanaleigh. When you draw upon it, do not strain yourself. It should not be painful. The life we draw upon to hone our abilities is delicate. Treat the energy with care. It is a gift—you have to be kind to it." He lets his hands fall, then turns his palms upwards. His fingers stiffen as the lightning spreads around him. It grows in strength. He moves each beam of light in wide arcs. Gracefully sliding the lightning through the air with his mind. He coaxes it back and forth. Rais gives the electricity some freedom so that it can move naturally and not be confined to a specific pattern or rhythm.

He releases his hold on the energy, and the lightning pulls back into his hands. It dissipates as he lets the energy fall back into the world around them. "Try again. Use both your mind and fire like you were working on before."

They stand out in the middle of the snow. Ava shivers across from him. He sends a thought to her. *You have to focus on the task, not on the cold. If you let something as menial as cold stop you, then you will not survive for very long.*

She furrows her brows. He can feel her anger building up inside. He reaches out to her mind again. *I can only access your mind because you are letting me. Hold onto that anger and use it to drive you.*

Ava reaches out her arms again, and her energy buzzes out in a line. She closes her eyes, and the energy alights in a blue flame. It flickers and blooms in huge waves.

Fantastic Ava, now try shutting me out of your mind.

She's too focused to respond to him. Oddly enough he finds amusement in watching her train. She never believed in herself before, she never put any effort into her tasks. Alys had always forced her into interests she hated. She tried desperately to make Ava in her image, and Ava retaliated by working against her. Seeing her now, becoming the daughter Alys always wanted is both amusing to him and melancholic. If Alys were to see her now, she would be so impressed by her daughter.

And I'm the one who needs to focus? Ava sends to him.

He looks her dead in the eye, fire burning bright around her in the snow and a boyish smile on her face.

She silences the fire with a sweep of her hands and runs back to the manor. Her coat pulled tight to her.

Rais alates into the back foyer. Ava shuts the door behind her and shakes her head at him. "You still have yet to keep me from entering your mind," he reminds her.

"I know, I know," she says. "I'm trying, but it's not working. Every time I think you can't break through, you do. What if when we get to this city, they get in my mind? What happens then?"

"Nothing, because it will not happen. You are perfectly capable of protecting yourself, but something is stopping you."

They are planning on leaving in a few days, and she needs to be able to protect herself. He won't tell her see he's worried, but he is. He can protect her, but only to a certain extent. He doesn't have the ability to stop someone else from entering her mind. If they do, he won't know until it's too late.

"I don't know what's stopping me."

He walks to her and looks her in the eye. "Our psyche is fragile, sensitive, and complicated. If you are holding onto negativity or issues from the past, it can affect your abilities."

"I thought I let it all go," she says. Rais assumes she's lying to herself. Because how can she believe that? He can barely stand close to her without being hit with the heaviness that leaks from her mind.

"Maybe you are still repressing feelings," he suggests.

She stares off at the floor. Rais hates seeing her lost, but every day comes with improvements and setbacks. "It might take time, so let's focus on another aspect," he says.

"Okay."

He offers his hand to her, and she takes it. He leads her to her mother's office on the third floor. It's one of the few rooms centered in the manor, overlooking the fountain through the trees.

Rais releases her hand once they are inside and pulls a folder from one of the desk drawers. "In Rebynrock you are going to encounter a few different Wyntryn diplomats. Each specialize in a different field. I assume there will also be a high-ranking official from the Society and from Goldryn."

"Goldryn is holding the city as well?" Ava asks.

Rais has yet to tell Ava that her sister is the Queen of Goldryn. He isn't sure how to approach the subject, especially since he doesn't want to add to the struggles she is already facing. Ava is a trusting person, and he is afraid that she will go to her sister as soon as she learns of their relation. She wouldn't know any better because she can't remember the crimes Stygian has committed.

"The Queen of Goldryn is allied with Grymyr. In turn, it is likely that both regions have a hand to play in overthrowing the city, but there's no way of knowing until we are there. I will cover as many bases as I can with you so that you will be prepared for whatever we show up against," he says.

"What if it's something we can't prepare for?" Her voice is timid and quiet.

"Then we will figure it out as we go. We can start here." He hands her a paper covering the diplomat of Rebynrock, the third protector of the region. "In Wyntryn there are ten protectors of the region, and they are ranked on a hierarchy. The first protector is the Queen, in this case, the heiress to the throne—you. The second protector either being the King or an appointed head of the Wyntryn defenses. The third protector is the diplomat of the High Mountain, Eieran Hynrule."

She chuckles. "I swear I have met this Eieran before. And I probably have."

"You have, he was here at the manor quite often. He was your mother's most trusted advisor."

"Who is the second protector?" Her blue eyes meet his, and he shakes her gaze away.

"At the moment, no one. The diplomats elected me to take on partial duties based upon Alys' request. Although once you are made Queen, it will be your decision to choose who to trust in that position," he says.

Surprising even himself, he has no interest in the position. He wants to follow Alys' wishes and hunt down the talismans instead. He feels he would become desolate in the position, as he has in the manor. Being by himself is soothing, but he despises being in the same place for long periods of time. He wants to travel the world. Alys had promised him she would send him to represent Wyntryn in the Eventyr capital, but that seems an unlikely event now.

"I suppose that's something I'll figure out when I get to it," she tells him.

He nods, but his mind is someplace else. In a world where his dreams stay, isolated from possibility. Like the dream that Ava had never died. He still enjoys learning about who she is now, but it isn't easy to see her and know that she may never remember the time they spent together. The resurfacing of that memory the other day gives him hope, but he knows it's unfair of him to work against something she can't control. She never asked for this, and it would be unfair to let her see how much it really affects him.

Ava pulls another paper from the folder and sets the one covering Eieran down. "The Queen of Goldryn. Stygian," she reads out.

Rais walks around the desk and pulls it from her hand, she shoots him a look of confusion, but to cover his tracks he begins to talk about Stygian. "The Queen of Goldryn is allied with Grymyr and Eventyr. That means the three most powerful regions are working together. All with their own agendas. Stygian is the blood of the Goldryn ancestral line, but she was not first in line for the throne. With the help of Kalenti Alberona, Queen of Eventyr, she found a way to rise into power. Her people adore her, but she treats the rest of the continent like ants waiting to be squashed."

"And the Wyntryns are those ants?" Ava speaks her thoughts aloud.

"Precisely. We only have to hope that there is some sympathy left in her heart," he says.

Rais slides the paper back into one of the desk drawers. He points out another protector of the region to her instead. "Here is another diplomat that might be present in Rebynrock. The sixth protector, Hyacin Moore, diplomat of the Frozen Rivers. His land is along the northern coast of Wyntryn, he hails over the lands just beyond the mountains. It is likely he has taken mages to Rebynrock to help. The other diplomats could be there too, but I know two of them are currently residing on the eastern continent helping our people in Aysand refugee camps."

Ava reads over one of the papers. "Is this the fourth protector, Osidias Donsen?" she asks.

"No, that's the eighth protector, diplomat of the Western Coast. The fourth protector is ..." He shuffles through the parchment until he sees the right one. "Here, Anya Petrichor."

Ava moves the paper towards her. "What does this symbol mean?" She points to a small eye drop shape by the woman's name.

"It means she shares blood of the Wyntryn line, but she is ineligible for the crown. Anya is your distant cousin, your grandmother had a sister, who had a son, who had Anya." Family lines are always a mouthful to say.

"When I was in Grymyr, Levi told me my last name is Beckett. Is Petrichor my true last name?" She looks down at the paper as she asks, studying the summary of her cousin's history.

"No. Your name is Ava Beckett Wyntryn. Your father's last name is Beckett. The lies of that boy make me curious as to what his intentions are."

Ever since Rais met Levites at the Society, he knew there was something off. Similar to Saira, Levites had an unexplainable emptiness. A lack of emotion that slowly grew every time he crossed paths with him. Possibly it was a cause of the Society, or it was simply in their shared blood. Whichever it may be, at least Ava finally saw the danger in them and got away.

"I wonder the same thing." She stands and forces him to look back at her. "That emptiness you noticed ..."

Rais freezes, his heart stuttering. What could she see in his mind? He did not open it to her or even feel her pass his defenses.

"I felt it too, not with Levi, but with Saira. He was disturbing, unsettling. He could laugh, but it was almost robotic. He seemed from another world, but he wasn't. What causes something like that to happen to a person?"

Rais stares back at her. He lets out a breath of relief that she hadn't heard all his thoughts. But he's uncomfortable at the thought that she could enter his mind without him knowing. It was something that had never happened to him before. He pushes past the thoughts. "He lost touch with reality, or he lost his tether to this world. It is also possible that whatever the Society forced him to do broke him mentally."

"Do you think that might happen to Levi?" As soon as the words slip from her mouth, she seems to pull back into herself. Embarrassment washes over her and sinks out into her aura. She must be uncomfortable showing him that she still cares for the boy who helped murder her mother.

"It could, but that is out of your control."

She bites her lip and moves to leave the room. "I think I'm going to take a walk. Thank you, Raiden, for helping me today. Maybe we can work on protecting my mind later, but I need a break."

Rais wonders if she will ever stop calling him by his full name. It was Ava who first called him Rais, and he clung to the nickname as a child. Everyone in the manor seemed to cling to it too.

"That is perfectly fine," he says. But she's already out the door by the time the words escape his lips.

Rais had a feeling she felt something more for Levi than she let on, but he supposes this is proof enough. He will do his best not to let it bother him, but no matter what he tells himself, it will. He has to accept that she's living a life different from the one before. And that might not include him. The dream of traveling the two continents suddenly becomes more of a possibility. He only wishes that when she is Queen and becomes the brave woman he sees her to be, she won't forget about him.

His eyes glass over, as he realizes she already has. He's wishing for something not to happen, that's already become true. The day Ava died—she lost all memories of him. Which leaves him with a sinking feeling of loneliness that is likely to never fade away.

Chapter Eighteen

She pushes herself through the manor as quickly as she can physically go. She makes it to the opposite end of the hallway and tries the last doorknob. Ava falls into the room and closes the door behind her. She settles against the floor and pushes her back to the door. Her mind is filled to the brim with emotions and thoughts that spin in broad, endless circles. Heavyweights that fly in opposing directions. Her muscles are sore from straining herself this morning and her head aches from overstimulation.

Ava rubs her temples with her forefingers, hoping to soothe the growing headache. She is learning everything so quickly, but when it comes to protecting her own mind, she is helpless. Absolutely helpless. She was able to hold fire in the snow while keeping conversation with Raiden through the Sonder, but it seems impossible to keep him out. How can she feel so powerful, yet so useless?

And Levi—she wants to hate him. Wants to despise his very soul, but she can't. She can't stop thinking about him, and it hurts. He was there every day for months, by her side, comforting her. It was easy to avoid him in Grymyr because she knew she could see him if she wanted to. But now she is in a different region entirely, and he is so far away from her. She wants to be near him again, to feel him near her, but she won't ever be able to do that again. Because she has responsibilities now, to the home her mother left behind. The future foretold to her by her ancestors' generations ago. She has no choice in the matter and there is an entire region of people needing her. *But what could I possibly do?* She's not these people's savior.

The same thoughts probably plague Raiden. How can he be relied on for such important tasks when he is so young? No matter how Raiden presents himself, she can't help but think that he too has a fragile mind.

He must be hiding his pain on the inside so that no one will see. And that's what he wants her to do as well. To hide it all inside, to protect herself from people seeing her vulnerabilities. But what's wrong with people feeling her emotions, seeing her pain, knowing her struggles? Everyone has them, she doesn't need to hide them. Maybe that's what stops her from being able to block Raiden and build those walls because deep down she doesn't want to hide from the world. She likes the freedom of having a free-flowing mind. If she is never able to build the protective walls, she doesn't see why that's a bad thing.

Ava hugs her knees to her chest and lets her gaze stray around the room. It's shrouded in darkness, but she can see the shapes of furniture highlighted by the minimal sunlight that filters through an open curtain. All the other windows are fully covered, except for one in the back. That window has the blinds slightly pulled apart and lets in those few rays of light.

She gets off the floor and slides her feet slowly around the room. Her hand strays across the dull purple comforter of the large, framed bed. She claps the dust from her hands and moves to the mahogany dresser stretched beneath the window in the back. Framed photos cover the top of the dresser, and a vase sits in the center, with dead flowers hanging loosely over the side.

She picks up one of the pictures and gazes over the image. Her heart sinks at the sight. This is her mother's room. The photo is of her mother and another girl. Her mom looks happy, she wears simple clothes and stands next to a girl with dark brown hair.

Ava places the frame back on the dresser and backs out of the room. She lets it stay there, exactly the way her mother left it.

She closes the door behind her and lets out a sigh. Everywhere she goes she runs into another emotional strain. Another memory she isn't ready to face. Ava pulls the thick fabric coat off and lays it over her arm. She holds it close to her stomach as she walks back to the room Raiden took her to.

When she enters, he isn't there. So, she slips into the Sonder and searches for him. She follows the remnants of his mind in the Sonder. It leads her to a room down the hall.

She knocks on the door, but there's no response. Ava twists the knob and enters the room.

The floors and furniture are covered with books and parchment. He flicks through his tracker, looking from it to the parchment covering his desk. "Raiden?" she asks tentatively.

He sets the device down on his desk. "I thought you were going to take a walk."

"I was," she begins to say. Ava's not sure why she's there. Something drew her to find him. "I don't like always worrying about things I can't understand or remember. I want to not have to worry."

He sits there, not saying anything. "I know, I should prepare to go to Rebynrock, and I want to ... but I also want to live a little," she says. He still doesn't respond and his lips bend inwards. "I want to fly. I want to smell jasmine and cinnamon. To fall to my back in laughter."

Her gaze wanders along the high set and smooth lines of his face.

He sucks in a breath and looks up to her. "Living sounds nice." Raiden looks swamped in his thoughts, in whatever he is researching or looking for through all the books. But he stands and walks to her, taking her hand. "Close your eyes and hang onto my mind."

"Okay ..." she says. Her coat drops to the floor.

She closes her eyes and tightens her grip on his hand as a vision bursts through her mind. The Sonder tugs all around her and she feels herself falling through the Plane of Verity. The world bends and blurs, and then there is the squawking of seagulls. A breeze billows against her skin. Her hair is thrown behind her and her clothes tighten to her skin. Raiden's voice flows out into the air. "You can open your eyes now."

Her eyes open and are instantly stung with salty air. Ava's mouth opens in shock. Raiden has alated them to a cliff that hangs over the ocean. She feels warm, her skin slowly becoming sticky with sweat. "Where are we?"

"Goldryn. But a place far from any city," he says. She looks down the cliffside, to the deep blue water beneath them.

"You ready?"

"Ready for what?" Raiden's hand is still tight around hers, and he looks to the water below. "You're kidding," Ava says.

"If you fear it, imagine you are flying. Trust me, I have done this before. It is nothing but exhilarating." His whitish hair is thrown out of place by the wind. The perfect soldier loosened by the freeness of the moment.

"I didn't mean I actually wanted to fly." The wind presses against her, she has to fight just to stay standing upright.

"Trust me?"

Ava teeters on her feet. She did ask to live a little, so she might as well. Though the water is very far below them. High enough to make nerves rumble through her.

"Fine, okay," she reassures herself.

Raiden looks to her, raising his brows in question. She nods back to him in confirmation.

And they jump.

She closes her eyes. The pit of her stomach clenches and adrenaline rushes through her. For a few seconds, she hangs in the air. Hand in hand with Raiden and everything disappears. For just a moment, she's flying.

Until they hit the water, and she sinks beneath the surface. The heavy water engulfs her, swirling her downwards. Her hand slips from his. She feels the softness of the ocean water sucking against her skin. Then she kicks her legs and pushes upwards. The open ocean moves her back and forth across the surface.

Ava spins in place looking for Raiden. He appears almost ten feet away. Soft laughter echoes out into the open air. She swims to him, and he pulls her against him. Their clothes are heavy with water and dragging them downwards. She treads the water, keeping herself on the surface, but her clothes are a nuisance.

Raiden tugs her along towards the shore. Once their

feet can touch the sand, she throws water against him. He spits out the salty water and throws it back towards her. She turns her head against it and lets out a genuine laugh. Her heart as open as her mind. For once, the worries are gone. No expectations, no grief, no sadness, no emptiness … in that moment, in the cold ocean, she soars.

And then it all comes swarming back. Her clothes are muggy, her hair knotted, her skin cold. The sharp wind only adds to the discomfort. And those huge overlaying realities come falling upon her mind in chunks. Her memories are gone, her father left, her mother died, her best friend a culprit in her mother's death, and she's destined to become the Queen of a region she barely knows anything about. Then there is Raiden. Bright eyes staring back at her, laughter written all over his face. His heart blissfully open and his mind shut tight. And she has a hardened snake in her chest. A snake that keeps her from giving her heart to another. Keeping her from letting anyone break her down anymore.

She pulls away from him and swims to shore. The sand scrunches between her toes and spreads across her clothing and skin. Ava stands on the sand looking out to the massive and layered cliffs of the Goldryn coast. Oranges, browns, and grays swirl together in uneven lines. Crowned with bright green grass. Trees grow from the rock face, covered in flowers that are saturated in varying colors.

Raiden comes up behind her and reaches a hand out to her shoulder, but she moves away. No longer focused on the moment—her mind falls back into a muddled mess.

Ava wants to fall through the air, over and over, but no matter how much time she spends escaping reality, the burdens will never go away. She has to meet them face to face and do her best to keep surviving. "I'm ready to go to Rebynrock," she says. Her adrenaline fades into the waves as they wash up against the sand and then retreat into the ocean.

"What about protecting your mind?" he asks. Sand is spindled up and down his skin. His eyes rimmed with red from the salty ocean.

Ava shrugs. "It might be weeks before I get a hold of myself, but I can tell when someone is in my mind. And I have some control over my fire now, so I'll be fine. We have all the time in the world, but Wyntryn doesn't have that luxury."

Raiden seems lightened by her introspection and glad that she shares a common goal with him. "There is not a safe way to alate into the caves, there are too many risks of stepping out into the wrong place. So, we will have to travel by horse. We can head back to the manor and leave tomorrow at sunrise."

Raiden has every little detail thought out, but of course he does. Everything happens so quickly in his life. She will have to learn to move at the same pace, but like everything else, it will take time. And it may be a long while before she feels in control of her own life.

Chapter Nineteen

The front door swings open, clashing loudly into the window frame. Ava drops the cloak she recently found. It swishes against the wood of the stairs. A figure steps into the manor and the door slowly closes behind it. The shadow that haunts her nightmares.

"Miss me, little Wyntryn?"

Saira.

Ava quickly recedes up the stairs. Her foot misses the next step, and she stumbles backward. Her back hits the edge of the stairs with a thud. Saira moves towards her with a disturbing speed. *Raiden?* She calls out.

Saira is at the foot of the stairs and Ava has nowhere to go. She presses her mind into the Sonder, picturing her room in the manor. She moves through the Plane of Verity in a panic and tumbles out onto a cold floor. She recognizes the bed frame, the armoire, her shoes—she made it into her room. Saira couldn't follow her, but he is still in the manor. She can hear him singing out her name. Ava closes her door and presses her back against it.

She can hear him down the hallway. He kicks open

the doors and throws furniture around in search of her. With each room he searches, his anger grows. Ava reminds herself to breathe. Because her lungs are moving far too fast.

"Little Wyntryn? Did your Sparrow leave you?"

He is close to her room. So, so close. Ava never locked the door. She spins to it. As quietly as she can, she turns the lock. Click.

She practically feels him turn to her door. The doorknob wobbles. Then he yanks on it. The door lets out a low groan. Ava moves away from it, placing one foot behind her until she is backed against the wall.

There is silence. A terrifying moment of unknown.

Then Saira slams something into the door. The door shakes. It pushes inward until the hinges break and the door flies towards her. She jumps to the side, landing on the floor behind her bed. Saira runs in with a wide grin on his face.

He struts to Ava and yanks her onto her feet.

Raiden alates into the doorway and sends a bolt of lightning into Saira. Ava pulls her shirt from his grasp. She crawls over her bed. Saira sends an icy wind at Raiden. It pushes him out the doorway. Saira turns to her. A dagger slides across the floorboards. Ava glances to Raiden and bends to the ground. Saira moves around the bed and grasps her shoulder. Before he pulls her up, she slips her fingers around the leather grip.

A sharp pain rushes through her head. He tries to force her into the Sonder with him.

The dagger is a phantom in her hand. She doesn't want to do it, but she has no other choice. She tightens her fingers around the dagger and stabs it into Saira's arm. He lets out a sharp cry and releases her from his grip.

Ava wants to burn his touch from her skin and clothes.

Raiden stalks towards Saira and throws a single punch, hitting Saira's temple. Saira collapses to the ground unconscious.

"Do you care to know why he's here?" Raiden asks.

He says it in a way that sends a chill down her spine. "I would like to know why," Ava says. She hopes that answer will keep Raiden from doing something he might regret.

"Can you help me get him downstairs then?" he asks.

She forcefully nods She doesn't want to, but there's no reason she can't help. Raiden lifts Saira's shoulders and Ava grabs his ankles. They carry him out of the room and down the hallway. Raiden instructs her to back down the stairs so that he holds the brunt of the weight. They go down step by step. Her hands slip on Saira's dark slacks, but she doesn't want to touch his skin.

They eventually get him down the stairs and into the room with metal walls. They leave him at the far end of the room.

"I can keep watch if you need to tack up Oberyn," Ava offers.

"I do not trust him enough to leave you here alone."

"I don't know how to tack up a horse. And I don't even know what to pack."

Raiden bites his lip. "Will you notify me as soon as he regains consciousness?" he asks.

"Yes. You don't have to worry."

He glances at Saira. "If he tries to attack, do not be afraid to fight. You are only as strong as your own will."

Sunrise comes and goes, and they don't leave for

Rebynrock. Ava stands in the odd room with metal walls, staring into Saira's eyes. He tilts his head at her, his eyes flashing with false amusement. The morning light ricochets through the room.

Only minutes ago, Saira awoke. He sat up, pushed himself against the wall, and proceeded to stare at her with dull green eyes. She has yet to break eye contact with him. Bottled-up energy gushes from his pores. His face is paler and deadlier than ever. His eyes hooded and dark.

A disturbing feeling sits in the space around them—slinking and crawling through the air and into her head. Despite her unnerve she holds his gaze. Animals value their dominance. And she isn't planning on letting Saira feel dominant over her. She is not his prey to hunt down and kill.

She will never give him the pleasure of killing her. Not after Grymyr when he tortured her mind. Not after he killed Ms. Ethelle and countless others. Not after he shot her very own mother. She can never forgive him for what he has done. She would only be belittling herself to let him think he is above her. Ava has to hold her ground. Not only for herself but for everyone who has fallen victim to his torments.

The room's temperature drops as Saira sends a cooling breeze across the floorboards. Ava lets the blueness of the Sonder rise within her and opens her mind to the plane. She draws her energy out across the floor and adrenaline tingles through her.

After discovering her abilities, she has begun to feel a need to use her energy. It sizzles within her veins, asking to be released.

She is shrouded in flickering blue as she sets his cool breeze aflame. Saira's eyes widen in surprise, and he brings himself to his feet. Ava's own excitement runs through her blood at the vision of fire. Her fire.

Saira begins to twist the cool breeze around her. The whirlwind gets faster and faster. She can feel icicles crystallizing against her skin. A tantalizing cold, begging her to fight back.

She lights the fire within herself. It burns from her core and through her skin, but the icicles don't melt. And Saira only moves closer. His frozen energy spindles around her.

She pulls her energy back in and directs it towards Saira. But he invades her mind, and her head is thrown back, breaking their eye contact. Saira's confidence grows and stretches around her. She coughs against the chill rising through her and tries to push Saira's mind from her own.

"Seems your Sparrow isn't here to save you now, Your Grace," he whispers into her ear. He stretches his spindly hand to her neck and clamps down, his skin freezing against her own. His nails dig into her fragile skin.

She kicks against him, but he doesn't budge. Panic rises from her gut, and she doesn't know what to do. Ava scratches her nails against his hand, his arm. Tearing at his flesh in desperation.

Fight back. He throws at her.

She can barely breathe, her eyelids fluttering against her own weakness.

Fight back. He screams into her mind.

Ava clamps her hands around his wrist and focuses her energy on the inside of his arm. In a last-ditch effort, she pulls herself into the Sonder and sends fire through him. A wretched scream pours from his mouth, and he lets go of her neck. She falls to the floor, gasping. In shock that she ever let him get to her that quickly. And now she can barely force a breath from her lungs.

She forces herself to stand, her neck aching and burning with each breath she takes. Ava runs towards Saira and throws her hand against his face, digging her nails in and burning his skin with her touch. He screams again, clawing at her. She doesn't let go until Raiden enters the room. She pulls her hand away. Saira's face is melted and destroyed.

She backs away. Her body still shaking. Her mind and neck still aching, her heart racing.

Raiden hurries to her side and she falls into him. He strokes her hair away from her face and looks over her. He focuses on the quickly bruising mark across her neck. His eyes burn with a golden fury. He steps away from Ava and moves to stand over Saira. She can feel the electricity bursting through him and into the air around them. The whole room prepared to explode with a single spark.

Saira's flesh is mangled on the right side of his face. His mind can't seem to calculate the damage, because he laughs. Unphased by the harm she inflicted. "What fun that was," Saira says.

Ava bends in disgust, her throat bobbing. Vomit rises from her stomach as it churns within her.

"Really, Your Grace, I love to see you in action. You are simply wonderful." His mouth stretches into an empty smile.

Ava meets his eyes once more. "Leave this place, or I won't stop next time," she tells him. Ava fights to remain steady despite her pain and the gagging taste in her mouth.

"Ah, well I won't stop either," he says. "Oh … and please do attend." His body dissipates into the Sonder.

There is nothing left before them but Raiden's anger and a letter resting on the floor.

Raiden bends to pick it up and opens it. His eyes narrow and he folds it back up, moving to shove it in his pocket.

"Give it to me," Ava says. Her voice comes out hoarse.

Raiden looks down at the letter and unwillingly passes it to her. Ava pulls it from his grasp and opens it up. She reads it aloud slowly, her voice cracking against the pain of her throat, "Dear Ava Beckett Wyntryn, The Society of the Collective invites you to a celebration of the rising moon. A night of festivities catered to the unity of the Western Continent. We hope you join us for this evening of acceptance and peace. You can join us at our headquarters in the center of the Grymyr capital, at the Library of Mystical Creatures."

"The ball is a trap," Raiden informs her. He continues when she can't seem to speak. "I got an invitation as well. It is two weeks from now. They have invited the most important people from every region in the continent. It is either a slaughter or a way to show off their dominance. I reckon we avoid it entirely."

Ava gazes at the floor. Her eyes burn with the pain vibrating from her neck. She can barely focus on what the invitation implies.

Raiden goes to her and helps her sit down on the cushions. "I am sorry I left you in here alone," he says.

Ava shakes her head and speaks through to his mind. *You need to realize that you can't always protect me.*

"I know, but if I can, I want to."

He gently touches her neck. Ava does her best not to flinch, but slow tears fall down her cheeks. His eyes study her with worry, and she brushes the scar on his jaw with her hand. He stares at her. "Please don't."

She draws her hand away from him and lets it fall against her lap. *I'm okay, don't look so worried.*

"I am worried. You are not even able to speak," he insists. "I can alate you to Rebynrock, and we can find a healer. It might not be the safest idea, but you need medical help."

Ava shuts her eyes, not wanting to look at him. To see the worry, she doesn't want him to have. Ava doesn't think she deserves his worry. What has she done to deserve it? There's no reason for him to drain himself over something he can't control. She also doesn't want to try to respond to him. Her mind isn't in a good place to make decisions.

Raiden lets out a disgruntled sigh, his mind clicking through every option as he calculates what is best. She watches as he runs from the room and comes back with her jacket and a large sword strapped across his back. Along with it, he holds a belt, with a dagger attached.

She moves to sit upright and shrugs the warm fabric over her arms. She shifts forward to let Raiden pull the belt around her hips. Her fingers tread over the smooth metal of the dagger. She can tell it's different than the one she stabbed Saira with hours before, but she can't bend her neck to see.

"We are going to go now." He pauses. "Something is blocking me from accessing Rebynrock through the Sonder. I am not able to alate within the cavern walls, but there is a village right outside of the mountain. There are people there who can help us."

He takes her hands. She nods to him, her mind foggy and her consciousness slipping. Raiden sends the images of where they are going, and she clings to his mind. She is dragged through the plane of verity and into heavy snow. Raiden places an arm behind her back and one beneath her knees and lifts her into the air. She can't see much, but she feels him pulling his feet through the snow. She wakes slightly to the feeling of warmth on her skin and the sound of a crackling fire.

"Golden Sparrow, you are back so soon." A woman's voice calls through the room. Ava hears her feet shuffle across the floor.

"I need a healer," Raiden tells the woman.

Keys clink together. The woman leads them up a flight of stairs. "You can stay in here. I will fetch the healer right away," she says before hurrying out of the room.

The door shuts, and Ava's head falls against a pillow. Her mind swirls and her vision blurs over even more than before. *What did he do to me?* She pushes to Raiden.

"We will know soon enough, but take solace in the fact that you fought back. His face will be permanently marked by your wrath."

Are you trying to be funny, Golden Sparrow? She muses.

The bed shifts as Raiden leans against it. "Always trying, but failing dreadfully." Raiden's voice is filled with light, but she feels his mind swarmed with apprehension and restless nerves.

She can't seem to keep her eyes open any longer. The blurriness too heavy. Her mind too foggy to stay present. She falls into a quiet sleep, the pain subsiding with her resting mind.

Chapter Twenty

Rais leans against the bed. There's an ache in his back from the wooden frame. He hasn't moved because he wants to be as close to Ava as he can. That way he can hear if her breathing slows and know when she moves without having to watch her. If he watched her while she slept, she'd be uncomfortable, so he doesn't. Instead, he leans there, his back to her, and his annoyance rising with every passing minute.

The healer has yet to show up. Clearly, the healer doesn't realize who it is lying asleep in the inn. His nerves are spiked, and his mind is agitated. Rais gets to his feet and begins pacing back and forth.

He forces himself to focus on the room. It is similar to the one he stayed in before. With a small furnace in the corner and a bed too small for anyone taller than Ava.

He looks over the wooden walls and floors. And then to the ceiling, the same as the rest of the room. Wooden and dull. He moves to the window and looks out at the street. The laughter of two kids playing echoes into the air. Their small hands throw snowballs at one another. Normally their enjoyment would bring a smile to his face, but he can only think of Ava. His gaze finds its way back to her and the darkening purple and blue across her neck. He knows she will be fine, but what worries him is the damage to her vocal cords. The way her voice croaked out in the manor. The way her breathing has been unsteady and berated for the past hour.

He has been waiting for that woman to return with the healer. *Why has she not returned? I need the healer now.* Rais' patience has reached its end. He picks his sword up off of the ground and leaves the room. He doesn't want to leave her, but getting a healer will be more useful to her than his presence. He shuts the door carefully behind him and then leaps down the stairs and into the lobby. The small woman isn't there, so he goes through the lobby and down the front steps. Once outside, he reaches into the Sonder in search of the woman's mind. Once he locates it, he stalks past the two joyful children and to the front of a quaint home.

He steps up to the front door and knocks. His anger reflected through his knocking and the ringing in his ears.

The woman from the inn opens the door and looks up to him. "I am sorry, he has been busy this whole time. I have been trying to get him to go check on her."

"Excuse me," he says. He tries to keep his tone controlled. Rais pushes past her and into the house. He spots a man in the corner sitting over an old lady and spooning hot soup into her mouth. "Do you know who I am asking you to treat?" he shouts. His hands flinching at his sides.

The man turns to him. He's young with spindly hair and tired eyes. "I do apologize sir, but I have other patients."

"The heiress," Rais says. "I am asking you to go

heal Alys Wyntryn's daughter, and you sit here taking your precious time." He directs his words at the fragile woman on the bed. "I am sorry ma'am, but you must see there is someone who needs more help right now?"

The old lady looks to the healer, who looks from the old lady to Rais. "How do I know what you say is the truth?" the healer asks.

The woman from the inn speaks up from behind Rais. She says, "he is the tenth protector of Wyntryn, the Sparrow. You will trust his word, Daryn."

Daryn sets the soup down and stands hesitantly before Rais. "I apologize for my mistake, Sparrow Hynrule."

"You can call me Rais. But please, help Ava."

"I will go there now," Daryn says.

"Good."

Rais leaves the house and watches the healer go to the inn. He waits for the door of the inn to close, before walking out toward the trees. The woman follows him, but he pointedly ignores her.

"Sparrow, was that really the heiress who you brought here?" she calls to him.

He keeps walking, wanting the snow to shake down from the trees and cover him in a blanket of cold.

"Will she be the one to save us? Can I share news of her presence with others?"

Rais spins to her. "Believe what you want. Do as you wish." She flinches, a look of hurt crosses her features.

She moves to say something but takes a step back. Then turns and walks away from him then. He knows he should act more formally around citizens, around everyone really. But his mind is unpredictable sometimes, especially when it comes to his anger.

Rais stands there in the snow. His skin frosting over. His toes and ears numb in the cold. The sharpness that comes with Wyntryn's seasons is soothing to him. It reminds him of the home he is fighting for. And it grounds him in the moment. It draws him to a single undeniable feeling, cold. No matter where he is in the region, seven out of the twelve months in a year, his favorite weather is there to greet him. To help him feel himself and feel closer to the land he protects.

He returns to the village and looks up at the outside of the inn. The raggedy building with no more than ten rooms. In all the times he has traveled through this village, he has never tried to learn people's names. He supposes it is his fear that keeps him from pleasantries. A fear that makes him avoid getting too close. That's why the people he does trust, he clings to. Almost too much.

I'm better off on my own. I have lost so much, and I will only burden people with my suffering.

He chuckles to himself in response to the thought. Because everyone he knows has lost as much as him. That is the cruelty of this world he supposes, a world of war and hate. It means there will never be a person who doesn't have to fight to survive. Even the rich, living in excess of whatever they please, suffer too. Burdened by their own loss, hate, loneliness. The rich aren't happy because they are rich. If anything, the poor have more to live for. Because they must fight for everything they have. Every Wyntryn in the past ten years has had no choice but to fight for their lives. In some way or another.

His mind strays away from the thought, at the sight of the two kids still laughing with each other. Their father calls out to them from two houses over asking for them to come inside. And then they go, two innocent minds, oblivious to the dangers of the world they live in.

He goes into the inn and apologizes to the woman at the counter. She doesn't respond to him, so he continues past to the stairs.

He stops in the doorway to Ava's room, his hand loose on the handle. Ava is fast asleep. A herb paste is plastered across her neck. Even in sleep, her mind is empty. The pain is great enough that she isn't even dreaming.

Daryn stands silently in the corner by the furnace. He walks to Rais and pushes him back through the door. Daryn follows him out and shuts the door behind him. "She needs her rest," he says.

"I want to see her."

Daryn shakes his head. "You can wait."

"How bad is it?" Rais asks.

"Mostly surface injuries, but there may be inner damage that I haven't been able to locate yet. I will return every hour to check on her and do what I can, but my energy is limited these days. A new injury appears around every corner," Daryn's thoughts stray for a moment. "Can I ask who did this?"

"The Society," Rais replies flatly.

"To do that to our heiress on top of all their other actions… Grymyr will pay one day for the treachery they have caused our people." His eyes are wide with dark circles ringed below them.

Rais looks to the door. As if he can see the answers through it. "There has to be an end eventually, and with that end, we will have justice for our families, for our people." Daryn bends his head down. His body reflects his lack of energy. *The man needs his own healer*, Rais thinks to himself.

"You are a protector of this region, sir. You and that

girl are two of the few people that can truly make a difference. Even if what's left of this region fights back every day, the changes must be made on a diplomatic level. When it comes to rulers, the only people who can stop them are their equals. There will be no end unless someone takes action," he says. Daryn shifts his grip on the small case that holds his supplies. "If you have any care for her, you will fight back. All you protectors have done is sit around and wait for somebody else to act. But there is no one else. We have already lost Rebynrock." His voice is a whisper, full of pain.

Rais bites his tongue, waiting for the man to walk away. He can't face him. The guilt he has been holding in for so long crashes down upon him. And he yanks his mind into the Sonder. His mind ragged with a fury stronger than anything he has felt in a long time.

As Daryn slips down the stairs, Rais steps through the Plane of Verity and into Grymyr. He finds himself outside of the tall brick building on 32nd street. And begins the hunt for his prey. Rais' mind searches through the entire library before he even reaches the threshold. He can sense the mind barriers on the lower levels, but what he wants isn't there. It is at the very top floor, locked between a spiral staircase and a circular window.

Saira knows he is coming.

Rais stalks through the door and into the quiet library. He focuses his mind in the Sonder, slowly gathering energy within himself. Rais flies through the stacks of books, his body high on the feeling of unused energy. He bounds up the stairs, the wood creaking loudly beneath his feet. He reaches the highest floor in no time.

He steps through the opening to meet his adversary face to face. As he enters, a wave of icy water flies toward him. He reaches out and blocks it, sending it flying through the window. The glass shatters and sprays out onto the ground below. Saira leaps towards Rais, his hands landing square on his shoulders and pushing him backward. Rais throws a jolt of electricity towards Saira, but he pushes it aside with a flick of his wrist.

They stand between the attic and the banister of the stairs. Their breathing steady and each of their minds a well-protected fortress. Rais thinks about Ava and the gnarled bruising across her neck. His rage filters through his body sending uncontrolled sparks into the air around him. Saira's face is melted and gory, his right eye bloodshot from the morning's events.

He leaps again towards Rais, his movements erratic. Rais dodges him. He centers his energy in his hands and brings spheres of lightning to life. When Saira lunges again, he strikes him in the side. Saira falls back against the wall and moves forward forcing Rais back to the staircase. Icicles spray from Saira's hands and one hits Rais in the shoulder. He yanks it out and throws it to the side, but Saira is already in midair again. He hits Rais backward, and he falls through the banister. Nausea hits him as his body twists in the air. Rais pulls himself through the plane and alates to the floor. He stumbles into a bookcase, but rights himself.

Above him is a large metal dragon with an arrow piercing through its skull. Excitement rifles through him. The last time he saw that arrow, it was in a heavily guarded area kept hidden within Wyntryn. But the Society must have found it and taken it for themselves when no one was watching. And there it is, hidden in plain sight. The Society may be made up of expert minds, but they can be so mindless sometimes. It may not be where he thought it was, but despite that, he still somehow found it. In the Library of Mystical Creatures, of all places.

Saira appears behind him, and Rais throws out a bolt of lightning in his direction. Saira dodges it and appears farther down in the pathway of books. Saira is blindly alating. Which only puts him at risk. A person can never be sure of where their feet may land next when acting in such a manner. The mind and the Sonder are delicate. And if an irregular isn't careful, they can easily hurt themselves.

When Saira alates again it's closer to Rais. Rais grabs the creature by his shoulder and throws him into the bookcase. He slams the heel of his foot into Saira's gut. The bookcase teeters over, already unstable from years of neglect. Saira and the bookcase collapse backward. Books fall in large heaps from the blow. They scatter across the floor onto everything but Rais.

Rais rips Saira from the bookcase and drags him to the front of the library. He kicks him to the ground and pulls his sword from his back. He drops his knee onto Saira's thigh and holds the sword to his throat. Rais forces his mind through Saira's tightly built madhouse. He throws his anger into Saira's mind, screaming into his skull. *You will pay for the lives you have tortured and ruined, Saira. You killed my Queen. You killed my people. And you will find your way to an afterlife of misery. Where people like you get to witness your crimes over and over and over until even you can't handle being trapped in your own head.*

As he sends the thoughts, his mind finally sees through to Saira's. And he notices a familiar pattern written into Saira's brain. Webbed tendrils of what once were Saira's thoughts and memories are tied and twisted together. He is slowly being consumed by the same sticky glue that plagued the man Rais ran into in Goldryn. The Society isn't only destroying the minds of irregulars in other regions, they are doing it to their own people. Even Saira, a high-ranked commander, is being targeted.

Rais retreats from his mind as Saira smiles up at him. "I already can't handle it." He laughs quietly. "It's okay, do it. I deserve it, don't I?"

Rais pulls away from him, sheathing his sword. Killing Saira won't make Rais feel any better. And the poor man has already been broken and tortured beyond repair. It isn't Saira who deserves to die, it's the people who made him this way.

A sour taste grows in his mouth.

He may hate him, but Saira has been suffering.

Rais leaves Saira's mangled mind and body on the floor and looks up to the hanging dragon. He shoots a bolt of lightning through his finger and up into the ceiling. It bursts across the chains, breaking them, and sending the majestic creature plummeting into the bookcases. Rais climbs up to the top of one of the sturdier shelves and walks across to where the dragon's head rests. He gently wraps his fingers around the obsidian arrow and yanks it from the eye of the metal dragon. The arrow is hot in his hand. A life inside of it, bursting and thriving at the touch of his energy. He slides the thin talisman into a pocket on the inside of his jacket and nods to Saira who watches from the floor with wide eyes. For once, the empty, tortured boy shows a genuine emotion.

Rais slips back into the Sonder and through to his familiar world. Where the trees are barren, and nothing falls from the sky but soft snow. In the middle of the village, he drops to his knees and bends his face to the ground. He whispers a prayer to his ancestors, asking them to forgive him for his neglect of their people and for letting his anger control his actions.

Rais is only human but expected to be more. Given a title prematurely that writes his destiny for him. He locks his emotions back inside his mind, and rises from the ground, ready to face the next challenge.

It's early morning, and Rais can't sleep. They have been in the small village below the Mountain of Rebynrock for five days. His eyes are closed, but images flash through his head. Images from the days when his family's home stood steady. His mother weaving blankets together in preparation for the coming winter. His father carrying home gray rabbits slung over his shoulder. Rais remembers them working synchronously. They were building a steady and happy life for him. But then the Queen came. She had gotten her hands on the tanzanite talisman and heard that the painite talisman was hidden in his home village. Alys became obsessed with the power the talisman gave her. She needed more. Alys went to his village in search of the talisman. Stygian came after Alys and tried to stop her mother, but his village was in their way. His home and parents became collateral damage.

He sees flashes of his childhood home being scorched by a powerful blaze. Images of the manor, of Ava. The wonderful and horrible twisting together in a tattered tapestry within his memories. He wishes he could go back in time. Wishes he could carry Ava back through the plane of verity. Bend the laws of the land and take her back to the manor. Back to when they sat on the wooden floors of the study and chastised each other. When they threw thoughts at each other's minds and shared dreams of a future filled with life and adventure. Not one shrouded in death and malicious minds that threaten their lives.

Rais wants to go back in time and stop Ava's memories from being erased. He regrets not being able to save her. He was in Grymyr that summer. He was there, but Alys asked him to leave. And he left. He wishes he could tell Ava everything that has built up inside of him over the years, but the Ava he knew is gone. If she only knew—if she could only understand. If only she could hear the words he never got to say. If he could just go back. Maybe, just maybe, time would never get the chance to erase him from Ava's memories.

He lays still, staring into the darkness.

The door opens and closes quickly. Her footsteps are light and careful. She slides onto the sheets beside him. His muscles tense in her presence. Does she even realize that he is awake?

Ava? He speaks through to her mind.

Did I wake you? She sends back to him, the thought tinged with worry.

No. I have been awake.

She turns to her side. *How did you get the scar?* she asks.

The muscle between his eyebrows flinches, and he closes his eyes. "I was at a village along the Wyntryn coast, just above the Goldryn border. The village had been overrun by Atane. A group of Goldryn soldiers were on our land helping to fight the beasts off. But once the Atane were cleared, the soldiers began to loot what was left of the village. I tried to stop them, but it was five to one. They knocked me out, and when I woke up ..." There's a tingling behind his eyes. Pressure building with the resurfacing of the memory. "I woke up tied to a tree outside of the village. I had to watch as the soldiers killed the villagers, and when they were done, one of them decided tying me up wasn't enough. He carved his knife into me, and then they left me to bleed out."

She rests her hand on his arm. "I am so sorry Raiden. That cruelty is ... unforgivable," she whispers. Her voice is still tainted by the damage of Saira's hand.

"It's all in the past now." His head falls to the side, and he meets Ava's eyes in the dark. The depths of the blue drags him back into his regrets. Back to all the words that sit on his tongue, forever unsaid. He forces the folds of his mind back within his tightly built defenses and cuts through the moment by saying, "if you feel good enough to travel, it is time we head for Rebynrock. We have already been here for five days. We can't risk losing another."

Ava nods against the arm she has tucked beneath her head. "I feel fine now, it still burns a bit, but there's nothing stopping me from going."

"Good. We can leave once the sky is bright. There's a man who offered to take us to the city. I was going to meet him this morning whether we chose to leave or not." Rais rolls to his back.

"You never take the time to enjoy the moment, do you?" Ava asks.

He tilts his head to hers. "What do you mean?"

"Everything happens so quickly. You seem so eager to keep moving. Do you ever take the time to simply cherish the moment?"

He huffs lightly and his eyes narrow. He used to thrive off the little moments in the day. Like when he would stare up into the sky and his imagination would fly him away from the world. When he would soak up every last drop of the present, no matter how irrelevant it might have been. If only life was as simple as living in the moment, but the world refuses to allow him that pleasure. He is burdened to live the life set for him by Alys, by his ancestors, by everyone who is incapable of doing what they ask of him to do. Rather than sharing his true thoughts with her, he simply states, "sometimes."

Ava's breath escapes in a hush. He can see her throat bobbing and her eyes holding a heaviness that he doesn't understand. Why is she reacting that way?

Before he can figure it out, Ava shuts her response down and pries herself off the bed. She pulls the curtains open. "The sky is already bright," she states.

Rais sits up, pulling the sleep from his mind. Ava watches him closely for a moment, before breaking away. She says, "I'm going to get ready to leave."

He watches her retreat from the room. His curiosity begs him to figure out why she responded in such a way, but he shrugs it off and begins to pull himself together. They are leaving for Rebynrock, and he has no idea what to expect of the city when they arrive.

Chapter Twenty-One

Ava returns to her room, closing the door behind her. She leans against it for a moment. A blissful smile on her face. She is almost annoyed with herself for feeling this way, but she doesn't hate the feeling enough to push it away. She slips her pants over the warm tights she already has on. Tucks in her white blouse and then slides the belt with the dagger around her hips. She picks up her jacket and slides it over her arms.

Ava asked Raiden about the dagger the day before. It was the first time she was able to talk in days. He told her that the dagger belonged to her. Evidently, when you graduate from the academy her mother ran, you sign an oath. Afterward, you are given a dagger connected to the Ancestral Fountain and a mage coat. Each dagger and coat are designed with their owner in mind. Which is why her coat and dagger have the twin dragons. It was the symbol given to her at birth. Whereas her mother is represented by a dragon with four wings.

Going into the small bathroom in her room, she sees the wreck of her hair and the grotesque bruising covering her neck in the mirror. The darkest bruising is located where Saira's fingernails dug into her skin. She pulls her hair into a bun, fastening it in place. Her gaze stays on the bruising. Her hands fall slowly to the counter. She never really looked at the bruising until now. In the mirror, Saira looks back at her. His dull eyes bore into her. His hand reaches out towards her neck. Ava stops breathing for a moment. She reaches up to her neck and brushes the tarnished skin with her fingers. It aches. She closes her eyes as a ragged breath shakes through her.

She leans against the wall of the bathroom. Her palm presses against her sternum. As soon as she buries the memory of Saira's fingers wrapped around her neck, she opens her eyes. Ava quickly buttons her coat up. The collar hides the bruising. She can't help but stare at her reflection. At the dragons that twist up the lapels of her jacket.

In the mirror, she sees herself. Not a stranger or a girl lost in grief. She sees someone who is broken, and hurt, but surviving. There's a strength within her. A power that she has only recently found. It was buried in her for a long time, but she found it.

There's a soft knock from beyond the bathroom. She straightens the collar of her coat and goes to the door, opening it to see Raiden. "Ready?" he asks.

She responds with a smile and follows him down the stairs. At the front desk the woman, Chenea gets up and walks up to her. Chenea takes her hand and presses her lips to her knuckles. "Safe journeys, Ava Wyntryn."

"Thank you, Chenea, for everything you have done for us." Ava offers her open hand as she had seen Raiden do. Chenea places her fist in her palm and nods to her. Raiden had taught her that the gesture is a way of showing vulnerability and respect to another. It is commonly used when greeting others or showing someone your gratitude. Raiden takes Ava to the stables at the south end of the village.

A tall and broad-shouldered man stands at the entrance. "Thank you Erka for offering to take us to the city and sending a mage to ride Oberyn back to me."

"I owe you one for saving our village, Raiden. And I need to pick up supplies for the village, so it'll be nice to have you two to escort the extra horse I need," Erka says earnestly. He leads them around to the other side of the stables where three horses are tacked up and tied up to a post.

Raiden instantly moves to Oberyn's side, greeting his old friend. She leans her large head into his chest, and Raiden runs his hand along her neck. He unties the rope attached to her bridle and pulls her away from the other horses. Ava's entranced by the connection between Raiden and his horse.

"Here, my lady, I will help you onto your horse," Erka offers.

"Thank you," she says. Ava goes up to the rusty brown horse Erka' unties from the post. Erka stands to the side of the horse and offers her a leg up. She places her knee against his hands, and he boosts her up onto the back of the horse. She swings her leg around and shifts back into the saddle. She doesn't remember ever riding a horse, but her muscles do. Her body tells her how to hold the reins and how to hold her feet in the stirrups.

Erka gets up on his own horse and begins to trail off towards the towering mountain beyond the village. Raiden brings Oberyn into step beside Ava and her horse. "If you need help, let me know," he says.

"I think I got it," she says. Her body and mind entirely focused on her balance and the horse's shifting muscles beneath her. Through the saddle, she can feel every movement and stumble the horse makes.

Erka picks up to a trot. She presses her legs against the horse's ribs. asking him to change strides to match Erka's horse. As the horse speeds up, her heart flutters. She's vulnerable on the horse and could easily fall off. She holds her legs firmly against its soft pelt. Ava lets go of the reins for a second to pull the hood of her cloak over her hair.

The horse tosses his head, and she slips her hands around the reins. With a slight panic, she looks to Raiden for help, but he's far ahead of her now. Ava tries to settle her nerves and regain her balance. The horse seems to sense her calming down, and its movements become more fluid.

She follows close behind Erka. Mount Rebyn fills the horizon now. They move along an invisible trail leading to the base of the mountain. There are soldiers dressed in armor with the Goldryn sigil stationed at numerous outposts along the way. Despite the extensive number of guards out in the snow, they are only stopped once. As the day passes by and they continue to the mountain, the guards seem to ignore them—only watching from a distance. Ava can feel them stalking around her mind, but none of them try to invade her thoughts.

The three of them slip into a sparse gathering of trees, and Erka leads them to an outcropping in the mountain. The path opens into a cave that leads to a twisting pathway. The horses move slow and steady through the darkness, not even fazed by the peculiar and echoey space.

A bright light shifts through the tunnel up ahead. As they approach it, she struggles to see through to the other side. When the three of them finally exit the tunnel and into the hidden city of Rebynrock, Ava's breath catches in her throat. Her gaze carries over everything quickly, taking in the spectacle.

Three wide openings crown the top of the cavern, hundreds of feet above them. Each letting in rays of sunshine. The floor of the cavern is covered in neatly built structures stacked upon each other, reaching high into the cave. Crossing the space above them are walkways carved from stone. A huge statue reaches down one side of the cavern, vines, and trees twisting around its shape. It's a woman, a warrior covered in armor and holding a blade pointed up towards the main opening of the cavern.

"This way," Erka says.

She follows absentmindedly, her eyes still taking in the beauty of Rebynrock. People crowd the streets. There's a beautiful life to the city, in the region she thought had been destroyed and deserted. The colors of the buildings a vibrant shade of orange and red. Light posts flicker throughout the streets, illuminating the cave. Despite the impression of a city filled with life, she notices the overwhelming amount of Goldryn soldiers sitting atop roofs and by entrances holding weapons.

When they reach the stable, two guards wearing the sigil of a three-headed dragon walk up to them. "What is your purpose of being here?" the taller of the two asks.

Raiden responds, "I am Sparrow Hynrule, the tenth sworn protector of Wyntryn."

Ava turns to him, in all the papers he had given her to read, there was nothing about Raiden. She had no idea that he was one of the ten protectors. She knows he has the title of Sparrow, but she doesn't know much about the duties that come with it.

The guard says something to his partner and turns back to them. "Sparrow Hynrule, I must request you and your party leave your horses here and come with us."

"On who's authority?" Raiden asks.

"Queen Stygian's. You don't have authority here."

Raiden dismounts Oberyn and hands the reins to Erka. He moves to Ava and offers her a hand. She slides off the side of the horse. Raiden catches her and helps her land steady on her feet. He moves to the guards. "This man has nothing to do with our affairs. He will take our horses to the stables."

The guards share words with each other and then nod to Erka. They hold out metal collars. "As irregulars, you are required to wear these."

Raiden gawks at the guard. "We are not placing Eventyr steel around our throats. You will take us to who is in charge, or we will escort ourselves."

"Your position in Wyntryn is not viable here. You will follow our directions," the guard insists.

Raiden smiles and locks eyes with the guard addressing them. The man flinches, and Raiden reaches out his hand to the man's temple. His eyes go blank, and he collapses to the ground. "Will you take us now?" he asks the remaining guard.

His throat bobs. He says through gritted teeth, "you may follow me."

What did you do to him? Ava asks Raiden.

I convinced his mind to fall asleep.

That's something you can do? Ava stares at him in shock.

Raiden shrugs. *There's no limit to what our minds are capable of.*

They follow the guard quietly the rest of the way.

They pass through the streets of the cavern city and up a set of steps to one of the hanging walkways. They move across the stone bridge to a large fortress carved into the mountain's side. The rest of the buildings in Rebynrock are made of wood and tile, but this one is built into the side of the mountain. Made from solid stone. It has wide openings carved out on the highest floor, but there are no other windows on the rest of the fortress. Rather, there are false indents built into the rock. Each one is filled with pine, ivy, and flowers that hang against the stone. At the end of the walkway, are two large doors made from the same rock.

They walk along candlelit hallways. The inside of the fortress is delicate and reflects the aesthetics of royalty. With candelabras, ornate runners, and large tapestries that hang along the walls.

The guard stops in front of a set of double doors, knocking on them with a steady hand. He steps to the side and the doors are opened by a guard from the inside. Raiden enters with Ava following behind him.

"Rais," a sharp toned voice calls out. A stunning woman dressed in a black bodice dress moves from around a large desk. "What a pleasure to see you again." There's a sarcastic tone to her voice. A large crown sits upon her head. Her blue eyes flick to Ava. "You brought me a prize?" She stalks towards Ava and reaches her finger to her. Her nail presses beneath Ava's chin and lifts it up. "The dragon rises from the ash," she says while inspecting Ava. The woman returns to the desk, leaning delicately against it. Her fingers twist against the wood. "Now, tell me why you have come."

The dark hair, the lean figure—she looks identical to the girl in the photo. The one she found on her mother's dresser.

"You know why, Stygian," Raiden says.

She's the Goldryn Queen. Why is Stygian and her mother in a photo together, on her mother's dresser of all places?

A coarse smile stretches across her face. "Let me guess, you want to take Rebynrock back. You want to tell me that I do not have claim over the Wyntryn throne?" Stygian blinks sweetly. Her narrow face shining with a dark beauty.

"You have no claim," he tells her.

"Silly boy, anyone of Wyntryn blood has claim. Or am I to believe that this girl is capable of taking what's hers?"

Ava starts to talk, but she can't grasp onto her thought. She doesn't know how or what to add to the conversation.

Ava hates how the dark woman lifted her face and looked over her like a piece of rare jewelry. And this Goldryn queen has Wyntryn blood, but how is she related to Ava? Stygian looks to be in her mid-twenties. Does Ava have more cousins than Anya Petrichor? And if Stygian is related to her, why hasn't Raiden talked to her about it? If Stygian has a claim to the throne, why is Raiden so adamant that she is to become Queen? The questions relentlessly fly through her mind.

"She is the heiress. Not you," Raiden retorts.

"True. And luckily for you Rais, I must return to Goldryn. The Society has failed to give me what I asked for, but unluckily my soldiers will remain in the city. And I have to say, I don't trust you and this pathetic waste of space to keep my city intact. I will, unfortunately, have to lock you both within the city under strict watch until I can return. You will see soon enough, I've already placed charms on this city. I doubt anyone will be able to break through."

What charms did she place that would require them to break through? The only thing Ava's ever encountered like that is the basement at the library. When she entered that lower level, she lost all connection to the Sonder. Maybe Stygian can do something like that to Rebynrock. If she can, they don't stand a chance to free the city.

"I am not here to fight for what you have unrightfully claimed. I want to negotiate a treaty between Goldryn and Wyntryn," he says.

"To do that, you will need to gather approval from not only me but at least five of the protectors of Wyntryn. And it appears there is only one of you. How unfortunate." She twists her finger in the air, spinning fire around it. "When I return, if you have the agreement of the Wyntryn diplomacy, I will consider negotiating. I'm sure some of those misfits are around here somewhere. You Wyntryns do seem to be around every corner these days. It is deeply unsettling." She walks straight towards Ava, meeting her eyes. "Silenced by my presence darling? Hm ... it is amusing that you are so unlike Alys. She would despise you."

Ava's throat tightens. She can't remember much about her mother or anything else in her life. But Stygian's words still hurt—cutting through like a knife. *She would despise me.*

Stygian continues past them and out the doors. She calls for the guards and tells them to not let Raiden and Ava leave the city upon her departure.

Ava spins to Raiden. "Is that what you wanted to happen?"

"No, but she's willing to negotiate a truce. That's more than we have gotten from Stygian since she was coronated four years ago," he tells her.

"And what about us being trapped here? What does the Society have that she would risk her own people for? And the truce isn't a sure thing. Stygian said if half the protectors agree, she will think about it. Why risk an entire city over a chance?"

"We will deal with one thing at a time. For now, we should try to find out if there are any diplomats already within the city," he says.

"This is insanity." Ava moves around the room, looking over the walls covered in maps and trinkets from Wyntryn's past. "What if in your negotiation, she chooses not to give up the city?"

"Then we will fight for it."

"Why not fight for it now? What's stopping us?"

"There are soldiers spread through the city and stationed around the mountain. I would rather us walk away with our lives. There is a diplomatic way to deal with this," he explains.

"The diplomatic way is giving another region power over us?"

"Right now, yes. A war cannot be won with one uprising. If we were to fight and win this city back, Stygian has an entire army she can march right through Wyntryn and take the other two caverns. Right now, Rebynrock is the only city under siege, and I would like to keep it that way."

Ava lets out a short laugh. "You would like to keep it that way. I may be overstepping here, but I am the heiress to Wyntryn. Shouldn't I also have a say in the decisions you are making for the region?"

"I am not trying to—"

"I trust you, I do. But you have made every decision on your own. I know I don't know what I am doing yet, but you can't leave me out of this."

"Ava, you never even tried to say anything to Stygian."

"You are right, I didn't," she admits. She wanted to say something. She did try, but she couldn't find the words.

Ava isn't entirely sure why she's arguing with him, but she does feel like she's being pushed aside. Both Stygian and Raiden spoke about her as if she wasn't in the room. A toy for them to toss around.

It's just that she has all these expectations she has to live up to. Levi expected her to be someone she wasn't. Raiden expects her to be a Queen. The people in the village looked to her as if she was a savior. But she's not. She's not the girl she once was, or a Queen, or a savior. She's ... she's just Ava.

"Excuse me," a lady calls from the open doorway. "One of our mages within the city let me know of your presence."

Recognition crosses Raiden's face. And as always, it is another person who Ava doesn't know. She is a stranger in her own body.

"Thank the gods you are here," Raiden says.

"I am shocked you got yourself in the presence of the Queen so quickly. I have been begging her guards to let me in for days," the woman tells him. Her black hair is tightly braided along the sides and hangs low down her back. She wears a flowing blue dress, with a covering of fur resting on her shoulders. Attached to the front shoulder of her clothing is a golden pin. Ava can't see it clearly, but it appears to be a dragon flying upwards, with a sword held between its wings.

"If she's been here for only three days, who is giving the orders?" Raiden asks.

"A commander from the Society, he is inhabiting the historic headquarters on the east side of the city. I suppose Stygian wanted her own fortress, so she came here. To my surprise, she didn't kick any of Eieran's workers out and I was allowed to remain in my chambers."

"I will never understand her. She floods the streets of our city with soldiers but doesn't attack. You should know, she has offered to negotiate a truce with Wyntryn if five of the protectors can agree to it," Raiden says.

The woman nods in response to Raiden, then looks to her. "Are you okay, Ava?"

Ava doesn't know what to say. The woman looks to Raiden in confusion. Raiden must have sent a thought to the woman's mind because her expression changes. She says, "I apologize. My name is Anya. I am your second cousin and one of Wyntryn's diplomats. If it makes you feel better about not remembering who I am, I have not seen you since you were six and I was ten. Our memories are short and few, so we will have to become better acquainted." Her smile is radiant and kind. "I can bring you to your chambers if you'd like."

"Please."

Anya holds her hands delicately below her ribs. "Wonderful." Her eyes flick to Raiden, "I hope we can speak this evening. There are matters to discuss regarding the capture of Rebynrock."

Ava's gaze falls on Raiden. His face is unreadable and his mind impenetrable. Anya loops her arm through Ava's and pulls her from Raiden, leading her through the fortress to her chambers. The thought of Ava having her own chambers is odd, but she supposes it is what she should begin to expect as the daughter of a Queen. But she still misses her father's small apartment in the city. It is simple, and she loves everything about it. From the pictures of her parents to the out-of-date furniture.

They arrive at the end of a hallway and Anya draws her arm from Ava's to open the door before them. "These were your mother's rooms. Hopefully, they will feel familiar to you. Your mother always made her rooms feel like home, so that no matter where she was in Wyntryn, she could find rest in a familiar place."

"Stygian didn't claim them?"

"No, she took Eieran's chambers. Since he's the protector of this mountain range, he has the nicest rooms. Although they all look the same to me," Anya says.

Ava walks into the large rooms. The first one is a sitting area with paintings covering the walls. The next is the bedroom, almost identical to the rooms in the manor. A large four-poster bed in the center and detailed wooden furniture is scattered along the walls. The last room is a bathroom with white tiles and a large tub.

She finds her way back to Anya in the sitting room. "Thank you for your kindness."

Anya bows her head. "It is the least I can do. Please know that while you are here in Rebynrock you can come to me for anything you need. My father should be arriving soon from Mount Meta, so I must leave to meet him. Will you be fine here?"

"Yes, but can I ask you a question first?"

"Of course."

"What do you think of negotiating a truce?" Ava asks.

Anya straightens her shoulders. "It seems you are in disagreement?"

"I am. Negotiating a truce is giving into the threats of the other regions. Shouldn't we show them that they can't walk on our land and take our cities? They need to know we will fight back, that we are a threat to them," Ava says.

"I agree. The Society and Stygian's soldiers walked through our borders and into our city without having to lay a finger on one of our citizens. Our defenses are scattered, and our borders are weak. Showing vulnerability is not the way to protect ourselves. And a truce is only viable if both sides are a threat to one another." Anya moves to Ava. "You have the instincts of a Queen. Learn how to share those instincts with others. I am grateful for your honesty, cousin, but I must go."

She leaves the room, her blue dress swirling around her like waves of the ocean.

Ava's eyes are heavy, and her inner thighs are begging her to rest. Riding the horse that morning had caused her to work muscles she never uses. She goes to the bedroom and sits on the quilted comforter. The bed is a blessing in comparison to the small uncomfortable one at the inn.

On the side table is a tray of various fruits and nuts. She picks up the tray and sets it beside her in the bed. She lays down and picks at the food while staring up at the overhanging cloth above the bed.

She is so lost in this world. She is constantly going from feeling strong and confident, to defeated. Her mind is never able to decide on what emotion to focus on. What overwhelms her now is the Queen of Goldryn, Stygian. It was terrifying to stand in her presence.

There is something about the woman that is both mysterious and disturbing. And she saw a familiarity in the Queen's face and recognized the aura that surrounded her. Ava wonders when she previously met the Goldryn Queen. The woman with Wyntryn blood and a claim to the throne. The one who stands by her mother in a photo—a photo that resides on her mother's dresser.

The Queen's voice echoes in her head, "the dragon rises from the ash."

Chapter Twenty-Two

Rais sets the gleaming arrow on the table before him. Its black metal reflects the light of the candles. He slides his finger across the cool surface, wondering if this is the prize the Society promised Stygian in turn for the use of her army. Although, it is entirely possible that they had another equally powerful weapon stored in Grymyr.

Rais picks up the thin talisman and stores it in his jacket. He conceals its presence with his mind. But he knows concealing it is not enough, because its pull can be followed anytime its possessor uses the Sonder. The more energy used by the possessor of the talisman, the brighter the beacon in the Sonder. By alating long distances, anyone within a certain radius will see the excessive amount of energy being used. They can follow the remnants of that energy through the Plane of Verity if they are skilled enough. He mindlessly put a target on his back by alating from Grymyr to the village. Anyone searching for it in the Sonder may be aware of its location now. He only hopes that if people are after it, no one will be able to track the energy traces to Rebynrock.

The arrow is one of five talismans in Kanaleigh. Each originating from the lands of Wyntryn. The arrow, the scale, and the three rarest gemstones from the Wyntryn mountains—tanzanite, taaffeite, and painite. Each talisman is infused with the soul of a powerful irregular. The fusion causes each of the items to become an amplifier of the possessor's abilities.

In Alys' letter to Rais, she requested for him to hunt them down. She also enlisted the help of her most trusted students. It was her last request and it's been kept secret from the ten protectors of Wyntryn. Rais is the only exception. And as far as Rais knows, he's the only one of them who has been able to locate any of the talismans. He's in possession of one and has the possible locations of two others. Nina has given up on the search, Willow never began, and the other two have not appeared in the Sonder for over a month. Rais might be the only one left.

He buttons his coat and gets up to leave. His room is quaint but well furnished. And despite his body telling him to rest, his mind can find no peace. So, he leaves his room behind to go check on Ava.

Rais passes numerous guards lining the stone hallways. Goldryn soldiers with unmoving faces and blank minds. Besides Saira, he has yet to encounter a mind webbed and destroyed like the one he found in Goldryn. He searches for similarities in the guards he passes.

It's a possibility that the culprit of destroying people's minds is working under Stygian. But to his surprise, every guard he passes has a clean and untangled mind. It is only their physical presences that are controlled by Stygian's influence. For each soldier stands straight, their hands by their sides, and their eyes unwavering.

Their gazes follow him through the hallway and

search his own mind. Which Rais' finds amusing, because even if he had nefarious intentions, they would be hidden away behind mazes that the guards would have to fight through to find.

Ava's free-flowing mind leads him to her chambers. He knocks on her door and waits for her to open it. She eventually does, but she makes him wait a few minutes before getting to it.

When the door opens, it reveals Ava tightened into a corset overlayed with a forest green gown. He stares at her clean face and bandaged neck. Her hair is pulled behind her in complex braids, sweeping into curls. At the sight of her, he is at a loss of words.

"Nadia forced me into it. She told me I should get used to not wearing a mage's coat and boots," Ava says. She scratches at the braids on her head.

He doesn't move or respond, still taken by her.

"Despite it looking great, it's extremely uncomfortable. And I was actually sleeping when Nadia came in. She told me Anya had sent her." Ava stops speaking when she notices Rais' silence. "Are you okay?"

He swallows. "Yes, of course, I am. It's only that you look—" He searches for the words, skipping over the ones he truly wants to say. And landing on, "you look like a Queen."

Her face reddens into a soft smile, and she glances behind her to the maid standing in the corner of the room. Her eyes go back to him. "So, you came to check on me?"

Rais is lost for a moment because she has somehow seen right through him. Nadia's quiet voice cuts through the silence. "They are serving a meal in the dining hall for Sir Petrichor's arrival. Anya has asked you both to attend, but it seems no one has informed you … I can lead you there now if you will let me."

"That would be great, thank you," Rais says.

Nadia walks past him Rais and into the hallway, gesturing for them to follow her.

Ava sends a thought into his mind. *I'm not sure what I was expecting at Rebynrock, but I didn't expect it to involve cordial meetings and dinners.*

You will find that unless you are fighting for your life, the times between wars are surprisingly uneventful and often lonely. He shares with her.

I am glad I won't be lonely then. Her words break through his mind with a gentle flicker.

He likes the thought, that he no longer has to be lonely. That Ava is not only willing but wants to stay with him.

Nadia takes them inside the dining hall. Extravagant in its decoration. Wyntryn marble statues sit within alcoves along the walls. Large chandeliers hang low. A large wooden table stretches through the room, with tall chairs. A runner of dark blue and gray runs down the center. It's embroidered with images of Rebynrock's history. From the discovery of the cavern to the creation of the mines, and then on to the building of the city.

In midst of the glory of the room, there's a tensity in the air. There's a subtle smile on Ava's face and warmth in her skin, but her eyes don't meet his. She strays from his mind, keeping to herself.

Nadia leaves them standing before the dining table. The doors swing shut behind her. Rais pulls out a seat for Ava, but she hesitates before she sitting down.

Rais moves across from her. As he sits he sends a thought to her, *these chairs are clearly designed for luxury and not comfort.*

She doesn't even react to the words that spin from his mind. "Do you hold an indifference towards me?" he asks.

She bites down on her lip. "No, Raiden."

"Then why?" he asks plainly.

Ava tilts her head as she stares at the embroidered cloth. "When it's only us, I like being with you. But with Erka, with Stygian, you push me away. Talk for me as if I am some child. I may have lost my memories, but I haven't lost my instincts or my mind. I can speak for myself, and I deserve the courtesy to at least know what you are doing and thinking behind my back," she explains. Her voice steady.

Rais gulps. "I have only been honest with you."

She takes a sharp breath and looks to him. Her words escape quickly. "When we first arrived in the village and you came to check on me, I saw blood on your coat. And when you asked me if I was ready to leave this morning, Erka happened to already have the horses ready. When we were talking to Stygian, you already knew what you wanted to happen."

"Yes, you are right, but I didn't want to concern you with those things. You are already dealing with so much."

Rais' heart is moving quicker than comfortable. He fears that Ava is considering that she doesn't need his help. That he is just another person to pass by in her rediscovery of the world. The sad truth is, he has lied to her. He's never told her anything that wasn't true, but he's withheld things. Like Stygian being her sister, or as she's pointed out, what he plans in his head. He supposes he's never thought to share his thoughts with her, but he should.

"I have to deal with struggles, yes, it's a lot. But you

don't have to treat me like I'm going to break. I am stronger than you think. I do have breakdowns, but after I get through them, I am stronger and more capable of dealing with the next stumble." She looks up and straightens her shoulders. Her voice comes out quieter than before, "I can only trust you if you put your trust in me. And that starts by you telling me how you were injured and why your mind feels different."

Rais flinches. What does she mean by his mind feels different? If his mind is different, he doesn't know why. But it is an unnerving revelation.

"I was angry after you were injured. I didn't defend you and I did nothing to protect you and Wyntryn all these months. I swore an oath, and I felt like I was breaking it. My instincts led me to Grymyr, and I found Saira. I was going to kill him, and I almost did. But I realized he was as much a victim as the rest of us. I righted my mind and came back to Wyntryn. To protect you."

After Saira attacked her, she got her own revenge. Rais got Ava to a healer, but he let Saira go. That's why he went after him because he didn't think Saira deserved to get away. But next time someone hurts Ava, he will not wait to go after them.

"Saira caused the injury?"

"Yes," he says. He honestly had forgotten about the icicle that Saira threw into his shoulder. Daryn treated it so soon that the pain was gone before he could even feel discomfort.

"You should know that I don't need—"

The doors to the dining room swing open and Anya and her father enter arm in arm. Rais and Ava break from their conversation and push their emotions down. Keeping them from the viewing of the Petrichors.

"My Queen," Sir Petrichor calls from the door. He pulls from Anya and offers his open hand to Ava. Ava reaches out her fist to his palm, and he sets his other hand over hers. "You are as lovely as ever, Ava. You bear such resemblance to your radiant mother. We are glad to host you here in Eieran's absence."

"I am grateful," she says.

Aran Petrichor sits at the head of the table, Anya pulling the chair to Ava's left.

"Sir Aran, might I ask where Eieran is?" Rais asks.

Aran Petrichor nods. "Your cousin is in the high mountain gathering mages to help take Rebynrock back. He should be here by the end of tomorrow. Word of our Queen's presence has spread like wildfire."

"Is that a good thing?" Ava asks. "Considering that I am not even the Queen ..."

"Rebynrock is already aware of your presence. They can feel our ancestors in the Sonder following you here in protection. Even without a coronation, the land and people recognize you as our Queen. And if you are concerned for your safety ... a tenth of Queen Stygian's army is already within our borders. No greater threat should appear against you than that."

Anya's brows furrow. "Don't scare her, father. They are our guests and they have only just arrived. Even if we are surrounded by enemies, all of us here are powerful mages. And there are many soon to arrive."

"On the topic, I would like to discuss negotiating a peace treaty between Wyntryn and Goldryn," Rais says. He wants to save the region. And the best way to do that is to make a truce with Goldryn.

Anya smiles and looks to Ava. "What do you think?"

Ava shifts uncomfortably in her seat. Rais watches her uncertainly. Aware now that she has shared something with Anya that he doesn't know about.

"I don't think we should negotiate with Stygian. She knows she has the advantage and will use it to put us in a position where we will need her to be kind to us. A negotiation will never work unless she sees us as an equal threat. Otherwise, Wyntryn will end up with the shorter end of the agreement," Ava explains. She avoids his surprised gaze.

Does she know what will happen if they don't make a truce? They will lose even more Wyntryn lives. He'd rather work with Stygian than see another village destroyed and deserted.

Sir Petrichor nods along with her. "I no longer have a say in these decisions, but I understand your perspective, Your Grace. Queen Stygian is known for her ego. She sees herself as doing us a favor in offering a negotiation."

"Not only that, but she is also allowing us to come and go from the city. She has not harmed a single citizen. It makes me believe that her intentions are not as they appear. She is filling our streets with soldiers as a threat. If we ignore it, we are proving to her that she can take our home without a fight. Even if we lose people in a war, we will prove to Grymyr and Goldryn that we are not a broken region," Anya says.

Have any of them even considered what Wyntryn might gain from a truce? For the first time in decades, they could have peace between the regions. Rais shakes his head. "You are willing to lose the lives of our people by risking a war? If we make a treaty our people can have more sources of food, of supplies, it is more beneficial for our economy and overall health to lose some dignity and pride over a treaty. Why put up a façade of being strong when we are not? Our region is broken. We need help, and right now we cannot provide for ourselves."

"I disagree," Anya says.

"Almost half our people are in refugee camps across the ocean! Eventyr is an ally to Goldryn, if we are to begin a war, what will happen to our people there? Will they become prisoners of Eventyr? And what about our people in this very city who are surrounded by enemies? Stygian may have not attacked us yet, but what if she does?" Rais glances between the three of them, unphased by his questions. Except for Ava, whose gaze is intent on him.

"I hear you. But what would our ancestors want? You have expressed how important they are to our people, to our past and future. Would they want us to fight for our land or give in to the abuse of another region?" Ava asks.

Rais is at a loss, all of them so ready for another war. And he is still waiting to recover from the last. "Alys would choose to fight," he admits.

"When our Alys became Queen, she was not liked by the people. They found her cold and harsh, but she turned their hearts through the fire in her own. She fought for our people with every breath she took. Even when she knew she was going to meet her end, she still made sure Wyntryn would be taken care of," Aran says to Ava.

Anya speaks up, "to negotiate, Rais mentioned we need five protectors in agreement. Eieran is on his way, and I can send word to Osidias. In place of our fallen protector Maya, my father can fill the temporary position as a past protector. That will give us more than the necessary votes, we will only have to come to an agreement. I don't agree with making a truce, but we should continue to discuss it."

Servers bring in food, and for the duration of the meal, Rais keeps to himself. He listens to Ava and Anya reconnect. There is a distance between them. He never meant to make her feel pushed aside. He's only ever wanted to protect her. But if she needs space, he will give it to her.

When he finishes his meal, he excuses himself from the table and leaves the room. Desperate for a breath of fresh air. Not the damp and tense air that has filled his lungs since he's arrived in Rebynrock.

"Raiden." Ava's voice flows out from behind him.

He doesn't trust himself not to say the wrong thing or something that will hurt her. So, he keeps walking to his room. She follows him, not breaking stride. It stays that way until he reaches his door, and then he finally turns to her.

Her eyes lock with his, but she doesn't say anything at first.

"I am sorry for protecting you. I know you are strong and capable. I have looked up to you since we were kids because of that. Because of your confidence. But—"

"An apology is not an apology if you are making an excuse," she says. Her forehead creases. "I hear you. And seeing me that way is not treating me that way. You can apologize all you want. It won't change the fact that you are keeping secrets."

"If I could take it all back, I would. I am a wreck without you, and I swear I am only keeping things from you because I fear how you will react. But as you said before, for you to trust me, I need to trust you." Rais opens his door and holds it for her to go inside. He slides the arrow from his coat and holds it lightly in his hands. Ava shuts the door behind her and stares down at the talisman.

"This is the secret. Alys did not only ask me to help

you but to find the talismans created in Wyntryn and use them to help save the region. This is one of them. I found it when I went to Grymyr," he admits.

"I've seen this before. It was in the metal dragon in the library. But how can something so simple help us?"

"It is a talisman. It was created by a group of powerful mages who sacrificed themselves and sealed their power within five objects. They can amplify one's abilities. They can turn the flame of a candle into a wildfire."

Rais realizes in that moment, that Alys let Ava and herself die because she was making Ava into a living talisman. When she came back to life, her power was amplified and with the loss of her memories, her body was able to focus on her abilities and not the inflictions of her past.

"If this one was in Grymyr, where are the rest?"

"There is one in Eventyr, but the rest are currently unattainable."

She takes the arrow from his hands and sets it on the table behind him. She steps back to him and presses her fingers to his temple. His eyes stray over her. The way her hair is braided and pulled back makes her look like a true Wyntryn warrior. Even the dress that hugs her in forest greens is that of the region's style. She may not remember being a Wyntryn, but she certainly looks like one.

Her voice comes out calm and collected as she tells him, "that talisman is clouding your mind. You may not feel it, but that's the difference I've been feeling in you. You should find a place to hide that arrow. We shouldn't use these talismans."

"I suppose we do not need them," he says.

"Why?" she asks. Her fingers fall from his temple.

"We have you."

Chapter Twenty-Three

Ava sits in on Raiden, Anya, and Aran's meetings all day. They discuss going to meet with the Society's commander across the city. They argue about negotiating versus retaliating. And what steps they need to take to find a proper replacement for the position of the ninth protector of the region. She listens particularly to Aran because he was the author of one of the poems in her mother's journal. He wrote about a songbird that flew away from the manor. She has been trying to figure out what that poem means, but so far, she has learned nothing. Ava doesn't provide much in the meetings either. Only her presence and small commentary on the topics that she understands.

Her mind is focused on how grateful she is to be wearing a tunic and pants instead of one of those elegant yet restricting gowns. Her hair is still pleated back into loose braids that mix with her wavy hair, but she can at least breathe. She also thinks of Raiden. Of the secret she keeps from him. The truth that Levi was more to her than a friend. That she possibly loved him, in some way or another. Ava doesn't really know what love means anyway. She just knows that she cares for Levi. And how does she tell this boy from her past, who cares for her more than himself, that her heart lied elsewhere? Or at least she thought it did, once. Levi will always be her best friend, but she's beginning to see that whatever relationship they did have was built with a shaky foundation. She relied on him when she was grieving, so of course she cares for him, but what if it is only that and nothing more?

She cares for Raiden too, but her time with him has been so short. Ava can feel the emotions of her past self and see the few memories that have resurfaced, but besides that, she has little to no knowledge of him. Only a day ago she learned that he is one of the protectors. And only last night she realized that Eieran Hynrule is his elder cousin.

What about the secrets he hid from her? Even if he did come clean to her, she can't help but think about how much Levi told her, and how much he was still able to withhold.

Her heart is delicate, and she is not willing to risk letting it shatter in the same way her mind has. She doesn't ever want to lose the emotions that have been written into her soul. Because even with the loss of her memories, and the hardened snake twisted around her heart, she has retained her emotions. The feelings that drive her, that make her feel like herself. The love she has for her family, for this mystical land, and for the ghosts of her past.

Ava's mind drifts back to the conversation happening around her. Raiden's white hair is ruffled from his hand running through it. And in his left hand, he holds a paper that he crumpled in a bout of frustration. Anya is the most civil of the three, sitting properly with a calm and composed expression on her face.

Ava, Aran Petrichor asked you a question. Raiden's voice tumbles through her.

She looks to him for help.

He offers a look of understanding and turns to the others. "We both got invitations."

"We did too, but we assumed it was an outreach of kindness. That was before they took over Rebynrock," Anya says. Her face looks more worn to Ava now that she is paying attention. There's a slight strain in Anya's voice.

Raiden says, "I recommended to Ava that we avoid the occasion. They might use it as an ambush."

"Actually, I would like to attend," Ava speaks up. To her, the ball is not only a way to learn about the other region's leading officials, but an opportunity to see Levi. And although she knows she should permanently leave him in her past, she wants to see him one last time before leaving the life she knows for what awaits her as Queen. That is if they can get out of Rebynrock unscathed.

Those months after her mother's death were short, but they make up most of her physical memories. That's why Levi is still so prevalent in her mind, because he was there when she had no one else. Besides the lies and the deceit, he is still all she knows. Even if that time did not reflect her life before, where she is now and the people she is with, are all new. So even if this rising moon celebration is a disaster, she wants to take the risk. To see Levi, and to remember what it was like not to remember. What it was like for the only weight on her shoulders to be grief. When she could lay around all day wearing baggy clothes. With no expectations or responsibilities. What it was like to have a life that was constant and predictable.

"Is that a good idea?" Raiden asks. Not directing it at her, but the other two at the table.

Anya looks to Ava. "You can make your own choices, but if you wish to attend, we will make sure you are not alone in enemy territory."

Ava shrugs. "It's not enemy territory for me. I am assuming this Library of Mystical Creatures, is the library I spent almost every day in for well over a month. If something does happen, I'll have an escape route. But I think if we are trying to rebuild Wyntryn, it will only be detrimental if I don't present myself as Queen before the other regions. This ball is the perfect opportunity to do so."

"Then you shall be in attendance," Aran tells her. "Rais, you should be there as well. You entered the Society last summer as the Wyntryn representative. You at least have some familiarity with their headquarters. Until then, we will discuss with Eieran and Osidias our conundrum and make a formal decision on whether we fight back or negotiate."

"Very well, and I will go to request an invitation with this commander across the city. If he allows us to meet with him, Ava and I will go," Anya says cordially. She then lifts herself from her seat and leaves the room. Shortly followed by her father.

The prospect of facing a commander of the Society is not appealing to Ava. If this commander is anything like Saira, she wants nothing to do with him. But she can't refuse to go because there are people relying on her now. At least if she does have to go, Anya will be there with her.

Ava feels Raiden watching her. She stands and walks around the office. It's the same room they were brought to when meeting with Stygian.

"I've found out about the charms Stygian mentioned," Raiden says.

Ava stares up at a large map of the continents,

listening to Raiden as he continues. "I attempted alating, and it is impossible. I almost found myself stuck in the Sonder. I also cannot access my energy. I can speak with you through the Sonder, and enter the plane, but it's as if my energy is completely depleted. I would be curious how it is affecting you."

Ava walks back towards the table and focuses her energy on the unlit candle in the center. She draws herself into the Sonder and alights it with her mind, but no fire burns. Her energy only evaporates into the air and restores itself back inside of her. "How can she do that?"

Raiden leans his elbows against the table. "Some irregulars have gifts that are rare. For Stygian, she is able to create barriers in the Sonder; blocking the use of certain abilities without the use of the ancient language. For example, no one can alate into the City on the Sea, the capital of Goldryn. Here, I think she has somehow blocked our use of elemental magic and alating."

"There are symbols in the library, the Society's headquarters. When you pass through them, you are unable to access the Sonder at all," she says.

"Yes, most barrier charms are not based on one's power alone. They are put in place with the use of the ancient language of our lands. Irregulars with enough energy to complete such tasks only need their energy, the ancient language, and will. But even having enough energy to execute such tasks is rare. Many irregulars are incapable of bringing another back to life, incapable of alating, or creating an element with their energy. Abilities differ greatly, but all can be incredibly dangerous."

"In one of the memories that resurfaced at the manor, I wasn't even able to catch another's energy in the air. It fell right through my hands. What was I capable of before everything happened?" she asks. She slides into the chair beside him.

"You could only sustain very small fires, such as a candle or sparking a fireplace to life. Never in impermissible weather or an entire city block." There's a spark of amusement in his words. As if his mind is recollecting a series of memories she may never see.

"Where did all of my energy come from then?" she asks. Ava reaches down into her seemingly bottomless pit of power. In all her practice and outbursts through the Sonder, she has yet to reach an end or a point of inability.

"I have no idea," Raiden admits. "Your mother knew things we may never be able to find out ourselves. But from my understanding, bringing you back to life re-ignited you as an irregular. Because you were born with abilities, it was heightened when you were brought back through the Sonder. Almost as if you were a talisman yourself. An already powerful object overwhelmed with even more power."

"By bringing me back to life, I became a physical amplifier of my own energy?" she thinks aloud.

"That is my theory." His voice is low, something deep in his mind bothering him.

"You never say much about yourself." Her shoulders slump forward, and her head tilts to see his expression.

He has a quiet and quick laugh. One that is less of amusement and more of a troubling thought. Where the breaths are quick, in and out, without a change of face. Only a blank expression, with eyes that bore into a random spot on the wall. "There is not much to say."

"That's not true." She comforts him with a warm smile, offering her hand. But he doesn't move to accept the gesture.

"I am not special Ava. I am only a boy who died with his parents in a fire. And by some luck, the Queen of Wyntryn decided to save my life. Offered me a home, an education, training. I have no interests beyond survival and instinct. If I was not the Sparrow, sworn to an oath that gave me a purpose, I would have nothing to live for." His eyes are still unfocused, staring at the wall.

"That's not true," she says.

"How would you know what is true about me or not?"

"Because I see you. I feel what you feel. You do not act because of an oath. You have a passion and drive to protect people, to protect me, because of who you are. Not because you swore to some dead people that you would, but because you want to. When you encountered Saira, you said you didn't kill him because you saw that he was a victim too. If you were following this oath, you would have killed him for what he did to me. But you restrained yourself. You can see beyond people's actions, to who they are. That is your gift. You don't want to agree to an uprising because you don't want people to die. You want to give them a life worth living, under an enemy or not. That makes you special because you have a view of the world that no one else sees."

As Ava says it, she realizes that she does know Raiden. That even in missing her past, she can still recognize the people she once knew. She can still see and care for Raiden. A comforting thought to her, but it only proves to her that she sees Levi for who he is too. And that despite his flaws, she's not mistaken that his feelings are genuine.

Raiden breaks his desolate gaze to meet her eyes. "If my view is unique to you, Ava, know that I do not see you as someone who needs protection. I know that you are more than capable of fending for yourself, but that does not mean that you must fight on your own. If you want to know more about me, I like keeping my mind to myself. I do not make a habit of working with others. I had to learn how to speak for myself, and because of that I prefer doing everything on my own."

"You can prefer to do it on your own, but as you just said—it does not mean that you have to."

Raiden glances at her. As he looks back at the wall he smiles. At least she's not alone.

After leaving Raiden to work out his plans, Ava finds herself past the fortress guards and onto the stone walkway. She feels safe exploring on her own. Her clothes are dull, and her hair matches the styles of everyone else she sees. She hopes no one will recognize her.

Ava left her mage coat behind but kept the dagger on her belt in case there were to be any trouble. Although, she doubts there will be. As Anya had kindly pointed out, the Goldryn soldiers do nothing but stand in the streets. A warning to the people, not a tangible threat, yet.

Ava can care less about the prying eyes of the soldiers. She is simply glad to be out of the dark and damp corridors of the fortress. She wishes she could go out into the snow, but for now she has settled for the sunlight overhead that stretches into the city from the large opening above.

She walks freely across the stone bridge, not sharing the space with any others. The walkway gives her a good vantage point of the city. The view allows her to see the towering buildings. Made of redwood and covered in paintings of symbols and creatures. On the ground level, the streets are crowded with market stands. They sell everything from fresh meats to handcrafted jewelry. She can even see one table covered in furs for those traveling out into the snowy landscape.

Ava finds herself leaning over the walkway and watching the people, her people, go about their days. She has a fascination with the hairstyles of Wyntryn. Each woman possesses loose braids of all kinds. Pulled back and hanging like tapered silk. Those with thicker hair either have tighter braids that hang down their back or dense curls that frame their faces.

The citizens wearing fancier clothing return to homes on the highest of the buildings. The ones only reachable by pathways above where she stands. Another curiosity to her, are the animals that roam the lower grounds of the cavern. Dogs and cats of all breeds, stalk along the streets. Their fur scraggly and unkempt.

She starts down the stairwell at the end of the bridge, but a man with white hair steps in front of her—blocking her from going any farther.

"I was hoping to run into you, little Wyntryn," he says. His teeth showing in a broad, drunken smile.

"Who are you?" Ava asks. She squares her shoulders.

"No worries, little Wyntryn, it is only your great mentor Eieran." His hand slaps down onto her shoulder.

She plucks it off her and steps back up the stairs. "Eieran Hynrule?"

"That's me. I hear you and my cousin are friends again. I have been pushing for the two of you since I saw little cousin's face get all red when he talked to you." His voice bellows out.

Ava uncomfortably walks back down the pathway, Eieran in step by her side. "So, you were my mentor?"

"Right. I keep forgetting that you've forgotten. You'd think I would've noticed when you asked who I was. It's a miracle people think I'm wise ... or something like that." Eieran chuckles. "And it is true, I was tasked with your training in the Sonder. Your mother thought it would be ill-advised for her to train you herself. Anyways, how are you getting along these days little Wyntryn?"

"I'm surviving," she states.

"Aren't we all?"

Eieran's mind is well concealed. Ava can't even detect it in the Sonder. His abilities must be far beyond anyone she's encountered. She knows that Raiden chooses what emotions he allows to escape him, but to have enough control to remain entirely undetected is impressive. Especially when her mind is uncontrollable and free-flowing. An easy target for any attacker.

They reach the doors of the fortress and Eieran throws them open. He calls out into the dark hallways, "ah, the moldy fortress of Rebynrock! My great home, you smell of death."

Ava can't help but be put off by Eieran's open confidence. She expected all the protectors to be like Anya and Raiden, proper and concealed in their ways. This Eieran is the opposite. His mind is a mystery, but his presence is most certainly not.

Eieran glides through the hallways. He's clearly very familiar with his surroundings. Too nervous to speak up, Ava continues to follow behind him. Eieran finds his way to Raiden's room and then barges inside. Ava stays in the hallway, watching as Raiden lights up and greets his cousin with a bear hug. Eieran ruffles his hair and pushes him. Raiden looks to Eieran in admiration. Which makes Ava even more curious about her past mentor.

Are you going to stay standing out in the hallway? Raiden's voice flows through her mind.

She steps cautiously into the room, her gaze staying on her golden-eyed friend.

"Have you already reacquainted yourself with Ava?" Raiden asks Eieran.

Eieran crosses his arms before him. "I have. We ran into each other out in the city."

Raiden looks to her in silent surprise. Ava assumes the narrowed eyes are a sign of him disagreeing with her actions. But she ignores the look and nods along with Eieran. "Yes, he arrived while I was out on the bridge. Reminded me that he was my mentor and your cousin."

Raiden shakes his head. She shrugs back at him in response.

"It's as if you two purposefully run an entirely separate thread of communication when in the presence of others. I hope you'll never change." Eieran pats Raiden's shoulder and walks through the door. "I have to discuss endeavors with Anya, I'll leave you guys to it."

The door lightly shuts behind him, and Ava is left with a reddened face. Instead of them awkwardly avoiding each other, they begin to laugh at themselves. Ava speaks into Raiden's mind, *are we that obvious?*

"To my cousin, we are. Although it is entirely possible, that no one else has been honest with us," he says. A laugh still rumbles through him.

"How rude of us," she retorts. Her face contorting in disgust.

He takes her hand and pulls her into a spin. She

twists to him. A happiness rises in her chest. But she stops him from spinning her again by grabbing onto the lapel of his coat. The laughter in their chests quiets as they lean into each other. A lurking feeling twists around them, begging them to fall closer. She can't help but keep his gaze even though it causes her heart to strain. Staring into his eyes, she feels the snake coil around her chest, and she glances away. Ava pulls her hand from his jacket and takes a step back. She sees the same stricken look on him. And as she steps away, his mind closes her off.

"Sorry." She stumbles over the word. Her mind flickering and telling her to leave before she makes it any worse. He runs a hand through his hair, and Levi clouds her vision. "I should go, but I'll see you at dinner."

Ava leaves the room. She stands still in the hallway outside. Not sure how to decipher the feelings that have arisen inside her or how to push away the thoughts of Levi. And she hates that she thinks of Levi when she is around Raiden. Guilt riddles her with a further influx of anxiety. She seems to tilt. Her mind overly aware of the guards whose eyes stray to her.

She begins to walk through the corridors to her room. Her pace quickens with each guard she sees. The stone protecting her heart is ready to shatter. She holds steadfast, throwing her thoughts far behind her. She hopes to console the adrenaline that refuses to subside.

She stumbles into her chambers and runs to her bed, but the surfacing tide in her mind hits her before she can lie down. Her knees hit the ground and send a shock wave through her bones. Her mind fizzles into a memory from the past.

"Sweetheart, I am here to bring you home to Wyntryn." Her mother's voice sings through the dusty apartment. Ava picks up her already packed bag and goes to her mother. Alys' hair is tied into a bun. Her face tired and drained of the life that usually shines through with great vibrance. "Did you say goodbye to your father?"

It's the end of the summer, and Ava's time to return to the Wyntryn Manor. "We said our goodbyes before he left for work." Her voice comes out smooth and young. Not tainted by the maturity of emotional turmoil.

"Very well, let us leave now," her mother says.

Levi walks up behind Ava and says goodbye to her. He crosses the room and slips through the door, throwing a wink her way.

"Who is that?"

"Levi, he's a part of the Society," Ava states plainly.

Her mother's face hardens with anger. "You are no longer allowed to see that boy."

"I'm already leaving the city, mother. It will be awhile before I even get a chance to." Ava rolls her eyes.

"If you don't want to go back, don't. Stay here then, but don't come crying to me when you have the responsibilities of an entire region on your shoulders. If you keep prioritizing the enemy, you will never be a Queen," her mother bites out.

Ava drops her bag to the floor. "I never want to be one anyways. At least Grymyr allows for the people to vote."

"And what about the irregulars here? They will never have a vote because they are openly murdered in the streets." Her mother's eyes are bloody with anger.

Ava doesn't respond to her—she picks her bag back up and slings it over her shoulder. "I'm not trying to say Wyntryn is worse. I'm only saying that you shouldn't expect me to become you, because I'm not. And you won't even let me choose who to be friends with!"

"That's not true. I adore all of your friends at the manor," she says.

"Only because you also get to control their lives." Her mother stares back at her with a steely gaze, unwavering. "Are we leaving?" Ava asks.

Her mother reaches her hand out, and Ava takes it.

Ava blinks the memory away. Her gaze falls to the stone floor of her chambers. She sits back on her heels, wishing she could still argue with her mother.

Chapter Twenty-Four

Rais keeps his mind in the moment. Even as she retreats through the doorway, his mind stays on her. On her laughter and the silence they shared. In those few moments, he felt as he did with her before she lost her memories. The blissful happiness. The way they teased each other and brought each other to life. But every time she feels any happiness now, she contorts back into herself. Hardens her heart and runs away.

He doesn't expect them to ever be what they once were. But it only hurts when she leads him on. He can't ask her to choose either, because then he might lose her entirely. He would rather his heart be thrown around than lose her. It is a risk he takes gladly because the worst time in his life was when he was away from her.

Rais pulls his coat off and leaves it on his bed. He finds his way through the corridors to Alys' office. Anya is in the room when he arrives. "Sorry, I did not intend to disturb you," he says.

"No, you aren't bothering me," she tells him.

He meets her by the table side and looks down at

the map of Wyntryn she has laid out. Every village that has been attacked is represented by a red figure, the surviving ones with blue, and the ones under siege with white. Rebynrock and three of the coastal cities are marked by the white fawns. There are only two cities and three villages marked by the blue. The rest of the map is riddled with red fawn figurines. At the sight of the map, he imagines every torn apart village he has seen. And seeing what is left of their region on the map, makes him understand Anya's perspective. Why it is so important to her that they fight for their region, and not give up what they have lost for something as fragile as a truce. If they give up now, they won't ever get justice for those who died at the hands of their enemies.

"Its disturbing, isn't it?" Anya whispers.

"It reminds me of when you couldn't go more than a mile without running into a thriving civilization. Everything fell apart so, so quickly," he says. His voice quiet.

Anya rubs her thumb against her home village, marked with a red deer. "We are lucky to have any family left."

"Anytime Alys spoke in front of a village or city, she would say what made our region so strong is the loyalty we have for our neighbors. Because Wyntryns are not coexisting, we are a family who protects one another. Wyntryn survives because Wyntryn is one," Rais recites.

Anya repeats Alys' phrase. "Wyntryn survives because Wyntryn is one."

"Maybe we should fight back," he says.

"What made you change your mind?" Her words are heavy on his mind, but he knows why. He has always known.

"Wyntryn."

She smiles. "I don't want to fight either you know. As protectors, we are meant to keep our people alive. But what I find our people value most, is our past, our ancestors. We have already lost so many, and the ones we have lost would want us to fight."

"We signed an oath to protect the Queen, the people, and the land. If we make this truce, it is only the beginning of our losses," he says. Rais so desperately wants to give the people the ability to live fruitfully, but to do so they can't give up the generations of values and land that their ancestors have fought for.

She slides a golden pin across the table to him. "You never got yours."

He picks it up and rubs his thumb against the smooth metal. It's the pin every protector wears. A dragon holding a sword between its wings. "I thought they weren't able to forge any new ones."

"This one was my father's. He told me to give it to you."

"Thanks Anya."

"Mhm." She looks to him. "I know your home village was destroyed, but do you know why?"

"I claim it was the aftermath of a war. But it wasn't. Alys got her hands on dark energy, and Stygian wanted to save her from it. Alys set the entire village ablaze, and Stygian took the power for herself. But it corrupted her as easily as it took Alys. When Alys finally found her conscience, I was the only one she managed to save. My parents, home, and village were gone. And I was all that was left. It was years before I met my cousin."

"You don't hold any ill feelings for Alys?"

"No. I did, for a while. But her mistakes gave me a life I would not trade for anything."

She pushes from the table and moves to the couch on the wall. She sits and lets out a heavy sigh. "I never wanted to be a diplomat, but it came with my family name. When there are only four true-blooded Wyntryns left, you don't really have a choice."

"No one gets to choose their life. You must deal with what you are given and make the most of it. We make small choices, here and there. But what happens is meant to happen, we only have to react in our own ways and keep going. We are protectors for a reason. Something greater than our own preferences put us here. We have to keep on going and do our best to make the choices we have to for others."

"I hear you. It doesn't make it any easier though."

He chuckles. "No, nothing does."

"I spent the past two months going to every recorded village to get an accurate census of our population and recruit soldiers." She pauses, her gaze crossing past him to the map. "I thought we had more. In our prime, this region had the upper of fifteen million people inhabiting it. My current calculation is roughly two million still inhabiting the cities and villages. Eventyr and Aysand have at least half that in refugee camps. I can only assume there are more scattered throughout Kanaleigh. But … whatever Wyntryn was, may never be again. Not for decades, for generations." He can feel her heart cracking before him. Her head lightly bobs from side to side in her own disbelief.

"What of an army?"

She looks to him. "With a good strategy, we have a chance. But what is left of our mages is dismal. Enough to clear the soldiers from Rebynrock, with luck."

Rais sucks on his teeth. He turns from Anya. "What

if we consider the talismans."

"We don't have any. They were hidden decades ago by the Queen and King of the first great war," she says with a breath.

"What if we did have one in possession?"

Anya's brows furrow. "Well, if we did, it would change the entire game. A talisman turns an irregular into a physical source of energy. It doesn't only amplify the possessor's power but gives any irregular the possessor allows to draw from their source. It turns a group of soldiers, into an army. A sword into an avalanche."

"Then we have a chance."

"What are you withholding from me, Sparrow?" Her eyes brighter now with the prospect of hope.

"I have an idea."

Rais explains his far-fetched plan to her. A way to take Rebynrock back, without needing to encounter Stygian again, and without having to reveal the talisman to the Sonder. They would be able to keep their special weapon a secret until they needed it. If they have to start another war, they need backup. This plan would make Stygian and the Society look one way, while they attacked from another.

Anya stands and goes to the map. She looks down at Rebynrock and the white fawn that stands over the city's name. "How do we know she will be able to do it?" she asks.

"*Vaye chessya ta mey mata,*" he says. His voice twisting around the ancient tongue.

Anya presses her hand to her heart. "Have faith in our ancestors. Well, I really hope you're right."

Chapter Twenty-Five

The wires of the dress cause her ribs to ache. And besides the several points of pain across her, the gown is beautiful. It flows to the ground in layers of orange and red. Fluffy chiffon that is loose enough to look airy, but layered enough to provide warmth in the winter weather. The dress has sleeves that run across the top of her hands. She wears heels that constrict her feet. The lady Nadia even went out of her way to design her braided hair around one of her mother's crowns. A simplistic black sun that shapes to her head. And lastly, she wears a heavy maroon cloak that brings warmth to her in the cold air.

She has never felt so elegant or uncomfortable.

"Are you prepared?" Anya asks.

"Not at all, but it's too late now," Ava says. Her face slack with fear. As they begin their trek across the city, she swears her fear is causing her to physically shake. It is equally plausible that the culprits are the demons on her feet. *The things women do for beauty,* Ava thinks. She is about to face one of the Society commanders. Anya talked her through what to be prepared for, but she is still terrified.

With Anya at her side and an escort of Society members behind them, they make their way through the city. Even with the electricity in the air, Ava is grateful to finally get out in the streets. Watching from above is not the same as moving through the chaos. From the ground, she can see the faces of the people. Unlike Grymyr, they don't hide under extravagant clothing. They don't wear masks or hats. The people in Rebynrock have nothing to hide. Despite their circumstances, they greet each other with kindness and walk freely through the city. Men and women carry baskets of food and goods to and from the markets. She sees a man buy and give fresh food to a family who can't afford it. The genuine empathy in Wyntryn almost brings her to tears. To see people in such poor situations give to others, be selfless, is beyond admirable.

It gives her the confidence she lacked before. Their kindness lessening the anxiety prickling inside her. And she supposes that the freeness of her mind is a gift. A gift from her ancestors, so that she can share in the ways of her people. And so that they can see who she is. Know if she is lying or telling the truth. Know if what she does is for herself or for others. Both a blessing and a curse, but something Ava can learn to cherish.

They approach a large outcropping of the cavern. The building is made with the same redwood as the others in the city, but rather this one has pillars across the front and a large door at the top of many steps. Anya sends Ava comforting thoughts as they move up the steps. Ava's thighs burn with the effort. She should have convinced Nadia to find her a pair of boots that were appropriate for the occasion rather than heels.

They finally reach the top step, and Ava wipes the sweat from her brow. The Society members walk past them and to the guards at the doors. The doors open to reveal a singular man standing in the center of a mosaic floor.

"Welcome, daughters of Wyntryn. It is a pleasure to finally meet you." His voice rumbles out. He wears a fitted suit with his coily hair neatly brushed back. The man's head tilts to the side at an unnatural angle and slowly rightens as he says, "my name is Damon. I am a commander of the Society of the Collective. Now, introduce yourselves."

For once, Ava speaks up. "I am Ava Beckett Wyntryn, heiress to the Wyntryn throne. This is Anya Petrichor, fourth protector and diplomat of Wyntryn."

"Hm … lovely. My Levites had much to say about you, Ava. Did you know I had to go against the Grymyr government to keep you alive? What a pity too, because you slipped right through that fools' fingers. And you melted off my Saira's pretty face."

Ava doesn't let herself react to his information. Albeit shocking news that the Society meant to kill her, she keeps her gaze steady. Levi may be the reason she is still alive. Her muscles quiver, but she won't break character before Damon. She distracts his mind with irrelevant thoughts. She pushes the thoughts into the sonder, hoping they will take his focus away from her unnerve.

Damon says, "now what I want to know, is why you believe you can change my mind? After all the favors I have done for you, especially you, Ava. Clearly, you are here for the city, and why would I ever give it to you?" His voice is like Saira's, lifeless with an eerie amusement.

"What I want to know, is why you think keeping someone alive is a favor," Anya spits out at him.

He widens his eyes in shock. The Society members lining the edges of the room straighten their stances, shifting their hands to their weapons. "Because no irregular is meant to live. Let alone deserve life," Damon says cordially.

Ava fights the urge to roll her eyes, the hypocrite is an irregular. The room is full of them. Her chest burns with disgust for the commander.

"Is that so? Then why take over a city of innocents. Our mages typically don't live inside our cities, they live on the outskirts in case of attack," Anya says.

The way Anya speaks is unusual. Ava hasn't ever seen her be so bold. She's usually more formal. But it's not as if Ava has known her for long.

"Because Wyntryn scum don't deserve any place on this earth, dear Anya. You both are lucky we have allowed you to remain in your little home. If it were not for Stygian, I would have sliced both of your throats by now."

"I would love to see you try."

Ava looks to her. Is she trying to get a reaction out of him? They are surrounded by enemies with weapons, and Anya is being reckless.

Damon's mouth twitches. "Do you wish to die, scum?"

"I find death rewarding." She chastises him, "in reference to yours of course."

Damon twists his fingers in a signal, and a Society member grasps onto Anya's arm. She flicks her hand and the man crumples to the floor. "Oh dear," she says as she looks to the man. "Well, I suppose he is an irregular."

Damon frantically signals to more of his people, and before they can even reach Anya, she has them collapsing to the floor. Ava takes a step back in surprise. It's the same technique Raiden used at the stable. She's shutting their minds off through the Sonder.

They aren't entirely weaponless. With Stygian's

charms, they can't alate or act with physical energy, but they can still use their minds.

"What are you trying for?" he yells.

"Poetic justice, I suppose. Because you killed my Queen."

What is she doing? Ava is frozen in place. Damon reaches for his dagger. Time slows, and to her horror, Damon flings the dagger at Anya.

It slams into Anya's side, and before she can get her bearings, a member of the Society throws her to the ground. Damon runs for Ava, and slams his hand to her chest, pushing her backward. She clenches onto his wrist and fights him back. She feels her energy building up within her, but she knows it's useless there because of Stygian's barrier charm.

"What, you have no power here child?" he taunts.

"You don't either." She spits on his face.

Damon practically snarls at her and his grip tightens. She tries to break through his mind, but she can't. She feels useless, powerless.

She twists his arm and throws him to the side. He clenches onto her shoulder. "You get no more favors, Wyntryn. You will die just as your mother did. Let me call for one mind-shattering bulle—"

Her energy builds to a crescendo within her and breaches the surface. The energy rises through the city in billowing waves. This man planned her mother's death, planned her death. He calls her people scum. Threw a dagger into her cousin's side. If anyone deserves her mother's fate, it's him.

She throws her hands around his throat and her energy moves with a life of its own. She pulls herself into the Sonder, breaking through Stygian's barrier with ease.

She lights the commander on fire from within with nothing but a flicker. He lets out a wretched scream. The fire quakes from the inside out. Her fingers begin to dig into his neck with her fury, but as the fire engulfs him, she loosens her grip. Throws him to the floor, and the other Society members come racing towards her. She does not want to stoop to Saira's level, but she will do what it takes to save Rebynrock from the parasites inhabiting it. Ava flicks her hands, and her energy consumes those running towards her with flames. They are engulfed in a flickering blaze of blue. They quickly scramble for their own energy, for water, to alate. But Ava doesn't stay to find out if they escape.

She steps out of her heels, releasing the pressure from her feet. She stalks out into the city. Her soul on fire for her people. A dragon inside her birthing new life. Ready to release fire upon the world.

For so long the Great Wars have tormented her people, this very land. And even now, long after the last resurgence of the war, other kingdoms think they can take Wyntryn. Their arrogance blinds them, because Ava will not let Wyntryn go without a fight. They have taken her family, her very memories. They even went as far as killing her. But even in that, they failed. Because she came back to life far more powerful that before. The very soldiers in this city have mocked her. Watched her with their eyes, judged her. No long will she allow them to threaten her people. Her enemies have taken everything from her. She will not let them do the same to the Wyntryn people.

Her body convulses with the pain of her tarnished mind, and she lets out a scream. It echoes through the cavern with unrelenting power. The fire rages through her veins with the release. It frees her from the burdens of a tangled mind and opens her to the world around her.

Bursts of blue flame go off across the city. Fire sparks beneath the feet of every Goldryn soldier and every Society member. Those who don't run, she hunts down with her mind and begins lighting the flame inside of them. She forces them to feel the pain that her people have felt.

Her ancestors rise from deep within the land, reaching for her. Their energy rifles through her body, and strengthens her fire. They work through her to fight for their people. For her people.

Pieces of the fortress behind her crumble down from the quakes of her energy being released. She alates to the bottom of the stairs. A Goldryn guard charges at her with a bleeding passion. Ava throws him to the side with a wave of embers and steps to his side. She bends over him. Ava wrenches the sword from his hand and places her fingers to his left temple. *Go home to your Queen. And tell her what has happened here. Tell her the dragon has risen from the ashes. Tell her that she will regret ever invading my region.*

The soldier scrambles to his feet and pushes away from her. He begins to sprint through the city. Fear paving a path to his homeland.

Ava's eyes find their way to her hand, covered in dirt and grime. She spins a blaze around her fingers. Burning away the dirt and leaving her hand clean. For once, she is in absolute control. Her vision is filled with the flickering blue of the flames; the power passed down to her through generations of brave souls, destined to spend their lives fighting for their land and people.

She clasps her hand shut, putting out the flame. As well as every flame she lit inside the city.

People stand in the streets looking around in a panic. The soldiers are gone, the Society evacuated. The only dead are those who dared to fight back.

In midst of the travesty, her heart rises. With the flames she soars. Her mind clearing with the gusts of energy that pass through her. The blue awakens deep within her and banishes that petulant snake from her chest. She opens her hand again, watching as a steady blue flame dances across her skin.

When Ava dares to look up from the fire in her hand, she sees everyone's eyes on her.

A silence blankets the streets of Rebynrock. People run from their homes to crowd along the walkways. They all stare. And finally, the world is quiet. Ava has no fears or worries, no emotions tugging on her soul.

Anya stands atop the steps. "*Mey chessya* Queen Ava!" she shouts to the crowds.

There is a silence, and then a singular voice from somewhere in the crowd of people calls out, "Queen Ava!"

The streets erupt in calls of blessings, a chant of faith for their heiress, no, their Queen.

She drowns out the noise when she feels his mind. She looks to the nearest walkway, and her gaze locks with his golden irises. A soft smile warms his face as he sees her. She reaches out to his mind, *what do I do next?*

Be their Queen.

Chapter Twenty-Six

Rais runs from the fortress at the sounds of screaming and crumbling rock. Every Goldryn soldier along the walkway has fire below their feet. Those who don't run are slowly consumed by the blaze blanketing them and tearing at them. The soldiers run down the walkway in fear, screaming commands to each other. They attempt to alate but fail to break through Stygian's charms. Their very own Queen, the cause of their downfall.

The soldiers who run from the fortress behind him aren't plagued by the same treachery. At the sight of the chaos, they turn to Rais. He pulls his sword from its sheath as a red-haired man swings his own sword down on Rais. Rais ducks and jumps to the side. He meets the man's next swing with his own sword. They twist around, and Rais drops down, shoving his shoulder into the man's stomach and throwing him off the walkway.

Another soldier comes careening towards him, her dark purple cloak flying with her movements. She throws a dagger at him, and he ducks to the side. A soldier behind him slashes at him with his sword, and Rais has to spin around to block the blow with his own weapon. He dances around the soldiers, clashing and dodging their attacks. His mind follows their minds, predicting each of their next movements. So that when one soldier throws their sword, he can block it. And when another gets too close to the edge of the walkway, he can force them over the side.

"Cousin!" Eieran calls out. The broad-shouldered man falls into step beside Rais. "You need to get to her," he commands.

"Let's get through these soldiers first."

A soldier lands a punch against Rais' temple. He falters, and a sword slices cleanly across his thigh. He falls out of the way of their blows and corrects his stance. He fights through his stinging leg and continues the dance. Rais slices his sword to the right and falls back two steps. He notices a soldier's vulnerability and slices their side. He has to jump to the left to block another attack. He elbows the soldier to his right and spins his sword, hitting the man to his left. He keeps up the back and forth, and back again until no more soldiers stand in his way.

Looking out at Rebynrock, he sees the flames subside. Crowds of soldiers and Society members crowd the tunnel leading out of the city. He lets out a ragged breath and begins to search for Ava. The citizens of Rebynrock cover the streets and walkways. He has to fight through the people to make it to her. He can feel her close but can't see her. Ava's energy flows off her in waves. An endless source of power.

He eventually catches sight of her as Anya's voice rings out into the cavern. "*Mey chessya* Queen Ava!" After her call of blessing, the people erupt into their own cheers and chants.

He shoves his way to the edge of the walkway and

looks down towards her. The fire in her hand goes out and her eyes go straight to him. Her mind flies through his with ease. *What do I do next?*

Be their Queen.

Whatever power she has just unleashed is unfathomable. To reach through the entire city and breach her sister's barrier. The way she attacked the soldiers is grotesque, but it worked. He hates it, but it's the only reason the city is free. He only hopes that Stygian won't tear them apart as soon as she hears.

The crowds begin to disperse, but he can't get through. He swings his leg over the edge of the walkway and drops to the one underneath. He has her in his sights, but she is being consumed by people singing her praises. Rais drops down to the ground and shoves through the people. He sends them anonymous commands to move away from the Queen. She may not officially be Queen, but that's how the people see her.

Her eyes catch on his and relief flowers from her mind. He grasps her hand and pulls her through the crowd. "What about Anya?" she asks.

"She can find her way back, but you are currently a goddess to these people. It is best we get you back to the fortress."

Her hand tightens around his, and they bolt through alleyways until they make it to a set of stairs leading to a bridge. They follow the bridge to another, and he helps boost her over the divide between that one and the walkway leading to the fortress. Once her feet are steady on the other side, he jumps over and takes her hand again. At the sight of her, people flock towards them. Rais keeps a grip on her hand and brings her to the entrance. He shoulders the door open and lets her slip inside. He sends out silencing commands to those trying to get through the door. Then he shuts it, holding the doors closed while he slides the locks in place.

He lets out a long breath and turns to Ava. She smiles. "They're all gone."

"Because of you," he tells her.

He pulls her into an embrace. She holds her arms tight around him. She really did it. Alys would be so proud of her.

There's an undeniable change in her mind. He could recognize every time she forced herself to ignore the pain, but he can tell she isn't faking it this time. Somehow she has freed herself of the emotional burdens that have been consuming her.

She pulls from him, her hand still held against his upper arm. She searches his eyes. "Because of you, I was able to find that fire you always talk about."

"Possibly, but you are the reason Rebynrock has been freed. You had to find that fire yourself. You are the one who showed those Wyntryns that you are a worthy Queen. You have given them hope for a future where Wyntryn survives," he says. His hand braces the side of her face.

She lifts her hand to his. It's clammy against his own, but also comforting. She pulls his hand from her face and places it over her heart. He watches her steadily with rising curiosity. "In my mother's chambers, there are words embroidered on the cloth hanging over the bed. Wyntryn survives because Wyntryn is one. The soldiers are gone not only because of me, but because of you, Anya, and Eieran. The fire itself didn't even feel like it was coming from me. It felt as if our ancestors were working through me. The flames moved with their own life, guided by those who came before us."

His body warms at the thought of their ancestors being the ones to save them. That was the goal, the plan Anya and he had devised prior to the meeting with Commander Damon. He noticed that when people attack the ones Ava loves most, she fights back. When she found out how her mother died, she lit Grymyr on fire. And she was the same way before her abilities grew into what they are now. If anyone ever hurts her loved ones, she fights back with a fiery passion. He knew that if Anya could pull cruelties from Damon's mouth and even hurt Anya, Ava would not be able to stand by in the face of his treacheries. He wasn't sure if she would release enough energy to completely rid the city of their enemies, but she did. And she gained the loyalty and admiration of every Wyntryn in Rebynrock.

He and Anya weren't wrong when they spoke the ancient tongue, *vaye chessya ta mey mata*. And their words must have reached their ancestors because when they needed them most, they were there. As Ava said herself, they worked through her to help them free the city.

Rais' hand is still pressed over her heart. She speaks slowly, "all of this feels strange. I had so much anger inside of me. And now, it's gone. The pain, the sadness, all swept away by the same tide. I feel—good. It's strange because I can't remember a time when I felt this free."

He lifts her chin. "Don't waste a minute of that feeling. It's rare. Especially as you step into the role of Queen. There will be days when it will feel like you are isolated like no one understands that fire within you. People will hate you and they will love you. When you feel like the world is against you, find me. Take my hand, meet my eyes, and I will remind you of who I see when I look at you," he tells her. His voice barely a murmur.

Her chest rises and falls, her eyes glassy. "Only if I can do the same for you."

He nods. And her mouth stretches into a smile. She pushes to her toes and presses her lips to his scar. She shifts back to her heels and sends a message into his mind.

Rais graces her jaw with his fingertips at her words. He senses a presence outside of the fortress doors and turns from her, unlocking the doors to let Anya in. She steps inside and instantly moves to Ava—pulling her into a hug. "Cousin you are a godsend," Anya says to her.

"We need to get you a healer right away," Ava says.

Anya pulls from her cousin. "I will be fine. The dagger cut pretty deep, but the blood is slowing." She looks to Rais. "I doubt we will have much time to prepare once Stygian hears word of what has happened here."

Rais knows Anya is right, but he wants to celebrate the victory for a while longer. "We should speak to Eieran about what we will do next. And I will send word to Osidias to stay where he is."

"I agree. Ava if you wish to go rest, you should. The three of us can work out the next steps and let you know what we decide, if that's fine with you. You can of course stay and speak with us if you wish."

Ava rolls her shoulders and tugs on her fingers lightly. "I trust you. You guys can do your thing ... I want to be alone for a bit anyway." She looks to Rais and then flicks her gaze down the corridor. "I'll go now, and I can catch up with you all tomorrow. And Anya, please let someone look at that wound."

Rais watches her stumble down the hall. He can tell she is favoring one foot over the other. And based on her fidgeting, he assumes that something is nagging at her. He wants to ask her, but he maintains his patience.

"I'll meet you in the war room, Anya. I'm going to go find Eieran," Rais tells her absentmindedly.

"Very well, I'll go speak with my father," Anya says.

Even though he takes a different path through the fortress, his mind keeps tugging him to Ava. His mind asks him to go to her, but his legs keep on track to Eieran's rooms.

What riddles his mind so fervently is Ava telling him that the arrow changed the feeling of his mind. He wants to follow Alys' wishes and use the talismans to fight against their enemies. But if they tainted his mind, he has no interest in them. The worry is that if Ava is a walking talisman, guided by their ancestors, then how is that affecting her mind? Will she too be changed and meddled with over time? She described the ancestors as working through her. That she wasn't thinking through what she was doing. And if she is a talisman, how is she effecting the people around her? Simply the thought is terrifying.

She wields a deadly ability. Fire is a dangerous power that can be manipulated easily. There's a difference between using the power to help save Wyntryn and using the power to kill. He doesn't want to kill in this war. He knows it's inevitable, but he doesn't know if Ava realizes what pain she may cause to others. What pain she has already caused. All of those dead soldiers have families, people waiting for them in Goldryn in Grymyr. The only way he can reconcile their deaths is in rememberance of all the Wyntryn lives taken by those same regions.

Rais wasn't there when Ava attacked the commander, but he saw the soldiers in the streets. Fire burned beneath the feet of every single one. And those who didn't run and tried to fight back, were burned from the inside. A horrid and evil end to life. Despite his pride in her saving Rebynrock, he can't help but feel sick. Sickened by the way they gained the city's freedom.

It makes him wonder how it felt to die in such a way as a child. Fire took his parents from him. Fire corrupted Alys' eldest daughter Stygian. And fire is the weapon used most by the Atane to destroy the Wyntryn forests and villages.

When fighting others, he never intends to kill. He only goes as far as taking one's life if they won't stop until they take his. Raiden couldn't even kill Saira, a man who has killed hundreds if not more. The same man who killed their Queen and desires to kill Ava. He can't bring himself to such darkness unless he has absolutely no other choice. No human should ever kill another. It's unnatural. And yet it is a common occurrence in their world.

He knocks on his cousin's door, and Eieran yells for him to come in. Raiden walks in, a yawn overtaking him.

"Need a nap, oh great Sparrow?" he pesters.

"It is just one of those days, cousin." Rais sighs. He slumps onto the couch. He stares up at the stone ceiling while Eieran shrugs on his coat. The pain in Rais' leg is more prevalent now than before.

"Our Ava showed great courage today. The people see her as a Queen now, which will be helpful when recruiting troops," Eieran says.

Rais covers his eyes with his arm, blocking the light from going through his eyelids. "She seems to have found herself. But if I am entirely honest, I am worried for her."

"About what?" he asks. His tall figure moves closer to him as he goes to stand before the door.

"The way she attacked the soldiers … lighting a fire inside of them. It is nothing but vicious. I know it saved Rebynrock, but what if the violence corrupts her?"

Eieran lets out a low laugh. "There is no reason to worry for her. There is darkness in Wyntryn blood, but if your kind soul stays by her, she will never fall to it. The fact is, war is violent. It is dark and it is cruel. It corrupts us all in different ways. She did what she had to do to save our people. You should be celebrating this, not sending your mind into its own war."

Rais slides his leg off the couch and moves to stand. "What if I am not always by her side?"

Eieran reaches to wrap his arm around Rais' shoulders and then covers Rais' mouth with his hand. Rais glares at him. "Hush, cousin. You annoy me with your worries." Eieran moves his hand and shoves Rais out the door. Eieran follows behind him, and they make their way to the war room.

They enter the room covered in maps. Anya sits and stares down at the map. She has a thick bandage wrapped around her waist. When it comes to Anya Petrichor, nothing stops her, not even an injury like this.

On the map, there is now a blue fawn atop Rebynrock. Rais sits down at the table and Eieran slides into the chair next to him.

Anya looks up to them. "I think Ava needs to leave Rebynrock. If anyone comes after her, the first place they will check is here," she says pointedly.

"Rais will go with her then. It is best if it is only the two of you traveling, that way you won't attract too much attention," Eieran adds.

"If we stay here, we can continue to defend Rebynrock," Rais argues.

Anya bites her lip and points to the village on the outskirts of the mountain holding the city. "This village is full of mages who have signed an oath. If we need assistance, they are within a day's ride of getting here and many of them are able to alate."

Anya is right about the mages from the village. Rais met them all himself when they took down that group of Atane. At least the city will have some defenses. And maybe it is best to get Ava out of there. "What about our invitations to the rising moon festival in Grymyr?" Rais asks.

Eieran leans back in his chair. "I think Anya or I should attend. It would be incredibly dangerous for Ava to go."

There are benefits to Ava going to the ball in Grymyr and they did mention before that he should go with her. "If the other regions are to respect her as our next Queen, she needs to appear before them. The Isles, Goldryn, and Grymyr will all have their highest authorities present. I can go with her, make sure she is safe. Any sign of trouble and we will return to the manor," Rais says.

"What if you can't alate?" Eieran asks.

"There are safe places in Grymyr I can take her. If we are entering a war, it is best that Ava knows who she is up against and for the other regions to see that we are not a broken kingdom. If you or Anya were to go, they would think us cowards for hiding her." Rais knows it is important to Ava to go, so he will make sure she gets into that library.

"I agree with Ava attending," Anya says. She looks to Eieran, and he nods, confirming his own agreement. "Good, then we are decided. You and Ava will leave Rebynrock, and in three days you both will attend the ball in Grymyr. The only other topic I think we need to cover before we all disperse is finding an army."

"Your father mentioned going to Metarock to gather recruits," Rais mentions to Anya.

"Yes. He left right after I spoke with him. He will go to the next hidden city afterward. I figured I can stay here until Osidias arrives, and then I will return to the coast to gather what people I can."

"There are training camps remaining along this area of the region." Eieran points to the land west of the Wyntryn Manor. "We can gather the more inexperienced mages here and work on training while we can. The armies are still underground in Metarock along with what is left of our armor. We can transport what we can to the camps."

"We should also reach out to the protectors overseas. They might be able to bring a few groups back to Wyntryn to help fight," Rais adds.

"I can send a representative to each refugee camp while I stay in Rebynrock. We should keep the Wyntryn Manor as our headquarters. Once you and Ava get back from Grymyr, Rais, you can see if she is able to hold a charm on the land. That way we can have at least one safe place to go if that area is attacked," Anya says.

"When I do get back, I would like to lead the training for irregulars."

Both Anya and Eieran agree. They each take the time to write out letters to the other protectors. They sign their names at the bottom and seal them shut with Wyntryn's sigil. Anya continues to discuss logistics, but the main issues have been resolved. Rais eventually excuses himself from the meeting and walks through the shadowed fortress.

He breathes in the smell of damp stone and the

winter's cold. Dark velvet tapestries cover the walls.

He runs his fingers across the rough stone as he makes his way through the hallways. The fortress is more welcoming and grander now that it isn't being stalked by their enemies.

Rais is fond of the architecture in the region. The redwood buildings, with swirling murals covering the surfaces. The stone and dark wood fortresses and manors. The most appealing part of the hidden cities are the arched pathways that zigzag through the caverns and the sculptures that are carved from the cave walls. He even has an appreciation for the villages made of warm wood and crumbling shingles. The Wyntryn aesthetic is one of dark shades, cool temperatures, and fire. Fire in the land's blood and fire in every home at night.

Rais slips into Ava's chambers. He sees her through the open doorway of the room, sitting on the bed with a book in her hands.

"I thought you were supposed to be getting rest," he says. His voice stark in the still room.

"I thought you were supposed to be in a meeting," she retorts.

Rais slides onto the bed next to her and leans against a pillow. His body welcomes the comfort. "What is the book about?"

She closes it and sets it on her lap. "The story of my grandparents. I found it on one of the shelves. Someone, somewhere, decided to write their story down."

"Ah, I have heard they had a grand reign."

She pushes her head back and stares up at the cloth covering the bed. "It seems like it. It makes me wonder if someone will write a story about my mother or about me someday."

"How could they not? What you did today has already been written down. Left to the history books for future rulers of Wyntryn to admire," he says.

Her cheeks redden and she tilts her head to see him better. She changes the subject by asking, "what did you all decide?"

Rais crosses his arms across his chest. "We decided you aren't safe staying here. You and I will leave for the manor tomorrow. We will ride there, as to not risk alerting your's or the talisman's presence in the Sonder. Then you and I will attend the ball in Grymyr. When that is over, we will return to the manor. I have taken on the role of training irregulars in the art of the mind. Anya and Eieran have their own tasks as well. Hopefully, when the time comes, we will be able to hold our own in battle."

"We will. But if we are leaving tomorrow, then, for now, I will gladly sleep until I am dragged from this bed." She sits up suddenly and reaches towards his thigh, running her finger lightly across the sliced flesh. "When did this happen?" she asks with a slight panic.

"Your fire missed the soldiers in the fortress. Eieran and I were fighting them, and I faltered. Lost sight of my predictions for only a moment and got a sword slicing through my thigh," he says. Injuries aren't something unusual for him, so he doesn't see it as a big deal. Rais can still walk, so there is no need to worry.

"You haven't even cleaned it you fool," she snaps at him.

Ava gets off the bed and places her book on the bedside table. She retreats into the bathroom and comes back with a damp cloth and herbs. She settles beside him with her legs crossed. Before he can stop her, she pulls the dagger from her belt and slices what's left of his pant leg off. Her hands move slowly as she cleans the wound. Rais flinches and bites down on the inside of his mouth, but he does his best to not show her he's in pain. No matter how hard he tries, he is sure that she can see right through him to the truth.

With the cut clean, she places the herbs neatly against the wound and then wraps a cloth around his leg, fastening it with a clip. "I should've let you get an infection for ignoring it," she states matter-of-factly.

"There were more important things to do, like saving you from swarms of adoring fans," he teases.

She narrows her eyes at him. "I think I'm capable of fighting through a crowd myself." She falls to her back, relaxing into the mattress.

"Then next time, I'll leave you to it," he says with a smile.

"And next time, I'll let your wound heal into a nasty scar."

Rais looks to her in amusement. But she has already rolled onto her side and closed her eyes. "Goodnight, Your Grace," he says quietly.

He carefully gets up from the bed and leaves her room. He returns to his own, where his mind stays awake all night. His lack of melatonin causing him to drown in tired thoughts.

Chapter Twenty-Seven

As the sun rises over the mountain, light cascades through the city of Rebynrock. It covers the delicate buildings in a myriad of colors. Alights the redwood into a fiery shade. The light warms the roofs of the city, allowing the cold to be washed away until the sun passes over and the cavern fills with darkness once again.

The dawn light is slowly disappearing beyond the alcoves now. Ava listens to a woman telling stories on the streets below. The woman sits on wooden boxes while crowds of people listen with interest. Her graying hair flutters around her face. The creases around her mouth show when she smiles. "Before the first great war, Wyntryn was born from the fusion of man and dragon. Our founder Kataar Wyntryn joined blood with a great winter dragon. When all thought he had died, he was reborn with a connection to the land. His very life force was made with the energy that runs through Kanaleigh. He became an irregular. The first man to ever walk the Plane of Verity. Following his lead, the other founders of Kanaleigh fused their blood with a mythical creature. And across the land, the race of irregulars was born. These people are our mages, our protectors. Even Wyntryn's royal bloodline comes from the first Wyntryn, Kataar. It is said when you are rebirthed with the energy of Kanaleigh, your eyes shine brighter, your hair grows thicker, even your very bones grow longer. I've seen this change with my own eyes ..."

Her mind twists around the woman's stories while she waits for Raiden to meet her outside the fortress. She leans against the edge of the stone bridge, attracted to the aura of the crowd.

The doors open behind her and she turns expecting to see Raiden, but Anya steps out instead. Anya meets her farther down on the walkway, where Ava looks out at the city. She offers Ava her palm. Ava places her fist in her hand, and Anya places her other hand atop. "I will miss you greatly cousin, but we will see each other soon enough," Anya says.

Ava hugs her cousin, and promises her, "I will see you soon, Anya." Ava pulls from the embrace. "I am so thankful I got to meet you. You and my uncle are all the family I have left."

"I feel the same. You should know Ava, that all of Wyntryn is your family too. Our people are gracious and will always be here to catch you when you fall. That is what makes this kingdom so special. We are not built on fear or war, we are built on our shared connection. We are loyal to our own, always."

The doors open again, and Raiden walks through with two bags thrown over his shoulder and a sword at his back. She runs her fingers along the dagger at her own waist, checking to make sure she hadn't forgotten it.

Raiden says his goodbyes to Anya, and they start off down the hanging walkway. Ava sweeps a heavy cloak over her shoulders. The deep blue cloth slumps over her, falling low to her feet.

"Safe travels to the both of you!" Anya calls from behind them. Her voice suddenly rushes through Ava's mind, *search those who search you. Don't let yourself be blinded by the lack of memories.*

Ava twists to look at her. Ms. Ethelle had given her the same warning, search those who search you. *What is it that Anya believes I have blinded myself to? Or is it a warning of what is to come?* Her cousin raises her hand and waves.

Ava waves back. Unease lurks through her skin. She turns away from Anya and catches up to Raiden. He looks down at her with a happiness that laces through his mind. "Did you get any sleep?" she asks him.

He gently shakes his head. "No, but it allowed me plenty of time to sort through my thoughts. And because I was up so early, I was able to say goodbye to Eieran before he left."

"I was wondering where he went," Ava says.

They move down the stairwells and alleyways until they find their way to the main road leading to the stables. As people recognize her, they leave their homes and filter out onto the streets. They wave and shout their blessings to the two of them. Ava waves to her people, listening to the thoughts they throw through the air to her. It's overwhelming, but she's grateful for their confidence. Because even with a lightness in her chest and mind, she still struggles to find confidence in her words and actions. But if these people can believe in her with such a passion, maybe she can believe in herself.

A worker at the stable brings them Oberyn and an unfamiliar horse. A grey, with splotches of dull white and dark grey dappled across his coat. The horse's legs and face are darker than the rest of it. Its eyes are a deep brown. The worker tells them the grey's name is Nimbus and that he is a gift from the people of Rebynrock, given in gratitude for her freeing the city.

She leads Nimbus to a tree stump on the side of the barn, and braces her foot in the stirrup, pushing through her other leg to swing around into the saddle. Nimbus shifts beneath her, getting used to the added weight. She sits back in the saddle, balancing herself on the lengthy creature.

Raiden walks Oberyn up next to her, and they begin their trek through the tunnels of the mountain. The walls of the caves shimmer in the faint light of the fire she holds in her hand. Ava's vision is mostly filled with black, but in the darkness, her other senses are heightened. She can hear the flapping of bat wings overhead and the echoes of sounds from the city behind them. The farther they go the quieter and colder it gets.

When they emerge from the tunnels, they walk a path that cuts underneath an overhanging ledge. The air swirls with a thick fog. The misty land is frigid and pecks at her skin. She rubs her hand along Nimbus's neck, trading warmth with the beautiful horse.

Raiden estimates that they can make it to the manor before dark, but they will not be able to stop for more than an hour. Ava looks forward to getting back to the manor and then on to Grymyr. She wants to stay in her father's apartment one last time before leaving for Wyntryn. Ava assumes Raiden will be against the idea, so she doesn't bring it up. But the thought rests in her head. Along with all the curiosities of Kanaleigh that spin through her mind.

They approach the village where Erka and Chenea live. And as they pass by, Ava sends her regards to them, thanking them for helping her heal and reach Rebynrock. They continue past the village and into a dense forest. It's known as the Brockade forest. A large area that stretches from the Goldryn border to the Wyntryn Manor. The ground there is covered in frozen moss and thick undergrowth that cracks beneath the horse's hooves.

The trees in the forest reach high into the sky. Barren of leaves and riddled with rot. The only color in the landscape comes from the evergreens.

The sun rises to a peak in the sky when they finally exit the forest. Ava and Raiden are quiet up until then, their words only short observations of their surroundings. And as they leave the forest behind, they walk up on a dismantled and burnt village. The buildings are ghosts of their former selves. Roofs are caved in, fences in pieces on the ground, and windows shattered. Raiden brings Oberyn to a halt. He whispers to Ava, "drop behind me. I sense an Atane here."

Ava slows Nimbus and pulls him behind Raiden. They stay there for a few moments listening to their surroundings. Each of them on edge, ready to react to whatever appears from behind the burnt buildings.

Raiden reaches his hand to his sword and slides from Oberyn. He walks slowly towards the nearest shell of a home, pressing his back to the wall. Ava senses the beast now—its mind erratic and wild.

A roar sounds from farther within the village, and the Atane comes storming through the snow on large hooves. Its head resembles a large cat with the body of a stunted horse. It sets its sights on Raiden and opens its mouth wide. Ava jumps from Nimbus in that moment. She watches in horror as it careens towards Raiden. It's teeth are huge and fire swells within it's white belly. The flame moves through its throat and builds in its mouth. Raiden lunges underneath the body of the creature and slices the back of its legs. He catches his balance and runs to the other side. The creature whirls towards him and lets out the red-hot blaze.

The fire swarms towards Raiden, too fast for him to dodge. Raiden tries to push his legs underneath him to jump to the side, but his injured leg keeps him from moving. Ava runs through the veil of their world into the Plane of Verity. She pulls the fire toward her.

It listens to her, and she draws the energy into herself—silencing the flame. The Atane rears onto its hind legs and lets out an angered roar. Raiden catches his footing and runs towards the creature again. Ava yells at it. It turns towards her, gathering fire within itself again. With its attention drawn away from Raiden, he can make his move. His sword slices into the neck of the beast. Fire billows from the mouth of the Atane and into the air in an uncontrollable cloud. Raiden yanks his sword from its neck and moves out of the way of the fire. It burns bright before the winter landscape. The creature collapses to the ground. Its blood flowing into the snow. The eyes of the Atane move wildly, and its legs shake.

Raiden moves to the suffering beast's head and slides his sword through its skull. Her hand goes to her mouth at the sight of the poor beast. Raiden pulls the blade out and wipes it off in the once pristine snow. He slides it back into its sheath and goes to Ava.

Ava looks tentatively to him and reaches her hand out towards the animal from a comfortable distance. She draws herself into the Sonder and sets it aflame. So that the Atane may return to nature and give back to their lands.

Raiden bends his head to her. "Thanks for the

help."

"Did you expect me to only watch as you vitiated the poor creature?" she asks.

"Atane are not poor creatures. They were genetically modified to kill our people and ravage our lands," he says with a sigh.

"At least you didn't let it suffer," she says. Her eyes still burn from the sight of the fallen Atane.

Raiden walks to Oberyn, still standing silently waiting for them. "Do you need a break, or do you want to keep going?" he asks her.

She goes to Nimbus, whose nose is deep in the snow as he tries to find grass to nibble on. Ava grasps the reins and leads him to Raiden and Oberyn. "I'm fine to keep on going."

"Great, we should be able to make it back soon. This is the last village before we reach the manor," he says.

Raiden lets go of Oberyn's reins and goes to the side of Nimbus, offering her a leg up. She takes it gratefully and slides into the saddle atop the horse's back. Raiden returns to Oberyn and easily boosts himself up and into the saddle regardless of his injured leg. "You're going to reopen the wound," Ava says.

"I already have, but the wound is wrapped tight. I will be perfectly fine," he tells her.

"And you were calling me the fool when you first met me."

Raiden stills. She pulls Nimbus up to Oberyn and keeps him at a steady pace. Raiden stays quiet, his mind shuttering itself from her. Ava narrows her eyes in confusion but keeps her focus on the balance between her and Nimbus.

They move through a few more groupings of trees

as the day moves on.

As the sun begins to dip into the western side of the sky, they enter a wide clearing. Ava relaxes her shoulders, loosening her posture. She turns her head up to the sky and breathes in the prickly air. When she opens her eyes, she sees white flecks falling from the sky. A snowflake lands on her nose, and she brushes it off. She returns her gaze ahead of her and notices Raiden's eyes on her. He watches her in amusement. She pulls up beside him and reaches her hand out to him. She tries her best to stay balanced on the grey's back.

He takes it and kisses her knuckles. She laughs at his proper ways. She always found it odd that one of the common gestures was to kiss the top of a woman's hand. She brings her hand back to the reins and stares off into the trees lined along the edge of the clearing. There's a moose standing still. It grazes through the tall grass that pokes through the snow. Its ears flicker as they move by.

Raiden turns to look that way and keeps his own gaze steady on the marvelous creature. "For such a large animal, its so calm."

"Looking at an animal like that in the Wyntryn lands, it should give us hope that we can still recover."

"We will recover, but it will take time," he admits.

Her mind dreams up a future for her people that brings happiness to her heart. "I like to think that we have plenty of time. In our lives we will live to see the day when the forests are full of creatures and the land is full of thriving cities," Ava says.

"I would like that," he mumbles. His thoughts are distant from her.

They continue through the snow and forests until the sun is low. The sky bursts with oranges and pinks, throwing color across the peaceful land. In the distance, she can see the shape of the manor. The tall stone walls fill an area surrounded by barren trees.

Raiden glances at her with a mischievous look and kicks Oberyn into a canter. She clicks her tongue to Nimbus, asking him to speed up. She and her horse chase after him. They fly across the land, the horses churning up the snow and throwing it around them. Wind flies through her hair and against her skin. Her body surges with freedom and subtle calm. Her mind is clear.

As they get closer to the stable, she glides Nimbus into a walk. Oberyn slows before her, and Raiden holds her still until Ava catches up. They keep the horses at a steady pace until they reach the stable doors.

Ava pushes her aching leg around and slides off the side of her horse. She loosens the girth as Raiden pushes the doors open. They guide the horses in and pull off the saddles and bridles. Raiden puts feed in the horses' stalls and fills their hay and water. While he does that, she brushes Nimbus and Oberyn down. The horses' breathing is ragged, and their legs move stiffly. Ava's own muscles are tense. She's ready to lie down for another long rest. She can't imagine how Raiden is feeling after a night of sleeplessness and a day of riding on an injured leg.

Raiden leaves the stalls and carries two fur blankets towards the horses. He passes one to her and throws the other over Oberyn's back. She slides the blanket over Nimbus, pulling the straps underneath the horse and securing them.

Once the horses are both taken care of and in their stalls, Raiden and Ava grab their bags and retreat to the warmth of the manor. Raiden wordlessly goes to his room. Where she assumes he passes out underneath the blankets of his bed.

Ava takes her time traveling up the steps and to her own room. Her thighs and calves ache. When she reaches her room, she drops her bag to the floor and pulls the book she was reading the night before from her bag. She tosses the book onto the bed and then pulls her clothes off. The clothes are drenched in melted snow. She slips into the bathroom and runs warm water for a bath.

She sinks into the soft water and falls into a vibrant memory.

A boy with white hair chases her down the stairs of the manor. She looks back and sees a broad grin on his face. She yells something unintelligible at him, and he throws a spark of lightning towards her. Ava twists through the maze of the main floor. She throws open a door and hurtles out into bright green grass. Before them is a field of lavender plants. Ava runs towards the field, throwing her head back to see Raiden right at her heels. He lunges at her and grasps her arm. She falls into the plants. Purple covers her vision and sunshine ricochets across the high stalks. "I got you!" Young Raiden teases with pride. She yanks his arm, and he falls into the lavender next to her. They stare up at the blue, cloudless sky.

"Rais?" she asks. Her young voice high. Raiden throws his arms above him, looking at his hands in the sun.

"Yes?"

"Do you like me?" she asks.

"Everyone likes you, Ava. You're the best," he chimes out.

Her younger self smiles at him. "No. Do you like me?"

He shrugs his shoulders. "Why does it matter? No

matter what, you will always be my person."

She pokes his cheek. "And you will always be mine."

Chapter Twenty-Eight

Willow looks out at the near-empty streets. She swore she heard shouts from the city. The harsh sun shines down on her. The sandstone is hot underneath her fingertips. She keeps her eyes on the streets beyond the palace. No one really travels through the city during the day, but there are also never any screams. Especially not like the one she just heard.

The outcropping in the palace she stands on gives her a view of the main city gate. The iron gate swings in and out. There are no guards along the wall. No one there to keep watch. "What in goddesses name?" she whispers.

Then she sees them, the swarms of deep purple. They alate right beyond the gates. Hundreds of Goldryn soldiers appear from seemingly nowhere. They run through the gates in a panic, screaming.

Willow needs to get to Stygian. She runs from the balcony and into the palace. The halls are silent. She sinks into the Sonder and searches for the Queen. But wherever she is, Willow can't detect her. Willow slips down the stairs and through the hallways of the first floor. She goes into the main courtyard.

What guards are there stand stagnant, staring into the city. She can't see the returning soldiers from here, but she can hear them. They cry out in pain from within the city.

Willow spins to the guards around her. "What are you doing? Fetch the healers!"

They don't move. "Now!" she shouts.

A few run off into the castle, but the others still stare out towards the bellowing cries. Willow runs towards the bridge, but Aliras catches her by the wrist. "Don't go," he says.

"They are suffering."

His eyebrows dip. "I need your help."

She forcefully turns from the bridge and follows him to the edge of the courtyard. They descend a series of steps that lead to the docks. He pushes open a door for her that opens to the armory. A soldier paces back and forth within.

He has burns on his hand and his temple. Red spots cover one side of his face and neck. *What happened to these people?*

Aliras steps up to the soldier. The man flinches and backs away. His eyes are filled with terror. "Please tell Willow what you told me," Aliras instructs.

The soldier dips his head and says quietly, "Alys Wyntryn's daughter … she's back."

Willow blinks idly for a second. Before it resonates within her, Ava. Did Ava do this to these people? But she couldn't have, Ava can barely access her elemental abilities.

The soldier gulps. "I tried to stop her, but she knocked me to the ground. She told me to tell Queen Stygian that ... that the dragon has risen from the ashes and that she will regret ever invading Wyntryn."

Willow reaches her hand out and steps towards him. "Will you show me what happened?"

He backs away from her.

"I won't hurt you. I promise. If you let me access your mind, I'll do the rest. It won't hurt if you allow me to see what happened," Willow says.

Aliras nods to the soldier. "I command you to comply."

The soldier gawks at Aliras, but he lets Willow touch his arm.

She flows into his mind. It's dark and filled with waking terrors. She slips through to his memories and opens what appears as a door. The vision consumes her, pushing her physical body to her knees.

Her mind is placed in the soldier's as he watches fire alight beneath his feet. Around him, fire rises underneath the feet of every soldier in the city.

Ava alates down the stairs of the fortress. Her body vibrates with energy and power. Flames cling to her body like armor. The soldier runs at Ava as she reaches the bottom of the steps. He swings his sword, and Ava throws him to the ground with a flurry of embers. Willow doesn't feel the pain the soldier felt, but she can imagine it.

Ava wrenches the sword from his hand and throws it to the side. She places her fingers to the soldier's temple and words spindle into Willow's mind. *Go home to your Queen. And tell her what has happened here. Tell her the dragon has risen from the ashes. Tell her that she will regret ever invading my region.*

The soldier stumbles away from Ava and gets to his feet. He then runs away, his legs barking beneath him with pain. The streets are filled with retreating soldiers. They are all on fire.

Willow yanks from the soldier's mind. She falls backward onto the stone floor and lifts her hand to her forehead.

Aliras watches her curiously.

She glances to him. "Ava Wyntryn destroyed the army sent to Rebynrock. Whatever is left of them are at our gates now. I'll deliver this man's message to Stygian."

"Do you really think that's a good idea?" Aliras asks. He offers her a hand. She takes it and he pulls her to her feet. "Stygian will lose her mind when she hears this. Think of the repercussions."

Willow is already aware of how Stygian will react. She will be furious but keeping it from her will only make her angrier. "I am aware, Aliras. Make sure your soldiers get to healers before you worry about the Queen's reaction."

Aliras doesn't look happy at what she says, but she isn't trying to convince him of anything. She wisps out of the armory and up the stairs. Willow finds her way to Stygian's chambers. She knocks on the door and waits for a response. There is none, so she pushes the door open and goes inside.

"Syn?" she calls out.

Willow steadily moves through the wide marbled chambers. She steps down into the area with Stygian's desk and rounds the furniture to the glass door. Outside the crystalline glass, is Stygian. She leans against the railing watching the horizon.

Willow slides the door open. "Hey."

The Queen doesn't look to her.

Willow walks up beside her and presses her forearms against the stone. "I know you can hear them."

Stygian's purple eyes glare at her. Willow fidgets her fingers together. "They are the soldiers you sent to Rebynrock. Ava was able to break through your barrier charms. Those who survived have suffered severe burns and other wounds. But there was one soldier whose mind I entered—"

"Why would she do this?" Stygian asks.

"Ava isn't who she once was. Her actions are based on what people have told her. As far as she's aware, you aren't family. You are a tyrant Queen who filled the streets of her home with enemies."

Stygian lifts her chin with the oncoming breeze.

"Syn, she sent a message with a soldier. Ava told him the dragon has risen from the ashes and that you will regret ever invading her region."

Stygian keeps her gaze ahead of her. "Tell me of the prophecy once more."

"You have heard it a million times. If you are asking if this proves it to be true, then yes. Ava has unlocked the power of your ancestors. War is on the horizon, and it will rise before the flowers bloom."

Stygian pushes from the wall and meets her gaze. "I sensed a talisman on Rais when I was in Rebynrock."

"What?"

The talismans are holders of great power. But they are only useful if the soul inside connects with the possessor. Otherwise, the talisman can destroy its possessor's mind. Mold them into a weapon of destruction. Rais already has an immense amount of power, but if the talisman doesn't conform to him, then he will be driven into madness.

"I want it for myself. I do not trust the Wyntryn

protectors with a talisman." Stygian looks off into the ocean and her expression hardens. "If there is to be a war, then so be it. However, I will make sure my sister is acting with her own thoughts and not the thoughts of others. If I must fight her in the end, then at least it will be of her own choosing."

Stygian is a dangerous woman. She has been broken by the people she trusted the most. Willow doesn't know how this war will turn out, but she knows Stygian will fight with everything she has.

Willow notes that Stygian didn't get the talisman Grymyr promised her. And now her soldiers have been terrorized by her own sister. It is a miracle Stygian is so calm. It is intriguing to think that she is conscious enough to be aware that Ava is not in her right mind. She would have expected Stygian to fall into an untamable rage over this. The Queen must be able to look past her sister's actions because she knows Ava lacks her memories.

There are many people pulling the strings in Ava's life. Willow supposes only time will tell before the strings fall, and Ava has to start moving on her own.

Because there will be a downfall. There always is. A point where everything tumbles apart and there is nothing to face but the cruel, undeniable truth.

Chapter Twenty-Nine

The halls are silent. The dust hangs heavy in the air. Sunlight floats through the open windows bringing warmth to the landing. Rais pulls his coat around him and watches the trees bend in the wind. Their branches ebbing and flowing like the waves of the ocean.

He can feel Ava's mind awake on the bottom floor of the manor, but he doesn't bother her. They have plenty of time to spend together, so he wants to give her space. To let her mind and body recover from the past few days. He is still in need of rest as well, but he doesn't mind the pressures and restrictions of stress. He almost enjoys keeping busy and forcing himself to the brink of breaking. He loves the allure of adventure and change. His mind its calmest in the face of danger. His worries do cause him to not get much sleep, but it's a part of who he is, and he wouldn't change it for anything.

Her footsteps are soft against the stairs. She walks up beside him and pokes him with her elbow. Ava passes him a mug, and he looks down at the steaming liquid. "I found a coffee maker hidden away in the pantry. I thought you might want some caffeine in case you weren't able to get much sleep," she says. Ava's mind swirls quietly around her—void of the burning pain that once flew around her like a tornado.

"Thank you." He takes a sip of the slightly bitter and creamy drink.

"I know we have only just arrived, but I would like to leave for Grymyr early," she says with hesitation.

Rais keeps his eyes on the snow-covered trees. "It is dangerous to have you in the city for longer than you need to be."

Her head is bent towards the floor when he turns to her. "I know it's dangerous, but I want to stay in my old bed one last time. I want to say goodbye to what is left of that life. Of the home my father built for me there."

Rais doesn't want the Society to get their hands on her again, but he can see the desperation in her. The importance of being able to do this for herself. To truly move on, she must say goodbye. "All right, we can leave tonight instead of tomorrow. You should get your things together though. I believe you have dresses in your room, but I'm sure there's some in your mother's room as well."

"Okay."

Ava walks away, and her warmth goes with her. A chill passes through him, tingling across his chest and down through his arms. As he walks down the stairs of the manor, his legs send pangs through him. The aftermath of riding horses and overexerting his body. Rais finds his way down the hall of portraits to the study. Where he settles onto the couch and sends a spark of electricity to the wood in the fireplace. A flame comes to life, sending heat through the room.

Rais pushes a pillow beneath his knee. It raises the

wound on his thigh, allowing for some of the pain to subside.

He stares at the fire. It sends his mind through flurries of memories. He doesn't remember the exact day his parent's died. He was too young. But he remembers the pain, and that pain turned into a fabricated reality. A memory created by trauma.

The oranges and reds of the fire bending together reminds him of Alys' wrath, of the wrath Ava shares. His mind floats through images of the past, taking his mind back to the days when he was nothing but a child. When he chased an easily angered Ava through the manor. The bliss he felt in those days is unfathomable to him now. He doesn't have much emotional pain, but his head is swarming with stressors. Even as he sits there on the couch, relaxing and floating through memories, he is still worrying about Wyntryn. About what will happen in Grymyr and about how Stygian is reacting to the news of Rebynrock.

He closes his eyelids and screams inside his head for it all to go away. To give him a moment of silence. Because even in sleep, his dreams are vivid and full of his fears. He may never find silence in his mind, but he wants to find peace in this world. So that one day his dreams will not be filled with fears, but with a semblance of blissful happiness.

He wakes from an unpleasant and sordid dream. He sits up and reaches into his coat, pulling out the thin metal arrow. The likely cause of his mental displeasures. He considered leaving it in Rebynrock but figured he had a safer place to hide it here at the manor.

He twists the talisman in his hands, feeling it pulse energy through his skin. He finds his way down the stairs and to the main entrance. Rais pushes through the doors and walks out onto the snow-covered terrace. His boots are instantly covered. The icy crystals soak into his pant legs. He pushes through the snow and towards the pathway into the trees.

He struggles to keep himself standing while walking along the path. The wind whips harshly against him.

His footsteps falter, but he keeps going. The path narrows ahead, the trees denser. He fights through the snow and into the fountain's boundaries. Where there is no heavy snow or icy wind. Only a pleasant calm that buzzes through his mind.

He feels the souls there circling him, prodding at him, and reaching for his thoughts. He blocks them out, tightening the folds of his mind. He walks to the fountain and bends before the pale stone. The water splashes on him, but he doesn't move. He takes the arrow and slides it into the water. The particles feel as if they are attacking him, the water somehow tightening around his arm and hand. He sets the arrow at the bottom of the fountain and yanks his arm free of the water. He sends a command to the Wyntryn ancestors present there, *protect the talisman. Keep enemies of the crown from entering this place.*

Pressure builds inside of his head, and he begins forcing his way back through the fountain's barrier. The air is colder and wind stronger beyond the fountain, but his mind is quieter. Raiden returns to the manor. Where he gathers his things and waits for the sun to set. At least now, they can alate to Grymyr without the fear of the talisman putting them in danger.

Hours later he stands outside of Ava's room, his

back pressed against the wall. He keeps his weight off his injured leg. The effects of the infliction finally force their way through him. The door to Ava's room cracks open and she slips out with a dress covered by a cloth bag. "Show me the way?" he asks.

She reaches her hand out to his and sends him an image of their destination. A beige hallway with numerous doors and an elevator at the end. He slips into the hazy blue, and she pulls him through the Sonder.

His eyes slowly adjust to the bright lights of the hallway. She slips a key from her pocket and into the door handle. She twists the key and opens the door to reveal a plain room. With worn furniture and framed newspapers on the walls. The back wall is covered with tall, curtained windows that overlook the towering metal and glass buildings of Grymyr. Ava walks through the room, her presence fitting easily into the essence of her old home. She goes down a hallway to the right and he hears the hinges of a door squeak.

He roams through the room. Across the floor is a swirling ornate rug, like those in the Wyntryn Manor. There's no fireplace in the apartment. Instead, there are vents on the ceiling that blow air at controlled temperatures.

Grymyr is known for its technologies. They created trackers, cars, and numerous other inventions to support the people who don't have the abilities of an irregular. Raiden owns a tracker, but he only uses it to communicate with the other protectors. There's no reason to call someone when you can alate to them or reach out to them with your mind. Although, Alys was one to use her tracker often.

She spoke of implementing similar technologies

in Wyntryn. Rais always assumed she was influenced by Ava's father. But their relationship broke off after the Society began executing irregulars. Alys didn't feel safe spending so much time in Grymyr or with someone connected to the Grymyr government. She only stayed in Grymyr for a week or two when she brought Ava to her father in the summers. And somehow after only being in Grymyr for a week this past summer, the Society attacked her.

"Sorry it's such a mess," Ava calls from the hallway.

"No, I think it is nice. I have never seen a residential building in Grymyr, I find it, plain, but it feels more ..." He searches for the right word.

"Personal?" she suggests.

Rais nods, it does feel more personal. In the apartment, there are framed images of Ava and her parents. The details and decorations reflect their family and interests. Unlike a village home in Wyntryn, the way this apartment is built is made to cater to all a person's different needs. The modern architecture of Grymyr is a nice difference to what Rais is used to.

Rais walks to the windows and pulls open the curtains, revealing the vibrant city outside the building. Looking down, he sees they are high up. From his perch at the windowsill, he overlooks the cars on the road, the crowds of people moving across the sidewalks and in and out of buildings.

He also notices the char along the streetlamps and the building across from them. This must have been the city block Ava set aflame.

"Rais?"

"Yes?" he asks. The city lights shine against his back. His face is dark as she looks up at him. The lights in the apartment have yet to be turned on.

"Do you like me?"

His brow bends and his expression changes. He recognizes the words from their childhood. "Everyone likes you, Ava. You're the best," he recites from memory.

Her blue eyes glimmer in the low light. "No, Rais. Do you like me?" she asks quietly.

There are no lavender or blue skies like when they first shared this conversation, but she's there. And she is as vibrant as the sun that shined down on them that day. He steps closer. "Why does it matter? No matter what, you will always be my person."

She reaches up to his scar, running her thumb along the protruding skin along his cheek and neck. For once, he doesn't flinch. He is comfortable with the gesture. "And you will always be mine," she whispers. She looks from the scar to his eyes. His breath brushes against the bridge of her nose. The emotions that leak from her mind make his chest tighten and tangle. He lifts his hand and cups her jaw.

He wants to lean into the feeling, but he knows Ava might pull away. And he doesn't want her to pull away. She's right there in his arms, and yet he feels as if she's half a world away.

Rais hesitates, pulling his hand from her. Her brows dip, and she breaks from his gaze. "I'm going to get some rest. I'll see you tomorrow," she says.

He watches her walk away. She runs her hand up her neck and through her hair.

Rais walks to the door of the apartment, but he stops himself and turns back towards the windows. He goes and sits on the couch, pressing his face into his hands. They were close in that way before, but there is something between them that's different now. Maybe it's that she doesn't remember or that she's changed. What he fears though, is that as she gains memories like the one of them in the meadow, she is only choosing to be with him because of what they once were.

That is his hesitation he supposes. He wants what they have, to be authentic, real. Not because of a lifetime that is now in the past.

Rais pulls his head from his hands and looks to the dark hallway. He stands and takes a breath. He goes to the hallway, unsure of himself. But in the dark, he sees her standing in the doorway to her room. He moves to her, and she stays stagnant. But then she moves too, meeting him halfway.

His hands reach out to her, and he pulls her to him. Their mouths bend together, and he lets those fears fade away. Ava runs her hand up his chest, and his heart collapses against her. The world twists with them, bending as they move with each other. A steady beat thrums in his ears. It silences the world and cuts off everything, but her.

Rais breaks from Ava and studies her expression. The slight smile, pink in the cheeks, eyes wide and encompassing him. "You are my person, Ava. You have me, all of me if you choose it."

She brushes his hair from his face, "I choose you, Rais. Even before I found you again, I think my soul missed you." She laughs softly.

"Your soul missed me?" he asks in amusement. "I refuse to lie to you, so you should know that my soul really missed you." He grabs her hand and pulls her to her bedroom. He sits on the floor with his legs crossed. She sits across from him shooting him an odd look. "Trust me?"

"Always," Ava says.

There is one secret Rais has been keeping from her. It is something she deserves to know, but he doesn't know how to say it. He has been hiding the truth of Stygian from her for her protection. But maybe it's best if she has the opportunity to come across the information herself.

He presses his forefingers to her temples and sends a memory to her. He closes his eyes and focuses on the memory, allowing it to resurface clearly in his mind.

The night is warm, and they sit on the roof—staring up at the stars. It was not even a month before her mother's death. The next day Ava would leave for the summer to go to Grymyr with her father. And that was one of the first days in Wyntryn that it was warm enough to be outside without a coat or blanket.

"I hate you," Ava says. His brows furrow as he looks to her. His head rests against the shingles. "I do," she reiterates, knowing he doesn't believe her.

"Why?" he asks.

She sits up and looks down at him. "Because you are everything my mom wanted me to be."

"What?"

"You're proper, respectful, caring. You are an expert in the mind. Your energy source is endless, and you've mastered your abilities. I understand it myself, but I am barely capable of what you can do. She adores you and despises me. I mean gods, she ran my sister out of the family because of her expectations. And now, you're the Sparrow. As soon as you turned sixteen, she gave you the position. It's aggravating," she yells out into the air. Her mind burning with the words.

"Ava ... no. You are all of that and more. You do not need to be a master of the Sonder to be the perfect daughter. You are the perfect daughter because you are you."

She shakes her head, upturning her face to the stars. "I hate you, Golden Sparrow." She draws the words out.

He rests his hand on hers and sits up to meet her eyes. "If anyone is to hate me, I would want it to be you."

"See? This is why I hate you. You always know what to say."

"I do not. If you could see into my mind, you would see a tangle of nerves and fear. I am good at making people think I am an expert, that I am fearless. But I am terrified that one day, I will break. Everything will fall apart, and I will disappoint everyone who put their faith in me," he admits.

"No one believes in me," she whispers.

"I believe in you."

She rolls her eyes. "I hate you."

He grins. "You love me."

"Ugh. I know, I know. You are my person, whether I like it or not." She sighs. In the memory she leans against him, hugging him on the roof. Underneath the stars.

"I'm going to miss you while you are in Grymyr."

"I will be back in a month. So be prepared to be pestered golden eyes!" she says dramatically. "But I will miss you too. It won't be long though, and you have another task at the Society's headquarters, right?"

He nods.

She stands up, balancing on the tilted roof. "Then you can stop by and see me. My dad's place is plain, but it has a nice overview of the city."

The memory fades from view. Blue scratches at his eyelids as he pulls from the Sonder. He opens his eyes to see Ava sitting across from him with an unreadable expression on her face.

She reaches out to him and brushes her hand across

his face. Then she stands and lays down in her bed. Her thoughts spinning off in directions he can't follow. He gets up and lays next to her, she holds his hand, but she doesn't say anything to him. So, he simply holds her hand and hopes that showing her that memory, doesn't push her away from him. But it's his last memory of her before she went to Grymyr. Before she died and lost her memories.

He never saw her apartment that summer. Never got to see her when he was visiting the Society. Alys had pulled him aside and sent him back to the manor. She sent him home with the letter that he would not open until after she died. The letter that told him that Ava would lose her memories in death. That instructed him to hunt down the talismans and be there for Ava when she was finally called home.

Chapter Thirty

The city lights flash against her pale skin. He watches her sleeping soundly. Her mind and soul quieted by a long-awaited peace. Rais' mind, on the other hand, is far from rest. It is awake and moving around itself, churning up thoughts and fears.

He slides from the bed and walks into the main space. Rais pulls out a chair from beneath the dining table and sits. He gazes out at the buzzing city with interest.

A thought flows into his mind, but not a thought originating within him. The words are distant, mangled. *Come to the manor.* It calls to him. *Someone is after the talisman.*

He searches for the source of the message. The purpose is undeniable, but who could be warning him? Rais takes a long look through the hallway, hoping Ava will be able to protect herself if anyone intrudes. And then he steps through the Plane of Verity and into the Wyntryn Manor.

"Rais," Nina chides.

The sight of his friend is comforting, but his friendship with Nina is a temporary one. As are his relationships with all his friends. People come and go like tides in his life. They rush around him while he stays stagnant, caught in a rip current that fights to drag him under the surface. He supposes the cause of the pain is the friends he chooses. Nina is a traveler, a nomad with no set destination. Willow is a loyal friend, but shares allegiances with the enemy. Even his cousin is not a constant in his life since he's always being dragged away by his duties. And Ava, well she is something entirely different.

He catches Nina's gaze as she slips around the banister of the stairs to face him. "I hear you found the arrow," she states plainly. Her dark skin is speckled with newly formed freckles. And her outfit is that of the styles worn in southern Goldryn.

"Where did you hear that from?" he asks. His suspicion turns to Nina. She could very well be the culprit that the voice warned him about.

"Did you forget that entering the Sonder with it in your possession, exposes it to anyone looking for its traces? And to think you are the smart one," she chastises.

"Are you after it?" he questions.

She lets out a sharp laugh. "Oh, I wish. You want to look outside or do you want me to spell it out for you?" Nina raises an eyebrow to him. As she walks into the light of the window, he notices she's wearing her mage's coat again. He hasn't seen it on her in a long time. Possibly she's come back to help them fight for their home.

She looks back to Rais, gesturing for him to look out the window. He moves towards the glass slowly, and his eyes widen with surprise. A purple fire burns through the trees surrounding the fountain. Stygian stands before the path throwing fire and screaming at their ancestors.

"She was screaming *nasty Wyntryns* earlier, cursing the family name. It makes me wonder if she realizes that she's attacking herself with those words," Nina grits out.

"It makes me wonder if she forgot she is a Wyntryn altogether."

Nina pushes his shoulder. "You gonna take one for the team?"

Rais side-eyes her. "I would rather do anything else."

"I thought she'd be able to get through to the fountain, but I suppose she's angered the ancestors." Nina shrugs. Her thin braids fall over her shoulders with the gesture.

He rubs his neck. "Is it bad if we leave her out there?" Rais asks.

"I will feel bad if she burns down the manor in spite. I have a lot of connections, and I heard about what Ava did in Rebynrock. Stygian got outsmarted and you know how much she craves dominance."

"Fine. I will go out there. Will you back me up when she attacks?" Rais asks his friend.

She rolls her eyes. "I suppose." Her cheeks lift into a smile, and Rais shakes his head at her.

He decides to not give up his presence to Stygian. She is already distracted enough to miss the fact that he alated here. Instead of sliding into the Sonder and into the snow, he takes the stairs. He buttons his coat up and makes his way through the foyer and out the door.

Rais strides through the snow to Stygian. He calls out to her, "what are you after?" He decides to play an ignorance to the talisman in the fountain.

"My birthright," she seethes.

"You chose to leave, Stygian, you signed away that

birthright when you signed your oath to Goldryn."

Stygian's eyes are wild, and her purple flames flicker in the trees, burning them slowly. "I know what you are hiding, Rais. Did you tell Ava? You haven't even told her of me, have you? Humph, darling, you are in over your head. This war will end you, and I will take this region as my own. You can withhold truths from me, from your little Ava, but do not ever think it will lead you to winning. For now, I will give you the opportunity to get me that talisman and bring it to me in Goldryn. If you choose war, then I will gladly kill Willow. I will send you her severed head, then I will visit this calm little estate, and destroy Nina."

She walks to him and grabs his chin. She twists his head upwards, but he doesn't fight back, not yet. Fighting back will only upset her more. She leans towards his neck, her breath warm against his skin. His body flinches at her being so close. "I almost forgot … I want to see my sister. I owe her an explanation. If I go to find her, and you try to keep her from me, my threat of murdering your dear friends still stands."

Stygian's face twists as if she's smelled something distasteful and she lets go of him.

"Such a sad little soldier you are. Fighting for a region and girl that have done nothing but lie to you. For your own sake, and your kindness to me as a child, I hope you learn the truth. But cross me, and you and your companions will not see the light of day." She dissipates into the frigid air, her fire blowing out in her absence.

Rais stays in the snow, staring at where she disappeared. He isn't even scared of her threat. What terrifies him more, are the lies she spoke of. The awareness of ignorance is a bone-shattering feeling.

"What did she say to you?" Nina yells to him from the doorway.

His body refuses to move, and Nina senses that in him. She goes to him, offering a rarity, comfort. "Show me?" she asks instead. She reaches up to Rais' temples and he plays the words over and over in his head.

When Nina does pull away, her face is dark. "Do you know what she may be talking about?" Rais asks quietly.

"I'm sorry, but I have no clue. You should ask Ava yourself." Nina says.

"You really think it is something Ava's keeping secret?" His words fall hopelessly.

Nina bends her gaze to him. "She may not remember, but we know Ava was one for her secrets before the accident. Did you even know she became friends with Levites the summer before Alys' death?"

Rais doesn't want to believe she could be malicious or that she might be hiding things from him. But Nina is right. It is entirely possible. And he didn't know she was close with Levites for that long. He knew they had met before, but not that she had ever considered him a friend or anything more than that. "I… have to get back to Grymyr."

"What are you going to do with the talisman?"

He squeezes his eyes shut. "I will leave it here and deal with it later. Lies or not, I need to keep Ava safe."

"Do you want me to go with you? Keep an eye on the ball? I wouldn't put it past the Society to make a move on you or Ava there. I can keep you updated with what I notice through the Sonder," Nina offers.

"Actually, yes, that would be wonderful. Thank you, Nina."

"I try to be helpful sometimes, Sparrow." She grins.

"I'll be there tomorrow night, but I'll keep my distance unless you need me."

He nods, and steps through the Plane of Verity.

The apartment is warm. He unbuttons his coat and leaves it on the ground. He goes to her bedroom. At the sight of her darkened silhouette, he isn't sure how to feel. He hates not knowing what is really happening around him. What truths may be withheld from him.

Rais retreats to the living room and lays on the couch. He closes his eyes against his tormenting thoughts. Stygian can't be trusted, but she was once Rais' friend. He has an inclination to belive some of what she told hin, Part of him hates her, but the other part worries about her well-being. He prays that Ava will be strong enough to fight through whatever Stygian is planning for her. And that whatever lies are being told to him, are forgivable.

Chapter Thirty-One

Ava pulls on the dress she found in her armoire. She discovered it with a note attached. The dress was for when her mother and she were to attend a ball in Metarock. Ava figured she could wear it now because she will never attend that ball with her mother.

The dress is obsidian. The top two layers of the skirt are dark blue. The layers create an illusion of iridescence. It's like the one she wore in Rebynrock, layered thin fabric with a fitted bodice. Except this one is much more extravagant. The sleeves are not tight to her skin, but loose, flowing past her wrists. The cut of the bodice accentuates her waist and hips. It creates an hourglass figure that she doesn't normally have. She swirls in her mirror, watching it move with her. Waves of fabric, elegantly curving to her body.

She brushes her hair back and begins braiding loose strands. She pulls the various braids and loose hair into a half-up half-down hairstyle. She braids a few chunks of the hair that are not pulled back, imitating the look of the Wyntryn hairstyles. Lastly, she pulls a pair of black heels from her closet and slides her feet into them.

She looks at her reflection and a girl with confidence stares back.

She picks up her tracker from the desk. She had left it when she went to Wyntryn and hadn't thought of it since. It's not like she had anyone to contact. She turns it on and opens her mother's voicemail. She smiles at the sound of her mother's voice. She hadn't heard it in forever, but it doesn't make her cry. If anything, it makes her want to be the Queen her mother believed her to be.

The memory Rais shared with her the night before had taken over her dreams. The way she looked to Rais, the way he looked to her. The mention of a sister she had never heard of. What Ava doesn't understand, is why no one ever mentioned this sister. Did Rais choose that memory as a warning or a hint? But why go through such lengths when he could be honest about it. And why would Anya, her own cousin not know of this sister?

She checks herself one more time, touching the light makeup on her face, and the sharp earrings that dangle from her ears. Ava goes to her door and walks through the hallway. She's ready to present herself as the Queen of Wyntryn to the other regions. Ready to see Levi again.

She enters the living room and Rais instantly moves to his feet. His eyes running over her. "You look truly ethereal, Your Grace."

His white hair is neatly brushed back. He wears a cleanly cut black suit. Embroidered with the same symbols as his mage's coat. The symbols of the Sparrow. He picks up a glistening tiara from the coffee table beside him. It's made of the same metal the arrow is crafted from. Two thin dragons made of fire twist together at the center holding a sapphire with their teeth. "And this is for you. If you are representing Wyntryn as our Queen, you should be wearing your mother's tiara."

Ava still feels uncomfortable at the thought of being Queen. Some people still call her the heiress, and she is. She is not a Queen, or at least she doesn't really want to be. There is a desire within her to protect the Wyntryn people. But even with that desire, she feels like an imposter when she's referred to as a Queen.

She walks to him. He lifts the tiara up and sets it on her head, sliding it through her hair. She offers him her hand. "Ready to show the other regions that Wyntryn is not merely surviving?" she asks.

Rais takes her hand.

Blue creeps into the world around her. They step through the Plane of Verity and to the Warped Library together. Ava looks up to the circle window cresting the top floor, but the glass is gone. Even from far below, she can see the chunks of broken glass on the edges of the window's frame. It's sad to see such a beautiful window destroyed. She wonders what must have caused it.

Rais guides her up to the front doors. They enter side by side.

The library is entirely different than before. Turned from a fallen mess into sublime elegance. The metal creatures that hang from the ceiling are shining, covered in lights. There are no books piled up between bookcases. The chandeliers are alight and hang lower now. Ava looks around at the other people in the room. All dressed in formal attire that matches their home regions. She feels small in a room full of so many powerful people. She looks to Rais for confidence. He smiles at her and sends a train of thought to her mind, *remember the crown upon your head. Many of these individuals are merely diplomats or considerably rich in their region, but you are the Queen of Wyntryn.*

She hangs tightly to his arm, pushing her shoulders back and lifting her chin.

In place of the front desk, is a tall wooden table covered with a white cloth. They step up to it, and the man behind it asks, "names?"

"Ava Beckett Wyntryn and Raiden Hynrule," she says. She can feel Rais' surprise with her willingness to speak first, but she only feels pride within herself. If she doesn't feel confident, the least she can do is put on a façade of confidence, as Rais said in the memory.

The man looks at her with curiosity. "You may follow the path of lights to our ballroom. The general requests all guests remain in the main room."

"Thank you," Ava says. She and Rais move into the library. The room billows with music.

An orchestra plays an enchanting ballad that echoes throughout the room. She wonders if she has ever been to this event before. If somewhere deep within her subconscious, there are memories of her dancing across this very floor—dancing with friends who may have long forgotten her by now.

She meets Rais' bright golden eyes. His black suit makes the dramatic features of his face stand out. He smiles down at her and unlaces his arm from hers. "Care to dance?"

She matches his smile. "Actually I despise dancing." Ava speaks the truth, simply the thought of dancing in front of others makes her feel nervous. But the thought of dancing with Rais doesn't make her nervous. She wants to see the other sides of him that she can't remember.

"You are a menace, Ava Beckett." He clicks his tongue at her.

She sneers back, "if I'm a menace, then so are you."

He leads her through the thrall of the people. Their gazes catch on her crown, the winter dragons entwined together. Rais ignores them and keeps his gaze on her, but she can't help but want to break away from the crowds.

"Everyone is staring at us," she whispers.

He winks at her. "Your dress is backwards."

She stifles a laugh. She is almost tempted to check, despite being sure that it's not. Rais places his hand on her hip and grasps her hand with his other. They twine their fingers together. The music bursts with luscious harmonies. Rais twirls her to the beat.

The sounds fill the room, blurring her senses together. All she can focus on is his face. The prominent cheekbones and jaw, his hooded eyes, and his enticing smile. Whether she wants to or not, she can't deny that she has fallen for Rais. Maybe the feelings have always been there. Hidden deep within her subconscious. She looks to him and sees her match. A person with as much grace and wrath as her. With a mind as complex as her own. He puts his arms around her, and she's home.

Not the manor, her parent's apartment, her mother, or anything else she thought mattered stands against this moment. The feeling of safety and understanding. His presence is a safety net. A home she can fall into that does not stand still through time. And as he holds her closer, she is swept into a forgotten memory.

The stable stands sturdy around her and Rais. Beyond the slats of the barn, she sees the lavender fields and tall grass. The grass glistens with the first frost of winter. It is the last day that the flowers will remain in bloom until next year. Rais steps out of Oberyn's stall and walks towards her. He grabs her hand and spins her around. Her laughter echoes through the open barn. They fall easily together, looking at each other with the blissful happiness they both dream of. She reaches up and brushes the hair from his face. "I hate that I have to keep leaving. Grymyr doesn't feel like home."

He stares back at her. His eyes as golden as ever. "I hate that you have to keep leaving too." His voice is brisk, in the still, warm air. She leans into him, and he wraps his arms around her. "Luckily there's only one more summer, and then you and I can venture the world together," he says. The moment is so clear, so real to Ava. He is her foundation. He has always been, long before they ever danced in that barn. Before they ever began dancing in the library. He has spun her before, held her before. But has she ever been there for him the way he has been there for her?

She pulls from the memory, and tilts her head, watching him look at her. Seeing in his eyes what she feels in her heart. In the memory Rais showed her last night, he confided in her. And she simply brushed past his own torments to complain about her own. She doesn't deserve him. She breaks from those thoughts as the music changes.

Her smile grows wider with each turn and movement to the music. In his presence, she is undeniably falling. It isn't a person or a thing that pulled Ava to that balcony a month ago, it was herself. She brought herself back to the manor, to Rais. To her future and to her home. A phrase common in Kanaleigh is that your heart will find its home and guide you there. Simple and to the point, your heart will guide you home. And hers did just that. Even if she can't consciously remember, everything else inside of her remembers. Like muscle memory, she found him again.

Rais holds her close. Maybe it is because they were

at each other's sides through their childhood or maybe they have a rare and undeniable connection. Whatever it is, he is her person. And she is his.

As the music bellows through the room, Rais begins to speak to her. He says, "you know, I used to tell myself time was a trap. That it was useless, but now I realize that without it, I wouldn't get these moments with you. Right now, nothing matters but the time we have now. What time I have with you." He searches for the right words to say. "I would be happy to have a lifetime like this."

She presses her hand to his cheek. "What if I don't believe in forever?"

"Then I will take you wherever I go and never leave your side wherever you go. So that even if we never have a forever, we still have plenty of time to be at each other's sides."

"Then it's a deal," she whispers. "Promise to never leave?"

"I promise," he confirms.

When yet another song ends, Rais and Ava finally pull apart from one another. The lights of the room reflect off their faces as they keep each other's gaze. Ava doesn't want to let go, but she can feel a familiar mind entering the library and moving towards her. Rais glances in the direction of her thoughts, to the approaching mind. Levi steps up beside her and her hands drop from Rais.

Rais hesitates. He glances between the two of them and forces out, "come find me later?"

She nods and looks to her old friend. His face is chiseled and his hair still messy in a hopeless kind of way. An unsure smile sits on his mouth. "Uh … you look beautiful Ava."

Her heart lifts. "Thank you Levi." She is glad that

he found her. That he wants to talk to her, especially since she left Grymyr and hasn't been back in what feels like months. So much has happened since she last saw him. It feels like ages since she last awaited his arrival at her apartment door.

"Do you want to step outside?" he asks. "It feels weird with all of these people looking at us."

"Of course, we have tons to catch up on." She pushes her hair over her shoulder and follows him outside.

The air is warmer than Wyntryn, it doesn't feel like the breeze is biting at her with each movement. The air softer, but tinged with the scents of the city.

She watches Levi fumble over his thoughts. The distance between them is awkward. They have lived lifetimes away from one another. The friend she once loved, now nervous to speak to her.

"Can I ask you something?" he asks.

"Of course."

"If you had never alated that day in the attic, would you have stayed with me?"

Her breathing slows as she meets his forest green irises. She doesn't want to hurt him. It's possible that if she never found her way back to her past, that she may have forgiven Levi more easily. That with less knowledge of her world, she would have continued to fall for him. But she doesn't feel that way now, and it's hard to believe that she ever would feel that way still. However harsh the thought is, Levi did have a hand in the death of her mother. He may have a good soul and she will forever see him as a savior to her after her mother's death. But she can't see herself ever staying with him in the way that he is implying. Then or now.

"Levi, I care about you. You are still my closest

friend. I believe that what happens to us and the choices we make are the best choices for ourselves at the time. There's nothing you can change about the past. Despite how much you wish things to change. What has happened to each of us is what was meant to happen. The truth is that you and I were never meant to be, at least not in that way." She stares down at the broken concrete. She remembers the day he first took her to the library. "I owe you for leading me home. You saved me."

Levi keeps his gaze steady on her. He speaks barely loud enough for her to hear, "I may never have what you have with him, but I can be okay with that. Even if you don't love me, my feelings will never change for you. I am happy that you're happy, that you are finding good in the life I fought to keep for you. You were my first and only real friend. I know I've messed up, but I will never forget having you in my life."

Her chest tightens with every word. "Levi, I—" she starts a thought. But it falls from her mind.

She wishes she wouldn't have to lose Levi. That she could see what he was like before the accident. If she could know if he was worth the effort, the emotional strain. To know if she had a choice to do anything but say goodbye. Because he is still her friend. And it hurts to see him like this, to lose him. But cutting off whatever was between them is her only option. Another decision she must make. But part of her is already regretting it.

"You need to know something," Levi says.

"And what's that?"

"The summer before your mother's death, you found out she was planning on killing your father. He was working with the Grymyr government through the Society, and as the Queen of Wyntryn, she felt it was safer for the both of you for him to be taken out of the picture. When you learned about her intentions, you came to me. We had met through your father, and I was the first person you went to for help. You and I worked with the Society to plot the murder of your mother." As Levi says the last few words, Ava's heart drops. Her memories of her father are dismal at best, so she can't understand his importance in her life. But she had the memories of emotions towards her mother, all good and loving, except somewhere in that she once saw the benefit of a world without her mother in it.

Levi continues, "when the day came, my brother received word that your mother was aware of our plans. She figured if you were with her the whole day, the Society wouldn't attack. But someone in the chain of command decided to take you down with her. After your mother died, you were brought back to life. You still had your memories—your mother never had the chance to wipe them. The Society was planning on executing you ... but Ms. Ethelle and I convinced them otherwise. The negotiation came with the loss of your memories in turn for your life. You would be allowed to live in Grymyr under the supervision of a Society member, but once you left, you were out of our jurisdiction."

She feels herself falling backwards and slipping through the air. She had plotted her mother's own murder, her own murder. She had lost her memories because of the Society. She is only alive because of Levi. But he was only there for her every day because he had to be. Her mind, memories, and emotions are tangled and lost in a confusion. She isn't sure whether to have a hatred for herself or for Grymyr.

"I'm sorry you have to hear all of this now. I should have been honest with you from the start." His voice is distraught.

She draws her unfocused vision from the ground and looks to him. "No, Levi, you saved my life. You fought for me to be here. And to think I would drop you so quickly over something I did myself. Even if you had to be there at my apartment every day, you brought me from whatever coma I had lost myself in. You dealt with my anger and sadness. You were there when no one else was," she says. She's suddenly grateful for him. Thankful that whatever friendship they had was enough to save her life.

Levi shakes his head. He admits, "I don't blame you for leaving me. You are the heiress to Wyntryn, and a diplomat is in love with you, and you have so many burdens and responsibilities. Your life was destined to be more vibrant than mine."

"Nevertheless, I am forever thankful for what you did for me. Even if it meant losing my memories, I am here today because of you," she says. Her mind reaches to his, but he blocks her out.

"I will always be there for you, Ava. If you ever need me, I will be there. But you should take some time to yourself. There is no way you are dealing with all this with a clear head. If you still want to talk when you have processed everything, let me know," he says absentmindedly. He walks back into the library, leaving her standing on the broken pavement. Her mind is a flurry of churned-up thoughts and emotions.

She looks up at the stars above. Her mother is up there, and Ava wonders if she's looking down on her. Can her mother forgive her for the horrible things she has done? She thinks of her father too. Hopefully, when he dies, he will join her mother in whatever afterlife they walk. Or will he be a nomad there, as he is in this world?

She only hopes, that when she dies, she will have Rais by her side. That she won't be alone for an eternity.

Chapter Thirty-Two

Rais watches Ava leave the library with Levites.

His mind has been foggy since he had his encounter with Stygian. Her claws are still sunken into his mind.

If Stygian shows up to talk to Ava, Rais hopes that Ava understands why he never told her about Stygian. She has been through enough in this past year. And Ava trusts far too easily. If she knows Stygian is her sister, then she will want to get to know her. Ava will put her trust in a woman who will only stab her in the back.

It hurts Rais to see her with Levites. He trusts her, but he can put two and two together. If they have been friends since before the accident, and she referred to her relationship with him as more than friends … It pains him, but she is responsible for making her own choices.

Rais looks around the ballroom. He isolates the leaders of each region with his eyes. He keeps himself aware of what he can. Because there is so much that he can't control. And at least Nina's there. Which is comforting to know because she may notice something that he doesn't.

On the thought of Nina, he catches her mingling with a group of diplomats from the Dragon Isles. She glances at him and speaks into his mind, *Rais. Saira is being held in the attic. I overheard from the stairs that they are trying to trap certain people in the basement.*

Who?

She fake laughs to the people around her and says something to them. Her voice then reaches into his mind once more. *They didn't say, but what Queen murdered one of their commanders and almost a hundred officers?*

Rais' face drops. The area in the basement is sealed with an ancient energy charm. It blocks any irregular's access to the Sonder while they are within the boundaries of the symbols. Rais starts to go to Ava, to warn her, but he doesn't want to interrupt her closure with Levites. If she doesn't get it now, she may never stop wanting to return to him. The thought is selfish and sits uncomfortably in his conscience, but he thinks it anyway.

Rais runs his hand along the inside of his suit, feeling for the dagger tucked there. He glances at Nina, who gives him a nod, encouraging him to confront Saira.

His last encounter with that troubled mind had led him to a talisman. It also helped him see that the Society itself is corrupt, and that not every member is at fault. The disturbing fact is that any irregular in Grymyr is at risk of being killed if they don't agree to join the Society. In turn for their lives, they are forced to take the lives of others.

Rais slides his energy through the room, feeling for any sign of ill intentions towards the Wyntryn representatives. He moves through the small gatherings of people. Politely excusing himself from those who try to stop and talk to him. He is intent on Levites' mind. Which now moves through the room. Rais follows behind him, taking an alternate route through the shelves to avoid Levites seeing him. Rais rubs his fingers against the scar running from his jaw and down his throat. The old pain aches through him.

The words that swirl around Levites' mind are dark and shrouded in guilt. Rais reaches the bottom of the twisting steps, looking up to Levites who has already passed the second-floor landing. Rais pushes himself close to the wall and conceals his mind. He follows quickly behind his adversary. He tugs on his cuffs and slides the dagger from his coat. If he has to attack, he can't use his lightning, at least not at first. There are hundreds of people in the room below, and he isn't trying to attract any unnecessary attention.

Rais keeps his feet quiet and steady. Only letting his weight push through on the end of each stair to avoid creaking. He reaches the top floor but slides into the shadows outside the doorway as Levites' voice calls into the room.

"You here, brother?"

Rais watches from where he stands. He's able to see part of the room, lit by the light of the moon shining through the open window frame. Saira's figure steps into the moonlight. "Does she know the truth?" Saira asks.

"Yes, but do you really think she will switch allegiances?" Levites' voice is quiet and unsure.

"I think something … will draw her to it." Saira looks through the doorway and then turns back to Levites. "A war will be starting on the continent soon, brother. Our general has asked me to lead a search for the Wyntryn talismans, I would like you to lead a group to the Dragon Isles, I've heard word that their ruler has had possession of one of them. I suspect it has been moved, but you can start there."

"No, Saira. I'm sorry, but I have no interest in your plans. I befriended Ava for the Society, I got her and her mother killed for the Society. I am—"

Rais' hairs stand on end. Hearing them admit to it, makes it far more real than before.

"That is not your choice to make, Levi. As soon as you joined the Society you signed your life away." Saira's head tilts and a soft maniacal laugh escapes from him. "You fell for the dreaded girl didn't you? How very idiotic."

Anger sparks through Rais. A harsh glaring alarm through his mind, covering his morality, blanketing him with desperation to see them both pay for their actions. Levites forced Ava into a false friendship, used her for his own volition. And claims to love her. Claims to love the girl he had killed. The girl whose mother he killed. What a brutal and ignorant boy. Rais can agree with the unfairness of the Society since they make the decision to join an ultimatum. But he cannot agree with the abuse of one's emotions, of their memories, of their livelihood. Those months Levites spent with Ava, she was at her most vulnerable, and he used her as a pawn for the Society.

"What does that have to do with the matter at hand? I am done with the Society," Levites says.

"Remember, that if you cannot get the girl to change allegiances, then you are responsible for her execution. That is the agreement you made, isn't it?"

The alarm grows louder in his mind and before he knows it, he's throwing himself into the room and forcing his hand around Saira's throat. The same way Saira attacked Ava at the manor.

Saira's voice crackles out in a deep laugh. "It isn't I,

who you should be mad at. It is the boy—the one who was given orders to kill Ava if she doesn't agree to work with the Society."

Rais drops Saira, throwing him into the wall with a blast of electricity. He turns his anger to Levites. The dagger still tight in his right hand.

Saira chokes out from behind Rais, "are you guilty, brother?"

The green of his eyes fills with terror. Merely a boy in a powerful uniform. "I didn't do anything, I promise."

"You are guilty, brother. Admit to it, you were the one that confirmed Ava's identity in the car. You were the only one she allowed into her mind on that road, you could have let them go. Both Wyntryn's could have lived," Saira sings in an unearthly rattle.

"Is this true?" Rais asks him. He suddenly has a need for vengeance.

"Fine! I lied to someone who is innocent, a friend, for months. She was vulnerable and we abused her for our own benefit. But I don't care about the power, I am tired of being forced to do these things. I will not kill her, I promise. I will never lay a finger on her," Levites pleads with him.

Rage boils low in his stomach and bile rises in his throat. He had been using her, manipulating her for his own use. Rais' body ignites with an energy that ricochets through the room. "You already killed her," he says with deadly calm. Levi meets him with panic-stricken eyes, flashing like headlights in the night. "You murdered Ava that night, correct?"

A tear slips down Levites' face as his eyes bear into Rais. "I didn't know her then, not really."

"Lies," Rais spits. A killing calm sweeping through

him. "You have known her for years."

"I care about her. I love Ava, I wouldn't dare hurt her."

Rais' mind instinctively goes to his oath. The oath he made when he became a mage of the Wyntryn region, and again when he took the position of Sparrow. To protect the land, people, and Queen of Wyntryn with his life. He repeats, "you murdered Ava that night, correct?"

"Yes," he admits.

His lightning buzzes through the air, begging to be released. He focuses his rage in his gut and turns to Saira. "What are you planning to do with her if she switches allegiances?"

Saira stares blankly at him. "That is not for me to tell."

Raiden throws his arms out sending electricity careening through the both of them. "Tell me!" he shouts.

Saira's menacing voice picks back up. He says, "well, you see, after taking her memories we thought she would make a wonderful pawn. Levi was bringing her here daily, and we were training her mind to not be able to close itself off. To make it easier to manipulate her. If she switches allegiances, we can make Wyntryn ours. And once we are done, we will kill her."

Rais bites down on his lip until there is blood flowing into his mouth. He forces out, "who was the one to take her memories?"

Saira smiles across the room to Levites. "Brother? Tell this nice man what you did."

"No, what you made me do," Levites snaps back.

"How am I a threat? After the accident, I was locked up in here, so anything you did, is completely on you. Not me."

Rais stares at Levites, his mind blurry with anger. Levi caused the accident, Levi took her memories, Levi abused her for months. His mind swirls with a piercing cry of rage. Rais sends a bolt of lightning at Saira, knocking him unconscious. Levi runs to his brother, but Rais grabs onto his shoulder and pushes him towards the broken window.

"What truth are you still withholding about Alys' murder?" Rais asks. His body is on edge, ready to cause the whole building to collapse.

Levites gulps. "Do you really want to know?"

"Tell me," he seethes.

"Ava came to the Society a year ago and asked us to help stage her mother's murder."

Before Levites can finish saying murder, Rais' hand is already tight around the dagger, pulling his arm up, and slashing. Rais barely even feels the action or sees what he does. He acts purely on rage, on the pain fighting to the surface of his mind.

No one can know the Queen of Wyntryn killed her mother. The knife slides through Levites' throat. The brown-haired boy reaches up for his neck. He pulls his hand away to see it covered in blood. His green eyes go wide with shock, and then, he falls backward into the already splintering wood of the window.

Rais' arm doesn't move, but the dagger drops to the wooden floorboards. He watches the boy as he falls through the air. The sound of metal hitting wood still rings in his ears. Before he can even process what he has done, the life he dreamed of with Ava disappears before him.

He's left standing there, looking out at the city lights of Grymyr, already praying for forgiveness. Because he knows, deep down, Ava is about to break her promise to him.

Chapter Thirty-Three

The cars whiz by the library, headlights shining. Horns honk from a crowded street somewhere out of view. Ava soaks up the familiarity of Grymyr. The smoky air and blurry atmosphere. The lights are always bright at night, bringing the city to life. Levi went back inside, but she stayed out on the crumbling sidewalk.

Ava can't comprehend the thought of contributing to her mother's murder. The more she learns about her past, the more unsure she becomes of who her mother was. She thought her mother was a kind person, someone to look up to. But how can such an admirable woman have so many enemies? Why would her mother see reason in killing her father and how could Ava ever find reason in killing her?

She reaches into the Sonder to find Rais' mind, but it's somewhere out of reach. She turns back to the face of the library to go find him, but a tall woman with dark hair stands in her way. Stygian.

The woman stalks towards her, her hair swaying at her sides. The cold gray of her eyes stare through her in an unnerving way. Ava tries to close her mind off from the Goldryn Queen. But despite her efforts, Stygian's thoughts penetrate her skull.

Ava's hand shoots to her head as she winces. She tries to push Stygian away, but she only digs deeper. Stygian pushes a force that pummels any attempt at defense. Her tactical voice slips through her like a parasite, *if you dare warn your friends I am here, I will destroy each of them one by one.*

Her voice is as smooth as a flickering flame and dreadfully quiet. Ava stares back at her, meeting her sinister glare. *Darling Ava, I can feel you trying to block me out still. Every second you do, your Rais and Levi are closer to death.*

Ava collects her straying thoughts and calms her mind. She stands straighter and opens her mind to Stygian. She knows Stygian would get her way whether she let her in or not, but it still bothers Ava. She doesn't want to leave her mind vulnerable.

Bile rises in her throat as Stygian's mind slips through her conscience.

Stygian flicks her hair behind her shoulder. "Excuse me for hurting your little brain. After your actions in Rebynrock, I have found a distrust towards you."

"What do you want?" Ava asks.

She looks to the side and pouts her lips. "I want to clear up the lies that have been embedded in your mind, darling Ava."

"If anyone is telling lies, it is you," Ava says.

She gapes at Ava. "So brash. Have you truly not figured it out yet? You are completely unaware. Unaware of so, so much."

She struts to Ava, dragging her fingernail along the side of Ava's face. "My little sister, I thought you would have been smarter." She bends her face to Ava's ear. Ava's jaw clenches. Her worst fears have come true. Stygian isn't only related to her, she is her sister. How has no one told her this? Ava wants to run from Stygian, but she's so close to her. Her breath like fire against Ava's skin. "We both share the same features of mother, the same eyes, dark hair, the same energy manifestation. Fire."

Ava's breath tightens in her throat. This is the lost sister she learned about, the one who left the family and changed allegiances to Goldryn. She thought she had only Anya and her uncle left, but she really does have a sister. Alive, and here before her. A terrifying woman, but her sister. "How is this even possible?" Ava asks. She holds in her emotions and tries not to accidentally release a burst of fire.

Stygian draws her finger from Ava's face. "Before our mother met your father, she had me out of wedlock. Years later she found your father and fell in love. Married him, had you. But he wanted nothing to do with Wyntryn. He moved back to Grymyr and continued to work for the government as an ally. After losing him, Mother only had enough space left in her heart for herself. So, I paved my own path. Left Mother and you, and found a home where people respected me. Actually cared about me." She juts her hand towards Ava. "Before I even changed allegiances; Mother told me I was not allowed to return to the manor. Not allowed to be in your presence. And when I came home to see her, she kicked me out like some stray cat. Once I was gone, she needed to mold a new heiress. Thus, she began to covet you."

Ava's mind goes back to the journal she found in her parent's apartment. The poem written by Aran Petrichor, *a songbird flies only to be taken away by time. In a man-*

or, she flew until the wind pushed her away too soon. Too soon, they cawed, too soon they wept. Our structures now weep with the loss of our niece.

"Stygian, I am sorry for what she did to you. But why hurt me in the process?" Ava cries out, "I can't change the past!"

"Darling." Stygian laughs. "You aren't listening." She backs away from Ava. "I don't want to hurt you. Unlike mother, I don't cast aside my family."

Ava shouts, "you took over Rebynrock!"

"I didn't even know you were back. I thought you had died in the accident, and then I heard Mother took your memories. I thought I was the one to take care of our homeland after mother's death," Stygian explains.

"How were you taking care of Wyntryn by covering the streets with soldiers of an enemy region?"

"You may not remember Ava, but our mother was a horrible woman. Filling the streets with enemy soldiers is a far cry from the treachery she imposed," Stygian says.

Ava shakes her head, she suspected her mother wasn't the kindest, but the truth still shocks her. But how can Ava even rely on Stygian's word? Stygian has never done anything to earn her trust.

"Everyone told me she was a wonderful Queen," Ava says.

"Our mother was horrible," she corrects. "She left me to die alone and took away what mattered most to you. And yet you defend her. She is still manipulating you to this day. Rais was her perfect little soldier, and you cling to his word."

"Don't talk about him in that way. Even if he is under the influence of our mother, he is an honest and genuine person. He would do anything to protect me." Unlike

Stygian, Rais has never hurt her. He has done nothing but save her, over and over again. If anything, it is Ava who hasn't done the same for him.

Stygian bends to her. "Every person lives by their own wants and needs. They will burn you, use you, lie to you. I am sure he and that Levi have taught you how to use your power, given you memories that you've lost. The truth is sister, you are a Queen, as am I. They fear you, Ava. They are manipulating you for their own gain, because they know if you are against them, you will be the cause of their deaths." Her voice grows icier. "They lie to you because they fear what the world will become when you are reunited with me."

"Are you not also a manipulator Stygian? I have no reason to trust you."

"My dearest sister, you have got it all wrong." Her eyes go to the circle window at the top of the library. "When you learn the truth, find me. When you realize your mistakes, I will give you a real home."

"I am glad to know you are my sister, Stygian, but I am loyal to Wyntryn. They need me," Ava says. Her voice is ever so wobbly.

Tears beg to fall from her eyes. Because what her sister says is not entirely untrue. Levi and Rais have both shared memories with her. She is the heiress but seen as a Queen. She would never think that they fear her, but what if they do? In Rebynrock, Ava scared herself. It was as if something changed inside of her. She didn't want to hurt … to kill those people. But her rage took over, and she did. The most disturbing part is that she was in complete control.

"You know where to find me." She twists away into the air, stepping through the Sonder. Stygian leaves a lingering image in Ava's mind. An image she can follow if she ever has the need to find her sister.

She feels the presence of another stranger near. "Ava!" she shouts from the steps of the library. She runs down the steps to her and pulls her toward the street. "You need to leave here, now."

Ava whips against her hold. "Who are you?"

"My name is Nina. I am a Wyntryn mage. A friend of Rais," she says. The girl looks to be her age, with amber eyes and smooth skin.

"Why do I need to leave?" Ava asks. Her emotions already built up after running into Stygian. They're ready to break and flow into the night.

"You don't know me, but I need you to trust me. Something is about to happen, and it's safer if you aren't here for it," Nina explains.

A shout comes from the attic in the library. The voices become clear as Ava focuses on them. She looks up to the broken window.

"Ava, please."

But Ava doesn't move. She stares up at the window as a body falls. It shatters the wooden frame. Her eyes widen and her mouth gapes open. She slings her arms out and throws her energy forward in hopes of stopping the body's fall. It slows but doesn't hold still in her energy. It hits the ground and stills for a second. Then a shaky breath comes, and Ava recognizes the mind.

She gasps, then runs, then screams. His face is pale with a frozen cry. She looks to the window again to see Rais' golden eyes alive in the moonlight. A cry begins to grow within her. As she stares at the window, a dagger falls and clatters against the floor. The hand that held it is outstretched, stagnant in the air. The scream ejects from her with a violent, uncontrollable rage. She falls to Levi's side and brushes her hand against his face.

Her eyes well up with tears and the guttural sound that escapes her throat quiets the world around her. His hair lays stagnant across his forehead. His eyes stare blankly at the sky. Tears litter his bloody skin as if frozen in time. Ava's breathing grows heavier with each second that passes. She moves her eyes from his face to his neck, and another cry comes from her throat. She staggers back onto the pavement. She braces herself on her hands, but they feel sticky. She looks down at one of her hands in shock. It's covered in dark red. She can't hear anything but her own cries reaching up from her and flying out into the city. All she can see is the blood, and the slice across Levi's neck. The blood pools everywhere and she is sitting in it, sobbing into the night.

She pulls herself to Levi's lifeless body. She places her fingers against his temples. All she has to do is bring him back. She can bring him back to life. If she is truly as powerful as everyone says, then she can save him. She can save Levi.

A whisper of a voice curls out from behind her, "it won't work Ava." Nina stands quietly behind her, watching. She moves forward to kneel beside Ava and places her hands against her face. She nudges her from Levi's body. The empty vessel that was once her friend. "Ava, once you've been brought back to life, you can never be brought back again. I am so sorry, but he's gone."

"No. I can bring him back, I have to," she gasps out.

"He's gone," Nina repeats.

"No!" She stands up, but loses her balance, collapsing back beside Levi. It's a bloody massacre and there's nothing she can do to fix it. She wants to go back in time and stop it.

She had the chance to stop it. She could have kept talking to Levi. Maybe he would have never gone up to the attic. She could have found Rais and stopped him from following Levi. Raiden—his face fills her thoughts, he murdered Levi. And Stygian is right, they're all liars. Raiden killed her best friend, killed Levi. And this Nina had tried to drag her away from it before it happened. They were all working against her, all manipulating her with what they wanted.

Her heart seems to collide into her lungs, and what has already broken inside of her shatters.

"You killed him!" She shrieks.

Her eyes meet Raiden's. She shouts to him again, "you murderer! You killed my best friend! You killed him!" Her face is a stream of tears and manic rage. "You killed Levi!" Her voice cracks and her face falls. He stares back at her, his eyes glossy with tears.

He alates to the ground and walks to her. Ava runs at him, a blaze igniting in her path. His eyes widen and he falls back a step. "I'm so sorry."

"Why? Why would you do this?" she cries out. Anger boils and festers in her bones.

"You don't understand. He was lying to you," he says. He backs away even more, closer to the wall of the neighboring building. He stumbles backward into the grass.

"You are the one lying! All of you, all everyone has done to me is lied." Her mind drops to an eerie silence. "Well guess what Raiden?" He winces. Her blood burns with fire. "I don't trust you. The only person I can trust is myself."

"Ava—" he gasps, plundering for his words.

"Liar," she seethes. She builds energy within her hand and throws a ball of fire at him.

He blocks it, and the fire evaporates into the air. "Please let me explain."

"There is nothing to explain. You killed Levi," she says. She steps up to him and grips his neck with a burning hand. He grits his teeth, fighting the pain. Tears burn in Ava's eyes as she stares up at him. She looks into the eyes of the boy she believed to be the only person she could trust. Her person. Despite what Levi told her in that courtyard, despite what Stygian told her, she still cared for Raiden. But his own actions destroyed any feelings she had for him. "You are nothing to me."

A force blows her back into the grass. Ava turns to Nina standing across from her with her arm extended. She holds a blockade between Ava and Raiden. "Leave here, Ava," Nina commands.

Ava looks to the steps of the library, to see the doors wide open and crowds of guests staring at the situation in shock. Ava takes one last look at Raiden, her eyes burning with disgust and disappointment. She goes to Levi's side and holds onto his lifeless body. He's too heavy for her to carry, but she can still try to pull him through the Sonder. She closes her eyes tightly and alates to a beach outside of the Goldryn city. It's the image Stygian sent to her mind before leaving. The only place she has left to go. Because she doesn't feel safe going back to the manor. Because the manor is the first place Raiden will go.

She falls through the blue and into the sand. Staggering upwards, Levi falls through her grasp and onto the ground. She cries and falls to the sand by his side. She pulls him to her chest and places her fingers against his temples once more. Her insides are set afire as she presses as much energy as she can into Levi. She searches for him in the Sonder. But he is gone, his mind lost.

She digs her toes into the sand and collapses into herself. She holds tightly to Levi's body as she lays there, sobbing into the hot, stagnant air.

Chapter Thirty-Four

The waves crash on the sand. The water slowly creeps up the beach towards her. The salty foam nips at her feet. The sky above is different here. In the city, it is brimmed with a pinkish blur of light pollution. Here the only light comes from the stars, the moon, and the lanterns rising from the city. She can hear the cascading music from within the city walls, celebrating the rising moon and the changing of seasons with festivities.

She slides her hand across her dress, dried blood is singed against it. A lone tear falls down her face at the thought of the blood's source. Her other arm still clings to Levi as if he will wake any moment and grin at her with his crooked smile. Her heart stutters with thoughts of him, and she is drowned in the memory of him appearing at her door. The memory of the day he took her to the warped library for the very first time.

He walked into the apartment with messy hair. She held the door for him as he pushed past her and laid down on the couch. "Another day, another chance to put that beautiful smile back on your face!" he said to her.

Ava smiles up at the sky with his voice in her thoughts.

That day Ava made some snarky comment back to him and went to sit across from him on the carpet. At the time she was lost. Still trying to deal with her lack of memories and the grief that pulled against her mind. Now, she faces similar feelings. Grief that makes her feel hopeless. So, she stays in that moment, remembering Levi's voice.

I know you'll never not feel grief from this Ava, but it's been months. At some point, you have to wake up and come back to the world.

She repeats the words over and over, and over. She doesn't feel grief from her mother's death anymore, but she feels grief from Levi's. Sickening grief that bears into her heart.

The snake slips back into her chest and tightens around her heart, threatening her once again.

She turns her head to Levi, looking at his frozen face. She chokes on her own saliva, choking on the reality before her. She so badly wants life to come back to his pale skin. For him to look at her with those green eyes and chastise her for being so annoying. She wants to argue with him and be mad at him. She wants to live in the moment by the window when he bent his lips to hers.

With his last words, he told her he would always be there for her. That whenever she needed him, whenever she felt lost, she only had to go to him. But she is lost now, and he isn't there. His body is there, but he isn't.

Ava will forever be grateful for Levi, but from now on if she needs him, she won't be able to find him. She will have to look up to the stars and pray that he's listening when she calls out for him.

"Sister, you came," Stygian says. Her methodical

voice slithers through the air. Ava feels her walking nearer, but as her sister sees the corpse by her side, she slows. Her aura changing at the sight.

Stygian takes a knee by her side and lifts Ava up towards her. Ava reluctantly moves to her sister's side, letting go of her friend. Stygian brushes her hair back and meets Ava's gaze. "My condolences for your loss darling sister. You must not let this death rip you apart. Focus that sadness on another emotion, on happiness, rage, spite, disgust, but do not let the grief destroy you. It has ruined many good people, do not let it also ruin you."

Ava stares into the sand, not wanting to feel anything.

"Ava, there is a traditional funeral in Goldryn. It is meant to honor the lives of those lost. Let me help you honor your friend in this way," she offers.

Ava looks to her, unmoving.

Stygian reaches her hand out to her, but Ava moves away. She bends back over Levi, taking one last glimpse of his face before saying goodbye forever. She blocks out the blood on his neck, the gore, the death. She focuses on what life once flowed through him, the richness in him. She leans down and kisses his forehead. "I love you too, Levi," she whispers against his cold skin. She may not have loved him the same way he loved her, but right now, that doesn't matter. Right now, she misses him enough to say those words. And she believes them.

After all the time she spent with him, she so easily discarded him. Traded her time with him for someone who took his life. Every day Levi was there for her. When she thought everything was over, repetitive, or useless, he was there. Always offering her his presence. Being a friend, a genuine, and amazing friend. He wanted to share the world with her, and she pushed him away.

Now she stares down at him. She reaches out to his spirit one last time, but it's long gone. There is nothing in his body. She bites her lip, tasting metallic blood as it saturates her mouth. She painfully stands and moves away from him.

"I'm ready," Ava says quietly to Stygian. The breeze carries over the ocean and blows against them.

"In the ceremony, you lay the body in the sand and set it aflame, letting the ocean carry their ashes out to sea. That way they may return to the world they were taken from," Stygian says.

Ava looks out at the ocean. Levi's energy manifested as water. She remembers him telling her in the library one day after working with Saira. He would want this to be his funeral. It is fitting that he would remain in the ocean, a place where he may find real peace.

Stygian pulls his body down to the water's edge. With the rising tide, the ocean will reach him and carry him away before sunrise.

Stygian moves to Ava's side and grasps her hand. "Together?" she asks.

Ava nods.

Fire slips from their fingers and moves across Levi's body. The bright blues of Ava's flames blend with the purple of her sister's. They rise high above them, and then slowly fall as what is left of Ava's friend disappears.

They stand there for a long while, but Stygian eventually pulls her from the quieting flames and guides her to the gates of Goldryn. Where she leads Ava to the palace resting above the ocean.

Away from Levi and away from her home.

Chapter Thirty-Five

"Mata ta chessya malla mey fin," Ava's mother would whisper to her. May the gods bless us until our end.

She would recite those words as the moon hovered high above them, on the nights when they laid on the manor's rooftop looking out at the stars. Those same nights it would be too dark to see anything but the snow falling and the stars resting high above them in the sky. Every time she spoke in that ancient tongue, Ava would ask, "why?" Because her family didn't believe in gods or goddesses. Her mother didn't worship anything beyond herself. In response to Ava's question, her mother would simply rub her thumb against her cheek and shake her head. The memories of those shared conversations with her mother are some of the few that have returned to her since the accident.

The memories only remind her of how her mother had always been distant and passive.

I should've known better, Ava thinks while staring out at the ocean below.

If she knew all those months ago, the truth, the lies,

the deceit, maybe she would have done things differently. Made different decisions.

Now, a year after her mother's death, sitting in a cold room, Ava knows she can never go back. Doesn't want to. Instead, she lets the rage dwell deep inside her heart and spread across her mind.

Ava is sequestered in a small room that sits on the eastern side of the Goldryn palace. Since arriving in the humid region, Ava hasn't bothered to explore the city or try to learn about the culture. She misses Wyntryn too much. She misses the stone walls of the manor and the horizon filled with mountains.

The door to her room slowly opens. A woman Ava faintly recognizes from her distant memories appears before her. After all that has happened, she isn't surprised by her recognition of the woman. If anything, Ava wants to know more about her.

The woman is lean, with a cool look of sympathy in her eyes. Her hair falls below her breasts. Long curled tendrils of pale purple and lavender. Her skin is a deep tan, descended from a race that originated in the western lands of Eventyr. The woman, a lady of the Crystal Lakes, the daughter of a high lord that served beneath the Queen of Eventyr.

The woman tilts her head and examines Ava, eyes surveying her as if she hasn't seen Ava in a very long time. And she hasn't, not since before the death of her former mentor, Alys Wyntryn.

"Have I met you before?" Ava asks with a quiet, shaky voice.

"I'm Willow." She pauses, her eyes landing on Ava's, recognition crosses her face. "You truly do look just like your mother." As Ava hears the words Willow speaks, her stomach falls. As if she has fallen off a cliff and doesn't know if she will land safely on her feet. Willow continues, "well darling, I have heard so much about you."

"How do you know me?" Ava lowers her voice so that the Goldryn Queen won't be able to hear from beyond the sandstone walls. "How do you know my mother?"

Willow's eyes glint. "I'm here because of the boy you want to kill. He is a friend of mine, the same as you once were to me. I have information regarding your situation with him. Something you might find useful." Willow's voice is a merriment of smooth syllables that flow into whispers. Her voice is accented by the deep and ancient tones of the Eventyrians. The country on the east continent, that is far from the palace where Ava now finds refuge. A place she at first thought of as a sanctuary but has turned out to be far from it.

Ava takes a steadying breath. "I don't want to hear what you have to say. He killed someone I loved. I will never forget about that ... I can never forgive that." Ava has the urge to cry out. To throw the mirror across the room, set the world on fire, and scream until she loses her voice. But she has already done that, which is why she now feels empty. Whatever anger she has is stifled. Her heart and mind so broken, so shattered, that she can't decipher what is the truth and what is a lie. Ava has been lost for the past year and has only spiraled more and more into a flurry of emotions as time goes on. And now it is an endless nightmare of nothing.

"Well Ava, then you'll find the information I have to share a relief. Information your lovely captor is trying to hide from you. Truths even your lost friend failed to let you see," Willow says. Willow lets a piece of parchment drop to the floor undetected. Ava looks off into the ocean beyond them as Willow continues. "I have a respect for your mother, and I owe it to her memory to keep you safe. Know that you can't trust anyone Ava, especially not within these walls."

As Willow moves to exit the room, Ava turns to watch her leave. That's when she notices the ripped and folded parchment on the wooden floor. She bends down to pick it up, and as she opens it to read the words that are written on it with spindly handwriting, her heart stops. Her chest heaves, as she chokes out a cry. Not of relief, or sadness, but of regret. That her friend has died because of a single treacherous lie.

Ava's eyes are intent on the piece of parchment in her hand. Willow turns back to Ava. The woman's eyes are large and doe-like, the iris' a pale lavender. The roots of her hair are as dark as midnight, but she has the rest dyed a subtle purple. She is smooth, stealthy, a silent hunter. But she isn't here to hunt Ava, she hunts for something other. A goal, but Ava can't figure out what it is. Despite how hard she tries to enter the mysterious woman's mind.

"Why are you telling me this?" Ava asks. Only a strip of light shines upon them through the window.

"Because he needs you. You need him too, you know it. You know the Queen only wants you because you're powerful. Your occurrence is one in a thousand years, darling. And you know he doesn't care about that—he sees you for what's inside." Her words twirl into the air between them as if blessed by some ancient goddess.

"I am not anything special."

"Have you heard the prophecy? The one of the two all-powerful sisters, destined to destroy the world or each other? A test of fate, of control. It is one of the ultimate questions of our race, do we use our power to take control of the physical or the mind? Many believe we aren't meant to exist at all, this prophecy is the end all be all. How do we live or how do we die?"

"And what if I choose nothing? What if I choose that I'm better off not controlling anything? That prophecy you talk about is meant for children. A story mothers tell their kids to scare them. To make them think there are punishments for our actions."

Willow gawks at her, her darkly painted lips widening in a disbelieving smile. "After all this time being surprised by the peculiar, and you still believe it is all a story for children? Open your eyes, Ava. You are not living a fairy tale. You have a destiny. You have people relying on you to leave this place alive. Would you truly give up on thousands of people because of your own personal torments? I'm truly sorry he died, it's treacherous, but there are those who are still alive," she says.

Ava closes her eyes, not wanting to read what's on the paper again. "My people will survive without me."

"No, they won't. They need their Queen. Rais needs you too," Willow pleads with her.

"Well, if Raiden needed me, he wouldn't have killed Levi. And I need to be here, I might be the only one who can stop my sister from taking what she wants."

"Do as you wish, Ava, but remember what you can of your past. The prophecy you believe to be a child's tale is real. It was written by the Wyntryn ancestors, that two sisters would come to be born of a Wyntryn Queen. It said that the sisters would be overcome with a consuming power after the death of their creator. If that power is released into our world, no one will be able to stop it. But you can stop it before it happens. The Society wanted your memories gone for a reason. The answer to all your questions is in your memories, your past. Use that message I gave you as you will. I hope it brings clarity to your situation," Willow says. She then sweeps around, her white dress swaying around her as she exits the room. The door shuts lightly behind her.

Ava looks down at the piece of parchment in her hand. At the words scrawled across it. She flips it to the other side and drawn in black ink is the symbol of the dragon being hit by an arrow. The Wyntryn sigil. The arrow shatters the flaming circle, shatters the Collective.

With all that has tried to break Ava, she remains standing. Even with the message from Willow, she will continue to stand. She always knew that the consequences would inevitably come for her, and they have. They have forced her to have no choice but to face the past. Her mother would tell her to let the consequences take her. To let her emotions, her challenges, swarm her and carry her onward. So that when she begins to lose herself, she can follow the current to safety. The current knows, and she is the current. Ever flowing, ever raging, ever soothing. Rising from the depths of the ocean, she is the dragon, leaving behind nothing but ashes.

Acknowledgments

I started this book in March 2021, but I would have never been able to publish it without the help and support of numerous people. Including my editor, family, and friends. *These Shattered Truths* has been a creative journey for me. I have had to teach myself so many skills. From book formatting to cover design, each piece has been a learning curve.

One of the people that helped me the most, was my developmental editor, Natalie Cammaratta. She is the author of *Falling & Uprising* and *Scattered & Breaking*. If it were not for her, this book would not have been published. She helped me take a manuscript that I have rewriten far too many times, and turn it into something marketable. Most notably, she helped me fix my many grammatical errors. Who knew I started so many sentences with gerunds?

I would also like to thank my mother, Paige Sandford, who listened to me day in and day out while I rambled on about this book. She was also the only person who read my first draft. She helped me work through revising my book and rewriting it. Even when she had no clue what I was talking about, she still listened. And a lot of the times, that's all I needed.

I want to also give credit to my many inspirations for not only this story, but the world of Kanaleigh that I was able to create. My sister-in-law, Brittany Sandford, gifted me a young adult fantasy novel in 10th grade. That novel led to my love for fantasy. I began reading again, and that reading led to writing. In seventh grade I joined a community of creatives with a common fondness for the *Warriors* series. This community, pushed me to develop my artistic skills and my writing. They also introduced me to many people who have continued to support me throughout my writing journey.

I would like to also thank my family, for simply believeing in me. Sometimes, that is all a person needs to keep going. My brothers in particular, Parker, Micah, and Drew pushed me to keep writing and have supported me since the start. Furthermore, I want to thank my closest friend, Shelby Graham. She has listened to me rant about publishing, books, and my writing process for hours on end. She is a godsend, and I am so thankful to have her in my life. She is the Nina to my Rais.

Although I have created each part of this book myself, I have not done it alone. My editor, creative community, family, and friends have been there for me every step of the way.

Pronunciation Station

Unfortunately, telepathy is impossible in our world. So you can not see into my mind and know exactly what I'm thinking. This page is for those who read the weird words and names in this book and think, *my brain is simply refusing to comprehend this.*

Alate (Uh-late)

Alys Wyntryn (Al-iss Win-ter-in)

Atane (Uh-t-on-a)

Ava Beckett (Ava Beh-ket)

Aysand (Eye-sand)

Eieran Hynrule (Ee-err-on Hh-eye-nn-rule)

Goldryn (Gold-rin)

Grymyr (Grim-er)

Hyacin Moore (Hi-uh-sin More)

Kalenti Alberona (Cal-en-tee Al-ber-o-na)

Kanaleigh (Con-ah-lay)

Levites (Lee-v-eye-tiss)

Metarock (Met-uh-rock)

Oberyn (Oh-burr-in)

Osidias Donsen (Oh-sih-dee-us Don-ss-en)

Petrichor (Peh-treh-core)

Rebynrock (Reh-bin-rock)

Raiden Hynrule (Rr-eye-den Hh-eye-en-rule)

Rais (Rr-eye-ss)

Saira (Ss-eye-rah)

Sonder (Ss-ah-nn-der)

Stygian Liones (Stig-ee-en Lee-oh-ness)

Ancient Language

The ancient language is the original tongue used by civilizations of irregulars in Kanaleigh. It is a universal language used to harness energy and elements through the sonder. The language remained prevalent in the lands until the Great War. but was mostly eradicated after the most recent resurgence of the war (approx. 20 years prior to These Shattered Truths).

Alate – to travel through the Plane of Verity

Atane – wild beast or untamable animal

Ayatha – goddess

Chessya – to bless, to feel blessed, to be faithful

Drogon – dragon

Feya – fire

Fin – destination, end, final

Itzal – goddess of death, darkness, destinations

Gana – realm, region, plane of existence

Malla – to be possible, to express possibility, to have permission, to give permission

Mata – beings beyond their world, ancestors, gods, and goddesses

Mey – relating to or belonging to oneself; relating to or belonging to many

Pheyani – to fly, to be one with the air

Ra — the origin of something, where something begins or starts, family name.

Reyani — to rise, to lift through the air

Rynal — the goddess of life, light, and beginnings

Sonder — the plane of existence (Plane of Verity) that irregulars can access with their minds

Ta — a way to connect words or meanings, used in the place of words (the, in, is, it, to, etc.)

Tyral — the goddess of relationships, land, and war

Vaye — to possess, to own, to hold

Verity — walking amongst the many, collection of souls in one place

** not all words appear in book **

Words ending in YR or YN - in relation to location, territory, or region. Also commonly included in the names of ancestral lines. For example, Wyntryn. Both a location and family name.

For more information on the ancient language of Kanaleigh, go to **www.sirisandford.com**

Explore the Sonderverse

You can go to Siri Sandford's website to learn more about the sonderverse. You can view speical information and details about chararcters, regions, and upcoming books!

www.sirisandford.com

Items available on the website's shop:

Signed copies

Character art stickers

Sonderverse bookmarks

8x5 map print

Book two of the Sonder trilogy ...

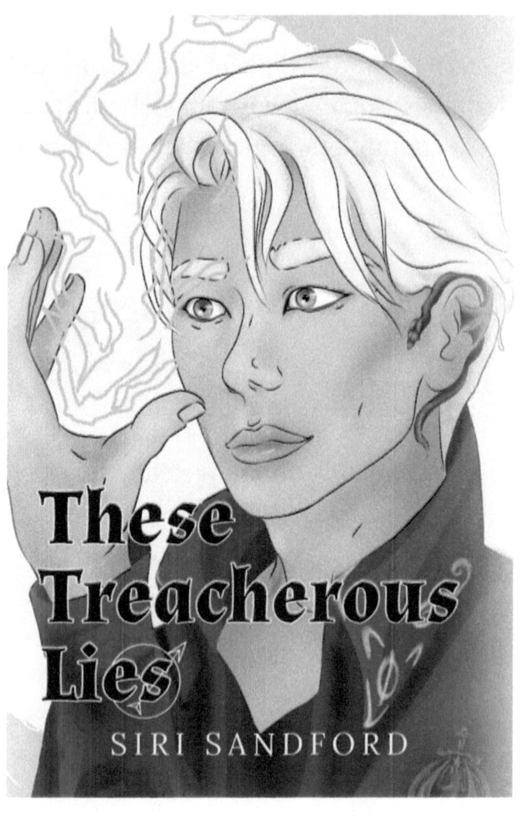

Go to www.sirisandford.com to learn more about *These Treacherous Lies*

On the plane of verity walks two souls.
Their fates ever connected through the sonder.
They will either be each other's savior
or destroyer.
Only through fire and ash will the truths sealed from their
minds be revealed.

www.ingramcontent.com/pod-product-compliance
Lightning Source LLC
Chambersburg PA
CBHW021622030826
48979CB00036B/1699/J
9798985726206